Murder Through the Grapevine

Teresa McClain-Watson

www.urbanc

Urban Books, LLC
78 East Industry Court
Deer Park, NY 11729

Murder Through the Grapevine ©copyright 2010
Teresa McClain-Watson

ISBN 13: 978-1-60162-855-8
ISBN 10: 1-60162-855-2

First Printing May 2010
Printed in the United States of America

10 9 8 7 6 5 4 3 2 1

This is a work of fiction. Any references or similarities to actual
events, real people, living, or dead, or to real locales are intended
to give the novel a sense of reality. Any similarity in other names,
characters, places, and incidents is entirely coincidental.

Distributed by Kensington Corp.
Submit Wholesale Orders to:
Kensington Publishing Corp.
C/O Penguin Group (USA) Inc.
Attention: Order Processing
405 Murray Hill Parkway
East Rutherford, NJ 07073-2316
Phone: 1-800-526-0275
Fax: 1-800-227-9604

Murder Through the Grapevine

MURDER THROUGH THE GRAPEVINE

A RONI JARRETT MYSTERY

TERESA MCCLAIN-WATSON

DEDICATION

To my father, Fred McClain, for his encouragement. I told him I think I may want to be a writer. He told me to take typing classes and then proceeded to get me paper and pens, a typewriter, and even a guitar (?). He covered the gambit for me. And I thank him dearly for it.

I also thank my husband and best friend, John, for all of his love and devotion.

Finally, I give honor to God Almighty for His love and salvation and for the gift of writing that He has given to me.

ONE

What looked like crazy was taking place at the Zion Hope Missionary Baptist Church as I walked into the huge, steeple-topped sanctuary and made my way toward the choir stand. I walked in slowly, because I couldn't believe my eyes. Sisters, good, church-going sisters, were having a fit about song selection, their shouting voices carrying high up in the rafters, and everybody and their mama was trying to get in on the free-for-all.

I almost turned around and walked back out. I wasn't with this, not today. Not after the kind of workday I'd already had. But I had no choice. Those wild-acting sisters, those card-carrying members of the lunatic society, also happened to be the choir that I directed.

"You can dry those eyes now," I decided to say above their yells, "'cause I'm here!"

I waited, standing in front of the chaos with my briefcase in one hand, my sheet music in the other, praying that my little show of humor got somebody's attention. But it didn't. Didn't stop one yell from coming out of the mouth of not one of those yelling sisters.

Not that I was surprised. Other than my best friend, Pam, who was twenty-four, and a handful of other choir members, I was the youngest thing there. And the fact that Alan Simms, the head of all of the church's auxiliaries, would have selected some youngblood like me to direct the choir never set right with Bernadette Finch, the former director, and the person who was undoubtedly the leader of this craziness.

I kept repeating," May I have your attention?" At my insistence, it took a loud drumroll from our drummer to get them to even look in my direction. When they did, I pushed my small glasses up on my small face and stared right back at them, anxious to find out just what brought on this incredibly inappropriate conduct.

"I want one person, and one person only," I said, "to explain to me why it is that the members of this choir, this Christian choir I remind y'all, are behaving like pure fools up in here. Nope, I didn't say everybody. I don't need everybody trying to talk at the same time. I said one body. One person." Then I turned to the one I just knew was behind the entire affair. "Sister Finch, why don't you enlighten us?"

She didn't hesitate. She stood up on her big bulk and folded her big arms. "You've been directing this choir for four months now," she said, all five-ten of her towering over me, "and we've been sitting back and letting you do your thing. But enough is enough."

A few of the other senior members hollered, "All right, now," causing me to roll my eyes.

I can't help it. When I feel I'm getting a bad rap, I get defensive.

"This is supposed to be a church choir," Sister Finch went on, "a good, hymn-singing, gospel choir, not some rhythm and blues band," she said with a sweep of her hand, directing it toward me first, and then to the equally surprised drummer.

Actually, I never cared for the blues, or any of the tunes of the day. I loved the classics, from Rachmaninoff's "Rhapsody on a Theme of Paganini," to Stravinsky's "The Rite of Spring," to anything Debussy, but it wasn't as if it mattered. Finch wouldn't have been any less outraged if she discovered that my taste in music was far less syncopated than what she'd thought. That woman wasn't complaining about my musical taste, she was complaining about me.

"Just what are you trying to say, Finch?" I asked her point-blank.

"I'm not *trying* to say anything," she said even more point-edly. "I'm *saying* that the type of music you been selecting ain't working. That's what I'm *saying*."

"And you saying right!" one of her buddies in the back row shouted out.

"Tell the truth and shame the devil!" another one shouted.

But Finch was her own encouragement. She went on without hesitation. "We're supposed to be here to sing praises to the Lord, not put on no Rick James concert!"

Since many of my younger members didn't know who Rick James was, and since they were generally tired of Finch and her mutiny anyway, they revolted too. Only, their angst was against Finch.

"What Roni trying to do for this choir is a great thing," Pamela said as she stood.

Pamela Tate was my closest friend here in Melville, the first person who showed me any kindness when I was a stranger here, just passing through my old hometown on my way to greener pastures, or so I'd thought. What I liked most about Pamela was her natural honesty. Girlfriend called it like she saw it and didn't worry about what grief it caused. When I'd first met her, I didn't like that particular quality about her; she was almost rude, it seemed to me. Now I was feeling the sister. Honesty was what folks needed, whether we could handle it or not.

"Y'all used to be singing all off-key," she went on, with her honest self, "didn't know the words half the time. Then got mad when people tried to tell y'all something. That's why Dr. Simms hired Roni. She's a professional. She's a graduate of the Juilliard School of Music, which, for all y'all that don't know, is one of the most prestigious colleges in this country. She knows her thing. The rest of us, including you too, Sister

Finch, wouldn't know sheet music from sheet rock. So, naw, I ain't wit' this. Count me out of this mess here. I say Roni Jarrett is our choir director, Dr. Simms hired her for good cause, and we should support her."

All of the younger members agreed, standing in support of Pamela's statement.

But none of the seniors agreed, standing too, in opposition, and before I knew it, they were all at it again.

It got so bad, and so loud, Luther Montgomery, the head of our deacon board, had to come down from his office upstairs and tell my members to knock it off. And even that didn't work.

I gave up, which wasn't all that hard, since I was already bone-tired, and decided to let them do their thing. I grabbed my sheet music and my briefcase and headed for the exit. "Let me know what y'all decide," I said to nobody in particular, since nobody was listening to me anyway.

I drove home, to Elkin Street, taking the longer route behind the high school and then pulling back out onto Spears, then Jacobson, and then Mark Russell Ridge. It was just past seven thirty on a cool fall evening, and the middle-class residents of Melville, Florida had packed up and gone indoors, leaving a calm quietness in the air that managed to relax me too.

When I got to Elkin, however, my neck of the woods, I was on guard again. That calm quietness was gone, as the sounds of nighttime in the hood came to life in its usual grand way with rap music blaring, loud and argumentative conversations, and constant activity.

One teenage kid was chasing another one across the street and they both ran in front of my car, causing me to slam on brakes. Meanwhile a no-nonsense-looking brother was slamming some strung-out junkie against the side of a house, and then pinning him with a crowbar. I stiffened, tired of all of this drama, although I wasn't exactly used to anything else.

***

I'd returned to Melville eight months ago from Newark, New Jersey, after the school I worked for found out about my past and fired me on the spot. I was devastated, because I was caught so off guard, because that past of mine seemed an eternal burden. But I also knew that the Lord Jesus Christ was my Savior and He would not leave me twisting in the wind. So I got myself together, said my good-byes to those few teachers who didn't suddenly see me as the scum of the earth, and moved on.

I ended up moving South, heading for Miami, but not before stopping through Melville. I'd lived in Melville for the first fifteen years of my life, up until that earth-shattering night when my parents died, and I wanted to see if I'd remember anything. Unfortunately, I remembered *too* many things, most of them stark reminders of how painful my life had been since I left Melville. So I decided it would be best to forget the memories, and move on.

But first I stopped at Mae's, a local diner, for a quick road break. It was then that two things happened within minutes of each other: I met Pamela Tate, who sat at my table because the diner was so crowded, and Anne Ziegler, the owner of the Queen Anne Beauty Salon.

Pamela and I hit it off right away, as she told me her entire life story in sixty seconds: was an attendee but not a graduate of Florida A&M University; used to work in her parents real estate business until her big mouth scared away too many customers; was now a teller at the bank, where she was too busy counting money to run her mouth; one dog, no children, and desperately seeking a good man. She talked fast and furiously, sometimes in a sister-girl street lingo, and sometimes like a valley girl. She was petite, as I was, but she was shorter and had more curves, the kind of phat sister that brothers went insane over. Ironically, she said the same thing about me.

"If I had your perfect, creamy brown skin, and those big beautiful Asian eyes, and all that long, thick, wavy hair . . . child, please," she'd said as she made herself comfortable at my table. "Nobody could tell me a thing 'cause I'd be Miss Thang. Hear what I'm saying? I'd be it."

She said this with laughter because she was probably only kidding, but I was in such a bad way eight months ago, and any kind word was welcome.

After staring at me for a few seconds longer, however, she reached a more certain conclusion, saying, instead, that I needed to ditch the glasses. "I mean, they're small and stylish, I'll give you that, but why not contacts or LASIK surgery?"

I was too nervous to put contacts into my eyes, and nobody was doing any surgery on me, those were the reasons, but I wasn't about to tell some stranger all of that. I didn't have to anyway, because Pam, being Pam, kept on talking.

"I can still see the beauty of your eyes even with your glasses on, so I guess that's why you keep wearing them. But they do make you look a little nerdy, girl, for real. And the way you keep pushing them up on your face makes you look a lot like the female version of Urkel."

When I asked her who in the heck was that, she laughed again. "Steve Urkel? The nerd with the pencil pile in his shirt pocket and the pants pulled up to his chest? Come *on*! He used to be on that old TV show when we were kids?"

When I still didn't appear to get it, she shook her head. "You are so not hip."

Anne Ziegler came into Mae's a few minutes later, talking so loud on her cell phone that everybody turned to see who in the world could be that obnoxious. She had her expensive handbag hanging from her shoulder, her white, tailored pant suit sparkling against her black skin, her four-inch high heels banging the mess out of the hardwood floor. She stopped by our table, just to say hey to Pam and to let her know that she was looking for somebody to manage her salon and wanted Pam, who seemed to know everybody, to spread the news.

As soon as Anne left our table and met up with her lunch companion, Pam spread the news to me, urging me to apply. All I had told her about myself was that I was on my way to Miami to hopefully find a decent job. How that translated into managing a hair salon in Melville was beyond me. But she was so insistent, and I was so afraid that I was about to let some grand opportunity pass me by, that I got up, went over to Anne's table, and introduced myself.

All I had to mention was that I was a graduate of Juilliard, that I'd received a bachelor of music degree with a major in piano, and she hired me on the spot. She didn't even care that I had absolutely no background in managing a beauty shop, or anything else for that matter, but that was the kind of strange turns my life had been taking.

Pam later said how she could tell that I was one of those elite-school-educated sisters, and that if she knew Anne Ziegler, she knew that such superficial credentials would impress her. I didn't care at all for the way she phrased that, especially in light of how difficult it was for me to receive those "superficial" credentials, but I understood where she was coming from.

And that was how I wound up back in Melville, alone and still not certain that this was the best move I could have made. But at least I'd made a move.

Less than two months later, when it appeared to me that I was in this for the long haul, I purchased a home in what Pam often said wasn't just the hood, but the sho nuff hood, a part of town bustling with so much illegal activity and poverty, everybody called it Dodge. Pam often told me that if she'd known where I was going to put down roots, she would have tied me up, kidnapped me, and knocked some sense into my head.

But I knew what I was doing. I knew my budget, and, if truth be told, the limits my less-than-stellar past placed on me being able to gain a bigger budget, and that little frame-styled, two-bedroom, one-bath home in not the best neighborhood in town, was barely within that budget to begin with. Forget what those houses in the so-called better communities would have cost.

So I proudly purchased my first home (with reasonable mortgage payments), painted it a bright yellow with grass-green trim, and reworked the entire yard. Soon my neighbors also caught the fever and started sprucing up their places too. All, except the owners of that apartment complex across the street. I can't even front. It was an eye sore, with faded gray peeling paint on the walls, dirt for grass, and a group of guys always hanging out on the stoop. They'd sit around smoking that dope disguised as cigars, shooting those dice and passing around dollar bills, listening to their loud gangsta rap and spinning around their souped-up rides as if they were proud to be a menace to society in general, not just to these poor folks in Dodge.

When I drove my red, aging BMW onto the driveway of my bright yellow house, I was treated to an unobstructed view of Juno Curtis and his boys on the stoop of that complex across the street. When Juno wasn't selling weed, he was our neighborhood watch, if you could believe that. If he liked you, he kept an eye out for you. His liking me, however, never stopped me from telling him about his behind and how wrong what he and his boys were doing. Although his boys wasn't having it, Juno would at least listen to me, nod his braided head occasionally, sometimes even act as if he was hearing what I was laying down.

But tonight I didn't even bother to lay it down. I was too

tired. My day job as manager of Anne Ziegler's salon had me running like the Road Runner on crack, all over the place, all because Anne came up with this bright idea to have a half-price hairdo day.

Quite naturally many of the sisters in the hood, who normally viewed Queen Anne's as a little too ritzy for their taste and pocketbooks, showed up in force. It was a madhouse.

Then I had to endure that madness at choir rehearsal.

Now Snoop was on the radio across the street dropping it like it was hot, and Juno and his boys were laughing and talking louder than Snoop was rapping. I barely had the energy to throw up a hand in a lame attempt at a wave, let alone lecture anybody.

That still, however, didn't stop Taneka Dupayne from running over.

"I'm broke, Neka," I said to her quickly, all too familiar with the girl's drug habit.

To my surprise, however, she wasn't looking for money.

"It's not true," she said in a voice that didn't even sound like hers. Even her eyes, which never looked clear, looked too clear tonight. "They gonna claim it's true, but it's not, and you can't let them get away with it, Roni."

"Girl, what are you talking about?" I asked her, more interested in getting my briefcase out of the car than paying attention to her.

"You can't let them get away with it!"

"Neka," I said impatiently, about ready to get rude, but then I looked at her more closely. What I saw stopped me cold. Sister looked bad. She was a crack addict, everybody knew that, but that's not what I meant. She looked sad, as if everybody was disregarding her and it was tearing her apart.

Taneka was only a year older than me, but that drug life had her looking an eternity older than my twenty-seven years. And she looked fed up, like somebody who never seemed to catch a break. That was what I saw when I looked into her eyes. Girlfriend needed a break.

"Why don't you come in, Neek," I said to her, taking her by her razor-thin arm. "We can talk inside."

I had known Taneka Dupayne since childhood, when we were both fast-tailed kids running around Melville as if we just knew life would be a breeze for us. We met when I was twelve years old and attending a public school for the first time in my life. My parents, who were jazz musicians, weren't getting as many gigs as they used to, and could no longer afford a private school education for me.

Public school was a cultural shock, as the girls there automatically disliked me, claiming that I thought I was cute, when I thought no such thing. And they especially hated my guts when boys started favoring me. I was bullied and beaten and threatened daily so much so, I often feigned illnesses to avoid going to school. As the year progressed and the violence and hatred against me only escalated, I even considered harming myself for real so that I could have a long convalescence and thereby avoid school altogether.

Before I could fully formulate my plan, however, I was attacked viciously by a group of girls who acted as if they'd planned to do the harming themselves. This wasn't their usual "knock-her-upside-her-head-and-pull-her-hair-out" fight, because one girl, JaQuana King, actually had a razor blade. Before she showed her weapon, however, I fought back as best I could, although I was greatly outnumbered and outsized. But when she whipped out that razor, my heart squeezed in fear.

She grinned, knowing she had me then, and said she was going to slash that cuteness right off of my face and cut that long, thick hair right off of my head. I had thought about doing myself some harm, it was true, but this was a far cry from what I had in mind.

During that same time Taneka had a reputation for violence far worse than JaQuana's. It was Neka, after all, who had been suspended for bringing a switchblade to school, bump a razor, and everybody knew she was somebody you just didn't mess with. She, in fact, had been watching the fight all along and was doing nothing to stop it. But when she saw that razor blade, she would later tell me, she knew that something had to give.

The fight was already one-sided, she'd said, five girls against my small self, but now, with the introduction of the razor, it was downright wrong.

Neka got in between JaQuana and me and told JaQuana if she wanted to slash somebody, to slash her. Since JaQuana had no idea what Taneka might be carrying, a switchblade or even worse, she backed up.

Neka reached into her windbreaker pocket as if she was about to retrieve her own weapon, and JaQuana took off running, her buddies right behind her. Neka bent over laughing.

I dropped down on my rump, stunned with fear, realizing how close I'd come to certain deformity.

We became fast friends after that, first at school only, and then after school, doing everything together. I discovered that Neka wasn't as bad as she let on, that she was actually a kind-hearted soul who had taken on that tough girl image when she had been bullied and beaten herself because boys found her attractive, too, and a few of the other cute girls couldn't stand it.

But instead of fighting back on their terms, the way I had attempted to do, she took the fight to a new level. That was why she brought the switchblade to school, why she'd jump into the face of any one of those girls who so much as looked at her the wrong way. She was determined to make them fear her. And they did.

And after that day I was suddenly associated with Neka, and was feared too. It changed my life. I loved school again, not just because those foolish girls had left me alone, but also because I could do my work without all of that pressure on my back. And Neka and me got tighter and tighter, hanging out more and more, until we discovered that we trusted no one else but each other. She told me about her alcoholic father and do-nothing mother, and how she wouldn't introduce me to them because of how they were.

"If they knew I had a good friend," she'd said, "they'd try to take that away from me too."

She never told me what else they had taken from her, and I didn't ask. She didn't need me judging her, but to be her friend. And I was.

It was a bond I thought would last forever. And it held strong for years, until that dreadful night when my parents left home for one of their jazz club gigs and never returned.

I'd called Neka as soon as I heard the news, and she rushed over. She was sixteen at the time and had left her parents home, deciding that she knew a little more than she probably did. She was living with Hakeem, some older boy she thought was in love with her, and he drove her over as soon as she got my phone call. She, in fact, wouldn't leave my side and even offered for me to stay with her and Hakeem, and that she would get a job and support us both.

But the social workers were already there, and they wouldn't allow me to spend so much as a night at Hakeem's. Neka herself was a troubled kid, they insisted, and Lord only knew what Hakeem was. So they carted me off, called my only known living relative, my father's sister, who lived in New Jersey, and made me wait in a group home until she could find the time to come and get me.

Neka and I tried to stay in touch by telephone, and we even tried on two occasions to bust me out of that prison of a group home, but nothing worked. And then my aunt showed up, and I was forced to move away from the only town I'd ever known and the only friend I'd ever had, only to get saddled with a relative who cared more about partying than she ever cared about me.

Neka had had her troubles too, during my group home days. Hakeem had kicked her out, and she found herself going from man to man, from nothing job to nothing job, until the last time we talked on the telephone, the night before I left for Newark, I could hear the desperation in her voice. Life was whipping her, and she was just about ready to lay down and let it.

Me and Neka both went through our own private hells in our own separate corners of the world after that night, where life turned out to be more like a whirlwind than any breeze for either one of us. And where now, looking at Neka, looking at the old friend I'd hardly recognized when I first came back to Melville, I couldn't help but wonder why it was that I made it through, while she, who used to be by far the tougher of us two, was still suffering from the choices she'd made when she was only sixteen.

By the time I got her inside of my home and gave her a glass of water, however, I could tell that she wasn't just suffering, but was on the verge of total collapse. She sat on that leather sofa in my small living room and stared into space, rocking back and forth and mumbling to herself despite my repeated requests that she let me in on her little conversation. Soon tears came to her large, staring eyes, and she looked at me as if she was seeing me for the first time.

I sat across from her, in my high-back chair, and that look in her eyes made my skin crawl.

"You can't let them get away with it," she said.

"What are you talking about, Neka? Who are *they*, and what are they trying to get away with?"

She began shaking her head, her dark, thin face hollow, almost skeleton-like "It's a mess. A mess, you hear me?"

"What's a mess?"

Taneka shook her head again.

"Neka, what's a mess?"

"You got to promise me. You're a churchgoing lady, Roni. You're the only one I know who can promise me. Promise me, Roni. Promise me you won't let them get away with it."

My heart dropped for Neka. She looked as if she was about to explode with anguish. For a hot second I got scared myself. What was wrong with this sister, I wondered. But then I exhaled, and gave in. I felt I had no choice.

"Okay, Neka, I promise." I pushed my glasses up on my face the way I was prone to do whenever I was nervous, and then I quickly demanded to know just exactly what I was promising.

She looked at me, stared at me, and then smiled a kind of sad, bitter smile. "She was gonna cut you," she said.

"Cut me? Who?"

"She was gonna cut you with that razor blade."

I stared at Neka. "You mean JaQuana King back in school?"

Neka nodded her head, smiling again, this time as if it was some inside joke.

"That was a long time ago, Neek."

"Long, long ago," she said. "So long ago." Her voice cracked. Then she added, "We had fun then."

I nodded, fighting back the tears that our old memories could still engender. "Yes, we did," I said. "We had a lot of fun then. But what's going on with you now, bud? Is somebody after you?"

"You got to stay tough, Roni, even when they try to stop you."

"Who's *they*, Neek? Who are you talking about?"

"It's a mess," she said again, shaking her head, that anguished look coming over her narrow face once again. And then, as if suddenly realizing that she shouldn't be where she was, she placed the glass of water on my coffee table, didn't tell me so much as good night, and took off out of my front door.

Now it was my time to shake my head. *That girl must have gotten hold of some powerfully crazy dope*, I thought. I decided to shower, say my prayers, praying for Neka and thanking the Good Lord that I didn't get hooked on drugs when I was out there, and take my behind to bed.

I lay in bed, thinking about my life thus far. After graduating from Juilliard, I'd landed a job with Branson Academy, a prestigious private school in Newark. But somebody, my ex-boyfriend Richard Pargeter, to be precise, told my employers a few things about my past, a past the dean felt rendered me, in his still painful words, "unfit to be around his students," and he fired me summarily. Dropped me like I was hot, in other words.

Now I was forced to apply for jobs as if it was my first time trying to work in my field, because no way was I going to mention Branson Academy on any resume I submitted. Thank God for Anne Ziegler, who gave me a job despite my lack of qualifications, and who still, when she wasn't being a witch on two legs, supported my desire to eventually work in my field.

I turned over, trying not to think about all of that worrisome stuff, still trying, after all these years, to get used to the solitude of my existence, when my phone rang.

Thinking it was Pamela calling to give me the final verdict on the choir mutiny, I picked up the receiver saying her name. But it wasn't Pam. Not by a long shot.

Like a blast from the past, like a nightmare I thought was long since over, it was, as if I'd conjured him up just by thinking about him, my ex. It was enough to make me sit up in bed.

"How did you get this number?" I demanded to know. *How did you know I was still alive?*

He laughed, of course. He never took me seriously. "You

can't ever get away from me, Roni Jarrett," he said between laughs. "Face it, girl, we were too good together."

"Yeah, right. What do you want?"

"I miss that gorgeous, smoky voice of yours, you know that?"

"What do you want, Richard?"

"Dang, girl!"

"I'm hanging up. Which I should have already done."

"Okay, okay. Goodness. I just wanna talk to your li'l chocolate butt, all right? Can't a man have a civil conversation with his woman?"

"*His* woman?" I said with a high-pitched lilt to my voice.

I'd dumped this player when I was twenty-three and just starting my junior year at Juilliard. He'd given me hell about my education the entire time I was in school, and I put up with it. Until I came home one weekend to the fancy Newark apartment we were sharing, and found him with some skanky female that stripped at his club.

It wasn't the first time I'd caught him cheating on me, I'm ashamed to admit, but it was definitely the last. But I didn't argue the way I usually did. I didn't trip. I didn't try to get him to feel my pain. I didn't care what he felt. My self-esteem already had to have been right around zero to put up with his mess as long as I had endured it, but I wasn't enduring it another second.

I threw my clothes into a garbage bag and left that scene. And left it, I thought, for good. Now all this time later, all that buried pain later, he had the nerve to still refer to me as *his* woman?

"We haven't been together in years," I reminded him, as if I needed to. "Four years, to be precise. And you're trying to act like you don't realize that? That you don't remember all that?"

"That's why I want us to talk. I've tried it with other girls,

Roni. Believe me, I tried. But it ain't happenin'. You're the one for me. For real, though. None of those other females got what you got, can do what you do for me. You're the best I ever had, Roni Jarrett, the best! We've got to try this thing again."

I wanted to laugh. So I did. "Forget it."

"Will you at least listen to me?"

"Take a hike, Richard. I'm not wasting another second trying anything with your trifling butt. You got me fired from a job I loved." I spoke with a bitterness I thought had long gone. "Fired, Richard. We weren't even together anymore. I wasn't even in your life anymore, and you still found a way to hurt me. And you think I would even consider trying to get back with you? That I'd be that desperate?"

"People change, Roni."

"Fine. And I hope you have. But that still has nothing to do with you and me getting together."

"People find religion."

Based on the way he said it, that lowering of his voice, I knew brotherman was up to something.

"I mean, take you for instance. You've found religion, haven't you, Roni? Playing that piano at that middle-class church in that middle-class family values kind of town."

How could he possibly know all of that? "Okay, what's the gig this time, Richard? What's the game? Hurt and humiliate Roni again? Is that it?"

"Ain't no game. I'm just curious, that's all. I'm just wondering if those good church folks know anything at all about their angel of a piano player's less than angelic background. I'm just wondering if I should school them on it."

My heart dropped. But Richard would never know it.

"Do what you have to do, know what I'm saying? If you're that petty, then be petty, show your true colors once again for all the world to see. Just leave me alone!" And then I did what

I should have done when I first heard his sorry voice, and hung up the phone.

I got on my knees and prayed fervently that that trifling Richard Pargeter wouldn't cause any more trouble for me. I was tired of trouble.

I'd only been a Christian for not quite a year, and that only happened because a teacher at Branson invited me to her church the week before I was fired. Her minister, who was telling his life story, seemed to be preaching about mine, from my days on the street, to when I met Richard, to when I left Richard.

At first I was suspicious. Then I realized that every sinner has a similar story to tell. Loneliness and rejection and desolation and despair have a way of sounding all too familiar. But when that minister said that my beginning didn't have to end that way, and that God could exchange my fate and write a new ending to my story, I heard him, and gave my life to Christ.

And He did rewrite my story, and He did give me a second chance, and Richard nor anybody else was going to take that chance from me. But that, of course, didn't stop them from trying.

I fell asleep talking to God as if He was laying right beside me. I was telling Him a mouthful: about Richard, about the choir, about my life thus far and how I could hardly wait for this day to end and for tomorrow to come and bring on a new day, a more hopeful day.

Tomorrow did come, and it was a new day, all right, but hope was another matter. I arrived at Queen Anne's late from oversleeping, and was treated to the usual beautician gossip about various citizens of our community, citizens who had no earthly idea that they were hot topics of conversation this early in the morning.

But when the talk shifted from who's sleeping with whom

to how the police found Taneka Dupayne, better known to them as "Crackhead Neka," in an alley late last night, and how she was beaten to death almost beyond recognition, my world as I had known it just the day before shifted too.

TWO

Melville, Florida isn't exactly your regular big city, but it's big enough, with nearly a hundred thousand bona fide residents and a college community that added to that number at varying degrees throughout the year. Sometimes the streets looked ghostly, and sometimes, like now, the streets were almost as crowded as any traffic jam I'd ever experienced in Newark.

I was on my way to the police station. The rag top of my Beamer down, my long, wavy hair blowing in the wind, my stereo pouring some serious Donnie McClurkin in my ears, and I couldn't believe I was doing this. Not that I didn't think I had a duty to go to the police. Thanks to my encounter with Taneka last night I knew I did, but it was just that I didn't get along with cops. I'd be the first to tell anybody that police officers were not my favorite people. Not that there weren't good, honest policemen—I'd never be so foolish to paint an entire profession with the same brush—but it's just that I'd never run into any.

When I first arrived at Queen Anne's this morning, flustered because I'd overslept, that promise my big mouth had made to Taneka wasn't even on my mind. That out-of-nowhere phone call from my ex was still occupying some space, and that choir acting a fool last night, but Neka was nowhere on my radar screen. I remembered stepping out of my car in front of the salon and looking around at all of the activity on Bay Street, and wondering, as I often did, how I ever ended up back in Melville. And working at a beauty shop, of all places. Not exactly my dream job come true.

Then I looked at that beauty shop, a white, one-story, gable-roofed building with gray awnings over the top and Queen Anne's Hair Salon written in large, black, semi-circled letterings across the enormous plateglass window. It shared an elongated lot with Berkmann's, a high-end clothing store, and Ethel Jean's Down Home Cooking, a restaurant with a great name but served food that had no flavor whatsoever.

When I walked into the salon, Anne Ziegler, my boss, was standing behind the long, marble-top front counter talking on the phone with a potential products vendor, doing the job I was hired to do. I walked up to her, ready to give her my best I'm-so-sorry-for-being-late speech, but she wasn't about to interrupt her business to listen to me. So I stood there and waited.

Anne, or Miss Anne as Greta and some of the other beauticians called her behind her back, was a well-proportioned, tall, bosomy woman, with jet-black, smooth skin, long, blond-weaved hair, and a wide, warm face made beautiful by her small, perceptive eyes, and rich, full lips. In many ways she was a kind soul, a sister who would give her last. But she was a no-nonsense businesswoman. And when she hung up that telephone she reminded me of that very fact.

"You're late," she said in that heavy, almost baritone voice she used whenever she wanted to make it clear that she wasn't playing.

"I'm sorry," I replied, trying to emulate that voice, but unable to get past alto. "I didn't realize."

"You know I don't play that, Roni."

"I didn't realize the time. I overslept."

"I'm sure you did, staying up all night messing with that choir."

I looked at her curiously.

"Oh, yeah," she said. "I heard about that. Heard folks were fighting in the stands and nearly gave poor Deacon Montgomery a heart attack when he tried to get those idiots to stop. But, hey, that's what you want."

"You act like it's something I campaigned for. It was a job that I applied for, Anne. That's all. Director of music. Directing the choir came with the package."

"You would have gladly done it even if it didn't come with no package. Don't even try me like that. I see your butt on Sunday mornings, all smiles when you walk into that choir stand, all teeth. You love that stuff."

"So that's a problem now?"

"Ain't no problem." Anne shook her blond head with a serious attitude. "But it's a fact that Bernadette Finch had been directing that choir for as long as I can remember, and it's another fact that Dr. Simms was wrong to take that away from her, and it's yet another fact that you was wrong for getting in the middle of that situation."

I shook my head. "It was a job that I applied for. Just like this job. I didn't get in the middle of anything. And why are you all on my case? Sister Finch is the one giving me a hard time, not the other way around."

"All I know is that every time y'all have choir rehearsal, you come bouncing in here late for work the following morning. That's all I know. And I'm not having it."

"Okay, Anne. Goodness. I didn't realize I had a pattern of behavior going on here."

"Lots you don't realize, college girl. That's your problem. You think because you're young and healthy and got your whole life ahead of you everything will just work itself out eventually. You've got everything, Roni. All Bernadette Finch had was that choir."

I've got everything? I was shocked that she would even think such a thing. But I didn't even go there. People believe what

they want to believe. "What's up with you and all of this praising of Sister Finch?" I said to her instead. "You don't even
like her."

"Yeah, well, I'm fifty years old today. Fifty years old." She
said this as if it was a disease. "And let's just say I understand
the sister now. I feel her. I know what time it is."

I wanted to ask, "And what time is that?" but the phone
rang again, and she snatched it up before I could say a word. I
started to head for my office in the back, but she held up one
of her beefy, perfectly manicured fingers to let me know to
hold on, to not go anywhere, that she's not through ripping
into me yet.

I stood at the counter waiting for her conversation to end,
and my inquisition to recommence. That was when I heard
about Taneka. Greta, the oldest beautician we had on staff,
although she was only thirty-five, was telling Ernest, our most
popular beautician, about the murder of a crack addict she'd
heard about.

At first I didn't think anything of it, especially since a crackhead being killed in Melville was hardly big news. I was more
interested in Greta herself, or E.F. Hutton, as Anne called
her behind her back. Anne explained that the well-known
brokerage firm ran commercials in the seventies and eighties
claiming that whenever E.F. Hutton had something to say,
everybody stopped and listened.

Our E.F. Hutton was removing braids from a customer's
head and running her mouth nonstop on the morning after
Neka's death. She was animated and confident and knew how
to keep a person spellbound with her gossip, one of those
females who knew everything about everybody but nobody
knew a thing about her. Her private life was her private life,
she loved to say, and when I'd point out that the same could
be said for all of those poor folks she was always gossiping
about, she'd tell me, although, technically, I was her supervisor, to mind my own business.

Tall, and stout, with big eyes and a messy mop of thick, shoulder-length, black hair, Greta was a fairly good beautician, the queen of the weave, but it was that mouth of hers that kept her customers coming back. Because she always knew the news.

Sometimes the salon would be just humming along, most of the conversation sedated, until Greta say, "Chile, did you hear . . ." to whoever's head she was working on at the time, and everybody would get quiet and listen.

As her supervisor, I once tried to have a little talk with her about all of that big gossiping she was doing, but Anne had a little talk with me.

"Greta's mouth keeps customers coming back," she said. "Leave E.F. Hutton alone. She's my best advertisement."

This morning, however, E.F. Hutton was advertising doom and gloom as she talked about this killing of a crack addict. She seemed to love to tell the news, I thought, watching her, as her entire plain face lit up with joy as she talked about something no one in their right mind could view as joyful.

But then Neka's name was mentioned. And my heart dropped. I hurried to Greta, asking for more details, and she gladly obliged. A friend of hers, she said, who knew a friend of a cop, had told her that Crackhead Neka's beaten up body was found in some dark alley last night over on Hazelhurst.

After the initial shock of it, after the disbelief finally began to turn into that hard, cold reality that made my stomach ache, I hoisted my small self up onto the large, hydraulic chair that sat between Greta's and Ernest's work stations and began swiveling side to side. I was still stunned, remembering that skeletal face of Neka's and her pretty, staring eyes, remembering that I'd seen her alive just last night, and now she was gone forever.

I shook my head and blinked a few times as if I still couldn't believe it, and then I looked at Greta and Ernest. It should be shocking to them, too, since they also knew Neka. But it didn't seem shocking to them at all. They kept right on talking about what happened, and about how bad Neka looked, as if they were talking about a minor matter, an everyday thing, another piece of gossip to add to their string.

"Do they have any suspects?" I asked nervously, pushing my glasses up on my still stunned face, knowing full well it was probably too soon. But given the way Neka was acting at my house last night, and that promise my big mouth had made to her about not letting them get away with it, I felt I had to ask.

"Suspects?" Greta said, amazed that I'd asked. "Already? The body's barely cold, Roni, okay, and you know good and well Gillette is not the kind of man that's gonna be beating the pavement looking for the killer of no crackhead like Neka. And if you don't believe that, you on crack yourself."

"Don't believe it," Ernest said to me, running his fingers through his customer's just permed hair, as if he was still trying to decide how best to style it. "Gillette's not like that."

"You ain't telling me," Greta said irritably. "Donald Gillette is one of those rich, uppity brothers who couldn't care less for the likes of Neka Dupayne."

"He cares," Ernest said.

I looked at him. He was tall like Greta, but was high yella, one of those impeccably groomed brothers with a slim body, a bald head, and an ever-present, colorful scarf that he'd always unwrap and sling around his neck again anytime things weren't going his way. He was also an unbelievably meticulous stylist who refused to release a customer until every strand of hair was perfectly in place.

Which always got on my nerves, especially when customers would have to wait sometimes for hours for him to get to them, causing them to start complaining to me, and causing me to complain to Anne.

But Ernest could do no wrong in Anne's eyes. "Let 'em

wait," she'd say, as if the stylist, not the customers, kept her in business. "If they want Ern, they gots to wait."

"Gillette is just somebody who thinks people should do the right thing," Ern went on. "He figure folks ought to take care of their responsibilities and act like they got some sense up in here, and I agree with him one hundred percent. He wants us to stop being complainers and victims and get ahead in this life. That's why he's hard on us. To me that's somebody who cares most of all."

"Cares most of all?" Greta said. "Man, please. The only reason he's so hard on everybody is because he don't have to worry about the consequences. Mayor Riles hired him because of who he is, not what he can do." Then she looked at me. "That job is just a hobby for him, Roni, just something for him to do in his spare time. Don't you listen to Ernest. Why should somebody like Donald Gillette care about Taneka Dupayne, or you, or me, or anybody else not up there with him?"

"Who's this Donald Gillette?" I asked, concerned that the brother sounded like trouble, like somebody who wasn't going to do right by Neek when I'd promised her that I'd make sure that they did, whoever *they* were.

Greta and Ernest looked at each other as if they couldn't believe my question, and then they looked at me.

"I know you didn't just ask that," Ernest said, his head downward as he looked at me over his half-moon reading glasses.

"Come on, Roni, where you been?"

"He's our police chief," Ernest said. "He also used to own Big G's, for crying out loud."

"Big whose?"

Ernest shook his head and looked at me with wonderment.

Greta laughed. "Big G's used to be this big deal nightclub in town. He owned it until his wife died. Then he sold it."

"For tons of green, girl. And how come you don't know no

Donald Gillette? I thought you said you was from Melville?"

"I am from Melville. But I left when I was fifteen. What would I have known about a nightclub at fifteen?"

Ernest laughed. "I knew plenty at fifteen. Plenty! And I shole knew Big G's. Just could never afford to check it out."

"So this Gillette used to own a nightclub and now he's a cop?" I asked. "Why did he give it up?"

"His wife died," Greta said as if I wasn't listening to her. "So he sold it, along with some other business interests he had. Made serious dollars off of the deal just like Ernest said, and then left town for what everybody assumed was gonna be forever. I mean, he was messed up after his wife died, I ain't kiddin' about that. The man was a wreck. But he came back. We was all shocked when it was announced he was the new chief. I mean, we all knew he had been a cop up north years before he went into the nightclub business, but it still didn't sound right. Not for a brother like Gillette. But it was true. He became our chief. He changed, though. Wasn't nothing like the easygoing dude we all used to know and love. Now he's all hard-edged, all about ridding the streets of this and that, and he ain't having this and that. I can't stand him now. And he's a player, too? A love-em-and-leave-em pro too? Please. He ain't nothing like he used to be. Now he's something else."

"He made it big as a businessman," Ernest said to me, spraying moisturizer onto his customer's head, all but ignoring Greta, "and came back to help out his community. In my eyes that shows character to be able to do that. Ain't too many people walking away with no big money like he had and coming back here. But he came back, shole did. With his fine self."

"Fine?" Greta said. "I don't know about all that."

Ernest stopped spraying and looked at her. "He *is* fine. What you talking about? He's the finest-looking brother in this country, maybe even in this world, and you know I'm telling the truth."

"I know you're exaggerating, that's what I know."

"I'm not exaggerating." Ernest leaned over toward the customer in his chair. "Miss Morton, chile, you know about men. Am I exaggerating?"

Miss Morton, who appeared to have been dozing through the exchange, tilted her head up. "What's that, Ernest?"

"Am I exaggerating about Donald Gillette being the finest-looking human being this world has ever known?"

Miss Morton laughed. "You're exaggerating,"she said then held up a finger. "But not by much."

Ernest smiled. "Thank you."

"What thank you?" Greta asked. "She said you're exaggerating."

"But not by much. The point," Ernest said, looking at me, "is that he's fine, okay. By anybody's measuring stick, the man is fine. Got those beautiful hazel eyes that droop a little, and that bod of his? Chile, chile. Makes you wanna holla." Ernest fanned himself with his hand, but got serious again when he saw that I wasn't with his clowning, that I still looked undoubtedly distressed. "He'll look out for Neka, Roni, don't you worry."

"Don't you believe it," Greta quickly interjected. "Donald Gillette won't be losing any sleep, not one wink, over what happened to some crackhead like Taneka Dupayne. And you can rest assured of that."

I sat still on that oversized hydraulic chair, hoping Greta was wrong, that her big gossip failed to be true and Ernest's assessment of this ex-nightclub owning po-po was far more accurate. For Neka's sake, anyway. But I knew Greta, and I knew Ernest, and if I ever had to lay bets on which one of them would know what they were talking about, it would be Greta Crenshaw in a walk. Unfortunately.

***

The Melville Police Department was located on the corner of Ricker Avenue and Laney Road, and it was a massive brick building with flags flying full staff and a large squadron of police vehicles parked out front.

The sergeant at the entrance desk had me waiting for nearly five minutes before he could find a moment to even ask me what I wanted. Then he told me that I had to wait even longer before Detective Vincent Delvecchio, the cop in charge of the investigation, could see me.

I sat down in an uncomfortable metal chair pushed up against a dingy wall and waited with more than a little anxiety for this detective. I pulled out some papers I had in my shoulder bag, some requisition orders I needed to review, but I was too antsy in a police station to be that calm. So I sat those papers on my lap and just waited.

But it was an impatient wait, as I found myself playing with my thumbs, leaning forward, leaning back, checking out my well-starched white dress pants and sleeveless yellow blouse that appeared to be as out of place in such a dingy building as the beautiful art that lined its walls. And I'm talking seriously beautiful art in massive frames and glass encasing. It was as if some local women's guild knew that a place like this was going to be depressing enough, so they got together and decided to liven it up with tasteful art.

It didn't work, the place was still depressing, but at least they tried.

I folded my arms and crossed my legs, and began staring at my glittery red-and-yellow stiletto heel as I swung my crossed leg back and forth. When I looked up again, however, a brother far more interesting to observe than any heel on my foot was walking through the entrance doors.

As soon as he walked through that door, before anybody had to tell me anything, I just knew he had to be that Donald

Gillette they were telling me about in the salon this morning. Although he was an older man, he was nowhere near as ancient as I thought he'd be. He wore a double-breasted, dark blue suit, one of those fancy-looking Italian jobs, and walked across the hardwood floor in his expensive wing-tip shoes with such an air of authority about him that you'd think he was the CEO of a Fortune 500 company rather than some local cop.

Why I automatically pegged him as Gillette, the police chief, I couldn't even say. He looked like no cop I'd ever seen. Not dressed up in digs like that. But somehow I knew it was him. Anyone who amassed a fortune in the business world and then decided to return to that high-risk world of cops and robbers had to be a noticeably different kind of man. And the brother who immediately caught my eye was definitely, almost incredibly, something different.

Ernest, of course, was exaggerating when he'd said he was the finest-looking man on the face of this earth. But I'm with Miss Morton. Not by much. He wasn't towering tall, just right around six feet was my guestimation, but he was powerfully built, a man with the kind of broad shoulders and thick, muscular chest that screamed workouts and athleticism. His face was a smooth, oak-brown complexion and appeared naturally stern, with a strong square jaw, a straight, elegant nose, and firm, luscious lips that commanded attention. He, in fact, made for such an awesome somebody to check out, this man who overwhelmed the room just by walking into it, I couldn't take my eyes off him.

But then I thought about Neka, and why I was in that police station in the first place, and my heart that had perked up just from seeing this guy, began to sink. For all of his commanding presence, he also had the look of a man who was all about business, all about getting the big guys and leaving peons like Neka to underlings who didn't want to be bothered with her either. I couldn't even begin to see a brother like him discussing why a crackhead was murdered. He'd be more concerned about the proverbial big picture, about why it was that drugs were so freely available in his town to begin with, and who were the suppliers. I could see him and his men straegizing about dealers and suppliers all night long. But about Neka? About who beat up a crackhead and tossed her body in some alley like she was a dog in the street? Not a chance. I was afraid that Greta's predictions about the man were beginning to seem right-on to me. Because if the brother who had just walked into the Melville Police Station was indeed Donald Gillette, all decked down like nobody's business, and this was the man who was in charge of investigating all drug-related murders and mayhem in this town, then who killed Taneka Dupayne was probably going to be an unsolved mystery for a long, long time to come.

There were many folks coming and going out of that police station that day, but for some reason this one particular man kept me enthralled. He walked up to the sergeant's desk, just as I had done, but was treated to a lively conversation by the same cop who wouldn't give me so much as a smile. They talked easily and companionably, which was all the more reason for me to peg him for a cop too.

But I still couldn't stop staring at him in his tailored-to-perfection suit, his muscular arms folded, his long legs spread eagle in a military, iron man stance. And maybe that, too, had something to do with why I didn't see him as the type who'd look out for the common man. Maybe it was that iron man in him, that steely look that came over his face as he listened intensely to the sergeant's long-winded story.

That same gaze finally left the still talkative sergeant and began to survey the busy room in the manner that cops seemed trained to do, with his eyes eventually settling, to my great discomfort, on me. Even from where I sat, I could tell they were sexy eyes, hazel in color with a slight but unmistakable droopiness about them that solidified their attractiveness. Oh, the brother was fine. Ernest was right about that.

Although the sergeant kept going on and on about something apparently serious, and he may have had Gillette's full ear, Gillette would not look away from me. I felt fire piercing through my entire body as those sexy eyes ever so slowly scanned me from head to toe, and then back up again, as if they were doing some serious assessing.

I was across the room, seated in a cheap chair against a dingy wall, but I would have declared he was right in front of me. That was how close he felt. That was how much fire he ignited in me.

"Hey, pretty lady. What up?" a voice said just above my head.

I jumped and turned. I let out a sigh of annoyance. A young brother was standing beside my chair, looking every bit the thug he undoubtedly was. Not that I was trying to be judgmental in calling the brother a thug, but I'd been around them since I was sixteen, and knew one when I saw one. And they always, I mean, always, found a way to hook up with me.

This one in particular had a gold grill in the front of his mouth, his hair spiked up and nappy, his clothes too big and baggy for his slender frame. And because, in my younger days, these had usually been the kind of brothers I was attracted to, I could immediately see the attractiveness in him. Which I knew was bad news, and which caused me to turn away from him and shuffle the papers on my lap.

"Whatever you're selling, I ain't buying," I said to him.

"Ouch!" he said playfully. "You know how to hurt a brother's feelings, though."

When I didn't respond to that, he kept going.

"What a classy lady like you doin' in a rat joint like this?"

Classy. I looked back toward Gillette, who was still staring at me.

He suddenly excused himself from his talkative sergeant and began heading in my direction. My heart began to pound as he came near, which was a first for me. My heart pounding just because a good-looking man was coming my way? It seemed almost laughable. But I couldn't laugh, not on my life. I was too excited, too jittery, and I didn't know why.

"Cat got your tongue?" the young brother I had already forgotten said into my ear.

I continued to ignore him and nervously pushed my glasses up on my face, my arms now folded, my legs still crossed, my head tilted up to see Gillette approaching, to see this big man suddenly before me with such unbelievable eyes.

"Get lost, Skeet," he said to the brother.

"Ah, man, Gillette, why you always buggin'? I wasn't doin' nothin' wrong. I was just talkin' to the lady."

The look Gillette gave him caused him to back up. "It's your world, cuz," Skeet said. "What? She one of yours or somethin'?" he kept backing up until he was back on the other side of the room, where he apparently had come from.

Gillette then looked at me. "You okay?"

I almost laughed. Did he think I was one of those prim and proper females who couldn't take care of herself? Or classy, as Skeet had called me? "Yes, I'm fine, thank you," I said.

He stared at me a moment, then extended his hand. "I'm Don Gillette."

"Chief of police Gillette?" I asked as we shook. His hand was so big, it swallowed mine.

"That's right," he said, still staring into my eyes. "And you're?"

I met what I felt was a slight resistance as I removed my hand from his. "I'm Veronica Jarrett. I'm waiting to see Detective Delvecchio."

He nodded and ran his hand across his low-cut, naturally wavy, salt-and-pepper hair. "Delvecchio. You need to see him about?"

"Taneka Dupayne."

"Dupayne? The young lady who was murdered last night?"

I swallowed hard, nodding.

"They found her body over on Hazelhurst."

"Right."

"You know her?"

"I'm a friend of hers," I said.

As soon as I'd said it, his look seemed to change. He was probably wondering if I was a crack addict, too, or bore some guilt by association. I felt a need to explain.

"We used to be tight when we were kids. But we weren't anymore. I hadn't seen her in years, not until I recently moved back to town."

As soon as I gave this justification I immediately regretted it, my face unable to hide my discomfort. I suddenly felt like a betrayer, trying to distance myself from an unsavory relative just to impress some man. Taneka didn't deserve that. I looked back up at Gillette. There was a softness in his expressive eyes that made me feel assured that he understood.

"You know something about your friend's murder?"

"Not really, no. I mean, I wish I did. I wish I . . . I just want to make sure that y'all understand what kind of person Neka was. She wasn't just a crackhead. She was a goodhearted person, a kind person. A person who would—"I couldn't finish.

All kinds of emotions began to well up inside of me, just thinking about Neka and how awful her death had to have been, and how her life was no picnic either caused me to suddenly feel vulnerable too. And before I knew it, tears began to fill my eyes.

I looked away from Gillette, embarrassed by my lack of control, expecting him to tell me to have a nice day and run, not walk, away from me and my emotional behind. But to my amazement, he didn't tell me any such thing.

He handed me his handkerchief. "Sure you're all right?" he asked as I wiped my tears away.

I looked up at him and nodded, but as soon as I saw the compassion in his eyes, my tears returned. I could have kicked myself for being so emotional. I had no intentions whatsoever of coming into this police station and acting like some simpering idiot. But, again, Gillette surprised me. He sat down beside me.

My heart hammered as his large body sat beside my small one, his nearness overwhelming me. And for the first time in a long time, not since my parents were still alive, I felt protected. Why I was feeling this way, however, given how utterly irrational it was, was the question.

For the longest time Gillette just sat there, his legs crossed too, his big hands relaxed in his lap. His men, some in uniform, some not, passed by and spoke to their chief then glared at me, as if they wanted to see for themselves what great powers I possessed to gain the undivided attention of their boss. It was the same question I was asking myself. Why was he doing this? Why was he wasting his valuable time sitting here with me?

He, in fact, stayed beside me, not long enough for me to wipe my tears and hand him back his handkerchief, but as long as it took for me to get my emotions totally back under control. It was such a kind thing to do, such a gentlemanly gesture, that I irrationally felt a connection to this man.

A connection to this man, I thought incredulously. *After a few minutes and I felt a connection to some stranger?* What was wrong with me? It was as if I was mixing apples with neckbones and calling it a tuna salad. My visit to this police station was about Neka's death, but I was acting as if it was all about my lonely heart. And it was too disturbing. Even Richard didn't used to have this kind of effect on me.

But then I remembered what Greta had said about this man I was fawning over, about how hard he was, about how little he'd care for somebody like Taneka, about him being a womanizer. Reality returned.

"Didn't mean to get so choked up," I said, confident now that I could speak without quivering.

"Perfectly natural. She was your friend."

I nodded. "Yes. And she was a good person too. Before the drugs. We used to run around Melville together, and she was the undisputed leader of our twosome. I was following her. That's why this is so incredible. For her end to have been so . . . so dismissive, like her life was nothing, like she deserved to be beaten up and thrown into some alley. Nobody deserved that. She didn't deserve that."

By now Gillette was staring at me again. A look came over his eyes, a look no longer fraught with compassion for me, but with memories of his own, of something or somebody, that caused him to look away from me. And as suddenly as he had sat down, he stood up.

I looked up, surprised, especially since I didn't tell him what I wanted him to know. That Neka had visited me the night of her murder. But his look was different now, more businesslike.

"Detective Delvecchio will be with you shortly," he said, as if I was now a stranger in his police station. Then he stared at me a moment longer, again looking me up and down as if there was some interest there, but not enough for him to make any moves. "You take care of yourself, you hear me?" He began heading for the elevators before I could so much as nod okay.

I felt a surge of disappointment when he walked away, as if I'd failed his assessment, which should have been fine by me, but for some crazy reason it wasn't. And I still couldn't take my eyes off of him, checking out his powerful body as he stopped to talk with a couple of his uniformed officers at those elevators.

I stared even more brazenly as he and his officers got onto the elevator and disappeared behind the slammed doors.

When I looked back around, the desk sergeant, who had apparently been staring at me the whole time, was now smiling and shaking his big, football head, as if my desperate housewife act just gave him his laugh for the day. As if the fact that he'd caught me profiling his boss was the funniest thing he'd ever witnessed.

I rolled my eyes.

"Miss Jarrett?" a voice said beside me.

I turned quickly to the sound. *Had he seen me too?*

It was another cop, this one taller than Gillette, but just as muscled, with brown, shabby hair that stopped at his shoulders, and milky blue eyes that seemed more than a little annoyed by my presence.

I grabbed my papers and my shoulder bag and stood up. He offered his hand.

"I'm Delvecchio," he said as we shook. "I understand you have something for me."

Something for him? What was that supposed to mean? Immediately my crooked cop antenna, which, I'd admit, was badly flawed and biased to begin with flew up. "Well, no," I said. "I mean, no."

Delvecchio's annoyance level jumped higher too, and he looked over at the desk sergeant. The sergeant sighed his impatience.

"You said you had something to tell the detective about that killing last night," the desk sergeant reminded me. "We ain't here to play no games, lady."

"I'm not playing any games," I said, remembering what he'd caught me doing. "And I do have something to tell him." Then I looked at the detective, a man who seemed as if he'd rather be anywhere than standing here wasting time with me. "I thought when you said that I had something for you, that you meant some physical evidence of some sort, or a bribe or something. I didn't know what you meant."

"A bribe?" He started looking around, as if he expected the Feds to break down the doors and cuff him at any moment. "What is this?"

"I misunderstood you, is what I'm saying. I'm sorry."

He looked at me longer and then shook his head. He concluded, I think, that I wasn't worth the energy it took to be angry. "Okay, give," he said as if I was boring him. "What you got?"

I looked around. The place wasn't exactly bursting with folks, but there were a number of them sitting around and coming and going. "Here?" I asked.

"Yes, here. Now what is it?"

"It's just that—"

"Look, you may not believe this, but I actually have things to do, all right. Now if you have something for me, spit it out, or go on back where you came from. Like Sarge said, we don't have time for games, lady."

Cops, I thought, I do not care for cops.

"Well?" he asked again, his patience about as tamed as a cat on a hot tin roof.

I started to tell him to just forget it, and leave. But I promised Neka. "I saw Taneka before she died," I said, swallowing my pride.

"Taneka Dupayne?"

"Yes."

"Where?"

"At my house."

"What time?"

I had to think about this. "Around seven thirty-five, seven forty-five, something like that."

"And this was last night?"

"Yes."

"So what went down? What was she doing?"

"She was acting really weird. She said that they're going to lie and say it's true, but it's not true, and that I can't let them get away with it."

He stared at me as if I had just spoken Swahili. "Okay, back up. Who are *they*?"

I shook my head. "I don't know."

"You don't know?"

"I don't know."

"So somebody comes up to you and urges you to not let them get away with something, but you don't care enough to ask just what it is she's talking about?"

"I asked, but she didn't say. Look, I know it sounds weird. It sounded weird to me too. But that's what happened, and I thought you'd like to know." I shoved my papers into my bag and hung it across my shoulder. My head was beginning to ache, which it usually did when I got upset. "If it's nothing you can use, then fine. At least I told you. I personally find it odd that she would come to me saying something like that then end up dead a few hours later, but hey, I' m no police officer. What do I know, right?"

Delvecchio didn't like me. I could see it in his eyes. He exhaled. "Where were you around eleven last night?" he asked me.

Oh, no, he didn't, I thought. "Excuse me?"

"Where were you at eleven o'clock last night?"

"I was home in my bed, that's where I was. Why would my whereabouts have anything to do with this?"

"Where do you live?"

"On Elkin Street."

"Where on Elkin?"

"Thirty-nine fifty-two Elkin."

"That's what, right across the street from where Dupayne lived?"

"That's right."

"So you and her ran together?"

"No, I didn't *run* with Taneka. She was just my neighbor,

who happened to tell me something strange on the night she died. That's the beginning and the end of it. I was just trying to help you, that's all."

"Help me do what?"

I couldn't believe he asked that. "Find out what happened to Taneka," I said, exhausted.

"Come on, lady. You know what happened to her. She was a crackhead looking for crack on Hazelhurst. What you think happened to her?"

"But why would she tell me to not let them get away with it, if it was as simple as that?"

"You tell me."

"What?"

"You heard me."

"Look, I told you all I know. Neka came over, she said those words to me, and that was it. She looked scared, and she looked worried sick. That's all I know."

"Ever been arrested before?"

"What?"

"Have you ever been arrested before?"

I stared at him. I also began praying to the Lord to not let this crazy man go snooping around in my background. "What difference does that make?" I asked as if I was offended. "I didn't kill her."

"I didn't say you killed her. Did I say you killed her? You said that."

Lord, give me strength. "Good-bye, detective," I said and turned to leave.

He caught me by the arm. "I'm not dismissing you yet."

"Unless you're arresting me, you are." I waited for him to make the next move.

When he didn't, I snatched my arm away from him and left that "sworn-to-serve-and-protect" building that wasn't serving and protecting me another second.

THREE

I drove back to work, which wasn't exactly a comforting thing to do either, but at least I never felt accused at Queen Anne's, or intimidated. That cop Delvecchio had gotten on my nerves, that's all, with his foolish suspiciousness, and that hazel-eyed Gillette, getting me all off-stride, didn't do my dislike of cops any service either, not to mention my already battered self-esteem. I told what I knew, and that was all I could do. It was up to them to take the next step. Maybe Delvecchio wasn't as much of a jerk as he let on, and he'd actually take what I had to tell him to heart. Somehow, however, I doubted it.

"How did it go?" Greta asked as soon as I entered the salon and tried to make my way toward the back. She was hot curling a client's very short hair, which required serious concentration, but she still had enough "got to hear the news" in her to dip into my business.

I looked at her, confused, although I had a pretty good idea what she was getting at. "How did what go?" I asked her.

"Your visit with the cops."

I apparently gave Greta a look something nasty because Ernest, who wasn't exactly the most diplomatic person in the room, stopped perming his client's hair and bent over laughing.

"Girrl," he said to Greta, "you done said the wrong thing now. I know that look. She ready to get a case. She ready to go upside your head."

"For what?" Greta said, as if she was offended. "All I did was ask her a question. Ain't nobody nowhere gonna stop me from asking questions. She ain't got to answer it, but I shole got a right to ask it."

"How did you know anything about my whereabouts?" I asked her, as if her little speech never took place.

"It's not like it was a secret, Roni. Dang!"

"Actually, it was."

"Actually, it was," Ernest said, mocking me. "Actually, you busted," he said to Greta.

"Forget you!" Greta said to him.

I folded my arms. "How did you find out about that, Gret?" I asked again.

Greta leaned back from her client, the curling iron still in her hand, and looked pointedly at me. "Did you or did you not tell Miss Anne that you was going to the police station on your lunch break? I heard you tell her."

"That was a private conversation between me and my boss. You didn't have any business eavesdropping on us."

"Now you can just step off, college girl. I wasn't eavesdropping on nobody. Y'all was talking loud enough for folks across town to hear y'all, so don't even flip that script on me."

I gave her a hard "talk to the hand" gesture and decided to go on about my business. Trying to reason with Greta Crenshaw was like reasoning with the devil. You always, but always, got tricked in the end.

"I heard you saw Crackhead Neka before she died last night," Minnie, another one of our stylists, asked as I walked past her station. "That for real, Roni?"

I started to ask her who told her that, and how would she like it if somebody called her Crackhead Minnie. "Just for a few minutes, that's all," I said.

"That must be weird."

It wasn't like it was a planned get-together, I wanted to tell her, but only smiled and kept walking instead, certain that if I answered one question, three or four would follow. It was a stereotype that most hair stylists were nosy. Not so, in the case of Queen Anne's. Because, in the case of Queen Anne's Beauty Salon, there was no *most*. Every one of those cosmetologists was a snoop, big time.

I stayed in my office a good two hours, letting the beauticians answer the phone and deal with the customers, telling them to transfer calls to me only if the calls dealt with authorizations, requisition orders, or other matters they couldn't handle. Unlike many beautyshop owners, Anne Ziegler didn't rent out booths to her beauticians and allow them to make their own money with their own clientele. They literally worked for her, and were paid a salary, regardless of the number of heads they did.

It worked well for a number of the beauticians, who knew they couldn't make the kind of money on their own an upscale shop like Anne's generated. Well-to-do folks weren't interested in going to anybody's hood salon or house kitchen to get their well-to-do heads done. Not in Melville, anyway. They were too brand-conscious, too image-crazy. Queen Anne's, though filled with very hood-like, kitchen-variety beauticians, was nonetheless the best brand in town. And the beauticians knew it, making sometimes more money on tips than they did on their regular paychecks. Although I was technically their supervisor, their pay was commensurate with mine or, since I wasn't allowed to receive tips, better.

I was also a supervisor pretty much in name only, especially since they didn't exactly submit to my authority. I could have gone to Anne about it, and she just might have done something, but I didn't see the point. Respect had to be earned, not forced, and I honestly didn't think that the staff at Queen Anne's believed I'd earned a thing. I was too young, they felt, too green, if you could believe it, to be taken seriously. That was why I often felt that I was in over my head. I had too many hills to climb, too many battles to fight, too much to prove every day.

I felt the same way when I was at Juilliard. Nothing came easily for me. I had to scratch and claw for every good grade and every opportunity I ever earned. And these sisters at Queen Anne's acted as if I was to the manor born. Me!

So I remained in the back, going over the books and trying not to think about Taneka. But all I thought about was Taneka. I wondered if her family was still in town, if she had anybody who cared anything at all about her. She could have been like me and pretty much alone in this world, with only one known relative, an aunt, who didn't care if I was dead or alive. Or maybe Taneka had still been connected to her family, but was just determined to live life on her own terms, only to have gotten hooked on drugs and had to reinvent the terms. Whatever her story, it was a tragic one. Because she was dead. Because those cops didn't give a darn. Because I was the wrong person to put her hope into.

Even after work, after I left the grocery store and turned onto my street, Taneka's life once again thrust itself into mine. It reared up again as I neared my little yellow house. I slowed my Beamer to a near crawl when I saw two cops, Detective Delvecchio and a uniformed officer, hanging across the street and questioning Juno Curtis, trying already, no doubt, to pin Neka's death on him. Which would be ridiculous. Not that Juno didn't have some serious moral deficiencies. The man did, after all, sell weed, and I could only imagine what else. But Juno was no killer. He looked out for you if you were a friend of his, and Taneka was in that category.

I parked in my driveway and stepped out. It was getting dark and Juno appeared to be getting worried. He didn't have that laid back, *what up* demeanor that I'd come to associate with him. But he had his pitbull face on, his Ice Cube scowl going big time. Then I suddenly realized, as I stared over at Juno, that Delvecchio was staring at me, as if he was seriously considering involving me in his interrogation.

Before he could attempt to execute any such idea, however, I grabbed my groceries out of my car and moved swiftly toward the side door that led into my kitchen. The phone started ringing as soon as I made it inside, and I hurried to answer it.

"Hey, babe. What's up?" Richard asked in that annoying baritone of his.

I nearly hung up the telephone.

"Don't hang up. I just wanted to say hello."

"Hello. Now good-bye!"

"Why you being like that, Roni? You know we had a good thing, girl. Why you wanna just throw it all away?"

"Oh, I see. *I'm* throwing it away. Well, Richard, in case you forget, *you* threw it away a long time ago. You did that. And now, looking back and knowing what I know about you, how petty you are, I'm so very glad that you did. So stop calling me, or I'll report you for harassment, and I'm not joking."

"Harassment?" he said, a laugh in his voice. "How can you harass a whore?"

I slammed the phone down then and had to lean against the kitchen counter just to regain my equilibrium. Tears stained my eyes, as my anger turned into dread. Was there ever going to be an end to all of this pain, this loneliness, this sense that nothing was ever going to go right in my life? Now here comes Richard, tormenting me too. "Lord, give me strength," I said aloud, and then, feeling depleted, I made myself a cup of coffee.

When I sat down at my kitchen table, however, I was unable to stop wondering what was up with Richard now. After the way he treated me, how in the world could he think for a second that I'd want him back? This was the same man who had become my family when I was so desperate for love but was too young and dumb to know bad news when I saw it. The same man who had tricked me into believing that he was the best I could ever get, that I had better hold onto him, regardless of how he treated me. The same man who cheated on me and lied to me and broke my heart in every way imaginable. And that same man, that same snake in the grass, expected me to want *him* back? Not even Richard was that far gone.

But something was driving this sudden need of his. Something, given Richard, that I wouldn't be able to figure out in my lifetime.

I looked out of my kitchen window at the night around Elkin Street. Young dudes were out in force, roaming the streets seeking young girls to devour, while those young girls competed for the devouring. I wanted to tell those fast-tail idiots to get away while they could, to not make the same mistakes I made, but I couldn't deal with that either. Just thinking about Richard, about Taneka, was too much as it was.

Taneka and Richard, I thought. Could there have been some connection between the two? I doubted it, since Richard still lived in Jersey, and they didn't even know each other, as far as I could glean. Besides, Richard was bound to rear his ugly head eventually; it was just a matter of time, although his timing was weird.

But coincidences do happen. And whether they did or didn't, it wasn't something I could even try to think about right now. Couldn't even attempt to wrap my brain around the implications of who could have killed Taneka. I was still trying to get over the fact that she had been killed at all. Killed like some animal in the street.

I stopped trying to think about it, or to deal with it, or to do anything that remotely resembled involving myself in other people's dramas, and got up, unpacked my groceries, and cooked myself some dinner.

In the evening of the next day the top of my Beamer was down as I drove into the parking lot of the Zion Hope Baptist Church. Alan Simms, the head of our church's auxiliaries, had phoned and asked me to arrive a little early for choir rehearsal so that I, along with Sister Finch, could meet with him beforehand and discuss the craziness that took place at the last rehearsal.

I parked in the slot reserved for music director and was surprised to see Pamela talking on her cell phone outside of the sanctuary. When she saw me, she got off of her phone and began heading my way. She wore four-inch heels, a skin-tight pair of leopard pants, and a long T-shirt. Whenever I'd see sister girl at the bank, I'd think she was the epitome of conservatism, usually wearing some blue or black skirt suit. Away from that bank, however, forget it. Pam was seriously fab.

"Look at you," she said as she approached, her pretty face beaming with cheerfulness. "All stylin' in your Beamer."

I reached across the passenger seat and grabbed my shoulder bag and briefcase. "Didn't expect to see you here this early."

"Like that outfit too," she said, staring at my red pantsuit. "Kind of match this bad ride. And it is a bad ride, Roni."

"I've had this car for three years, girl, and it wasn't new when I bought it."

"So? I still like it."

"And in answer to your unasked question, no, you can't borrow it."

As if a light once on was suddenly switched off, her smile left immediately. "You are so rude," she said.

"Why are you here this early? Rehearsal doesn't start for another hour."

"And?" she said in a frustrated tone. "You act like it's a miracle I'm a little early. But for your information, although it's none of your business, I work with the dance ministry, remember? We had an early meeting. But come on, Roni. I won't wreck your precious car. You know I'm careful. Just wanna show it out for a night, that's all." Then she smiled. "I'll hook you up with mine."

Pam drove a souped-up, gangster-looking bubba Chevy, and she just knew I wanted to get my paws on that. She'd been trying to get her claws into my ride ever since I met her, promising to hook me up with hers if I'd agree. Of course I never did. I wanted to drive a souped-up Chevy about as badly as a gansta rapper wanted to drive a souped-up moped, but she was insistent. Usually her insistence did nothing for me, but now, after Taneka's death, after seeing up close and personal how short life can really be, I wasn't so quick to completely dismiss her.

"We'll see," I finally said as I got out of the car.

She beamed and began doing the running man dance, where her feet and arms simulated running in place in slow motion.

"All right now," she sang. "Roni gon' hook me up."

"I said I'll see." I began walking toward the church entrance, smiling as I went, Pam smiling and walking right along with me. She knew it was a done deal, and I knew it too, but I always liked that wiggle room.

"So what was your problem all day?" she asked as we walked. "I called twice, but they said you were way too busy for conversation."

"I was just tired and stayed tucked away in my office. But why were you calling? What's up?"

"Nothing's up with me. Just wanted to see what was up with you. Word is, you was the last person to see that crackhead—"

"Her name was Taneka."

"Sorry. To see Taneka alive before she was murdered. That for real, girl?"

"I was probably one of the last, unfortunately yes."

"What she wanted with you? I didn't know you was all tight with Crackhead Ne—I mean, with Taneka."

"We weren't tight. Not anymore, anyway. She was just talking, that's all."

"About what?"

"Nonsense stuff, girl. Nothing."

"Nonsense stuff like what?"

"You don't wanna know, Pam, trust. It's nothing."

She folded her arms and stopped walking. "Like what, Roni?"

I stopped walking too, and blew air through my mouth. I knew I was wasting time I really didn't have. But Pam, like Neka, was a very persistent girl. "She told me to don't let them get away with it," I said.

She frowned. "Don't let who get away with what?"

"That's the question."

"Huh?"

"I told you it was nonsense."

"It's not that it's nonsense. I just don't get it."

"Welcome to the club," I said and began walking again, Pam keeping stride.

"Maybe Coop knows something."

I looked at her. "Coop?"

"Lester, child. He and Neka used to be an item, for real too."

When it was obvious that I still didn't know who she was talking about, she said, "Brother Cooper, Roni. He helps Sister Goshay run the mission ministry."

"Oh, Brother Cooper. Yeah, I know who you're talking about. Short, kind of chunky?"

"Right."

"And you think he knew Neka?"

"I know he knew her. They were gonna get married once upon a time."

I stopped walking. "Really?"

"For real. They was real tight."

"And you think he could know what Neka was trying to tell me?"

"Hey, he might."

"Is he around here tonight you think? I have a few minutes before my meeting with Alan. Take me to where you think he might be."

Pam laughed. "You sound like a character in a science fiction movie. 'Take me to your leader'. Come on, girl. I'll hook you up, especially since you're gonna hook me up with that fierce ride of yours."

"I said we'll see, Pam," I reminded her as I followed her across the parking lot.

We found him, not at the mission house where we had expected to find him, but in the conference room of the church where the deacons had finished a meeting and were now standing around in various private conversations. Lester Cooper, a husky, high-yella, freckle-faced brother with a fat boyish face was standing with our two senior deacons, Luther Montgomery and Ethan Wenn, listening intensely, but not speaking, as if he was hearing some super-deep conversation.

"They'll be back," Deacon Wenn said confidently, with Deacon Montgomery nodding his large head. "They just need a big-time quarterback, that's all. Bronson's good, I'll give him that, but he doesn't have what it takes to go all the way. They need a Moses to take them to the promised land, not some Judas."

"That boy didn't mean to throw that interception, Wenn," Deacon Montgomery said. "How many times I got to tell you that?"

"But he threw it. I don't care how many times you tell it. And it prevented us from going to the playoffs."

"Sorry to interrupt, folks," I said with a smile, knowing I had limited time while, given the conversation, they seemed to have all the time in the world.

"You aren't interrupting a thing, young lady," Deacon Montgomery said with a smile of his own. "Deacon Wenn's just upset that my team had a superior year, while his sorry team sucked."

"Don't you call my Dolphins sorry, Luther. And they don't suck. With the right quarterback—"

"We know, we know. They would have went all the way to the promised land. Anyway," Deacon Montgomery went on, "what can we do for you, Sister Jarrett?"

"Actually, Deac," Pam said, "she needs to talk with Brother Cooper here."

Lester Cooper immediately looked at Pam suspiciously. "Me?"

"Yes," I said, "if you don't mind."

"What you need to talk to me about?"

"I understand you knew Taneka Dupayne."

"Taneka Dupayne?" Deacon Wenn said. "Didn't I read about her? Isn't she that young'un that was found murdered in that alley the other night?"

"Murdered?" Deacon Montgomery said, and both he and Deacon Wenn looked at Cooper.

Cooper frowned. "I don't know nothing about no murder," he said anxiously to them then looked at me. "What you need to talk to me about? Just because I knew her a long time ago? Her murder ain't got nothing to do with me."

"I know that, Brother Cooper. It's just that Neka came to me a few hours before she died with some talk that doesn't make sense. I was trying to find out if you might be able to help me figure it out."

"I can't help you. I told you I don't know her anymore."

"I know, but if you could just hear me out, maybe something will come back to you. It'll only take a minute. I've got a meeting to get to myself."

He was still reluctant, however, which prompted Pam to get involved. "Oh, come on, Coop," she said. "Stop acting like she asking you for money. All she wants is a minute of your precious time."

"He's studying to become a member of the deacon board, Sister Pam," Deacon Wenn informed us, "and he knows how greatly we frown upon any, and I mean any, impropriety by our candidates."

"There's no impropriety," I assured the now curious deacons. "I just want to know more about Taneka, that's all."

"I told you—"

"I suggest you answer their questions, son," Deacon Montgomery said to Cooper.

"But I don't—"

"Answer their questions," Deacon Wenn concurred even more forcefully.

Cooper sighed. "Y'all excuse me," he said to them and then took me and Pam by an arm apiece and hurried us out into the hall, down the back stairs, and out of the church building through a side exit. And he wasn't pleased when we got out there. "Thanks a lot, Pam," he said.

"What did I do?"

"I'm trying to get selected to be a deacon, and you know it. You can't be asking me about no murder investigation. And in front of the two head deacons. I knew it was bad news as soon as I saw you."

"You are so wonderful," Pam said. "Just full of all this grief over the death of your girlfriend."

"She wasn't my girlfriend!" he yelled. Then he lowered his voice. "I told you that. I mean, she was, for a minute, but that was a long time ago. Years ago, before she was all into them drugs like that. I haven't seen her in I don't know how long."

"Quit lying, Coop. I used to see you not all that long ago talking with Neka up the way."

"About the Lord, Pam. I was talking to her about the Lord."

"This is the thing. Neka came to me saying that they're gonna say it's true, when it's not, and that I can't let them get away with it."

Cooper just stared at me. "And?"

"*And* she was wondering if you knew what Neka meant?"

"How would I know what she meant? No, I don't know what she meant. I wasn't down with Neka like that. Not anymore. Now I got to get back to my meeting."

"That meeting was already over, Brother Cooper," I said to him, reminding him that we saw it for ourselves.

"He means he's got to get back to his butt-kissing is what he means," Pam corrected me.

Cooper gave her one nasty look and then hurried back into the church.

I shook my head. "Colossal waste of time."

"He's lying," Pam said. "He and Neka were still tight."

"He admits he talked to her about the Lord."

"And you believe that's all he done to her? Please. I don't."

"Anyway," I said, opting to walk around to the front entrance rather than take that dark, narrow passageway back up, "that's his story, and he seems to be sticking to it. Which means he won't be of any help to me."

"He's all for self, child. He's not thinking about Neka."

"Nobody seems to be. That's the story of her life."

"I'll betcha he'll talk right if Gillette got a hold of him," Pam said.

I almost stopped in my tracks at just the mention of that name. Which was weird. "Gillette?" I said, as if I'd never heard the name before.

"Yeah, he's our police chief. And he don't take nothing from nobody. He'll probably have Coop hanging from a ledge or something, but he'll get him to tell it and tell it all."

"We don't need to go that far."

"I'm just sayin'. And, speaking of cops, have you had a chance to talk to our fine men in blue yet?"

"I tried to talk to them, but they weren't exactly interested."

"I can feel you," she said, nodding her head. "That's just how they are. Especially Gillette. He ain't wasting his precious time on no crackhead getting killed. He's in charge of keeping this town free from drugs, mind you, but when a drug addict dies, he couldn't care less. He probably figures she got what she deserved."

I looked at Pam, remembering what Greta had said about the brother. "He's like that?"

"Yeah, he's like that. I mean, he's cool, if you're a hard-working, productive member of this community. But if you ain't doing what you're supposed to be doing and something happens to you, he ain't wit' it. You're on your own."

"So you know him like that?"

She looked at me. "No, I don't know him like that. What you trying to imply? That I stay in so much trouble that I have this ongoing, longstanding relationship with the chief of police?"

I kept walking toward the church entrance, knowing I was treading on terrain I would be wise to just leave alone. But given the craziness of my life right now, I couldn't.

"You heard me, Roni," Pam said before I could respond. "What are you implying?"

"I'm not implying anything. I was just wondering if you knew him."

"I know *of* him, but I don't have any personal knowledge of him."

"Okay."

"There's a difference."

"Understood."

"So what's up with you?"

"Ain't nothing up with me, Pam. I was just asking a question. You were the one talking like you knew the man."

This brought on a smile. I knew it even before she grabbed me by the arm and stopped my progression.

"Now I get it," she said.

"I don't like the sound of that."

"You've seen him, haven't you?"

"Yes, I've seen him. So?"

"It happens all the time, Roni. All the time, girl. You are not the first female to find that tortured hunk of a police officer fine, okay."

"Fine?" I said, as if astounded. I even snatched my arm from her and began walking again. "Girl, you're out of your mind," I said as she began walking too. "I didn't say a thing about how fine that man was."

"And Fat Albert didn't say a thing about food, but everybody knows he eats. What I'm saying is, you're wasting your time with that jock. You've seen those sexy eyes on that brother. And that bod of his? And I know you heard about all that money he's got. I work in a bank. I knows what I'm talking about. You know good n well, ain't a woman in this town that hasn't tried to get next to that."

"Whatever, Pam," I said nonchalantly, though oddly disappointed.

"Lover boy has more females in that stable of his than the Kentucky Derby got horses. And I don't mean no hood rats either. I'm talking beautiful, successful sisters who can have any man they want."

"But they want Gillette?"

"They gots to have Gillette. I mean, these females be fighting over him, you hear me? Wealthy, successful sisters fighting like dogs. The last thing he needs is another somebody to be acting a fool over him, and the last thing you need is to be acting a fool over some man."

I smiled on that one. "Been there, done that, remember? You have nothing to worry about there."

"You don't wanna be bothered with some my-way-or-the-highway drill sergeant like Don Gillette. Okay?"

She was right, of course, but it didn't stop me from feeling at least slightly regretful. Why I would feel anything for a man I'd only seen once in my entire life, however, was anybody's guess.

"You deserve far better than some man who can't make up his mind," she added yet again, as if she hadn't made her point many times over already. "He is not your type. Not him."

"Didn't know I had a type," I said as we made it up to the double doors of the sanctuary, trying my best to steer the conversation away from talk of the unobtainable cop.

"I got a type, you got a type; all God's chillen got types."

"And who, Madam Pamela, if I may be so bold as to ask, is my type?"

"Oh, I don't know. Somebody nice, somebody good-looking, somebody successful. Somebody like Dr. Simms, for instance."

I rolled my eyes. I knew she was going to say that.

"He's a college professor, Roni, and the strong, God-fearing head of our church's auxiliaries. What more you want?"

Since that was a good question that I just couldn't answer, I didn't.

Pam shook her head. "You don't know a good man when you see one."

"If he's such a great catch, why don't you grab him for yourself?"

"Because it's you he wants. You know that."

I frowned. "Let's just forget it, all right." I pulled open the glass door. The last thing I needed right now was to deal with some misguided crush Alan Simms may or may not have had on me.

Inside the sanctuary a few of the choir members, mostly the older ones, had already assembled in the choir stands. I headed, however, not up front, but toward the side stairs, to Dr. Simms office.

Pam kept following me. "Guess what I know good?"

"If it's gossip, I don't care to know what you know good."

"Dr. Simms gonna side with Finch."

I stopped walking, causing Pam to bump into me in the narrow isle leading to the stairs. I turned around. "How would you know that? We haven't even had the meeting yet."

"She was in his office before you drove up. And she's still in there. Why would he be meeting with her without you there? I say it's so they can present a united front against you."

"So you think he'll fire me?"

"Not as the church pianist. They need you for that. But as choir director, yeah. That has to be what that meeting's about. Finch don't run no auxiliary anymore. Why else would he need to be meeting with her?"

I exhaled and kept walking. It would be a headache relieved if I didn't have to direct that contrary choir, no doubt about that. But for some reason I didn't feel relief at all, but dread and rejection, and that everpresent sense of failure where I never seem able to get it quite right.

Alan Simms stood up from behind his desk when I walked into his office, his oversized, ill-fitting dark suit hanging off of his tall, lean frame so markedly, I wondered if he knew what size he wore. But that was Alan. A sociology professor who looked like a sociology professor, and well-fitting, fancy clothes were not a part of that persona.

He smiled when he saw me. "There she is," he said as if Miss America had arrived.

The way he was looking at me, she had, but I knew better than that.

"Hello, Alan," I said, smiling too. You couldn't help but

smile at somebody like Alan Simms. The man's cheerfulness
was infectious.

But then I looked at Bernadette Finch, who was seated
in one of the two chairs in front of his desk, looking evil as
ever. "Hello, Sister Finch," I said with a little less enthusiasm,
meaning I didn't frown.

"Have a seat, why don't you." Alan looked as if he wanted
to rush from behind his desk and hold out the chair for me.

But I was already sitting down. I sat my briefcase and shoulder bag down, crossed the leg of my pantsuit.

Alan Simms was a young leader, just thirty, with a near-
shaved, perfectly round head and large, almost pop eyes. His
smile was endearing, a kind, compassionate smile, and every
time I was around him, I felt glad to be in his company. He
was my measuring stick, the kindest human being I do believe
I'd ever met. In my former life, before I knew anything about
living right, he would have been a chump in my eyes, a weak-
ling, somebody I wouldn't have given the time of day. Now I
knew better. Now I knew he was a good man, a gem, a good
friend.

But that was the problem. He wanted to be more than
friends. I saw it in his eyes every time he looked at me. I saw
it now as he walked from behind his desk and sat down on its
edge directly in front of me.

"I'm glad you both could come today," he said, sounding as
diplomatic as he usually did.

"Sorry I'm late," I said.

He looked at me and then at his wristwatch. "You aren't
late, Sister Jarrett."

"But weren't you and Sister Finch already meeting? I assumed it was about the choir."

He smiled sheepishly. So it was true.

"We did meet. I was hoping to get Bernadette to understand a few things."

"I understand," Finch interjected. "I told you I understand. I don't know why I got to still be sitting here."

"I just wanted to make sure we were all on the same page."

"We're on the same page. You said we can sing our hymns, since that's what a choir sings anyway."

"That's not exactly what I said, Sister Finch. That's why you needed to stay. Now, Roni," he said, turning his attention to me, "this is how it will have to be. During each rehearsal you will allow your senior members to select at least one hymn for the choir to perform."

"But, Alan—"

He held up a long, narrow hand. "Whether or not that song is sung during Sunday services, however, is up to you as choir director."

I could live with that.

Finch huffed. When she tried to add more, Alan cut her off.

"Good," he said, walking back behind his desk. "I'm glad you ladies, as the leadership of the choir, understand the importance of working together. Of being of one accord. The Good Lord requires it, and so do I. As you know, Pastor Burke appointed me to head all of the church's auxiliaries exactly to handle situations like these, when there is dissension in the ranks. We can't tolerate it, ladies. Pastor already said he will not tolerate it, so we all must get along, all right. That includes compromising, Roni, and that includes accepting Roni's leadership, Bernadette. Now if there's nothing more, I thank you both for coming, and you may both go to your rehearsal."

Finch stood up in a flash, as if she couldn't wait to get out of there and tell the other seniors about how this whole meeting was railroaded. In fact, she was out the door before I stood to my feet.

"Roni," Alan said, as I stood.

"Yes?"

He let out a deep exhale. "I heard some talk today that was rather disturbing."

What now? I pushed my glasses up on my nose. "What talk?"

"I heard you witnessed the killing of the young lady they found in that alley over on Hazelhurst."

I shook my head. "I didn't witness any such thing, Alan. That's just busybodies being busy. Taneka, the young lady, came by my house, that was true, but it was hours before." I pushed my glasses up on my face again. "It was hours before she died. I didn't witness her death."

He studied me through the prism of his large eyes. "Are you all right?" He looked so concerned, it bothered me.

"I'm fine. I'm sorry about what happened to Neka, especially since she seemed so upset when I saw her, but what can you do?"

"Put it in the Lord's hands."

"I have. Don't worry. I have."

"Good," he said with another one of his winning smiles.

"Anyway," I said as I grabbed my briefcase and shoulder bag, "I'd better get into the sanctuary before another riot breaks out. Deacon Montgomery had to come down the last time and quiet them down. I hope they weren't too disrespectful to the poor man."

"He can handle them. It's you I'm worried about."

"You mean Sister Finch?"

He nodded. "I mean Sister Finch."

"Nothing to worry about. You told her how it's going to be. I'm willing to live with it. She has no choice."

He nodded, although he didn't seem all that convinced. As I was about to leave, he looked me up and down, as if my red pantsuit fascinated him.

"How about we go and grab a bite to eat after rehearsal?" he asked, looking expectantly into my eyes. "Think you can spare a hungry boy like me just a few minutes of your time?"

I sighed as that strange burdensome feeling overtook me. *What more you want?* Pam had asked me, as if even she couldn't understand.

Alan Simms was a good man, a kind, considerate man of God, and, in a lot of ways, the perfect man for any woman, but he just didn't do it for me. He just didn't have any of that knock-my-socks-off vibe going for him that I told myself I would require before I'd even think about hooking up with somebody again. My experience with Richard had taught me that much. I'd hooked up with him because I was young and desperate, not in love, although I thought at the time that I was in love beyond compare.

But I declared when I left him that I'd never go down that road again. No matter how lonely I became, no matter how much I felt I needed the validation of somebody else to complete my life, I wasn't using people. I wasn't grabbing me a man just to have a man because he was nice and kind. I needed more. I demanded more. Pam said I expected too much from these men out here and needed to take Alan up on his numerous offers and count myself blessed. But I couldn't do it. I couldn't fall in love with him, not the way I wanted to experience love, and I'd be a liar to myself if I pretended otherwise. But that still didn't make it easy.

"I'm really tired tonight," I said to him.

He immediately began shaking his head. "No problem."

"No, really."

"Hey, Roni, it's me. You don't have to go into any details, okay. Just take care of yourself and I'll see you around."

He was hurt. I could see it in his eyes. And it hurt me too that I was such a jerk sometimes. But I couldn't pretend and I wasn't about to string the man along.

"Sure thing," I said as I left, trying to play it off, but not quite making it. Because I felt even lonelier; I felt almost disgusted; I felt as if I was a cross between a know-what-she-wants-and-won't-settle-for-less independent woman, and a fool.

FOUR

Mae's was a popular diner a few blocks from the salon, and often, at lunchtime, I'd walk over just to get away from the gossip. Anne sometimes walked over with me, calling it a business lunch, but I knew it was more like a tax write-off, and she'd bring that same gossip right along with her. Today was no exception. We were in a booth near the front of the diner, and she was going on and on about Greta Crenshaw and how some of our more, as she put it, high-end customers were beginning to complain that maybe the atmosphere in the salon was getting a little too ghetto for their taste.

I wasn't normally in the business of agreeing with snooty people, finding them a little too judgmental for my taste, but I had to agree with them there. The atmosphere was indeed ghetto, if ghetto, in this context, meant unprofessional. With Greta doing all of that gossiping, Ernest hollering every time one curl didn't curl perfectly, and Minnie sassing customers just because they didn't want the style she felt they should have, it was ridiculous.

I had tried to stop it when I first came on board, even calling a meeting to that effect, but they all went running to Anne, declaring who did I think I was, and Anne backed them, saying, "That's not your job."

Now it was really out of hand and she was asking what should we, *we*, mind you, do.

Before I could answer, our food arrived, a tuna sandwich for me, and a plain garden salad for her. Anne was on another one of her diets, although I didn't see her as fat or anything, just big-boned.

When I pointed that out to her, she cringed. "Big-boned? And that's supposed to make me feel better that I am, according to your perfect little figure self, big-boned? Please. Big-boned sounds like I'm some sumo wrestler, or some Amazon woman on steroids or something."

"Tell them to clean up their acts, or fire them. Simple as that. The reputation of the entire salon is on the line."

"Oh, stop being so melodramatic, Roni," she said snappishly, her small eyes squinting at her salad, while her long fingers lifted a leaf as if checking for bugs. "Most of those females that come to Queen Anne's love the atmosphere, they love that gossip, but there are some, I'll admit, like those professional sisters, like a lot of the preachers' wives, who just don't think it's proper at all. I need to find that balance."

"I don't know how you can pull that off, unless you open up a second salon with a totally different environment, and let them go there."

"Now there's a thought," she said with a smile, pointing her long fingernail at me, although she and I both knew that she wasn't about to open up a second anything. Her husband used to be a successful building contractor in town, and when he became ill and eventually died, he left her set for life. The idea that she'd take on the headache of being responsible for yet another beauty shop wasn't happening, at least not from what I could gauge, although she talked about it constantly.

"You know what I need?" she asked me, looking serious. Then she looked beyond me.

"What?"

She smiled. "Him."

She was looking toward the entrance, so I looked too. And my heart immediately did one of those inside flips. There he was, Donald Gillette, looking big and fine in his tailored suit.

I turned back around. I'd been in town for eight months, eight long months, and until three days ago I'd never laid eyes on the man before. Now I get to see him twice in three days? And was acting all nervous because of it? This couldn't be happening. My luck couldn't be this bad.

"That man right there used to own Big G's, Roni."

"I've heard."

"And my goodness," she said, shaking her head as she stared at him, "that's what I call a good-looking brother. Now if I got a hold of something like that, I'd be set."

"You are set."

"You know what I mean. Hello there, stranger," she said loudly.

Gillette glanced at our table, and then slowly, if not reluctantly, came over. "Hello, Anne," he said in that smooth delivery of his.

A jolt of excitement rushed through me, as if just hearing his voice was all I needed to get by, which was ridiculous.

"You're looking prosperous," Anne said with a grand smile.

For some reason Anne loved to put on that seductress queen act whenever a good-looking man was around, as if that made a woman of her age more attractive. In my opinion she was attractive enough without it, but of course, she never asked my opinion.

"Congratulations on your award," he said. "Miss Woman of the Year."

"Why, thank you, sir. Those garden club ladies must have been sipping on some serious liquor when they decided to select me, but hey, I'll take it. But how did you find out? It hasn't even been announced yet."

"I have my sources," he said with a seductive smile of his own.

He stood before us looking impressively distinguished, and surprisingly awkward, as his suit coat was open and revealed a shirt that was slightly protruding out over his belt buckle, as if he hadn't taken the time to properly tuck it in. That caught my attention, the fact that Mr. Perfectly Groomed could be like the rest of us and wasn't always perfectly anything. Naturally, he decided to turn his attention to me at the exact same time that my attention was on his midsection.

"Hello, Veronica," he said.

I swallowed hard, knowing how busted I was, and looked up into those eyes. "Hi."

"You two know each other?" Anne asked a little too suspiciously.

"We've met," Gillette replied.

Anne waited for more, and, in a way, so did I, but that was all he apparently was going to say on the subject.

"Why don't you join us?" Anne said, sliding over. "We'd love the company, wouldn't we, Roni?"

I wasn't about to agree to that, not the way my heart was slamming against my chest.

When he sat down, Anne asked him, "Meeting somebody?"

He shook his head. "No."

"I hear you and Liz might be taking a trip to Tahoe in a few weeks." Anne smiled. Gillette cut a sharp glance at me, as if I was going to be surprised he had a girlfriend. "No."

"What do you mean, no?" Anne asked, but Gillette didn't elaborate.

Anne let out a deep, throaty laugh. "Liz needs to quit. Lying to keep other women off the trail. She wants you bad, my brother."

"I doubt that."

Anne laughed again. "She needs to quit."

The waitress hurried over and took Gillette's order. When she had gone, I decided to jump in before Anne could. "Any progress on the case, Chief?" I asked him.

"What case?" Anne asked.

"Taneka Dupayne," I said.

"Who's Taneka Dupayne?"

"The girl they found murdered over on Halzelhurst."

"You mean Crackhead Neka? Why you so concerned about something like that?"

"They were friends," Gillette said, staring at me. "And, yes, there's been progress. Detective Delvecchio tells me that he's made an arrest."

My eyes widened. I could hardly believe it. "An arrest? Already? That's fantastic! Who?"

"Young thug named Juno Curtis."

"*Juno?* But—"

"But what, Roni?" Anne asked.

"Juno didn't kill Neka."

"You know him too?" she asked, shocked that I could know people who weren't what she considered upstanding.

"Yeah, I know him. He lives across the street from me. He and Neka lived in the same apartment complex."

Gillette looked surprised. "You live on Elkin?"

"Yes."

Anne shook her head. "You need to cut it out, Roni."

I frowned. "Cut what out?"

"You and your thug friends."

"What thug friends?"

When Anne didn't respond, I decided to forget her and look at Gillette. "Why would Delvecchio think that Juno did it? Juno wouldn't have killed Taneka."

"I haven't seen the evidence yet, but I'm sure it's solid if my lead detective felt he had enough to bring him in."

"But there's no way, Chief Juno was sitting right across the street when Neka came over to me with that 'don't let them get away with it' line."

Now it was Gillette's time to frown. "What 'don't let them get away with it' line?"

"Didn't Delvecchio tell you?"

"You tell me," he said.

I exhaled. I really hated bringing this up in front of Anne. "The night Taneka died she came over to my house and told me that they were going to claim it's true when it's not true and that I can't let them get away with it."

I waited for Gillette to ask, "Who are *they*, and what are they trying to get away with?" but he didn't even go there.

"And you told Delvecchio this?"

"Yes. That's why I came to the police station. What she had said to me didn't make any sense. And Juno was sitting right across the street when she said it. She wasn't scared of no Juno. She wasn't talking about him."

"That doesn't mean he wasn't involved with her death," Gillette said. "He could have wanted her dead for totally different reasons. He could have even been her drug supplier. Given their proximity, he probably was."

"Look, I know what you're saying. I know Juno ain't no saint. I know he sell his weed and who knows what else. He's a long way from being this upstanding citizen. But I can't see him killing Neka. I just don't see it."

"Lots of things you don't see, college girl. That's why people like Crackhead Neka was always running to you, because you'd fall for anything. This Juno character is probably the same way. But your face is too buried in them books to realize it."

What books? I shook my head. They didn't get it. A thug was a thug to them, capable of anything. They didn't understand street cred. They didn't understand that you didn't do your own friends in without some serious cause. They just didn't get it.

"Anyway," Anne said with a long sigh, "me and Roni were just talking about what to do about that salon of mine."

"She works for you?"

"She most certainly does."

Gillette looked at me, at my long, wavy hair mainly. "You're a hair stylist?"

"She wish. No, she's my salon manager. And we were just talking about how changes have got to be made."

Anne went on and on about her atmosphere problem, as if some cop could possibly be interested in such a thing. And he wasn't. Because while she was spilling her guts to him, his attention stayed on me. And I don't mean just every now and then either. No sneak-peek stuff. He was leaned back, looking way too comfortable, his hazel eyes glistening.

I tried to eat, I tried to drink, I tried to people-watch. I even tried to listen to Anne and watch her. But it did no good. He wouldn't relinquish his stare. A part of me, I must admit, was pleased that he was that interested, but another part of me, probably the bigger part, was pissed. He knew I wasn't exactly the picture of cool under his stare. But that certainly didn't stop him.

It wasn't until Anne finally finished her diatribe did he even think about looking elsewhere. By then, however, I was through dealing.

"So there's my dilemma," Anne said. "Either fire my staff or open up a new shop."

"Or make them behave themselves."

"Oh, come on, Gillette. Telling Greta Crenshaw and Ernest Livingston to behave themselves is like telling babies not to cry. Because, as our young college girl here likes to say," she said, causing him to look at me again, "that ain't happening."

"What college?" he asked me.

I glanced at Anne. She didn't like this unsolicited attention he was giving me one bit.

"Juilliard," I said, pushing my glasses up on my nose.

His eyebrows raised. "Good school."

"Yes."

"What's your weapon?"

"Her weapon?"

"Piano," I said.

He nodded. "Impressive. One of those child prodigies, I take it."

"Not hardly. It didn't come easily for me at all."

"Even more impressive."

"What's so impressive about it?" Anne scowled. "It's not like she's some accomplished concert pianist, now come on. Her only claim to fame is that she's the music director for Zion Hope."

"How did you manage it?" he asked me.

"How did she manage to become music director? Nothing to manage. Alan Simms happens to have the hots for her."

"Anne!" I said, stunned that she would go there. "Dr. Simms is a man of God, and you know it."

Alan Simms was the most straight-laced dude I knew, a man who hated even the appearance of evil, and she knew it too.

"I didn't say he wasn't. But the operative word is *man*. He's a man. A man who finds you attractive, Roni. There is definitely no secret about that."

"How did you manage to get into Juilliard?" Gillette asked.

"My parents were both jazz musicians. They taught me how to play piano when I was very small. I kept working hard at it too, for the first fifteen years of my life. Then I just . . . it's just that things changed."

"Her parents died in a car crash."

Gillette looked at me again. "Or was it a plane crash?"

I swallowed hard. "Car."

"Both of them?" Gillette asked.

I nodded. When our eyes met, the compassion I saw in his caused me to look away. Then a thought occurred to me. "Maybe you knew them," I said, looking back at him. "When you owned your nightclub, I mean. Roy and Marilyn Jarrett?"

Gillette had to think about this. "Doesn't ring a bell. But then it wouldn't. My club didn't feature jazz musicians."

"I see. Anyway, after they died I didn't pursue my music too much. Didn't have the chance to, really. But I guess all of that early training was enough. I went back to school, graduated, and eventually applied to Juilliard, more on a dare than anything else. And I got accepted."

"Graduated with honors too, I'll bet."

"Oh, yes. She never ceases to remind us."

I looked at Anne. I had never, not ever, mentioned to anyone at Queen Anne's about my graduation rank, which was nowhere near with honors, anyway. She may have had a thing for Donald Gillette and was upset that he was acting as if he was all into me at that moment in time, but it wasn't my fault. I wasn't forcing the man to ask me all of those personal questions.

I decided that Gillette's attention wasn't worth losing my job over. "Anyway," I said, grabbing my purse and scarf, "I'd better get back to the salon. I'll see you when you get there, Anne. Goodbye, Chief."

I didn't wait for either one of them to respond as I slid out of the booth. Although Anne seemed pleased, too pleased, if you asked me, I thought I saw a tinge of disappointment in Gillette's eyes, but that could have just been wishful thinking on my part.

By the time I made it home that evening, my conversation with Gillette, especially the part about Juno's arrest, was still on my mind. Taneka begged me to not let them get away with it, and the fact that they had arrested a man I still couldn't see as the killer made me feel as though they were going to do just that. Get away with it. Kill Taneka, if that was what she meant, but never pay for what they'd done.

The police weren't even investigating her murder. They couldn't have been, if they thought for a second that Juno did it. And even Gillette said himself that he hadn't bothered to check out the evidence. He seemed to be just going along with whatever a jerk like Delvecchio was telling him. Which meant Juno was in trouble for real, and Neka's premonition was right on target.

And that was why, when I arrived home, instead of going into my house and minding my own business, dealing with my own drama, I walked across the street to that apartment complex.

The landlord was an old husky dude named Pooh, although I'm certain that wasn't his real name, and he called himself infatuated with me. I asked, and was able to get him to let me into what had been Neka's apartment. He hung around the open door, trying to hit on me, but I was too busy checking out the crib, my heels clanging down hard against the bare floor.

The place looked bad. Bare to the bone. When I first saw it, I wondered if I was making too much out of my promise to Taneka. Maybe she was just pulling my leg, getting a last laugh off of her old friend, but the more I thought about it, the more it didn't add up.

I remembered the terror in her eyes. I remembered the urgency in her voice. Nobody, not even a crack addict, was that good an actress.

It was a small, one-bedroom apartment, tiny by even my standards, and it looked nearly abandoned. The living room had a broken-down love seat in a corner, and two old end tables, but that was it. No TV, no stereo, nothing of any value anywhere. Plenty of trash on the floor, however, and all kinds of crack pipes and tin cans and other drug paraphernalia. I guess it was what you'd expect in a drug addict's apartment.

"Pooh," I said, feeling foolish calling a grown man by that

ridiculous name, "how could Taneka afford the rent on this place? Was she working?"

Pooh looked at me as if I suddenly had wings on my head. "Neka working? Girl, please. That crackhead wouldn't have known a job if it walked up her legs and sat on her lap. You see this place."

"Who paid the rent then?"

He looked at me sidelong. "How should I know? They didn't pay it to me."

I frowned. "But aren't you the landlord?"

"But I ain't the rent collector."

"Who collects it then?"

He sucked his teeth. "You ask entirely too many questions, Roni Jarrett."

"Pooh?" I said, exasperated.

"Some dude, okay. I told you I don't be collecting no rent."

"Is he the owner?"

"I have no idea."

"Come on, Pooh. Give me some credit. You expect me to believe that you, the landlord, don't know who the owner happens to be? Do I look that dumb to you?"

"Sometimes . . . when you wear that little gray number."

"Pooh!"

"Roni!"

"You expect me to believe that you work for the owner, but you don't know who he is?"

"I don't expect you to believe anything. He's out of town somewhere. I don't know him. And the man I deal with ain't wit' this."

I frowned. "Ain't with what? His tenant has been murdered. I'm just trying to find out why."

"He ain't wit' it, Roni."

"What is he, a big drug dealer or something? Some cartel chief? Is that why Neka died? Because she knew too much?"

"Oh, yeah, those cartel chiefs always share their secrets with crackheads. All the time."

"It's not funny, Pooh."

"And I ain't laughing. You the one talking about cartel chiefs and junk."

"Did Taneka's death have something to do with the owner of this place? That's all I'm asking."

"You know what—I'm out of here."

"Pooh!"

"Don't Pooh me. I ain't gettin' in this. I got bills to pay too, and I'm not losing my job for nobody. The man I work for wasn't stuttin' no Neka. And he ain't got nothing to say about it either. You ain't gonna get him involved in this. You just feeling guilty because Neka came to you for help and you didn't help her."

"What? Oh, is that the talk now? That I let Neka down?"

"That's what they saying."

"It's not true."

"Whatever, Roni, I'm out of here. Just lock up when you leave, please, ma'am."

"It's like that, huh?"

"I'm Bennett."

"And you ain't in it."

"There ya go." And he went, swiftly, like the chump I always suspected he was.

I did a quick look around the apartment, through the empty cabinets in the kitchen, and the empty broken-down fridge.

I ended up in the bedroom. There wasn't much in there either, other than a filthy mattress on the floor and more drug paraphernalia. There was a picture taped up on the dingy wall of a younger Taneka, the Taneka I used to know, with her beautiful smile and pigtails. She was a pretty girl then, filled with life and vigor.

I looked away, and moved toward the closet. Inside had a

few Salvation Army-looking clothes, the kind of clothes too old and tattered to sell for drugs.

Just as I was about to conclude that nothing was happening up in here, and I was truly wasting my time, I saw a nice-looking red jewelry box in brass and lace trimmings in the back of the closet in a corner. I was stunned. Neka could have easily sold it for a dime bag at least, but there it was, the only decent-looking anything in the entire apartment.

I picked it up and opened it, as all kinds of thoughts raced through my head as to what could be in it. But I was let down again, because nothing was in it. It was empty. A nice, empty box.

It didn't make a whole lot of sense to me that she would still have it, until I went to put it back. Behind it was a loose baseboard, which barely caught my eye.

I looked closer, keeling all the way down to it, and that was when I saw a thin little book between the wall and the loose board. I quickly pulled it out, made sure nothing else was back there, and stood up.

It was Taneka's diary, apparently, dating back only a couple weeks. Considering what I had before I found it, however, it was some find. I smiled. Taneka was nobody's fool. Girlfriend knew exactly what she was doing. That was why she kept a diary in the first place. That was why she had that jewelry box in front of it. One of her crackhead friends get the idea to scope out the place, looking for what they could steal, he'll see the box, grab it, and take off, not even thinking about looking behind any baseboard.

I decided right there to take it with me and check it out, but just as soon as I slipped the diary into my pant pocket, I heard the creak of a floorboard behind me.

Startled, I turned quickly. I held my hand to my chest and exhaled. "You scared me half to death, Juno!"

He looked at me suspiciously. He was out of jail, which

was good news, but that still didn't lessen my concern that he'd seen me with that diary. He looked kind of rough, with stubble on his chin and braids that were beginning to unravel.

"'S up?"

"Ever hear of knocking?"

"Yeah, I heard of it. So?"

"It would have been considerate of you not to sneak up on me like that."

"What I wanna sneak up on you for? And what you doing in here anyway?"

"What *you* doing in here?"

"Pooh said your li'l butt was up here doing your *Charlie's Angels* act again, so I decided to come up and thank you."

"*Charlie's Angels?* What is Pooh talking about? I'm just looking around, that's all, seeing what I can see."

"Saw anything?"

I decided to ignore that. "Thank me for what?"

"Huh?"

"You said you wanted to thank me, but there's no need for that. I'm not the one who put up your bail."

"What bail?"

"What bail? Don't tell me you broke out? Are you crazy?"

"Roni, just chill, all right. You know I didn't break out of no jail. Gillette personally let me go, all right, thanks to you."

"Thanks to me?"

"That's what the man said. Didn't want him releasing me and then claim, like you just did, that I broke out, or whatever they wanna call it. So I asked him. That's when he told me that you said I was innocent. Said he checked out the evidence and figured Delvecchio didn't have enough to hold me."

"Wonder why he even arrested you?"

"Why you think? Because I'm an easy collar. Them jurors look at my criminal record and they ready to convict me on principle alone, forget the evidence."

"No way you would have killed Neka."

"Got that right."

"So Gillette said he checked out the evidence because I thought you were innocent?"

"That's what the man said."

My heart raced a little. But it had to be more to it than that. "And what else?"

"What you mean, what else?"

"What other reasons did he give for releasing you, Juno? Work with me, brother. Maybe they found the real killer."

"Get real. Wasn't no other reasons. That was it. Apparently your word was good enough for him." Juno smiled that obnoxious, gold-teeth smile of his. "What, Roni? You one of his women now too?"

I shook my head. "Forget you, Juno," I said and headed out the door, waiting for his smiling butt to follow so that I could lock up the apartment. I felt nervous for some reason, and perplexed, unsure if I should be flattered that Gillette would be so into me, or worried sick.

Later that night, after I'd eaten and prepared for bed, I went into my back bedroom, which I had converted into an office, and read Neka's diary. It chronicled her relationship with some dude named Jeffrey and how "she saw the guns, just the way she'd seen Willie's."

She wrote of being worried that Jeffrey was going to do something stupid, just as Willie had done, and how he thought she wasn't smart enough to figure out what he was up to because of her "problem."

She knew plenty, she wrote, although she didn't say what it was that she did know.

And the diary became more and more confusing, the more I read it.

But I kept reading, wondering why the girl didn't just spell out what was going on and cut all of the defensive crap. All of this "I'm not stupid," and "I know what he's up to," and "I might have a problem but I got plenty sense" wasn't cutting it for me. Until Willie's name came up again. Willie Barnes. I had somewhere, at least, to start.

I didn't know if Jeffrey and Willie were involved in drugs, too, or maybe even gunrunning, but I knew it was something illegal.

Maybe Jeffrey owned that apartment building Neka lived in. Maybe Pooh was being cagey on purpose, to get me to understand that there was a connection. But why would Pooh care?

I spent a good part of the night walking around my tiny office thinking about it and was just about ready to chunk it all and go to bed.

Suddenly, the silence changed into one of those loud, all-hell-breaking-loose sounds. First I thought there were firecrackers popping off outside, in an odd kind of rapid succession. Then there was the sound of chattering glass, not from outside, I quickly realized, but from inside my own home.

I hit the floor, and I hit it hard, crawling on my belly until I was under my desk. My heart was ramming so fiercely against my chest, I thought I was having a heart attack. Gunfire was ringing out as if I was in the middle of a war zone.

I was breathing heavily and in tears, angry at myself for being so alone in this world. I cried out to God, for protection, for mercy, for help. Somebody was shooting into my home. Somebody was trying to kill me! I couldn't believe it. I covered my head with my hands, praying and crying, unable to handle the truth.

Then just as suddenly, silence penetrated again. A tense silence, but it was very brief. Because almost immediately after, I heard a car speed off, and the neighborhood dogs started barking.

I'd heard about drive-by shootings all of my life, saw many pictures of them in newspapers and on television programs, but as I lay under my desk, frozen, terrified to move even as I heard what sounded like the voices of my neighbors, including Juno, calling out my name and banging on my front door, I had a feeling I was about to join the ranks of those who'd been through the fire too. Only, in my case, that fire, I had a sneaking suspicion, was just beginning to burn.

FIVE

Uniformed cops were all over my house taking pictures of my broken windows, interviewing neighbors, asking me all kinds of questions I just couldn't answer. I had no idea who would have done something like this to me. I wasn't the kind of sister who had all of these enemies, and especially not one that wanted me dead. One cop, a rookie if you asked me, said that from the looks of things they weren't trying to kill me, but frighten me. Well, they'd succeeded beyond their wildest dreams, because I was out of my mind with fright, still shaking, still trying my best not to break down and ask the Lord, Why? Why did this have to happen to me?

But I counted my blessings still. For if I was in my front bedroom, or in my living room, my body would have been scattered over the floor, right alongside the glass. So that rookie could talk all night about what it looked like, trying to minimize it all he cared to, but my nerves told me differently.

I was seated at my kitchen table, still scared half to death, trying to drink the coffee Pam had handed me, and to drink it without jiggling the cup too badly. I was in bad shape. That's why I had called Pam over. She was so worried when she arrived, she immediately placed a blanket across my shoulders, to keep me warm, to keep me from going into some serious shock. And as horrible as the actual incident was, where I probably would never get that sound of crashing glass out of my head, the idea of what happened was worse. Someone had tried to kill me. Someone had tried to do me in, just as they'd done Taneka.

When I explained this to Pam, she shook her head. "You think Neka's death is related to this?" she asked.

"Of course, they're related," I said, unable to suppress my anger over this crazy disruption. "Has to be. I've been alive on God's green earth for twenty-seven years and never had anybody shooting at me. Taneka's murdered and a few days later somebody wants to gun me down too?"

"Neka wasn't gunned down."

"You know what I'm saying. There has to be a connection."

"I guess you're right, girl," Pam replied, looking as worried as I was feeling. "Something's up, that's for sure."

And even if something was up, all I could come up with was a lot of maybes. Maybe asking questions about Neka unnerved the wrong person; maybe Pooh had told his mysterious boss that I'd been snooping around; maybe Juno wasn't as uninvolved as I had thought and when he saw me take that diary he ran and told somebody; maybe the cops were crooked and Neka's murder involved higher-ups they were being paid to protect. I couldn't answer any of those maybes, but I couldn't stop obsessing on them either.

Pam finished pouring herself a cup of coffee with one hand, balancing her baby brother Kyle in her arm with the other, and then she sat back down at the kitchen table. Kyle, usually a very robust two-year-old, ended up in her care tonight when her dinner party-bound parents asked her to babysit. Now he was asleep in her arms.

"Why don't you take that boy home and let him get back in bed?"

"And leave you here by yourself? Like no way."

"How would I be by myself, Pam? Half of the Melville Police Department is in my living room. And the other half is on my front lawn."

"Yeah, they're here now, but what's gonna happen when they leave? And they will leave."

"I'll be okay."

Pam shook her head. "You're staying with me tonight, Roni. Stop being so stubborn. You don't know what these people are capable of. They might come back."

"I doubt that."

"But you don't know that. That's the point. Kyle is fine. You just do what you gots to do and then come on home with me."

I smiled weakly, the best I could do under the circumstances. "Yes, Mother."

Detective Delvecchio, of all people, came lumbering his tired self into my kitchen when he finally arrived. He looked first at Pam and then at me. He hesitated. "You again?" he said, a frown on his face.

"Not by design, I assure you."

"You're Veronica Jarrett, the homeowner?"

"Yes."

"Terrific. So what's the story this time?"

"Excuse me?"

"What's the deal? First a crackhead gets herself killed and you're real concerned about it. So concerned that you come running down to the police station to just let us know what a saintly crackhead she was. Then your house gets nailed within days of the crackhead's murder, a crackhead you also just so happen to live across the street from. I'm beginning to figure something fishy's going on here."

I rolled my eyes. What was it about cops and me? "Look, Delpissio, or whatever your name happens to be."

"Delvecchio."

"I don't know what you're trying to prove, and I don't care, but you won't stand in my home disrespecting me."

"I'll stand in your home and do whatever I want."

"Vince?" a short, uniformed cop hurried in and said before I could jab him back.

Delvecchio, however, didn't take his eyes off of me. "What?" he replied with a hard edge to his voice, his pie face almost beet-red.

The cop frowned. "What's the matter with you?"

"What do you want, Fontaine?"

"What did I do?"

Delvecchio exhaled and stared hard at his colleague.

"I thought you'd like to know that Chief just drove up," his colleague said.

Delvecchio looked as if he knew he hadn't heard him correctly. "Gillette's here?"

"He just drove up."

"What's he doing here?"

"Dispatch notified him. They have to give him name of victim, address of victim whenever it's drug related."

I wanted to say, *What drug related?*

"But this is a drive-by!" Delvecchio said angrily to his colleague. "Why would he come rushing over here on something like this?"

"How would I know? It's odd to me too. But he's here."

Delvecchio and the uniform just stood there, seemingly thinking hard about this, and then, as if they'd figured it out at the exact same time, they both looked at me.

"What?" I asked them.

"You know the Chief?" Delvecchio asked me.

"I know *of* him like everybody else in this town. I've met him."

"But you aren't a friend of his?"

"No."

"Not one of his *special* friends?"

"Whatever that is, no."

"He hears you're involved in a drive-by and comes rushing over, something he's never done. And you're telling me you're not connected to him in any way? Why would he even bother?"

"I have no idea."

"You expect me to believe that?"

I wanted to tell him that I didn't care what he believed.

Another uniformed officer came in, speaking in a near whisper, as if the subject of his conversation was close on his heels. "Chief's here," he said with a hand to his mouth, as if warning his fellow officers.

My stomach muscles immediately tightened in anticipation of seeing Gillette again, and when I did see him, when his now familiar figure rounded the archway and entered my kitchen, my heart began to pound. It was uncanny. All he had to do was show up and my heart started showing out, as if there was, as Delvecchio seemed insistent about, some real connection between the two of us. Although there wasn't.

But I couldn't deny my reaction to the man. Nor his reaction to me. Which stunned me.

He looked flustered and worried when he first came into my kitchen, as if he wasn't going to be satisfied until he saw for himself whatever it was he came to see. He even began to scan the room with impatient eyes, searching the faces of everyone present, until those eyes found me. And as soon as they did, as soon as they looked upon me with a sudden sharp awareness in them that made me even more nervous, he literally sighed relief and allowed all of that anxiety and frustration to evaporate from his handsome face.

He was dressed down in a pair of blue jeans, a gray T-shirt, and a dark green bomber jacket, and it was obvious, given the way he normally dressed, that he'd thrown them on and hurried over.

Delvecchio smiled and looked my way. It was as if Gillette's disheveled appearance alone was enough to confirm his suspicions.

That didn't stop Gillette, however, from continuing to stare at me, as he stood in my kitchen and focused on me and me alone. Which nearly did me in. His eyes looked so warm, and so compassionate, and so in tune with the devastating emotions I was feeling after being a victim of such a terrifying crime.

I began to have an urgent need to break down and cry. Hadn't done it yet, despite the madness all around me, but looking into those droopy, sexy, hazel eyes of Donald Gillette made me want to break down and run into his arms.

"What's up, boss?" Delvecchio said, all smiles now. "What in the world are you doing out here?"

It was hearing Delvecchio's voice, and the insinuation in his question, no doubt, that seemed to shake Gillette out of his tunnel vision. What did he think he was doing anyway, all focused on me? And just that quickly the compassion in his eyes left, and that commanding presence of his began to reassert itself.

He stood erect, placed his hands in the pockets of his jeans, and began to roam around my kitchen, looking at my white oak cabinets, my granite-top center island, my brown leather bar stools. He didn't stop walking, in fact, until he was standing directly beside me at my small kitchen table.

He smelled wonderful, like a sweet, fresh scent, and I half-expected him to swoop me up into his arms and say something remarkably comforting. But although he was standing beside me, he wasn't even looking at me. He was still checking out the room. I didn't know if he thought the crime itself had originated in this very kitchen, or if he was just odd like that.

He was just odd like that, I concluded, especially since Delvecchio didn't seem to mind that his question went unanswered.

"What we got?" Gillette finally spoke, still looking around, at my green-and-white checkered floor this time.

"Your regular drive-by," Delvecchio quickly replied, flipping open his small notepad. "Some of the neighbors claim they heard it, but nobody saw it, which is crazy, given this neighborhood and the way everybody's always hanging out. But on this particular night they were all snuggled safely in their beds like good little children, if you can believe that fairytale."

"What's that supposed to mean?" I could immediately feel Gillette's gaze on me, but I didn't care. I wasn't letting Delvecchio get away with a remark like that, I didn't care how ghetto that might have made me appear.

"I was talking to the chief," Delvecchio replied. "And last I looked, that ain't you."

"But I'm talking to you."

"For real," Pam said.

"And what I want to know," I continued, "is why you would think that it's so impossible for people in this particular neighborhood to mind their own business? When people hear gunfire, they don't stick around to get the number of the license plate, they run for cover. But, of course, this isn't the high and mighty suburbs, is it? Those little fearless folks out there would not only write down the number on the plates, but they'd jump in front of the speeding car and grab the suspect until you faithful men in blue arrive."

Pam laughed.

"Let you tell it, of course," I added.

Delvecchio just stared at me, as if he could have ripped my small body in two with his bare hands. Gillette had a similar look, which bothered me, but not enough for me to back down.

Gillette looked away from me and back at his detective. "Any damage beyond those windows out front?"

Delvecchio had to exhale first, to calm himself back down, I imagine.

"No, sir," he said, still staring at me. "Just the windows."

"And no eyewitnesses?"

"Not a one."

"Okay," Gillette said with what seemed like a sigh of exhaustion. "I want you to take a few uniforms and hit the streets. Put the squeeze on Juno Curtis and his boys."

"We did already, Chief, remember? We even had that clown locked up. But you let him go."

This seemed to embarrass Gillette. "I didn't say lock him up," he said a little more harshly than was called for. "I said to squeeze him, get him talking. And not just him, but check out Joey Lopez and Dice Grimes and Big Joe Hopson and every other criminal element in this area."

"In other words, everybody," Delvecchio said, a big grin on his face. Then he looked at me. I rolled my eyes.

"Somebody has to know something," Gillette went on, not bothering to correct his obnoxious detective, which disappointed me. "I want to know what the word on the street is, and I want to know tonight."

Delvecchio looked at Gillette as if he'd just slapped him. "Tonight? For this? You got to be kidding, Chief."

Gillette looked at Delvecchio as if he was anything but.

Delvecchio began nodding reluctantly, realizing it too. "I'm on it."

"Let me see the witness statements you already have," Gillette said to him, "and tell the guys out front to start wrapping it up. We won't get anywhere hanging around here."

Although Delvecchio quickly handed his notepad to Gillette, he didn't seem quite as ready to relinquish his staredown of me. But he had no choice. He gave me that evil eye one last time, and then left to do Gillette's bidding.

Gillette looked at Pam as Kyle stirred in her lap. He asked her, "You're Miss Jarrett's . . . ?"

"Friend," I said.

"Best friend," she said.

I smiled.

"Best friend."

Gillette moved forward and extended his large hand, which Pam, at first, just looked at. "Donald Gillette," he said, waiting.

Pam finally shifted Kyle's weight and shook his hand. "I know who you are."

Gillette smiled that amazingly charming smile of his. "That puts you one up on me."

"Oh," Pam said, smiling too. "I'm Pam."

When Gillette kept looking at her, however, she got it. "Pamela Tate," she added.

"Do you live around here, Miss Tate?"

"In Dodge? Like no way." Pam immediately looked at me, as if she just knew she had offended me. And ordinarily she would have. But this was no ordinary night.

"I'm going to have to ask you to excuse us for a few moments," Gillette said in his smooth delivery, "if you don't mind."

Pam looked into those eyes of Gillette's, and I could tell sister girl wanted to smile that seductive smile of hers and talk smack, tell the brother something real cute. But there was something about Gillette, something ingrained in that serious look he always had on his face that warned you not to go there, that he was not the one you could just clown around with.

She hoisted Kyle up in her arms and stood up. "I'll be up front, Roni. Holler if you have to."

When she left, he took her place at the table. I sipped from my coffee and snuggled deeper into the blanket that draped my shoulders. He looked at those shoulders.

"Cold?"

"Cool," I said.

"Yeah, temperatures really dipped tonight. And it's only October."

"Almost wintertime."

"I guess you got a point there." He leaned forward, his arms resting on either side of my plastic, frog-shaped place mat. For some reason I felt uncomfortable with him in my home like this. I felt laid bare, as if he knew all my secrets now, and I knew nothing about him. What could a man of his wealth and background think about my remarkably humble abode, I wondered. Was he impressed? Repulsed? Or just plain indifferent?

He reached into the inside pocket of his bomber jacket and pulled out a pair of half-moon reading glasses. When he put them on and began skimming Delvecchio's notes, he asked without looking up, "What happened here, Veronica?"

I got a warm feeling when he said my name, as if nobody said it the way he did, which wasn't even true. "I wish I knew," I said. "I was standing in my office."

He looked at me over his glasses, as if I'd just given him reason to hope. "Your office at the salon?" he asked. "You weren't here?"

"No. I mean, yes, I was here. But I meant I was in my office here at home. My converted office."

"I see," he said, a look of disappointment in his eyes. He then returned his attention to the notes. "Go on."

"I was walking around the office thinking about things."

"What things?"

"I hardly think that's relevant."

"Why don't we let me decide what's relevant?" he said, his eyes still reading through the notepad.

I huffed inwardly. Who did he think he was? "I was just thinking about things," I said stubbornly. "Personal matters. Anyway, I was walking around the office thinking, and that's when I heard all of this gunfire."

"And you have no idea who would do something like this to your home?"

"No. None."

"How old are you?"

I hesitated. What did that have to do with anything? "Twenty-seven."

"Tell me about your boyfriend."

For a split second I thought about Richard, and those back-to-back phone calls I'd received from him, but I dismissed that. I couldn't see Richard doing a drive-by on his worse day, or even ordering one. This wasn't his style. When he hurt you, like the way he got me fired from my job, he'd want you to know it was him.

"Boyfriend?"

He looked up at me. "Yes, boyfriend. And why isn't he here holding your hand?" He frowned, as if upset that some man wasn't here beside me.

"If I had a boyfriend, which I don't," I added, a little disappointed that he would be so willing to cast me off on somebody else, "but if I did have one, I doubt seriously if he would be involved in something this trifling."

"Somebody spraying your home with bullets is trifling to you?"

"Of course not. I mean, Why would I date somebody who'd do something like this? That's what I mean."

Gillette had a way of making my anger rise.

"And why are you here anyway? They said you were supposed to be notified on drug-related cases. This isn't some drug crime."

"All drive-bys are initially ruled as drug-related, until proven otherwise."

"All of them? Why?"

"It's the tactic of choice for drug dealers. We have to start there first. But what about any of your past boyfriends?" Gillette returned his attention to the notepad.

I didn't quite understand what he was asking. "Yes, I've had boyfriends before," I replied, although I'd actually had only one boyfriend in the past, but what was that his business?

"I wasn't asking if you've had any," he said, peeved that I thought he was trying to pry into my business. "I want to know, Who are they? Where are they? Did it end badly?"

"Oh," I said, feeling a little embarrassed. "None are here. In Florida, I mean. There was one back in Newark."

"Newark?"

"Yeah. I grew up in Melville, but left when I was fifteen—"

"After your parents died."

"Right," I said, still able to feel that tinge of pain. "I lived in Newark until I came back here. I met Richard, that's my ex, in Newark."

"Okay. Who else?"

I frowned. "Who else what?"

"Boyfriends, Veronica? What about the others?"

I paused. I really didn't see where any of this mattered. "There are no others."

He looked at me over his eyeglasses. "I'm not just talking about recently. I'm talking any boyfriend you've ever had. These things are almost always far more personal than you'd think, with some jokers holding grudges dating back years."

"Well, I don't know who they can be. I had one boyfriend back in Jersey, but that's it."

Gillette stared at me. "You mean to tell me that in all of your life, in all of your twenty-seven years in this world, you've only been involved with one guy?"

He made it sound like a crime. And, maybe, given who that one guy happened to have been, it was. "Yes."

"One, Veronica?"

"Yes, Gillette. Goodness, what's the big deal?"

He kept looking at me as if I'd just dropped in from the moon, and then his eyes moved from my face to my chest, and back down to his notepad. "How well did you know Taneka Dupayne?"

"I told you we were best friends once. Real tight. She saved my life."

"How did she manage that?" He said this as if he didn't believe it.

"She stood up for me on a playground one day," I said with a smile, remembering it. "I was bullied as a kid."

He looked up at me. "Bullied? Why?"

"Stupid kid stuff."

"Such as?"

"Some girls said I acted like I thought I was cute, and they didn't like it."

"And did you?"

"Did I what? Like it?"

"Think you were cute?"

"Oh, no. Of course not." I pushed my glasses up on my face.

"What did they do to you?"

"Little stuff at first, like gossiping about me, harassing me every time I walked near them. But then they started getting more and more creative, and one day a girl cornered me and pulled out a razor blade."

"A blade?"

"Yep. Her plan was to leave her mark on my face and a sizeable chunk of my hair in her hands."

Gillette stared at me, at my face and my hair. He stared so intently, I had to look away from him. When I did return his gaze, his look was so intense, yet so soft with concern, I almost wanted to run to him.

"They didn't succeed," he said, as if he had to remind me.

"No, they didn't, thanks to Neek. They were scared of her."

"And yet she managed to get herself hooked on drugs."

I nodded. "Unfortunately. She was so strong, so sure of herself. I don't know what happened."

"Life happened. And it probably wasn't pretty."

"Not for either one of us, you're right."

Gillette stared at me again, and so intensely, I found it almost unbearable to look him in the eye. But I did.

"You aren't into drugs, are you, Veronica?" He asked this with what sounded like a plea in his voice.

"No, I'm definitely not into drugs. I've seen what that stuff do to people."

He nodded, as if he needed that confirmation then flipped another page in his notepad. "So you came back to town and hooked back up with your old friend?"

"I wouldn't call it a hookup. She just so happened to live across the street from me, that's all. And we talked some, but she never really came around me that much, except when she needed money."

He flipped back two pages in Delvecchio's notes. Then he stopped and stared at them. "You were in her apartment today."

How did Delvecchio know that? I know Juno wouldn't have told him that, or Pooh. Or would they? "Just for a few minutes," I said cautiously.

"Why?"

"I was just looking around, that's all."

"Why were you looking around?"

"Because I wanted to check out her place, Gillette. Wasn't no big reason."

"What did you find?"

"You talk as if I went there looking for something."

"What did you find?"

"I didn't say I found—a book, okay. I found a book. Like a little dairy."

He immediately looked at me over his glasses. "Diary? Did you say *diary?*"

I exhaled and pushed my glasses up on my face. "Yeah. I found it in her closet. I wasn't stealing it or anything like that. I just wanted to see if it contained something that would help me understand what's happening."

"You still have it?"

"I wasn't stealing it."

He frowned. "Did I say you were stealing it, Veronica? Where is it?"

I hesitated. I didn't like his tone, nor his scowl. "I put it up."

He looked at me a moment longer, flipped shut the notepad, and then stood up, his big bulk towering over me. "Let's go get it."

I didn't see where an escort was necessary, but he didn't have the look of a man interested in debating the point. I removed the blanket and stood up, my short shorts and skimpy, skintight T-shirt revealing way too much.

Gillette's lazy eyes moved downward immediately, but I didn't even care. I was in my home. I had no earthly idea that I was going to have a houseful of guests tonight. I let him get his little look and then ignored him, letting him follow me to my office as if I wasn't uptight at all.

I had locked the diary in my desk drawer before the cops arrived, although I wasn't quite sure why. Probably my innate distrust of cops had taken over, and I hid it without thinking about it. But when I got to the door of my office, I wasn't even concerned about any diary of Taneka's or anything else quite so normal. I was concerned, instead, about the terror I felt in that very room not two hours ago.

I even thought I'd heard another gunshot, which caused me to wince and stop in my tracks, and Gillette, coming up behind me, bumped into me. As if knowing, and without asking the reason for my abruptness, his hands immediately moved to my shoulders.

I leaned back into him, to feel the warmth and protectiveness of another human being, and we just stood that way for more than a few seconds.

Then Gillette said softly and into my hair, "I'm so sorry this happened to you, Veronica."

I nodded, because I was sorry too, because I was not yet ready to accept what was too terrifying to ever accept. But for the grace of God I could very well have spent my last moments on earth in this very room. With no clue whatsoever that it was even coming. Yet here I was, shaken, confused, scared witless, but still standing. Still here. *When all of these cops finally leave my home, I have some serious praying and praising to do.*

I eased myself away from the warmth of Gillette's big hands and hurried to my desk. I felt embarrassed by my neediness, as I opened my desk drawer. When I handed him the diary, I refused to meet his eyes, moving away from him and taking a seat on the front edge of my desk. To my surprise he sat beside me, and just like that, he was warming me once again, even though he wasn't touching me, his sweet, fresh scent almost intoxicating.

It was impossible to ignore his presence, it was just too overwhelming, but I tried anyway. I even thought to stand up and move across the room, to prove to him that I wasn't some chickenhead female trying to get his attention, but that would have been too ridiculous. The man was just doing his job. He, in fact, was reading every word in that boring diary as if it was some exciting suspense novel.

I folded my arms and tried my best to show patience, but I couldn't pull it off. I was still too ramped up to calm down. I probably would have been strumming my feet against the floor, if they could have reached the floor.

Gillette's certainly reached, as they spread out away from him and were crossed at the ankle. He flipped page after page and read Neka's cryptic, defensive writings with seeming ease. And when he reached the last page, he looked up and removed his glasses. He pinched the bridge of his nose as if this night was just exhausting the mess out of him. Then he looked at me. "Where did you find this?"

"In her closet. Behind the baseboard."

"This all you found?"

"Yes."

"Sure about that?"

"Positive about that, although I don't know why your men didn't find it. Weren't they supposed to search the victim's apartment?"

"They did search it, smart mouth. What else did you find?"

"I told you, nothing else."

Gillette stared at me.

"I'm not a liar, Gillette."

"Just a thief."

"A thief? I didn't."

"You took property that didn't belong to you without the permission of its owner or rightful heir. In legal terms, Veronica, that's theft."

My heart dropped. Was he crooked too, like all those other cops I'd known before?

"I didn't intend to keep it," I said, desperation in my voice. "I just wanted to see if there was something there, something I could discover that would help make sense about what happened to Neka. That's all I intended to do."

"Your intent is irrelevant."

"Irrelevant? How is it irrelevant? I wasn't stealing it."

"Possession, Veronica"—He waved the diary in my face—"is nine-tenths of the law. It can be evidence of guilt in and of itself. You know that."

"So I'm under arrest, is that what you're trying to say?"

He hesitated. "We might be able to work something out."

My "crooked cop antenna" flew up. I'd gotten myself in a fix now. I was probably going to have to do him some unmentionable favor, or go to jail. Which meant I was going to jail. Which meant I should have never thought that I could trust a cop in the first place.

"Work something out?" I asked suspiciously.

"Yes."

"Such as?" I looked at him hard. He stared back at me, the

greenish gray of his iris stark and intense, and we were completely eye to eye. We were so close, in fact, I could see exactly
where his eyelid drooped and how his eyes looked more weary
right now than sexy.

"I want you to promise me that you'll stay out of this and
any other investigation."

At first I thought he was trying to be funny. That's it? That's
all? No kinky stuff? I kept my eyes on him. "And?" I just knew
there had to be more.

"And I'll pretend I didn't find Miss Dupayne's property in
your home."

Could it be possible? I wondered. Was I sitting beside an
honest cop? I wasn't trying to act like I didn't know that there
were thousands of honest cops out there. Just none had ever
crossed my path.

But then again, I thought, maybe none still hadn't. Maybe
Gillette was scaring me away from the investigation, not because he was suddenly so concerned for my safety, but because
he was trying to protect some big shot somewhere. Protect the
real killer.

"Is it a deal, Veronica?"

I sighed and looked away from him. "I'll stay out of your
way," was all I was willing to promise.

"Roni!" a familiar voice echoed from the hall, and me and
Gillette both turned in time to see Alan Simms, followed
by Deacons Wenn and Montgomery and, to my discomfort,
Brother Cooper, hurry into the office.

Alan hurried to me, his oversized suit coat flapping around
him, while the others squeezed in too. He glanced at Gillette,
at how closely we were sitting together, and then he looked at
me. "Are you all right, honey?" he asked.

Even I was amazed that he would call me *honey* so blatantly
like that. "I'm fine, Dr. Simms," I said in the best official tone
I could register. I wanted to make it perfectly clear to Gillette
that nothing undercover was going on between Alan and me.

But before I could go on to make anything perfectly clear, Gillette stood up.

"Chief Gillette, hello," Alan said, extending his hand.

Gillette shook his hand, but didn't say anything.

"Is she really all right?"

Gillette stared at Alan, as if sizing him up. "You are?"

"Oh, I'm sorry. I'm Alan Simms. Roni's friend." He said this as if our relationship was far more than he knew it was, which irked me. "I was worried sick about her. I can't believe something like this has happened to such a sweet soul as Roni. It just doesn't seem possible."

"We came right over," Deacon Montgomery hurried over and said, "as soon as we got the call from Sister Tate. Pastor Burke will be along shortly too, Sister Jarrett. He's as shocked as we are."

"One of our sisters the victim of a drive-by shooting," Deacon Wenn said, shaking his large head. "Who would do something like this?"

They all looked at Gillette after that comment, as if Gillette had the answers already, but from the look on his face, he wasn't about to tell them, even if he had.

"They must have shot off two or three rounds from the look of all that shattered glass," Alan said in the awkward silence.

"And don't you worry about the mess, Roni," Deacon Wenn said. "We placed Brother Cooper in charge of securing your house for the night, him and some of the other young men from the church. Don't you think for a moment that you're in this alone."

I looked at Lester Cooper. I really didn't want that brother securing anything for me. Just looking at him gave me the willies. Even Gillette seemed to notice my hesitation, but I didn't care. Brother Cooper just didn't strike me as the benevolent type. Besides, he stood by the deacons looking all frustrated, as if he didn't want to be at my house at all, let alone repair any damages. But what could I do about it? Turn down the offer? I didn't exactly have all of these other options.

"You okay, Veronica?" Gillette asked, looking at me intensely.

If I asked, maybe he'd repair the damages. Problem was, I wasn't about to ask. "I'm okay."

"Was it just the windows they shot up?" Alan asked.

I nodded. "Yes, thank God. At least, I think that was all."

Alan placed his arm around my shoulder, and I noticed Gillette's jaw tighten.

"You poor thing," Alan said. "I couldn't believe it when I heard it. 'A drive-by shooting at Roni Jarrett's house?' That's what I said to Deacon Wenn when he told me. I nearly fell out of my chair."

"Know what you mean," I politely but firmly maneuvered my way out of his grasp.

"And you're sure you're okay?"

"I'm fine, Alan, really. I'm fine." I looked again at Gillette. His entire demeanor, it seemed to me, had changed.

He slipped the diary into his bomber jacket and then zipped it up. "If you have any questions, you can contact Detective Delvecchio. He'll be the lead on this one too. Good night, gentlemen." Then he looked at me, his handsome face, his gorgeous eyes, looking suddenly morose. "Miss Jarrett," he added, and even while we were all yet voicing our good nights to him, he left.

SIX

"Melville Police, may I help you?"

I hesitated, as if it still wasn't clear to me why I was doing this.

"Hello? This is the Melville Police Department, how may I help you?"

"May I speak with Donald Gillette, please."

"Chief Gillette? May I ask who's calling?"

Another hesitation. I was not good at this, not at all. "Veronica Jarrett," I finally said.

She told me one moment, please, and placed me on hold. I leaned my back against the concrete wall and tried to get my nerves to act right. I was seated on the back steps of the salon, on my mid-morning break, phoning Gillette to see if he'd found out anything about those characters mentioned in Neka's diary.

It had been three days. Three days since the shooting at my house; three days since I heard anything at all from the Melville police; three days since I'd heard a word from Gillette. I knew Delvecchio was the lead detective on the case, and Gillette had told me to contact him if I had any questions, but I just couldn't pull myself to do it. Delvecchio couldn't stand me. Why would he tell me anything?

Besides, and this was a big besides, I really wanted to hear Gillette's voice again. I was actually enjoying the little attention he was giving me there for a while, as if he might have seen me as a possibility. Not that I was about to go down that road with him, especially if his womanizing rep was true, but I still couldn't help but be flattered by his attention. It wasn't until recently, when he had come rushing out to my house that night, did I realize just how starved for attention I really was. But then Alan showed up and so much for that. Gillette seemed to me to be the kind of brother willing to give a girl a chance, but only if he didn't have to work at it. For him I was probably way too much work, given who I was, given the violence suddenly associated with my name.

"This is Gillette," a firm voice on the other end of the phone said, and my heart dropped. The man wasn't even in my presence, and I still got a physical reaction.

"Hi. It's me. Roni." I tried to say this cheerfully. It sounded, however, too tinged with shaky nerves to come out smoothly.

There was a hesitation. "Hello, Veronica."

"How are you?"

"Okay. You?"

"I'm good. I'm here at work on break. It's kind of slow today, which is a good thing too because it's been a hectic week, know what I'm saying?"

He didn't say anything, as if he either didn't know what I was saying or didn't care if he did.

"Anyway," I said, to spare myself any further embarrassment, "I was wondering if you were able to find out anything about Jeffrey?"

"Who?" he said quickly, and I could just feel his frown.

"From the diary."

No response.

"Taneka Dupayne's diary."

"Oh," he said, as if he only vaguely remembered.

"She mentioned this Jeffrey dude, and this guy named Willie Barnes."

"Detective Delvecchio's handling that case."

"I know, but I just thought, since you're his boss."

"You'll need to talk with him about it."

I nodded my head. So it was like that then. He was through with me. Whatever interest he might have had, real or imagined, was gone. "I was just trying to find out what you might know about the case, that's all."

"I told you to stay out of it, Veronica."

"I am staying out of it. But it was my house that was the target of somebody's drive-by. I think I'm entitled to know if y'all are at least investigating."

"Of course we're investigating," he snapped. Then he let out this big exhale. "I'm sorry."

"Forget it," I quickly replied. "Will you please transfer me to Delvecchio?"

There was a hesitation on his end of the line. Then he said in an oddly regretful tone, "Hold on."

"No sweat," I said, as if his earlier bluntness didn't faze me at all. Yet, as soon as he placed me on hold, I hung up. "Jerk!"

Somebody behind me laughed.

I quickly turned around. It was Greta, standing at the door. She opened the screen door and came onto the porch to take her cigarette break. She already smelled like a pack of cigarettes, I thought, when she plopped down beside me.

"What's Gillette's problem now?" she asked me as if she'd heard my entire conversation.

"I wouldn't call it a problem," I said, "other than general irritation."

She laughed again and lit her cigarette. She never asked anybody if they minded if she smoked because she didn't care if we minded. "Don't take it personally, kid," she said, looking at her cigarette. "He irritates everybody. He used to be tolerable, sometimes downright friendly, but that was a long time ago. Before his wife died."

"Yeah, you mentioned something about his wife dying." I

was feeding Greta's hunger to gossip, which made me a hypocrite. But the truth was, in the matter of Don Gillette, I had a need, a literal hunger to know more about the man.

"Years ago, when you was probably still a little pigtail kid running around here, Gillette owned the hottest nightclub in town. Hot, successful, and infamous. He was a brother every girl in town wanted bad. You could just see the dollar signs in those females' eyes whenever they'd so much as mention his name. But it was Catarina that caught Gillette's eyes."

"Catarina?" Just the name caused a surge of jealousy within me.

"Oh, yeah. We all called her Cat though, to her mother's eternal disgust. They were poor as dirt, but because Cat was what you would call gifted in the looks department, her mother decided that she deserved to have the best. And Don Gillette, by far, here in Melville, was the best."

"So he married her?"

"He married her, which made his star rise even higher in the eyes of these country bumpkins around here. Here was a brother who remembered where he came from, they said, who didn't put some stranger on his arm to leave his wealth to, but a local sister. They thought that meant something, you know. Didn't mean a darn thing in my view, because Cat wasn't about Nathan Jones. I mean I knew the sister, okay. Everybody knew Cat. She was born and raised right over there in Dodge, same as the rest of us, but as soon as big-time Gillette put that ring on her finger, she changed. Wouldn't hardly speak to people. And when he married her, good golly Miss Molly, you could forget it. We was all beneath her then."

"I remember one day I saw her and I said, 'Hey, Cat, what's up, girl?' like I'd always done. Don't you know that heifer looked at me like I was pure dirt, Roni, and I'm being polite. She looked like I was just trash in her eyes. 'That's Mrs. Gillette to you', she said to me. Well, don't you know I stopped right where I stood, put my hand on my hip, and just looked at the heifer. But I didn't trip. I didn't act a fool on your girl, nothing like that. I just told her I saw her mama in the food stamp line the other day. Said it loud enough for all of her little snooty friends to hear it too, and kept on walking."

I smiled. That sounded like something Greta would do.

"But you know what, Roni, despite all that frontin' she was doing, despite all that high-society routine she was putting on, in the end she was nothing but a ho, and everybody knew it."

I was stunned. "She cheated on Gillette?"

"With every Tom, Dick, Harry, and Gary, too, in town. I'm talking nympho, you hear me? And Gillette knew all about it. But he wouldn't leave her, following her around and dragging her home from this bar, from this nightclub, from this man's apartment. And he would even beat up her boyfriends. But he wouldn't leave her. This big brother, this rich, gorgeous brother, almost got a sucker rep fooling with her."

"Ain't no almost in it."

"Yeah, but you don't know Don Gillette. He's nobody's sucker, okay. He just loved her, that's all. He loved that witch. And then she got pregnant."

"Pregnant? I didn't know he had kids."

"That was the problem. Word on the street was, the kid wasn't his."

"Now wait a minute. That's going too far. Unless somebody saw some DNA results up in there, how in the world would anybody on the street know that?"

"He used condoms with her. Always, from what I heard. Made sense. I mean, the woman slept with football teams, okay. But even though the kid wasn't going to be his, he kept her around, took her with him on all his business trips and everything, and he continued to treat the little slut like a queen. Then she had a miscarriage, and within weeks, Roni, girlfriend was right back on the corner."

"The corner?"

"You know what I mean. Right back ho'ing around. And she was even worse than she was before she had gotten pregnant. Everybody has their limit, and I guess that was Gillette's. He kicked her out. Wouldn't even take her phone calls, and whenever she came by his house or by the club, he wouldn't let her in the door. It was pitiful."

"Did she divorce him and get what was rightfully hers?"

"Listen to you. No, they never divorced. She got a check from him every month, a big check too, from what I hear. And she still lived in style, but he didn't divorce her."

"Probably because she'd get even more, like half of everything he owned."

"That's what you say. But you ain't hearing me. Gillette loved that sister. I'm talking *love*. She hurt him and embarrassed him daily, but he still loved her."

"So what happened to her? How did she die?"

"Drugs."

"Drugs? You mean like prescription painkillers or something?"

"Child, please. That female was a crack ho who died right where she started from. In Dodge."

"Crack?"

"Yes, ma'am. Miss Thang was a crackhead. When Gillette found out about it, he took her back for a minute. Yes, he did, and tried to help her stay clean. He even put her in one of those fancy rehab places out in California. But as soon as she got back to Melville, she was right back on the street. All she wanted was his money to get her drugs, but then he stopped giving it to her. He knew what time it was. He would find her on the streets, take her back home, beat up her suppliers, hired bodyguards to keep an eye on her, you name it. But she always got back out. That crack was calling her name."

"It was during that time that Gillette first started getting hard, first started changing. Cat was making him miserable, so he made everybody else miserable. And then she overdosed and died. And that did it. He was devastated, blaming himself and everything."

"How could he blame himself? He did all he could for her."

"He still blamed himself. If he hadn't kicked her out after that miscarriage, if he'd just understood her better, if he'd taken her away from here. Wrong or right, he blamed himself, okay. You digging me now? It had nothing to do with logic and facts. The man was a bundle of feelings. Hurt feelings. So he sold his club, sold all his other businesses, dropped out of sight for years then came back home. I guess it shouldn't have been no surprise that he came back to rid these streets of drugs, considering what drugs did to his wife, but it was still surprising."

"And he came back hard as steel."

"As steel, girl. And a big-time player, to boot. Somebody who you could just tell made up his mind that he wasn't going to be suckered again, or fall in love again either. His main squeeze nowadays supposed to be this chick named Liz Steward."

"Liz Steward? Who is she?"

"The district attorney here in town. Nasty sister. Tried hard to put my cousin Ducey in prison based on no evidence whatsoever, but it didn't work. I can't stand her. But that's the kind of woman Gillette fools with nowadays. They all have to be supersuccessful, superbeautiful, and superhateful, if you ask me. Like that woman doctor over at Memorial I see him with sometimes too. She ain't right either. But that's what he wants now, and they all want him, and try every trick in the book to get him too. But from what I hear he never, and I mean ever, let anybody get too close. I guess he figures he went through enough with Cat. He ain't going through it with nobody else."

"I hear that."

Depression came over me like a heavy weight on my shoulders, and I spent the rest of my workday trying to knock it off. But I couldn't. Because I got it. Maybe at first, when he saw me at the police station, and at Mae's, and when he rushed to my house after that drive-by, maybe then he thought I was different, that I was somebody he just might like to get to know better.

But then Alan Simms showed up and ended all of that. He now probably thought of me, not as some innocent potential, but as just another floozy, just another disappointment. Just like his wife.

I hid out in my office. With a can of Coke and a pastry from the vending machine, I tried to go over the stack of requisition orders sitting on my desk that I hadn't even looked at. I tried anyway, but I was still too down. What was happening to me? Was that drive-by shooting still terrifying me?

Gillette wasn't even somebody, in normal times, I would even be interested in. I mean, he looked good and had the bod going on, but he was a brother with baggage, the kind I definitely didn't need to be getting all excited about. But now I was getting depressed because he wasn't interested in me, as if my once calm, together life suddenly revolved around him. Please. It had to be the times and the emotions of just being a victim of anything, let alone a drive-by shooting, that had me this off-balance.

That was probably why I stopped pretending to work on requisitions and turned on my computer. Gillette wasn't going to do anything about Neka's murder or the attempt on my life, not if he put Delvecchio in charge, so I knew I had to get some answers myself. The only name I had to go on was that of Willie Barnes, since his was the only full name mentioned in Neka's diary. I typed his name into the Google search engine. So many Willie Barnes came up, I had to type in Melville, Florida to narrow the search.

I sat at my desk, sipping my Coke, eating my pastry, and staring at the computer screen. Gillette kept trying to get on my mind, and I kept trying to keep him off of it. He was bad news, and the sooner I admitted it, the better off I was going to be.

A few newspaper articles on Barnes did come up and, lo and behold, more tragedy, which immediately prompted me to sit erect and read carefully. It seemed that old Willie was killed during a foiled robbery attempt just a month ago. According to press accounts, Mason Lerner, the chairman of the board at Harbor House, a small, transitional housing facility for ex-offenders, was leaving the facility when he was accosted by Barnes and asked to turn over his wallet.

Barnes had to be some dumb criminal, I thought, because the crime occurred in the middle of the day, right outside this house for ex-criminals. And Lerner wasn't even alone. In fact, as a testament to Barnes' rotten luck, Lerner not only wasn't alone, he was with a cop. A cop. That floored me. Brother made up his mind to rob the next sucker that came out of Harbor House and a cop just so happened to be with him? I was more than floored when I saw that it wasn't just any cop with Lerner, but, amazingly, Vincent Delvecchio himself.

I know it's a small world, but it ain't that small. Something was up. And when I read further that it was Delvecchio who killed Barnes, that it was Delvecchio who silenced one of the two men Neka's diary indicated she had the goods on, my crooked cop antenna started going haywire.

Where do I begin? I certainly couldn't approach Delvecchio. He was a cop. He'd trump-up some charge against me, some dope charge or something equally reprehensible, and I wouldn't have a leg to stand on. Gillette certainly wouldn't come to my aid. Delvecchio, it seemed to me, was his right hand man.

I tried Google for any information on a Jeffrey in Melville, the other name mentioned in Neka's diary, but even then, I still got a whole bunch of articles on a whole bunch of different Jeffreys. When I cross-referenced his name with Barnes' or Taneka's, or even Delvecchio's, I got nothing.

I did, however, turn up a local article on Taneka that talked about her murder and the facts surrounding the case. It also mentioned that her parents had planned a private memorial service for her, with no details about when or where. But what struck me even more was that her parents, according to the newspaper, were the owners of the Hard Times Barbecue Pit, a local rib joint here in Melville.

When I was a kid with Neka, I had never known her parents or anything at all about their occupations. The fact that they'd owned Hard Times stunned me, because I passed by the place all the time, without once realizing that Taneka, whom this town had relegated to being just another crackhead, had connections there. And if I was ever going to get some answers about why anyone would want to kill Neka, or try to kill me, it seemed as good a place to start as any.

Hard Times wasn't exactly your idyllic family restaurant, but was a rough-looking rib joint in Dodge. I just couldn't bring myself to eat from, although the smell of those ribs always had me tempted. But the place was just too dingy-looking, from the dilapidated wood-framed exterior, to the winos and bums that loved to hang outside.

Those ribs were kicking when I entered the restaurant, and a near full house, including a few uniformed cops, were kicking back, eating them down to the bone and then licking fingers just to get that last taste. I hadn't had sweet-tasting ribs since leaving Jersey.

I was almost about to sit at that bar counter and order me a slab to go. Until I saw the cook, through a narrow fly door that led to the kitchen, picking up a bone that had fallen from his chopping table, and tossing it on the grill with the rest of the meat.

"Hello, pretty lady," an older man said with a big, bright smile. "What you havin' today?"

Nothing from here, I started to say. "Actually, I'm looking for someone."

"Here?"

"Yes, sir. I was wondering if Mr. or Mrs. Dupayne was around?"

From the look that came over his hard, leathery face, I knew I had hit the target. "Dupayne?" He began wiping the counter with a filthy rag he had in his possession. "What you want with them?"

"I was a friend of their daughter's, and I just wanted to offer my condolences."

He became less defensive. "I'm her father. You was a friend of Neka's?"

"Yes, sir. I'm Roni Jarrett. I don't know if you remember me." Especially since I hadn't exactly remembered him.

"Roni Jarrett? That name sure sounds familiar. You Gert Jarrett's child?"

"No, sir. My parents were Roy and Marilyn."

"Oh, yeah!" he said with some animation. "Yeah, I knew Roy and Marilyn. Musicians."

"That's right."

"Your mama had a right pretty voice. Could play that piano too, just as good as your daddy could. And Roy could play some piano. Shame what happened to them. And you they daughter? You little Roni?"

I smiled. "Yes, sir."

He stared at me. "I'll be darn. I remember you. Shame what happened to your people. And now you come here to give us sympathy over our loss. God bless you, child."

"Thank you, Mr. Dupayne. But what I was wondering—"

"Alma!" he yelled, startling me. "Get out here!" Then he looked at me again, shaking his head. "Roy and Marilyn's child, *mm-mm-mm*."

Within seconds, an older woman came out wiping her hands on an apron. She was the spitting image of Taneka. I wasn't sure of the apron's original color because it was nearly black with smudges.

"I'll be darn," Mr. Dupayne said, still shaking his head and looking at me. Then he looked at the woman who just had to be his wife. "This Roni Jarrett, Alma, a friend of Neka's. She Roy and Marilyn's daughter."

"Roy and Marilyn?"

"Yeah. You remember them. They were musicians. Got themselves killed in that bad car accident a few years back. Had the one daughter."

She stared at me. "That was twenty years ago."

Actually twelve, but I didn't go there. "Neka was a friend of mine."

She still stared at me suspiciously, causing Mr. Dupayne to jump in.

"Came to offer her condolences," he said. "And I shole thanked her for it."

"Then what you calling me for?"

"Well, actually, Mrs. Dupayne, I was hoping you could tell me a little something about your daughter."

A young couple came in, and Mr. Dupayne called for somebody in the kitchen to come and assist them. Then he looked at me. "I thought you said you knew her?"

"I did. But the way she died was so unbelievable. So tragic. I was just wondering if something was going on in her life, or—"

"We wouldn't know nothing about that," Mrs. Dupayne quickly said. "She left home when she was sixteen, thought she was forty, and we said good riddance. Ain't nobody gonna be acting a fool under my roof and expect to live there. Only time we saw that child lately was when she was up in here begging for money."

"We didn't give her a dime," Mr. Dupayne said, as if this made them somehow wonderful parents. But then he added, "not for them drugs anyway."

"Y'all paid the rent on her apartment, didn't you?"

Mr. Dupayne began nodding his head. "That's right. Paid it every month."

"To whom?"

The parents glanced at each other.

"What that got to do with you?" Mrs. Dupayne asked me.

"I'm just trying to find out what happened to Neka, ma'am. That's all."

"What you mean, what happened to her? She was a crack addict. That's what happened to her. She was a lost soul who didn't wanna be saved and who wouldn't listen to her mama no more. That's what happened to her."

"Yes, but she was also beaten to death. And that's the part I want to find out about."

Mrs. Dupayne's face became more pinched and agitated. Mr. Dupayne, however, seemed receptive, his wiping of the bar counter slowing down.

"We paid her rent every month to this young man named Juno."

Mrs. Dupayne gave him the eye.

"Juno?" I said. "Juno Curtis?"

"That's right."

"Juno owns those apartments?"

"I don't know all about him owning nothing. I just know he collects the rent."

"Not Pooh?"

"Who?"

"Never mind. What do you know about Juno's relationship with Taneka?"

"What relationship?" Mr. Dupayne said bitterly. "Other than him supplying her with them drugs?"

"You can just leave now," Mrs. Dupayne said to me. "We ain't gettin' mixed up with none of them drug people. They ain't coming here bothering us. We paid her rent to that fool because we didn't want our baby outdoors. We knew she'd always have a roof over her head. But that was all we did. We don't associate with no slime like no Juno Curtis."

I left. They'd given me about all the information I was going to get. Pooh was being all cagey about who the rent collector on Neka's apartment really was, not because of some big secret, but because that rent collector was drug-dealing Juno.

But was Juno more involved in this than I was giving him credit for, I wondered, as I stepped out of Hard Times and the evening wind whipped across my face. The fact that he may own the complex where Taneka lived, or at least collected the money for the owner of it, meant something. He had more of a connection to her than I had thought.

Mrs. Dupayne even said he was her drug supplier. I couldn't doubt that. I'd be crazy to think that Juno only sold weed. And what about that drive-by shooting at my place? A drive-by was the tactic of choice for drug dealers. Gillette had said so himself.

Did Juno see me take Neka's diary and contact somebody? Was that why I was targeted too? As I stepped off the sidewalk to head to my car across the street, I had more questions than I probably would ever find the answers to.

I was thinking about how awful that would be, to never find out what was really happening, when there was yet another happening. It was a speeding car this time, at the end of the corner, that managed to veer from one side of the street to the side that I was on in what looked like an out-of-control acceleration.

I saw the dark, old-styled Pontiac coming, but I wasn't thinking it was coming after me. When I realized that it wasn't slowing down, or correcting itself, wasn't trying to avoid me, terror gripped me like a light bulb finally coming on, and then I didn't hesitate.

I bolted, running as if my life depended on it, back to where I came from. I was running so fast, I lost a shoe. And even with all of my running, that car was still able to swerve as hard as it could in a thunderous squeal and still come within inches of knocking the life out of me. I slammed hard against the wood frame of Hard Times, only to find myself nearly knocked out anyway, not by the car, but by the impact of my own slam.

I slid down to the ground, nearly breathless, as the car veered back into the street and sped away, its squealing tires leaving the smell of burnt rubber in the air.

Most of the people inside of the restaurant rushed out, including the police officers, with one pulling out his radio and frantically calling it in. Those cops wanted me to go to the hospital, to get myself checked out, but I wasn't trying to hear that. I knew I was fine physically. Nothing there for a doctor to check out.

Emotionally was another story. Somebody was out to get me. That much I knew now without a doubt. And I was on my own. I'd be the first to admit that coincidences did indeed happen, but nobody was going to convince me that they happened this regular.

SEVEN

My eyes remained closed the entire time I talked with Pam. I didn't know if it was fatigue or just plain amazement. Somebody was targeting me for some crazy reason, and I was still shook up. I was constantly checking my doors, looking out of my windows, and under my bed. I was so nervous half the time, I wondered if I was starting to have panic attacks.

Yet, Pamela's suggestion that I change my entire lifestyle and come live with her "until this all blows over" wasn't working for me either.

"Why not, Roni?"

"I can hide out for a day or two, maybe even three or four, but what then? You think the Melville Police Department is that efficient that they'll solve this thing in a few days? Give me a break." I was lying on my living room sofa, the cordless phone resting in the crook of my neck and shoulder, my fingers twirling around a rubber band. Just the thought of what had almost happened to me in front of Hard Times was still reeling in my brain. *Who would want to kill me?*

"I hear what you're saying, Ron. Honestly, I do. But ain't no way I'd be up in that house by myself tonight."

"Maybe it was an accident, I don't know."

"Yeah, hon-hon. An accident. Like cars just come up on sidewalks running you down all the time."

"Well, what do you want me to do, Pam? Goodness. I believe in God. It's not just lip service with me. Sometimes you just have to trust the Lord."

"Yeah, but the Lord gives us common sense too, girl. And ain't no sense in what you're doing."

"Common sense is man's way of justifying a lack of faith. You know it, and I know it. No weapon that's formed against me is going to prosper. I believe that. I'm not about to let these people, whoever they are, have me on the run, acting like God's might and power means nothing to me. That's what they want. They want me acting all scared and crazy. Forget that. I can't live my life that way."

"But what's going on, Roni?"

"I don't know," I said honestly.

"And why would somebody be after you?"

"Maybe because I'm not letting them get away with Neka's murder."

"Whoever *they* are."

"Right."

"And you don't even know if you're letting them get away with her murder or not."

"That's true too." I took the rubber band and, with my thumb and finger, flicked it across the room. "I know it's all crazy. It's not making any sense to me either. But there's nothing hidden that won't be uncovered, and I'm believing in that uncovering. It'll all come to light eventually."

"Gotta give you your props, girl. I don't know too many sisters who can take that kind of pressure, with me chief among them, because let me tell you, if I knew somebody was after me, I'd be scared of my own shadow right about now."

I was plenty scared too, but what could I do about it? I had to rely on my faith and go on about my business. Either that, or just curl up somewhere and wait for them to take their best shot. And that wasn't happening. Not as long as I called myself a child of the Almighty God.

"Have you told Dr. Simms about what happened today?" Pam wanted me to be with Alan almost as badly as Alan did.

I cringed. "No, Pamela, I haven't told Dr. Simms. And don't intend to. This none of his business."

"You cold, girl."

"Well, it's not. He overdid it that night at my house, and I didn't like it. Calling me honey and putting his arm around my shoulder. He knew better than that. He knows we ain't down like that."

"Down like what? The man was just showing his concern for you, as any good church leader would have done."

"Yeah, right. I'll bet our police chief didn't see it that way."

"Our police chief? You mean Gillette? What does he have to do with—Oh my gosh! Now I get it. Now I got it. So that's it."

"What's *it*?"

"Roni wants Donnie!" Pam said in a singsong manner.

"What? Please. I can't stand that man, and he can't stand me."

"Yeah, uh-huh."

"I'm serious. Besides, he's too old for me."

"Too old for you? Child, please. He ain't that old."

"He's older than me."

"And? He'll run rings around any dude younger, and you know it. So don't even play me like that. You know you want him."

"Only in your gutter mind, girl."

"Sure, buddy. Whatever you say."

"Oh, forget you."

"Anyway," Pam said, "let me get off this phone and try to wash these dishes."

"You're way off base, but thanks for calling."

"Yeah, and I love you too. Anyway."

I smiled. "See you, girl."

"Sure you're okay?"

"I'm straight."

"'Cause I can come over. Ain't nothing for me to throw on some clothes and get there."

"I know, Pam, and I appreciate it. You know I do. But I'm straight. There's no need."

"Okay, girl. See ya. Truly wouldn't wanna be ya."

I smiled a smile I knew I didn't mean. I knew exactly what she meant. "Night, Pam." I hung up the phone.

That pain from a scrape on my elbow returned. I held it for a while, so that the throbbing could ease, and closed my tired eyes. The silence that permeated the room was unnerving. Maybe Pam was right. Maybe I was out of my mind just hanging around like some sitting duck.

But what other options did I have? Move in with her and make her a target too? Or maybe skip town and start over somewhere far away, forgetting about Taneka and any lame promise I made to her?

I had run away from Jersey when the heat got hot, refusing to even fight my firing, or at least try another school in the area. I'd just wanted a lot of real estate between myself and those folks at Branson Academy, who suddenly started looking at me as if I was trash. I ran away then, but I wasn't running anymore.

Branson Academy, I thought. It started out so great. I finally thought I had arrived, had finally done something right, when they hired me. It was a nice school, filled with good people, and they liked me, too. Really respected me. I was this Juilliard-educated sister who was going to lead their music department to heights previously unknown. And I was ready for the challenge too. More than ready.

Until Richard's phone call ended all of that. And those same people who used to look at me as their school's savior started looking at me as if I was the school's tramp.

I got up, deciding to forget all of this negative stuff that was taking up way too much of my thoughts, but before I could move away from the sofa, the doorbell rang.

Already jumpy, I jumped just from the mere ring and hurried over to my old-fashioned, double-pane living room window. I peeped out of the white plantation shutters and saw a new-looking silver pickup truck, a big Ford F-150, parked behind my Beamer. I'd never seen it before.

I hurried over to the peephole on my front door. And standing on my porch, to my utter surprise, was Gillette. My heart thumped.

I looked down. I was wearing the same shorts and skintight T-shirt I wore the last time he saw me. The man was probably going to think that this was about the only around-the-house outfit I owned. But what difference did it make? He was here, no doubt in my mind, on official business.

I heard the whip and twirl of that wind when I opened my door. I could smell his fresh cologne scent even through the screen. He looked as if he'd come straight from work, or from some business meeting somewhere. He had on another one of his expensive Italian suits and matching bowler hat, but this time he also had on a long brown overcoat, complete with a beautiful scarf hanging on either side. It was a windy fall night, but dang, the brother was a wee overdressed, if you asked me.

"Yes?" I said, without much warmth behind the word. He wasn't exactly kind when last we spoke, and the pain of that phone call, on top of what Greta had said about his new, hit-and-run attitude regarding women, was still burning in my memory.

"Good evening."

"Good evening."

He stared at me, as if he absolutely expected me to say more. "May I come in?" he finally asked, his words lacking warmth too.

I hesitated, as if I wasn't sure, and then opened the screen door. When I did so and felt just how bitingly cold that wind really was, I almost smiled. Overdressed my foot. He knew what he was doing.

He walked in, and as he squeezed past, I nearly closed my eyes, savoring the sweet scent of him. When he turned around and nearly caught me looking downright admirably at him, I caught myself and closed the door.

He gave my shorts and shirt his usual perusal.

I crossed my arms defensively. "Okay you're in. Now what do you want?"

A flash of anger crossed his face too, but then he tempered it. "Are you going to offer me a seat?"

I wasn't exactly behaving hospitably, I realized, so I uncrossed my arms, albeit reluctantly, and gestured toward the sofa.

Gillette walked slowly into my home, surveying it again as if he'd never seen it before. I was curious to know what he thought, but not enough to bring it up. This wasn't exactly a friendly visit.

I followed behind him as he slowly made his way. When he got to the chair that flanked my sofa, he removed his coat and scarf, revealing a suit so perfectly tailored to his body, it gave stark definition to his muscular frame. He placed his coat and scarf in the chair and then kept on moving toward my sofa.

We both took a seat on the sofa, him with his big legs crossed, me with my small legs tucked under my behind. He looked at those legs and then at me.

I adjusted my glasses up on my face.

"I heard about your little accident today," he said, his hazel eyes trained on me, his voice already sounding peeved.

"And what did you hear?"

He let out an exasperated exhale, as if I'd just said something provocative. Then he removed his hat with an angry snatch, rubbing his wavy hair in place when he did so. He tossed the hat onto the flanking chair. "What were you doing over at Hard Times, Veronica? Don't get smart with me."

"I wasn't trying to get smart with you."

"What were you doing over at Hard Times today?"

"What do you think I was doing? I was offering my condolences to Taneka's parents."

"And?"

"And nothing, Gillette. I told you I knew her."

"And I told you to stay out of this investigation."

"I'm not in any investigation, all right? Although I do think having Delvecchio in charge of it is a joke."

"Oh, is it now?"

"Yes, it is. He might be your right-hand man or whatever, and you might think he's all that, but I ain't feeling him. He doesn't care what happened to Taneka. He doesn't care about somebody shooting up my house. He doesn't care. And from what I hear around town, neither do you."

"Believe everything you hear?"

I didn't, of course, but I wasn't about to give an inch. "Why not?"

"Then you hear this—the next time you even think about interfering with my investigation—"

"*Your* investigation? Don't you mean Delvecchio's investigation? You did, after all, make that perfectly clear to me this morning. Delvecchio, you said and you said it repeatedly, is in charge of this."

"Just leave it alone, Veronica. And let the police handle it."

"Wonder why that doesn't reassure me?"

"It had better reassure you, because that's what you're going to do. Let the police handle this investigation."

I exhaled. I wasn't about to argue with the man, especially since he did have that *taking of Taneka's diary* theft, as he put it, still over my head. "Is that why you came all this way? To warn me off?"

"If that's the way you want to phrase it."

"And that's it?"

He hesitated. "And I wanted to make sure you were okay. Although, why I'm bothering, I do not know."

He didn't smile when he added this, but I did. He hadn't exactly come out and flat told me that he was worried about me, but it still couldn't have been an easy thing for a man like him to admit. Especially after what Greta had told me about the hell his deceased wife had put him through, and how he was determined to never let another woman get close to him.

But my smile didn't linger, because his look remained intense, as if he was still trying to figure me out, as if he still wasn't quite ready to go shopping for any friendship ring.

"Thanks for your concern," I said, in my best disinterested voice.

"Are you?"

I raised an eyebrow at him. Why would he question my sincerity? "Yes, I'm thankful. I'm very thankful."

"Are you okay?"

"Oh. Yes. I'm . . . okay." I looked away from him, as suddenly just looking into his eyes caused emotions to began bubbling inside me, deep-down emotions, as if I wasn't okay, as if I probably hadn't been okay for a very long time.

"Would you care for something to drink?" I decided to ask him, my way of changing the subject.

There was a hesitation in his response, as if he knew very well what I was up to. "What do you have?"

"Green tea."

"And?"

"And more green tea."

He smiled a smile so charming, I found myself staring at his bright white teeth. "That's all you drink?"

"That, and water. Would you like a glass?"

"No. Thank you. I'm fine. But what you can do for me is tell me why it was that you felt this sudden need to visit the Dupaynes."

The man was all about business, just as I'd thought. "I told you, I wanted to offer my condolences."

"I'm sure that was one reason."

"I need to know what happened to Taneka, all right, and why somebody's suddenly deciding to target me."

"Why do you think her parents would know anything about that?"

"It was somewhere to start. More than what Delvecchio's doing."

"That's what you think?"

"That's what I know. Remember Willie Barnes, one of the names Taneka mentioned in her diary?"

"What about him?"

"Delvecchio killed him."

"During a botched robbery attempt, that's right."

"You believe that?"

Gillette leaned his head back. He was tired. "I'm sure you don't."

"Gillette, it was broad daylight, in front of a halfway house for convicts."

"Ex-cons."

"You know what I'm saying. And that's the place Barnes decides to scope out for a robbery? A halfway house for ex-offenders? And then the man he chooses to rob just so happens to have a cop by his side? Come on, Gillette. This ain't no twilight zone we're living in. According to newspaper accounts, Barnes was robbing the man so he could get money for his girlfriend's drug habit."

"That's right."

"But why wouldn't he rob a convenience store, if money for drugs was what he was after? Or hold up a gas station, if he was that desperate? That's where the money is. What thief in his right mind would hang around a halfway house and rob the one man who just so happens to be coming out with a cop by his side, a man who might not even have any big cash on him anyway? No street dude like Willie Barnes would do something like that, Gillette. It doesn't make sense."

Gillette let out a heavy sigh, as if he was getting tired of me and my suspicions fast. "What's your point?"

"Don't you find it a little strange that the lead detective in Taneka's death also happens to be the man who killed one of the two dudes her diary said she had the goods on?"

"You sound like a television show."

"Taneka could have been Willie Barnes' girlfriend. That's why she kept mentioning him in her diary. It was probably Neka he was trying to get money to buy drugs for. And the man now leading the investigation into her death also happens to have killed her boyfriend? That's some coincidence, Gillette."

"It's not a coincidence at all. Melville isn't Newark, Veronica. This isn't some sprawling metropolis. We don't have an endless supply of cops when crimes happen around here. We use who we have. And we use them repeatedly."

"So Delvecchio's connection to one of the men in Neka's diary doesn't concern you?"

"Not in the least. I know Vince Delvecchio. He's a good cop, a careful cop. He didn't plan on killing Barnes that day."

"How can you be so sure?"

"Oh, for crying out loud!" Gillette uncrossed his legs and leaned forward. Then he looked back at me and exhaled loudly. "What are you getting at, Veronica?"

"The paper said Barnes was shot in the chest."

"So?"

"How did he pull his gun?"

"Barnes?"

"Delvecchio. If Barnes was there to rob Mason Lerner like the press reports claim, that meant Barnes had his gun ready when Lerner first came out of Harbor House. That had to be the case. Why would Barnes just stand there and let Delvecchio pull out his gun too? Why didn't Barnes kill Delvecchio, if he was already lock and loaded?"

Gillette didn't respond. Not that he was convinced by what I was saying, but at least he was listening.

"That was no robbery," I went on. "It couldn't have been. That was an assassination. Lerner came out of Harbor House, and Barnes immediately assassinated him because that was the man he came to get. That was the man he had to get. That gave Delvecchio time to take cover and shoot and kill Barnes. That's the only way that makes sense."

"Except for one small problem—Delvecchio himself said it was a robbery attempt."

"That's why I don't trust Delvecchio. He's hiding something."

"Hiding? Do you have proof of your allegations, young lady? Because if you don't, I would strongly suggest you knock it off."

"But if you investigate it—"

"So you're a cop now?"

"I'm just trying to get you to see how the official version is wack. It can't be true. If you'll investigate it—"

"It's been investigated."

"By you?"

"By Internal Affairs. By the community oversight committee. By newspaper reporters. By everybody, Veronica. Delvecchio was cleared. His explanation lined up with the facts of the case."

"They say."

"I see. So the members of the oversight committee, all of whom are regular citizens from all walks of life in this community, are liars too?"

I closed my eyes. "That's not what I'm saying."

"Sounds that way to me, kid."

"I'm just trying to find out the truth, Gillette." I opened my eyes. "Why don't you understand that and help me?"

This seemed to touch him. I could see it in his eyes.

"This is a matter for the police, and you need to let the police handle it. How many times do I have to tell you that, Veronica? This is no college sorority game you're playing. This is real, and this is dangerous. Somebody has killed your friend and has tried to harm you too."

He hesitated after he said this, as if he needed to convince me of the gravity.

"The more questions you keep asking, the more they will continue to try and harm you. How can you not see that? How can you not get that simple fact through your thick skull?" He placed two fingers against my forehead and pressed as he said this. Then he removed them.

He appeared so upset, so concerned, I didn't know how to take it. My butt was on the grill, not his. Seemed I should have been the one complaining about *his* thick skull.

He rubbed his own forehead, as if trying to maintain his composure. "Just let me do my job, Veronica. Is that too much to ask?"

"What have you found out about that Jeffrey dude from the diary?"

He looked at me. "You will not let up, will you?"

"Not until somebody starts telling me more than they're telling me now. Because it might add up to you, but it's not adding up to me." I winced as the pain in my elbow returned.

"What's the matter?"

"Nothing."

"Don't tell me nothing." His gorgeous eyes began roaming my body. "Were you hurt?"

"No. I wasn't hurt. Not really."

"Where, Veronica?"

"I told you—" *Why did I bother?* "My elbow."

He placed his hand underneath my arm and checked out my sore elbow. There was a small scrape on it that was already beginning to scab over, but from the look on Gillette's face, one would think I had a bullet lodged in it. He stared at it, as if all sorts of thoughts were running through his mind. Then he took his thick thumb and began rubbing it.

His touch felt so wonderful, so soothing, that I looked into his eyes, and we held each other's gaze for far longer than was reasonable.

Then he slowly released me. "Be careful next time."

"It's just a scrape."

"You could have been killed. My men were on the scene. They told me what happened."

I tried to smile. "Don't tell me the chief of police also investigates attempted hit-and-run accidents too."

"I investigate everything . . . that you're mixed up in."

His words warmed my heart, more so probably than was warranted, so much so that I didn't dare look into his eyes. "And why's that?" I asked him.

"Why's what?"

"Why are you taking this unusual interest in me?" I looked at him this time.

He shook his head. "Lord knows."

I smiled and then found myself laughing out loud.

Gillette couldn't help but grin himself, which was marvelous to see, but it was short-lived. He got serious again. "That's why I need you to let me handle this thing, Veronica. I mean it. I don't have the time, and my department doesn't have the resources to be tracking you, too."

"Then tell me what you know, Gillette."

He exhaled.

"Tell me what's going on. You knew about Willie Barnes. What about that Jeffrey dude? What have y'all found out about him?"

There was a pause. Then Gillette said, "His name is Jeffrey Collins."

My heart leaped. "You know his name?"

"Yes, we know him, all right. He's a local hood. Small-time all the way. Stolen goods mostly. Sometimes sells crack."

"You found him? You know where he is?"

He hesitated again. "Yes."

I jumped from the sofa, my excitement sudden and expressive. Surely this Jeffrey Collins had to be responsible for Neka's death and the attempts on my life. Maybe this nightmare was finally coming to an end. "What did he say?" I asked Gillette impatiently. "Did he mention me?"

"Hold on, Veronica."

"Has he confessed? I bet he won't confess. But he doesn't have to, does he? For a conviction, I mean."

"Veronica," Gillette said, standing, his muscular bulk overwhelming.

But I wasn't intimidated in the least. I was too relieved, too thankful, too filled with giddy anticipation to let his commanding presence bother me.

"We can convict on circumstantial evidence," I went on. "That'll work too. I've read where it can be just as powerful evidence as a confession, or even an eyewitness account. You know how people can be, anyway. Their eyes can play all kinds of tricks on them, have them so certain they saw something when they didn't see a thing. I read about this one woman who declared up and down that she saw—"

"He's dead, Veronica."

"Dead?"

"A couple of my men found him early this morning at a rooming house where we tracked him down. He apparently had been killed overnight. He was stabbed multiple times. I'm sorry."

I just stood there, unable to even acknowledge his concern.

Jeffrey Collins had been murdered too. Which meant that he couldn't have been the guy in the Pontiac outside of Hard Times, and probably wasn't the drive-by shooter either.

Nothing had changed. I was still in trouble. Still in danger of ending up just like Taneka.

For some odd reason, I started thinking about notification. Who would they notify? Neka at least had her parents. Both of mine were dead. My aunt in Newark hadn't seen me since she disowned me when I was still a teenager. I doubt if she could even identify my body, or would even bother trying. Pam was a friend, a good friend, but I'd known her for less than a year. She could hardly qualify as family.

I looked at Gillette. I could feel the tears trying desperately to escape. "Who would they notify for me?"

"Veronica," he said with deep sorrow in his voice.

And I lost it then. Tears flooded my eyes as I searched Gillette's for answers. And he looked seriously uncomfortable. I'm sure this wasn't quite what he'd bargained for when he decided to pay me a visit, to be sure, but I didn't care anymore. I leaned into him, resting my head against his chest, drinking up the sweet scent of him, crying outright for the first time in years.

Gillette just stood there, as if he was stunned by my display, but then I felt his big arms encircle me and pull me against him. That was what I had been longing for, to feel the warmth of another human being. But this was different. I felt safe in his arms. Protected for the first time since my childhood.

I leaned closer against him, and he pulled me closer too and held me tighter. And made me feel as if he understood, all right.

We stood there, holding each other, for a very long time. And I cried in his arms, not caring how it looked anymore.

When it looked as if my wailing was easing up, he lifted my chin and stared into my large, tear-stained eyes. He removed my small glasses and rubbed his thumb across my cheek, and then my lips, his look intense. "You okay?"

I nodded. I had no idea if I was, but I couldn't tell him that.

"You have beautiful eyes," he said, staring into them. And then he exhaled. "Nobody is going to hurt you, Veronica, I promise you. There'll be no need to notify anybody, because it ain't gonna happen."

Then he stared at me longer, contemplating all sorts of things, it seemed to me, and then, to my utter surprise, he kissed me.

It was a simple kiss at first, a kiss to comfort and relax, but then it became a long, passionate kiss. He kissed me so intensely and held me so tight, I found myself welcoming his affection as if I was hardly able to contain myself. I was so excited, in fact, that I found myself moving closer and closer to him, although we were already as close as humanly possible.

Then he removed his lips from mine and eased his grip on me.

I felt embarrassed because I knew I had carried on like I was starving for affection, but I'd never felt such intense desire, such longing, in my entire life. It was such a strong feeling, such a strange, tender feeling. I looked up at him, to see if he felt it too. He felt something. I could see it in his eyes, but he didn't say a word.

He wiped what remained of my tears away, and placed my small glasses back on my face. Then before I could say another word myself, although I wasn't sure what exactly I could say, he got in a hurry.

"Lock up when I leave." He grabbed his coat, scarf, and hat and began heading for the exit.

He looked back at me when I didn't reply. But I couldn't reply, still reeling from his kiss, from Jeffrey Collins' death, from all of the confusion. He seemed to understand my weariness because he stopped his progression and gave out one of those exasperated exhales of his. He stared at me with that "what-am-I-going-to-do-with-you look" in his eyes.

"Lock up when I leave," he said again, this time less forcefully.

I nodded. "I will." I began following him to the door, a sense of regret overtaking me. Why I was so regretful? And why he was suddenly in such a big hurry?

"I'll have one of my men keep an eye on your place tonight," he said as his big hand touched my doorknob.

"That's not necessary, Gillette."

"An officer will keep an eye on your place." He looked back at me one last time, as if daring me to object.

EIGHT

To my great disappointment, I didn't see Donald Gillette again until a week later, on Sunday. In church of all places. I was at the piano, playing a soft melody during scriptural reading, and the next time I looked up, there he was, looking fit and gorgeous in his perfectly tailored suit as he took a seat near the back of the church. At first I was elated. Just seeing him again gave me that kind of charge.

But then I started thinking about it and became more and more annoyed. It had been nearly a week, a whole week since that night he held me in his arms, since he kissed me, and nobody was going to tell me that he had been too busy to pick up a telephone and give me a call. No way. He knew I had problems. He knew how frightened I was that night. But he still didn't bother checking on me.

I had it so bad early on, I would hurry home from work and sit by the telephone, going so far as to pick it up a few times to make sure it had a dial tone. I even ditched my glasses, except when I had to do extensive reading, which was what they were designed for anyway. Pamela was pleased, declaring that I had been neglecting my appearance for far too long, and although I denied it vociferously, it didn't take a molecular biophysicist to figure out that all of my renewed interest in my looks was because of a man.

But even with all of my interest, even with all of my willingness to make some changes, he still never phoned, never came by, never so much as hinted at wanting to get in touch with me. And I was supposed to get all hyped up over the un-expected appearance of a man like that? *Like no way*, as Pam would have said.

Unfortunately for me, however, my proud stance was short-lived. For the one Sunday that Gillette decided to pay a visit also happened to be the one Sunday that I found myself suf-fering through the most embarrassing moment of my piano-playing days.

It started just before the pastor was due to preach. I was still seated at the piano, playing the opening chords to my rendition of Smokie Norful's "Just Can't Stop," a song the choir had known would be our praise number. Mark, our gui-tarist, and Hardy, our drummer, both were digging the beat and getting all into it too. Even the congregation, including Pastor Burke, who sat in the pulpit patting his feet, and Alan Simms, who stood up clapping his hands, seemed pleased by the selection. But before a word could come out of the choir's collective mouth, before I could raise my hand to signal that it was time for them to do their thing, Sister Finch and the rest of the seniors decided to do theirs.

I heard a deep, dragging sound that caused me to look up from the piano keys. *I hadn't signaled for the singing to begin*, was my first thought. After all of those rehearsals we'd had, all of those corrections and modifications, we were supposed to have this number together. What was up with this? Then I wondered if it was me, that I had failed miserably in training the choir. Because the sisters sounded like gurgling frogs, they were so off-key.

But then I realized what was really going on. To my amaze-ment, and to the amazement of everybody in the church, Sister Finch, along with the other seniors, had begun sing-ing a stirring rendition of "I've Been Buked and I've Been Scorned," an old, old, old-time Negro spiritual.

I nearly died where I sat. Pastor Burke stopped patting his

feet, and Alan Simms and the rest of the congregation members that had risen stopped clapping their hands, not because they wanted to, but because they had to. The beat was too complicated. They didn't get it. My drummer didn't either, staring at me as he tried to keep the "Just Can't Stop" up-tempo beat going while at the same time being drowned out by the much slower rhythm of the seniors.

Then, to make matters worse, the younger members of the choir, led by Pam, of course, decided to go on and start singing "Just Can't Stop," anyway, publicly "buking" Finch and her senior posse.

I had a royal mess on my hands. I was so embarrassed, not to mention so angry, that I didn't, at first, know what to do. But as Finch undoubtedly had already figured out, I really had no choice. The seniors outnumbered the youth in the choir three to one at least, and their deep, hymn-trained voices drowned out the young voices easily. I stopped playing "Just Can't Stop" and began playing "I've Been Buked and I've Been Scorned," too, feeling just like the song I was playing, staring at that Bernadette Finch the entire time that I played it.

After service, when all I wanted to do was get away from that church as fast as I could get going, I still managed to look around for Gillette, to see if he was laughing at me or, even worse, pitying me. But he was nowhere to be seen. Apparently he had already tipped out, deciding that I wasn't even worth hanging around to say hey to. Not some woman who couldn't get her own choir to treat her with respect.

And then, to make matters almost unbearable, Alan Simms detained me at the door. Sister Finch seemed primed for a confrontation, as she made sure she left just in front of me, but I wasn't having it. I ignored the sister, big time, and Alan seemed to do the same when she approached him at the door. He shook her hand, didn't even wish her a good evening, and then moved her along.

I must admit that pleased me. That was exactly what she

deserved. She knew the deal. She knew that no song was to be sung on Sunday mornings unless I personally authorized it. But she hadn't even consulted me. That was what she thought about me and my authority. That was what those folks at Queen Anne's thought about me and my authority. That was what Gillette thought about me. And that, I guess, was why it hurt so much. I was tired of being ignored.

When I came up to Alan, ready to extend my hand and keep going, too, he held onto my hand. "You've been buked," he said with one of his broad smiles.

"And scorned," I said, smiling too, although I really wasn't feeling it. "Talked about sure as you're born."

He shook his head. "I'll call another meeting. I just couldn't deal with Sister Finch today."

"You? I would have knocked her down if she'd even tried to get in my face."

He started smiling again.

"I'm not joking. She knew she was wrong."

"I know. And she knows it too. But let's not dwell on her. Life is too short."

"I know that's right."

"Have lunch with me."

My heart dropped. Why would he put me on the spot like this again when he knew I was already in agony? "Alan, I'm really not—"

"Okay."

"After what I went through with Sister Finch—"

"Hey, you don't have to run any lines on me."

I looked at him. He seemed almost rude. "It's not a line, Alan."

"If you say so."

"Look, I'm not trying to brush you off or—"

"Gillette was here today."

"What?"

"Chief Donald Gillette was here today. I know you saw

him. Or maybe you've forgotten who he is? He's the same man who was over to your house the night of that drive-by shooting. You remember him. The player. The one all these females want. The one who was seated so close to you at your house that night, I wondered if he was going to squeeze you to death."

I just stared at him. What in the world did he think he was doing? Everybody else was disrespecting me, so he decided to pile on too? I couldn't even bring myself to say what I felt, it hurt just that much, and so I started walking away. Alan, however, grabbed me gently by the arm.

"Roni, I'm sorry," he said quickly.

I hesitated. I almost snatched away from him. But this wasn't Alan. He wasn't normally obnoxious. I looked at him.

"I was just a little . . . jealous, I guess. And I know I have nothing to be jealous of, because we're just friends. You've made that perfectly clear. But I also don't want to see you hurt."

"Nothing to worry about there, Alan."

"Gillette has this reputation."

I didn't respond to that. When Alan realized I wasn't going to go there, he smiled. "Good," he said, and then extended his hand. "Friends again?"

I reluctantly smiled and shook it, shaking my head as I did. How could anybody remain angry with Alan Simms?

Later that same day I was at home in my backyard, sitting on the small swing bench I had near my rock garden. It was a mild day in Florida, almost seventy degrees, and I wanted to enjoy the temperature change with outdoor activity. It was during this enjoyment, while I was on break from pruning my hedges, that I heard footsteps on the side of my house.

It was rare that anybody came around to the back of my house. Only Pam did it to any regular degree, so I immediately became suspicious. I even sat my glass of tea down on the small table beside the bench, and was about to grab my hedge clippers, when Gillette's booming voice yelled out, "Anybody home?" and I just as quickly relaxed again.

He was the last person I expected to pay me a visit today, but I was so jumpy these days, so filled with unanswered questions in my life, that anybody familiar would have been tolerable. Even Gillette, who'd walked into my backyard as if he belonged there.

He was still dressed in his finely tailored clothes. Only, he didn't have on his suit coat nor his tie, and his shirt sleeves were rolled up, giving him the look of a man who'd been involved in something substantially more challenging than just hanging out after church.

When he saw me, hanging out in my backyard, his walk seemed to become slower, as if he saw something he didn't expect to see. I looked wonderful in church, I thought, in my nice dress suit, but now I was wearing a pair of gray shorts and an oversized white jersey, hardly anything worth slowing up over.

"You look startled, Gillette," I said as he walked toward me and my swing bench. "Is it me, or is it my amazingly beautiful backyard?"

He half-smiled. "Did anybody ever tell you that you've got a smart mouth?"

"You mean, other than you?"

This time he really smiled. "Exactly."

"Not really, no. Maybe my mouth isn't smart around anybody else."

"Just me, huh?"

"Just you."

His smile was more like a snort this time as he stood in front of me. His eyes seemed trained on me, as if he was trying to figure something out. He even placed his hands in his pant pockets and began jangling around his loose change, his gaze on me.

"Again, is it me, or is it the enchanting ambiance of my backyard?"

Gillette looked around at my backyard, at my rock garden, the hedges that surrounded it, the small waterfall in the middle of it. It wasn't my yard that had him so transfixed, I could tell, because I didn't see a flicker of anything in his eyes as they scanned it. Only when he looked back at me did something register there.

"No glasses."

"Oh," I said, touching my bare face. "Yes."

"Contacts?"

"No. I mean, no."

He continued staring at my eyes. "You play the piano very well."

"Please don't even mention that fiasco of a church service."

"What was that about?"

"You mean you noticed something was amiss?"

He smiled. "You can say that."

"It was awful, wasn't it? My choir thinks that sometimes we're Burger King, that they should be able to just have it their way."

Gillette grinned.

"They drive me crazy, I'm telling you."

"Well, your sanity aside, you handled it masterfully."

"Yeah, right," I said, unable to suppress a smile of my own.

But Gillette continued staring at me, looking me up and down, still jangling around his loose change, as if something heavy was on his mind. Maybe it was the case. Maybe he knew something about Neka's murder, or those two attempts on my life. Maybe he'd found out something bad and was reluctant to tell me.

"I've been meaning to call you," he said, still staring, as if my reaction was key.

"You've been meaning to call me?"

"Yes."

"But you didn't."

He hesitated. "No, I didn't."

"Then you didn't mean very hard, did you?"

He smiled as if my response surprised him, and then he leaned down toward me, placing his hands on the back of the bench on either side of me. I could smell his familiar sweet scent, and feel his big body pressing against my knees. He was so close, I could hear his heart beat, see the gleam in his magnificent drooped eyes. He made me feel so wired, so not myself, that it disturbed me mightily. But he looked as cool as a block of ice.

"Did anybody ever tell you that you've got a smart mouth?" he asked me, staring at that mouth.

My heart rammed against my chest. "I'm not sure," I said nervously.

"Not sure?" he said in a soft, soothing voice.

"No."

"Why aren't you sure, Veronica?"

The way he said my name. The way he looked at me. It was tortuous. "I don't know," I managed to say, screwing up my face. "I'm just not sure."

"Maybe I need to make you sure."

I nearly gulped. "Maybe you do."

He wasn't trying to smile this time, but was looking at me so intensely, I thought I was going to faint. And then he slowly leaned closer and rubbed his lips across mine, looked at me again, and kissed me. Then he pulled me up by my arms and began kissing me in that passionate way of his that made me immediately respond, as if all of his prior neglect meant nothing more to me than that old adage: *that was then, this is now.*

And I was in the now, returning his kisses and enjoying every moment of it. And when he pulled me into his arms and whispered in my ear, "I've missed you," my heart pounded against my chest. Tears almost welled up in my eyes. It was that beautiful. But I wasn't so far gone, so much in the now, that I couldn't realize what he was saying.

"You've missed me?"

"Yes," he said into my hair, pulling me closer against him.

"But not enough to phone me."

He continued to hold me, but his grip was loosening. I waited for his response; I waited for him to come up with some lame excuse. Because if he'd laid some line on me about how he was so busy and couldn't get around to one measly phone call, then whatever this was that was trying to develop between us would have been over. I would have personally seen to that. But to his credit, and to my relief, he didn't respond at all. Just held me. And then he let me go.

We stood momentarily awkward, as neither one of us seemed pleased by the fact that our relationship, such as it was, was probably going nowhere fast, but I recovered enough to offer him a seat.

"Any news on the case?" I asked as we both sat down on my swing bench.

It was small, just barely enough room for two people, and given Gillette's muscular build, he took up his half and a little bit of mine too, making for a tight fit.

I actually didn't mind, finding his closeness welcoming, and he apparently didn't mine either, as he took one of his arms and placed it over the back of the bench, effectively hugging me without touching me.

"We thought we had a few hits on that Pontiac, but nothing panned out."

"Nothing?"

"*Nada.* Without a license plate, it's going to be nearly impossible anyway. If it had been a new car, maybe we could have done some backtracking with the dealers around town.

But one as old as the one that attempted to take you out, that's another story. The owner could have purchased it from anywhere, or anyone."

"What about Neka's murder? Any progress there?"

Gillette hesitated. "Some."

I turned quickly to see his face. "What did you find out?"

"We found out that Jeffrey Collins was probably killed for reasons that had nothing to do with Taneka Dupayne."

I frowned. "Are you sure?"

"We're sure."

"But how can it not be related? He was mentioned in her diary, Gillette, before she turned up dead."

Gillette sighed as if I was too slow for him. "Let me back up," he said. "Jeffrey Collins and Willie Barnes were brothers. Did you know that?"

"Brothers? But they have different—I mean, no, I didn't know it. How did you find that out?"

"Good police work. What else? We also found out that it was Jeffrey Collins who killed Miss Dupayne."

I hesitated. The idea that they now knew the name of Taneka's murderer was unnerving. It made it all real again. "He killed her?" I asked, my voice shaky.

Gillette placed an arm around my shoulder. "It's all right, Veronica."

"He killed her?"

"Yes, we believe so."

Now I was confused. "But I thought you said his death wasn't related to Neka."

"It isn't related. He killed Dupayne because of his brother. He was killed because of his lifestyle."

"What lifestyle? Drugs?"

"You got it. He was a sometimes dealer for this dude they call Pac-man Joe. Word on the street is, Collins owed Pac big bucks and Pac decided to collect."

"But I still see a connection. Weren't drugs the reason why Jeffrey killed Taneka?"

"Collins killed Dupayne because he believed she was responsible for his brother's death."

"He believed Neka was responsible for killing Willie Barnes?"

"Right. Remember when you surmised that Taneka Dupayne was probably Willie Barnes' girlfriend? Well, you surmised correctly. We believe that Barnes attempted to rob Mason Lerner to supply Dupayne's drug habit. Collins probably knew it too and decided that his brother would still be alive today, if it wasn't for Dupayne."

"But Willie died months ago. Why would Jeffrey wait so long to kill Neka? And why didn't he go after Delvecchio? He was the one who actually shot and killed his brother."

"Delvecchio was justified, Jeffrey probably believed. Willie was, after all, committing a crime. But Taneka was the reason why he was committing that crime. She was the problem, at least in Jeffrey's eyes. And why did he wait so long? Who knows. Maybe revenge tastes sweeter the longer you think about it."

"So he killed Neka because his crazy brother was in love with her?"

"And because his crazy brother lost his life because of her, yes, that's what we believe."

"That doesn't sound like much of a motive, Gillette."

"Oh, it's a powerful motive. Don't you believe it's not. Men and women have done far worse in the name of love. Willie tried to steal in the name of love. Jeffrey killed in the name of love. Love will make a fool out of you if you let it."

At first I wondered if he meant me, that I was making such a show of myself right here and now, but it sounded too harsh to be about somebody else. He was making a personal statement borne out of personal experience. Gillette had been deeply in love with his now deceased wife and got burned, which could've been the root of his angst.

"We also believe," he went on, "that Jeffrey was responsible for that drive-by at your place."

"But why would he want to harm me?"

"Somehow he must have found out that you had Dupayne's diary."

"Her diary?"

"Yes. His name was mentioned prominently in it. Somebody could have told him that it existed, and that you had it."

"But who would tell him something like that? Nobody knew I had it but you and me. And Delvecchio, if you told him." I looked at Gillette, making it clear the confidence I had in Vince Delvecchio's credibility. "Besides, what about Friday evening at Hard Times when somebody tried to run me over? Jeffrey Collins was dead by then."

Gillette sighed. "And you're certain it wasn't just an out-of-control driver?"

"It could have been that. But it didn't feel like that."

"Didn't sound like it either." He pulled me closer to him. "That's an unanswered question, Veronica. It happens in investigations. Rarely do all the pieces fit. Let's just hope it was an accident."

"Yeah, because if it wasn't, that'll shoot your theory of Jeffrey doing that drive-by straight out of the water, wouldn't it?"

"I wouldn't go that far."

"But it has to. Unless there's some serious conspiracy stuff going on here, and more than one dude's gunning for me."

Gillette seemed alarmed by that, looking at me as if I'd just lost my mind, and then he looked away. "You'll be okay."

"Didn't say I wouldn't be."

"Even if I have to look out for you myself."

I smiled. "No need for that, Gillette."

"Let me worry about the need." He said this and then exhaled. "How long have you been a member of Zion Hope?"

"Not long. Less than a year. Why did you come?"

"I told you I missed you."

"And the answer wasn't you picking up a telephone and giving me a call, or just dropping by the house? Instead you get dressed, come to church, see me experience one of life's most embarrassing moments, and then leave? Without even saying hello?"

He looked at me and smiled. "Hello," he said.

I couldn't help but smile too.

"So you've been at Zion Hope for about a year?"

"About that, yeah. I mean, eight months, if you want to be precise about it."

"What do you know about a young man there named Lester Cooper?"

"Brother Cooper? I mean, I know him, but not personally. He came to my house the night of that drive-by."

"I know."

"He and Neka were tight though."

"What do you know about that relationship?"

"Not a whole lot. He blew me off when I tried to talk to him. He said he dated Neka a long time ago and didn't know a thing about her now."

"You believed him?" Gillette looked at me.

"I don't know. He gives me the willies, but I think it's just because of the way he didn't seem to care that Neka was dead. But as far as whether he was telling the truth about their relationship now, I didn't form an opinion one way or the other. Sometimes I can tell."

"You can tell what?"

"If your heart is right," I said.

Gillette, for some odd reason, literally gulped.

"But I don't trust my judgment lately. He seemed like an ambitious young man to me who didn't want Neka's death or anything else to taint his chances of becoming a deacon. That's my impression of him, which isn't saying much, I know."

"How can you tell?"

I frowned. "How can I tell what?"

"If a person's heart is right."

"I said *sometimes* I can tell. I don't know. It's just this feeling I get in the pit of my stomach, and it can go either way too. It tells me either yes, this dude's okay, or no, this dude is to be avoided at all costs. I used to live on the streets. You just get that sense."

"What did your stomach tell you about Lester Cooper?"

I shrugged. "Nothing."

"Nothing?"

"Not a thing."

"What did it tell you about me?" For some reason Gillette looked more terrified than amused.

I looked away from him. "All sorts of things," I said truthfully, and then gulped myself.

Moments of silence passed between us, as Gillette began rocking us slowly until, as if by happenstance, the awareness of how intimately he was holding me began to surface.

I looked up at him, and he looked down at me, and our eyes met once again. Only, this time it was me who ran my hand across his silky smooth face, and across his luscious lips, and into his incredibly soft, wavy, salt-and-pepper hair. Sexiness oozed from him, and he had to know it, and it made me wonder why was he bothering with me.

Pamela was right; he could have any woman he wanted. But why would he want me, especially with the baggage that I came with?

And what about his relationship with God? There was just so much I didn't know about him. Even Alan had warned me about getting hurt, as if fooling with a man like Donald Gillette almost guaranteed it.

It was too much, especially right now, and I wanted to say so. I wanted him to understand what I was going through.

But I waited too long. He started kissing me again. And I caved. Just like that. He had me at his mercy again.

He was going to give me nothing but heartache and grief. Somehow, deep down, I knew it to be true. But I still couldn't resist him. I still couldn't push him away from me and ask him to leave my life now, get away and stay away, before it was way too late.

NINE

He didn't leave, because I never asked him to, but he did eventually stop kissing on me and leaned his head back, as if fighting the feeling too.

I laid my head on his chest and allowed him to hold me tighter. The game had changed, it was clear, but I still wasn't sure of the rules.

"What is this about, Gillette?" I asked him, my hand flat on his barrel chest. We were still in my backyard, on my swing, trying our best to ease the emotions.

Gillette looked down at me. "What is what about?"

"Us. You and me. This. What is this about?"

"It's about a man and a woman enjoying each other's company."

"Why my company?"

"Why not your company?"

"You know what I mean, Gillette. The pickings are plentiful." I looked up at him. "But you're here."

We stared into each other's eyes.

"I make no promises, Veronica, no commitments, so don't expect any. Understand?"

I wasn't sure if I understood or not, so I let it slide, and leaned my head back against his chest. "What about God?" I asked him.

"What about Him?"

I looked at him. "Have you accepted Christ as your personal Savior?"

He exhaled. "I used to go to church—"

"That's not what I asked you."

"I used to go to church religiously every Sunday. Loved going. Felt my relationship with the Lord was just fine, thank you. But when my wife developed some problems, I prayed for her deliverance. I prayed fervently. Every day and every night I prayed. But she wasn't delivered. She died in her sin. And I never stepped foot into a church again."

"Until today."

He nodded. "Until today."

"Why did you let your wife's death affect your relationship with the Lord?"

Gillette frowned. "Why do you think? I told you she died. She wasn't delivered. And I wanted to know why He would allow her to die. He hasn't answered that question."

His bitterness was so deep, so searing, I silently prayed and asked the Lord to give me the words to say. "Maybe because you haven't answered His question."

Gillette looked at me as if I was nuts. "What question?"

"You want to know why did He allow your wife to die. Maybe He wants to know why did you allow yourself to love your wife more than you loved Him?"

Gillette looked away from me, as if startled by the question.

"And it's obvious that you did, Gillette. Or you wouldn't have allowed it to affect your relationship with Him. Everything the Bible teaches me is that God is a jealous God, a self-proclaimed jealous God, and that it's not only for His sake, but for our sake too. We must worship Him and Him alone. He won't share His throne. Not even with your wife."

He didn't respond. For the longest time, he didn't do anything. There was so much more I wanted to say about the Lord, but the spirit within me advised against it. Leave him to his thoughts, was the guidance I inwardly received. And I obeyed.

After an interminably long time, where no words were spoken between us, Gillette slowly began rocking the swing again. His hint, I suspected, that he had been left to his thoughts but now was ready to move on.

"You okay?" I asked him.

"So you don't hold Lester Cooper in any high regards?"

"Like I said, I don't really know him. Not like that, anyway. But do you seriously think that Brother Cooper may have had something to do with Neka's death?"

"I'm making sure all possibilities are fully investigated."

"So does that mean you're on the case now? I thought this was Delvecchio's baby."

"It was."

"Until?"

"Until they dragged you into it."

Inwardly I smiled. "Whoever *they* are."

"True."

"And you believe they dragged me into it because they found out I had Neka's diary?"

"It's possible. Your troubles didn't start until after you took that diary from her apartment."

"I didn't steal it."

"Kind of, sort of, right?"

I smiled. "Right."

"Are you sure, Veronica, that you didn't tell anybody else that you had possession of that diary? Not even one of your girlfriends?"

Ordinarily I would not have said a word. But Juno was the rent collector Pooh was so careful to protect, as if he was warning me to back off. "There was this one incident."

"Okay."

"Where Juno walked in on me."

Gillette sounded stunned. "Juno Curtis?"

"Yeah, but it was no big deal."

"He walked in on you where?"

"He came into Neka's apartment just as I was slipping the diary into my pocket, that's all. I doubt if he even saw it."

"But he could have?"

"He could have, sure. But you don't know Juno."

"I know, I know. He's an honorable thug."

That offended me. "I never said that."

"Did he ever mention the diary to you?"

"Gillette, I never said Juno was honorable. What I was trying to say was that he had a street code of honor, which is different."

"Okay. Now answer my question. Did Curtis ever talk to you about that diary?"

"No."

"Are you sure, Veronica?"

"Yes, I'm sure."

"Then why did you mention it to me?"

"Because you asked if anybody could have known about the diary."

"Yeah, but if you would have been as sure as you used to be that Curtis wasn't involved in this mess, then you wouldn't have told me anything about what he might have seen."

"But that was before."

"Before what?"

I didn't respond.

"Before what, Veronica?"

He sounded so anxious, it was beginning to scare me. The thought of Juno doing anything that would jeopardize me was hard to believe. Unless, of course, not jeopardizing me would jeopardize him.

"Before I found out that Juno was Neka's landlord."

Gillette looked at me hard. "Juno Curtis was Taneka Dupayne's landlord?"

"I thought Pooh was, but he's not."

Gillette frowned. "Pooh?"

"The dude who manages the building. I thought he collected the rents too."

"But he doesn't?"

"He said some other dude did. When I pressed, just trying to understand how a crack addict like Neka could afford to pay rent every month for any apartment, he got all defensive, like he was hiding something."

"And you think he was protecting Juno? That Juno is the rent collector?"

"I know he's the rent collector. Neka's parents told me so. They paid her rent, and they paid it directly to Juno."

Gillette exhaled. "You should have told me about this sooner, Veronica."

"And when did I have a chance? I haven't heard from you all week," I said, as if he had some obligation to stay in touch with me.

I glanced at him after I said it, and he glanced at me too, which didn't help, and then we both looked away.

"I had my men keeping an eye on you."

"Not exactly the same thing."

"It's standard procedure."

I smiled. I walked right into that one. "Oh, I see. Standard procedure. Got you." I swiftly slid away from him, which amounted to an inch or two, given the close quarters.

"I didn't mean it that way."

"Ain't no problem. I understand where you're coming from. You don't have to spell a thing out to me. I'm sharper than you think."

We fell into silence, which was fine by me, since I had nothing else to say to the brother anyway. And I wasn't even mad at him. I was mad at myself. Alan was too good, too honest, too pure for me. I had to want me some hardened, jaded, insensitive louse like Gillette. And I deserved him too.

He placed his hand on my arm, encircling it. "I didn't mean it that way."

"Whatever, Gillette."

"It's not whatever. I want you to understand that."

"I told you I understand it. I'm no idiot."

"Fine." He removed his grip from my arm and stood to his feet. "I've got to be somewhere, anyway, so I'd better get going."

Be somewhere, I thought. *On a Sunday evening?* If it wasn't a church house he had to get to, then it more than likely was some female's house. "Yeah," I said, standing too, "I'd better get a move on myself, or I'll be late for Sunday night service."

"Sunday night service?"

"At church. I have to play."

"With that same choir?"

I nodded. "We usually try to rehearse thirty or forty minutes before service, so I'd better hop in the shower and get on over there."

Gillette placed one hand in his pant pocket and began jiggling his loose change, staring at me or, more specifically, my chest. "A shower?"

"Like, yeah. I've been in this yard for quite a while."

"Want some company?" His smile made it clear that if he was kidding, he was only half-kidding.

"I thought you had to be somewhere," I said, teasing back.

He nodded. "Good point." He began jiggling that loose change of his again and staring at me. "Maybe another time."

It was a blatant invitation, but one I chose to ignore, especially after the way he all but relegated me to standard procedures, to just another person on his cop caseload.

"Well," he said, as if he was experienced enough to know when not to overplay his hand, "I certainly don't want to stand in the way of a woman and her music."

I smiled as we began walking toward the side of the house that led to my front yard. "I wish my choir felt the same way."

"Crack the whip. They'll come around."

"Yeah, right. I can just see myself trying to lord it over somebody like Bernadette Finch."

"Who's she?"

"Former choir director."

"And you replaced her? Now I get it."

When we got around to the front of the house, I realized that Gillette wasn't driving that big Ford truck he had driven over previously, but a sleek Porsche, one of those dark gold 911 Carrera models that seemed to scream pure power. I was taken aback, not just because of the kind of car it was, but because it seemed so like the kind of car a player would drive. And Gillette was a player. At least everybody was saying so, although earlier, when he looked into my eyes, when he kissed me and held me, he just didn't seem like that kind of brother.

It was wishful thinking on my part, I knew, but I also couldn't help from thinking, if it was true, if he did have this stable of women Pam and everybody else seemed to insist he had, it would be such a shame.

"You're driving the good car today."

Gillette smiled. "Maybe I'll give you a ride one of these days," he said as he opened the driver side door.

"It's fast, I'll bet." I glanced inside at the fine leather seats and all of the computerized gadgets.

"It's fast enough. But, of course, I try my best to adhere to all speed laws."

I laughed. "I bet you do."

Gillette was about to retort with a cute little line of his own, no doubt, but another sports car stopped in front of my house. This one, a Corvette, was banana yellow and with a motor so loud, it sounded as if it had been revved up even more than the original.

Gillette and I both looked as a man in his early thirties, decked down in FUBU and bling, stepped out of the car with a big, gold-teeth grin on his face. My heart nearly stopped when I realized it was Richard Pargeter, my ex-boyfriend from New-ark. He was still buff, still handsome, still with all of that jew-elry around his neck. And still slimy enough to make my skin crawl at just the sight of him.

"There's my baby!" he said boisterously as he walked to-ward us, his arms open wide. "How you doing, girl?"

I still couldn't believe my eyes. I even stretched them to make sure I was seeing what I saw. And it was true. Richard Pargeter was standing in my front yard skinning and grinning as if this shock he'd just laid on me was the highlight of his day.

"You know him?" Gillette asked me in that low, cop voice of his.

"Yeah," I said between clenched teeth. "Unfortunately."

Richard, sensing who was in charge of this scene, immedi-ately hurried toward Gillette, extending his hand as he came. "'S up?" he said in that friendly tone he knew how to turn on and off. "I'm Richard P. How you be?"

Gillette reluctantly shook his hand, his eyes never leav-ing Richard's. "Don Gillette."

"Don Gillette. Now that name sounds familiar. You doing all right? Just chilling with my girl, I see."

"I'm not your girl, Richard, so knock it off."

Richard smiled his big, gold-teeth smile again. "She likes to play me, man. Likes to act like she done forgot ol' Richard. But Richard remembers her. Remembers every inch of her."

I was about to move forward and tell Richard something real good, but Gillette's strong hand pulled me back.

"You're not from around here?"

Richard burst into a high-pitched laugh. "You're jivin', right? But, on the real, man, n'all, this ain't my scene. Ain't really Roni's either, if truth your game. Neither one of us are what you can call small-town folks. Ain't that right, sweetheart?"

Gillette looked at me.

"He's my ex-boyfriend," I said to him, my tone lowered. "And I'm not his sweetheart."

Gillette nodded. "Why don't you go inside."

"No. I mean, I need to talk to him, to set some things straight with him first."

Gillette looked at me as if he didn't like that plan at all. But he didn't have a vote. His scaring off Richard would mean nothing to Richard. He'd just take it as one man muscling out another man. I needed to talk to Richard. I needed to have a *come to Jesus* meeting with the brother, without Gillette running any interference, so he could understand once and for all that I was not the one, that I wasn't about to start playing any sick game with him.

"Bad ride," Richard said to Gillette, checking out his Porsche. "Must have set you back some cool green there."

Gillette was looking at that phony, smiling Richard with a disgust that warmed my heart. He saw right through that act of his. But when Gillette looked at me, and his look didn't change all that much from the one he had given Richard, my heart dropped. It was guilt by association once again, and so far my associates weren't making me look too good at all.

"Do you want me to stick around?"

I quickly shook my head. "I'm straight. Like I said, I need to talk to him. Alone."

Gillette looked at me without a whole lot of affection, which hurt. But at least he was getting in his car and leaving. That was crucial at this point. Because what I had to say to Richard would be unattractive, and it would be definitive. This had to be the last time he even thought about bothering me.

I wanted to tell Gillette that I'd call him, to reassure him that nothing was up with Richard and me, but from the look on his face, I let it slide. I had already told him that Richard was my ex. My word had to be enough. If a tenuous-at-best relationship fell apart because of his suspicions of some snake like Richard Pargeter, then anything would be enough to tip us over.

Which brings me back to the problem at hand. Richard. I had to set this brother straight.

Gillette backed his Porsche out of my driveway and drove away, shifting gears with such a jerk, it seemed he couldn't wait to get away from me.

I got in Richard's face with an anger I hadn't felt in years. I yelled, I pointed, I made the kind of scene neighbors could call 9-1-1 about. But I didn't care. His inopportune arrival felt just like when he got me fired from my job in Jersey.

"How dare you come to my home!" I yelled at him. "I don't want you! I don't want to have anything to do with your trifling butt! How could you do this to me again?"

Of course, brotherman wasn't even worried. He, in fact, was smiling, his hands up. "Take a chill, girl, aw'ight?"

I folded my arms and started shaking my leg. He was right, I did need to chill, but I was too furious to even try. All I felt for Richard Pargeter was anger, and I couldn't help but show it.

"What do you want, Richard?"

"Moving on up, I see. Ridin' around town with Mr. Porsche. Mr. Big Man. Who is he, anyway?"

"None of your darn business, that's who!"

Richard smiled. "Dang, girl! You cussin'? I thought you was religious now."

"You know what," I said, unfolding my arm and pointing at the street, and ready to show the street in me, "get out of my yard! Get your raggedy-behind showoff car and get away from me fast!"

A voice from across the street. "What's up, Roni?"

It was Juno walking over, with his boys behind him. Normally, his presence at a time like this would have been comforting for me. Now it was just another headache.

"I'm okay."

"Sure about that?" he asked, looking at Richard.

Richard extended his hand. "Richard P. How you be?" he said with a grand slapped-on smile. "I don't think we've met."

"Forget you, Richard," I said, refusing to let him put on that show of his for my neighbors. "Just leave."

"I thought you wanted to know how I found you."

"How?"

He shook his head. "It was too easy, girl. It was as easy as finding a hooker on a street corner. No offense, of course."

"Check him out," Juno said to his boys.

I immediately tried to minimize Richard's putdown, knowing that folks like Juno and Richard had no problem whatsoever escalating drama to dangerous heights. But not in my name, they weren't.

"It's okay, Juno, for real. He's not even worth it."

"I don't know, Roni. I think he is. I think the brother needs a serious attitude adjustment."

"And I think you need to mind your own business," Richard said.

I quickly moved in between them, and not a moment too soon either, because Juno was ready to make a move on Richard.

"I got this, Juno, all right. Just let me handle it."

Juno looked at Richard, looking him up and down. "You got a poor choice in men, Roni. First that old-ass Gillette, and now this loser. Need to check yourself, girl."

"Whatever, Juno."

Juno gave me one of his scowling Ice Cube looks, but then he and his boys started walking back across the street.

Richard smiled. "You always did like the thugs."

"Takes one to know one."

"For real, though."

"Good-bye, Richard."

"Good-bye nothin'. I need to talk to you. I wouldn't have come to your precious house, but you wouldn't answer my phone calls."

"What do you want?"

"Can we at least go inside?"

"Are you out of your mind? I wouldn't dare let you inside my house. You'd better be glad I'm even bothering with you out here. Now what is it?"

Richard exhaled. "I want—No, I need us to get back together."

"And I want—No, I need a million dollars. But that ain't happenin' either."

"This on the real, Roni. I need you."

"Tough."

"I said I need you."

"And I said tough. I needed you once. I was just a kid who had nobody when I met you, and you knew I had nobody. I needed you then, but all you was trying to do was figure out new and imaginative ways to use me."

"That was then, Roni. Dang! What you bringin' that up for? I wasn't but twenty-three myself."

"There's a big difference between being a twenty-three-year-old and being sixteen, so don't even go there."

"Okay, I blew it, all right. I'm sorry that I blew it. But I still need us to get back together, Roni."

"And again I say tough." I began walking away from him. "Have a nice life, Richard. Hope never to see you again."

He reached out and grabbed me by the arm, completely stopping me in my tracks, and his fake smile was gone. "You always been a cold female. That's why I could never feel the way I should have felt for you. Always hard. Always wanted a hundred and ten percent out of a brother, no matter what. Then you go to your fancy Juilliard school and figure you was going to just leave poor old stupid Richard in the dust, didn't you? But remember what I did before, Roni. You don't play with me, girl. When you least expect me, that's when I strike. Remember Jersey? Remember that stupid school you called yourself teaching at? Don't forget what happened there, because the same thing can happen here." He stood erect and smiled. "And Taneka."

I stared at him. How would he even know her name? "What about Taneka?"

"Just don't forget what happened to her either."

"How did you know about what happened to Taneka?"

"I know everything about your life, and always will. There's no getting away from me, that's all I'm saying. Unless you wanna end up like your friend."

I frowned. "Are you threatening me?"

He removed his hand from me and threw both hands in the air. And he smiled again. "Hey, I don't threaten. I'm just telling it like it is."

"Did you have something to do with that girl's death, Richard?"

He laughed.

"What about that drive-by shooting at my place, and that car outside of Hard Times?"

His smile left. "What drive-by shooting? Somebody tried to hurt you?" He looked deadly serious now, which surprised me.

"You know what I'm talking about, Richard."

"Wait a minute," he said as if upset. "Are you saying somebody did a drive-by on *you*?"

"What about Taneka?"

Now he looked confused. "What about her?"

"Are you involved in her murder?"

He laughed again. "You would love that, wouldn't you? Pin a murder rap on me. See me rot in prison. That'll be right up your alley. You can forget that."

"You still haven't answered my question."

"You still haven't answered mine. Not to my satisfaction, anyway. And that's the only answer I'll take, one I'm satisfied with. So you go on with your bad self, see your ol' sporty boyfriend, keep playing your church piano, and forget about old Richard. But I'm like bad days, girl. I ain't going nowhere. And you'll come around too. I guarantee it." He laughed, looking as if he was just daring me to doubt him. Then he got into his Corvette, backed out, and burned rubber, speeding away.

TEN

Pam said, "He's here?" so loud, I had to shush her.

We were back at church for Sunday night service, and the choir members were slowly trickling in. I was seated at the piano, and Pamela was leaning against it.

"What you mean, he's here?" she asked again, this time in a lowered voice. "He's in Melville?"

"He pulled up in his yellow Corvette."

"Corvette? The brother drives a 'Vette?"

"Snakes have taste too, Pammie, but that doesn't take away from what they are."

"I'd bet he's good-looking too, isn't he?"

"He's a dog, Pam. What difference does it make?"

"Big difference between a snake and a dog. Now which is it?"

"Pam!"

"Okay. *Dern*. I'm just playing. But a good-looking man is hard to find 'round here in Melville, girl."

"He wants us to get back together."

"Duh, Roni. Why else would the brother come all this way from New Jersey? Of course he wants you back. Question is—"

"Don't even go there."

"It was that bad, huh?"

I nodded. Even Pam didn't know the extent of my past, or the pain, and I wasn't about to school her either.

"It's kind of weird though, isn't it?" she went on, seeming to understand my limits. "Him suddenly all interested in you."

"I know."

"It's like, why now? Everything seems to be happening to you now, like some critical mass coming together. Maybe God is trying to get your attention, girl."

"He has my attention. It's Richard I'm worried about."

"You're worried about your ex?"

"Not like that. It's what he said."

"About what?"

"About Taneka."

"Taneka?"

"Hello, ladies," a male's voice said.

We both looked over and saw Alan heading our way.

"Hello, Dr. Simms," Pam said with a mischievous smile.

Alan, however, seemed to have eyes only for me. "I didn't expect to see you here tonight, Sister Jarrett."

"Why wouldn't you expect me tonight? I've never missed a Sunday night service yet."

"He means after that craziness in morning service, when Sister Finch decided to highjack the choir and do it her way."

"Oh, that," I said, although I doubted if it was that at all. "Sister Finch doesn't worry me."

"I did have a talk with her, however."

Pam nodded. "Good."

"But that's not what I was referencing. I was talking about your date with Chief Gillette."

"Her date?" Pam quickly looked at me. "What date, girl?"

"I didn't have any date with Chief Gillette."

"No?" Alan said. "I'm sorry. I thought that was why you turned me down. But who am I, right?"

"You're a wonderful person, Dr. Simms. That's who you are," Pam said patronizingly. "And I think Roni's just a fool not to want you."

Even Alan was shocked by that pronouncement. I know I was. I looked at Pam as if I could have strangled her. But Alan, as usual, was very gracious about it.

"I am rather transparent, aren't I, Sister Tate?"

Pam quickly shook her head. "No."

"It's all right. You're an honest person, and always have been. You stay that way."

Pam smiled. "Thanks."

Alan smiled too and then looked at me. "I need to go in prayer before service time. You ladies have a good evening."

"We will, Alan. Thanks," I said, feeling weighed down again, as he quickly moved away.

Pam looked at me. "You and Donald Gillette?" she said in amazement.

"Whatever, Pam, all right."

"You aren't gonna talk about it, are you?"

"There's nothing to talk about."

"So you're in his stable now? *Dern*, Roni! When did this happen? And why didn't I know about it? I know you liked him, but get in line. I didn't know he had eyes for you too."

"Pamela, you're grappling at straws, you know that?"

"Yeah." She sighed. "Something's undercover, but you ain't gon' tell. As usual. But at least you can tell me about Richard. What did he say?"

"He said a lot of things."

"But you said he worried you because he said something about Taneka."

I folded my arms and nodded. "Yeah, he did. He was probably just playing one of his mind games again, though."

"What did he say?"

"He said he wanted us to get back together."

"You told me that already."

"And that I'd better remember what happened to Taneka if I didn't get back with him."

Pam stared at me. "Oh, my gosh! Are you telling me that he threatened to kill you if you didn't hook up with him?"

"No. Not in so many words."

"But that was the implication?"

I hesitated on that. "He was just running his mouth."

"Roni, I don't know. This is getting kind of crazy now."

"What's crazy? Richard blabbing at the mouth is not news, okay."

"But how did he know about Neka?"

"It was in the papers, Pam."

"You know what I mean. How did he know you knew her like that?"

"We did live across the street from each other, okay. Look, I know what you're saying. I wanna know what's up with Richard too, believe that. But he's just blowing smoke like he always does."

"When did he get in town?"

"How would I know that?"

"You need to know it. Maybe he was the drive-by king at your house that night. Maybe he was the hit-and-run king at Hard Times that day."

I stood up, ready to get my choir's attention. "He wasn't."

"How can you be so sure?"

"Because I know him. Now let's get our minds off Richard Pargeter and onto the Lord. Shall we?"

Pam gave me her best "whatever" look and walked on up into the choir stands. I knew where she was coming from because she had a great point. Stuff didn't start happening until I got that first phone call from Richard. Although I still wouldn't believe for a second that he murdered somebody, something was definitely up with him. He didn't come all this way for his health, after all. And this idea that it was just to get back with me, I wasn't buying. I needed to find out, however, without having anything to do with him. The question was, How?

***

By the time I made it home and was walking through my front door, I felt something was wrong immediately. It was dark inside my home, as it should have been, but the outside lighting that usually illuminated in from my cracked blinds was not shining through. Which meant my blinds had been tightly shut, and definitely not by me. And there was a smell. Not a harsh one. In fact it was barely detectable. I prided myself on freshness, even artificially maintained freshness such as air wicks and potpourri, but I never prided myself on musk.

And that was the smell that met my nostrils when I walked into my home, a low-grade, musky, male scent. My first thought as I hurried to turn on the lamp on the table near the front door was that one of those neighborhood hoodlums had broken into my home. I never dreamed, however, when I turned on the light, that they'd still be there.

"She's home!" a male's voice shouted from my hallway as soon as the light flicked on.

I turned quickly in that direction. When I saw the side of what appeared to be a thin young man in jeans and a T-shirt running toward the back of my home, I screamed. Then another young man appeared. This one ran out of my bedroom and turned my way. It was too quick for me to ID him, but not quick enough that I couldn't see the number twenty-three written on the back of his jersey. And that was all that I could make out as he joined his partner in my office, and from the sound of it, they both jumped out of the window.

After I was able to stop screaming, I ran into the office to see if I could see anything. When I made it to the window and looked out, all I could see was an old souped-up Pontiac not unlike numerous ones in the area, but also not unlike the one that had targeted me in front of Hard Times, speeding off through the alley behind my house.

I turned and saw the chaos in my office. Papers and books were strewn everywhere as if they'd been tossed in the air, and my desk drawers were pulled out, emptied, and thrown all around my carpet. I looked at my stereo. It was intact. I looked at my keyboard. It was still there. I looked at my computer. That was fine too.

Had I come too soon? I wondered. Or was their aim totally different than your run-of-the-mill hood rat thief?

"Roni!" a male's voice yelled from my living room. "Roni!"

It was Juno. When I looked away from the mess, he and his boys were running toward me.

"You all right?" he asked me.

"They broke into my house, Juno."

"Who?"

"Two young dudes."

"Just now?"

"Yes, I saw them."

"Which way did they go?"

"They jumped a ride in the alley and took off. A souped-up Pontiac. Blue or black, I think."

"Let's go!" Juno said to his boys, and they took off.

I took off right along with them. Juno didn't realize I was even there until I was jumping into his SUV right alongside him and his boys. I was in the back, and he was up front, in the passenger seat.

He must have spied me through one of the side mirrors because he spun around as if he couldn't believe his eyes. "Ain't happening, Roni!" he yelled.

"Let's do this, Juno," I said.

"Girl, you crazy. Get up out of here!"

LoMan, the driver, asked, "What's the deal, Juno?"

"Come on, Juno, let's go," I said, ready to take care of business. "They're gonna get away!"

Juno threw his head back, shook it, but then he pointed for LoMan to get going.

And LoMan got going, flying across the street and through

the alley on the side of my house as if he wasn't driving a tank, but a tiny little sports mobile, everybody in the SUV bouncing with his speed.

Juno continued shaking his braided head and telling me how crazy I was, but I didn't even care. Those dudes broke into my home, not his, and more than anything, I wanted to know why.

Screech, the brother seated next to me in the back, pulled out his piece and started loading a round into it.

I suddenly caught some sense and got concerned. "Juno." I leaned forward toward him.

Juno had one hand on the dashboard as if he was braced. And he needed to be, given the way LoMan flew out of that alley and hung a right so sharp, we momentarily rode on two wheels. But LoMan drove as if he knew where he was going or, more specifically, where those thieves had gone.

"Juno," I said again.

"What, Roni?" he replied, an edge to his voice.

"What's the game plan?"

Screech, still checking out his gun, laughed.

Juno frowned. "What you talking about, girl?"

"What are you planning to do?"

"Catch those fools that broke into your house."

"And do what with them when you catch them?"

Juno gave a one-syllable snort and looked out of his side window. "What you think?"

"Juno, I don't want any violence."

Both LoMan and Screech laughed at that one.

"Check her out," Screech said.

"I mean it, Juno."

"Look," Juno said, "nobody told your li'l butt to ride along in the first place, now did they? In fact, some of us told you to keep your behind home. But nooo, not Roni. Not Miss Fearless. So don't even think about buggin' out on me now, girl. Don't even think it!"

We both swayed as LoMan made another sharp right onto Hargrove Boulevard.

"I'm not buggin' out, all right. I just need to talk to them, that's all, find out why they broke into my house."

"Why you think they broke in?" Screech asked. "They wanted what you got, stupid."

"But they didn't take anything, stupid," I replied. "Now how you figure that?"

"Probably didn't have time," LoMan said, "what with you screaming like somebody killin' you."

"But they'd been there long enough to ransack my entire office, and I'm talking tossing the whole room. I saw that much already. Yet they didn't touch my stereo, they didn't touch my computer, they didn't touch anything worth any value."

Juno asked, "What makes you so sure about what they didn't take?"

"I told you. I saw it. I'm observant, all right. They were after papers."

"What kind of papers?" Juno asked.

Everybody looked at me. I thought about Taneka's diary. I still wasn't certain that Juno didn't see me take it from her apartment that day.

"Like how am I supposed to know what papers those clowns were after? I don't have anything, and I mean nothing. But apparently they think I do. This wasn't some crackhead break-in delight, Juno. Those dudes were serious."

"Dang!" LoMan yelled loudly and started slamming the palm of his hand against the steering wheel.

"What?" I asked, afraid that I had said something to make him crazy. But before he even had a chance to respond to me, I heard what had him so animated. Sirens. Which meant cops were on our tail.

Juno looked back and then shook his head. Then he quickly sprung into action. "Who's packing?" he asked, pulling out his own revolver.

Everybody in the car, save yours truly, started pulling out guns and knives as if they were members of some SWAT team. I shook my head. *These fools need Jesus bad*, I thought.

"It's on you, Screech." Juno handed his and LoMan's weapons back to Screech.

Screech lifted a compartment under the rug of the SUV's floor and quickly stuffed all of the weapons down into it. Then he locked it back down, which took considerable effort. "If you still packing, tough. Ain't no opening this up again."

LoMan, meanwhile, began pulling over to the side of the road. "Everybody chill," he said. "Don't give them no reason."

"Ah, man!" Juno said as if he was in pain, as if he'd just remembered something. "I gotta lose this," he said, pulling what looked like a tiny bag of dope out of his shirt pocket.

"Ah, Juno!" LoMan said.

"I was about to make a sell when Roni screamed. Excuse me if I didn't have time to ditch the dope first."

"Open it back up, Screech!" LoMan yelled.

Screech immediately started shaking his head. "You know it's too late to pull that apart, man. Going down for a dime bag is one thing, but going down on weapons charges, man, forget that. We talking stupid years."

Juno looked out of the back window as the police car parked behind us. Then he looked at me, attempting to hand his weed to me. "Roni, please," he said.

"Are you crazy?" I said, staring at his dope.

"I'm already on probation. I got to be clean. They been looking for a reason to send me back up."

"And you just gave them one by riding around with dope in your pocket, by selling that crap in the first place, Juno."

"I wouldn't have been riding around at all if it wasn't for you, Roni, and you know this. I'm helping you out."

"I'm not going to jail for nobody, Juno."

"Get rid of it, Juno," LoMan said. "Five-O on the spot."

I looked out of the back window as the cop, some young

Clint Eastwood wannabe in his shades and boots, stepped out of his patrol car and began heading our way.

"Hide it under the mat," I said.

Juno started shaking his head. "If they find it, they'll have probable cause to keep searching under mats. That might expose our guns."

"Your arsenal, you mean."

"Do something, Juno!" LoMan demanded.

Juno threw the bag on my lap. "Please, Roni," he said as he turned around. "Please. They looking for a reason, though."

The plea in his voice stopped me cold. And I knew I was through dealing. This was exactly what I deserved for hopping into a truck with these fools anyway. But what could I do now? I didn't ask Juno to chase those thugs on my behalf, but I certainly didn't dissuade him either. I'd even joined in on the madness.

As Dirty Harry came nearer, I grabbed the bag and shoved it in my bra.

And ended up where I swore I'd never be again. Behind bars.

So much for starting over, I thought, *for rewriting your past.*

This jail cell looked eerily familiar to me, from the dingy walls, to the smells, to the hard-as-brick mattress. But that wasn't the worst of it. When I found out that the bag of weed had some crack cocaine, according to the cops anyway, I nearly gagged.

My stupid behind was caught with crack in my possession? For nearly an hour I sat there stunned, unable to move a muscle. I couldn't believe it. I couldn't believe Juno would do this to me. But even more than that, I couldn't believe I allowed myself to get into this kind of situation.

I was so hurt, so angry with myself, I didn't even have the nerve to ask the Lord to get me out of this. I felt too foolish, too guilty, too tired of being the victim of circumstances. That excuse was old even to me now.

And to top if all off, I wasn't alone in my misery, but was bunking with some female who made it her business to try and stay all up in mine. She was one of those big Queen Latifah-looking sisters and couldn't seem to keep her mouth shut. She talked, and she talked, and she walked, and she talked until, mercifully, the guard door opened and the young officer that had arrested me, the Clint Eastwood wannabe, came marching up to our cell.

"Let's go, Jarrett," he said.

I sprung to my feet. "I can go?" I asked, amazed and elated.

"Yeah, you can go." He unlocked the cell, a pair of handcuffs dangling from his hand. "To get processed in." He turned me around and cuffed me again.

"Very funny," I said.

And he walked me downstairs to Booking. Up until that time I was handling my business, trying my best to keep it together. But when I realized I was about to be officially processed in, that I was about to become their prisoner until some judge somewhere said I could go, I panicked. No way could I survive jail. Not now. Not after I worked so hard to turn my life around.

I told Dirty Harry and some big dude in Booking named Big Mac about my relationship, my personal relationship, I purposely emphasized, with their boss.

Dirty Harry laughed. "And?"

"And will you please get him on the phone?"

"So you wanna call the Chief? Fine with me. Call him. Call the mayor and governor too, while you're at it, because you ain't getting no results from them either."

"I'm a friend of Chief Gillette's," I said, making myself clear.

"Every female's a friend of Gillette's, let them tell it anyhow. Now come on." He tightened his grip on my arm and pulled me in front of him.

"I'm not just saying that, officer. Donald Gillette is a friend of mine. Call him. He'll tell you."

By now we were in front of Big Mac's booth and he, at least, seemed to take my pronouncement a little more seriously than his younger colleague.

I took full advantage of his hesitation. "He's going to have a fit when he finds out what's happening to me." I was being more hopeful than truthful at this point, I realized, but it worked.

The booking officer said, "Call the Chief, Stu. Just to make sure."

"You want me to call Don Gillette on a Sunday night?" Dirty Harry replied. "Are you nuts?"

"She might be on the level. I'm not booking her until you check out her story."

"She's just talking smack, dude, come on. I caught her with drugs, riding around with Juno Curtis and his gang of thugs. What would Gillette look like fooling around with somebody like her?"

"I don't know, but you got to check it out."

"Come on, Mac. What if she's lying? The Chief will have me for breakfast disturbing him at home on a Sunday night like this."

"What if she's telling the truth? He'll have you for more than breakfast then."

Dirty Harry shook his head. Then he got another bright idea. "I'll call Delvecchio. He and Gillette's kind of tight."

"Who's Delvecchio?" I asked quickly, knowing I was going down hard if he had anything to say about it.

"Call the chief, Stu," Big Mac said. "Gillette doesn't discuss his private life with no Vince Delvecchio."

Amen to that, brother.

Stu ordered me to sit down in a chair on the side of a nearby desk, and when I complained that I couldn't sit with these handcuffs behind my back, he uncuffed me and then cuffed me to the arm of the chair.

I almost got ugly then, real ugly, but I didn't. I just took my animal-like treatment like a woman, and sat my behind down.

Since there was no one else lined up to be booked, Big Mac came over and sat on the edge of the desk. Dirty Harry, so nervous that he looked unwell, took a deep breath, sat down too, and picked up the telephone.

Big Mac took the phone from him and sat it back on its hook. "Put it on speaker," he said, pressing a button on the phone.

Dirty Harry shook his head. Then he pulled a book from the drawer that had STATION DIRECTORY written on it, opened it, found a particular number, and began dialing. "I don't like this, Mac," he said as he dialed.

Mac nodded. "I know."

"You know how Gillette is. What if she's lying?"

"What if she's not? What if she is some special friend of his?"

That stopped Harry's dialing.

Stopped me, too, actually, since I never said anything about being any "special" friend of Gillette's. Not in the way that he meant, anyway.

We both looked at Mac.

Harry, however, did the talking. "That's what I don't like. You've seen the women Chief runs with. They're, you know . . ."

"Beautiful?" Mac volunteered.

"Gorgeous," Harry corrected him.

Mac and Dirty Harry both looked at me. Hard.

"I can't see nobody putting her in that category," Harry said.

Mac quickly shook his head. "She's not exactly gorgeous, I'll give you that."

Oh, thanks a lot, guys.

"But she's young and cute, brainy-looking," Mac added.

I nodded and adjusted my glasses up on my nose, just to help emphasize his point.

"But that's just it. She's too young. I ain't never seen Chief with no woman her age."

"That doesn't mean he don't be with them," Mac said, a little annoyed.

I nodded my head vigorously, but Dirty Harry still wasn't convinced. I guess he just couldn't see somebody like me fraternizing with his commanding officer. Either that, or he was trying mightily to find every excuse in the book to avoid that phone call.

In some ways I could see how he could be terrified of Gillette, who did have a way of keeping even me on pins and needles. But this Stu was, in my opinion, taking it too far. A citizen of this community was demanding that he call the head of the police department, a man she claimed to be her friend. What was the big darn deal?

Apparently it was a big darn deal, however, the way Harry dialed so slowly. He leaned back in his chair, lifting one of his booted feet up on the desk, while the other end of the phone line began to ring.

As soon as Gillette's voice came on the line, he quickly dropped his booted foot and leaned forward. Simultaneously, I quickly began to have "what-if-he-tells-me-to-take-a-hike" heart palpitations.

"Hello," Gillette's garbled voice said over the phone's speaker. He had either been asleep or engaged in other activity that had him in bed and drowsy.

"Hello, sir, this is Stu. I mean Stuart Joran. I mean Officer Joran." Stu scrunched up his face. He was blowing it big time.

"What is it?" Gillette replied in a voice that was already sounding irritated.

Harry seemed at a loss for words, as he just sat there. Big Mac had to push him with his elbow to rouse him to get on with it. Harry, instead, just looked up at him.

"Hello?"

Big Mac had to take over. He moved in closer to the phone's mic. "Hello, sir. This is MacDonald over in Booking."

"I thought I was talking with what's his name."

"I know."

"What's up, Mac? What's going on over there?"

"Nothing major, sir. It's just that Officer Joran arrested this young woman who claims to be a friend of yours, and we needed some guidance on how to proceed."

I couldn't have said it better myself, I thought.

"What woman?"

My heart began palpitating again.

"Um–" Mac snapped his fingers at Dirty Harry, who was catatonic, just staring at him.

"Veronica Jarrett," I said quietly.

"Veronica Jarrett," Mac said loudly.

That got an immediate reaction from Gillette. A sigh of exasperation. "Veronica Jarrett. What's the charge this time?"

This time? I'd never been arrested before. At least not in Melville.

"Possession of marijuana and crack cocaine, with intent to distribute, sir."

"What?" Gillette said aloud at the same time that I mouthed the same word.

I wasn't intending to sell no crack. I was just holding it. I didn't even know it was crack.

Mac gave me a withering look that brooked no debate.

"We caught her speeding up Hargrove with her thug friends," Dirty Harry suddenly said, regaining his voice, and pulse.

"What thug friends?"

"Juno Curtis and his boys," Harry said.

Gillette sighed again. "So she was running with Juno."

"I don't run with no Juno," I said loud enough for Gillette to hear. "And I wasn't intending to sell anything."

"How much was she holding, Mac?" Gillette asked, ignoring me.

Mac looked at Harry. "Dime bag," he said, "on both."

"So how can it be intent to distribute, when that was all I had?"

"You was riding around in a car with Juno Curtis!" Harry said, his young, round face beet-red with anger.

"And? Last I looked, it was still a free country and I could ride around with whomever I wish to ride around with, regardless of what you think of that person. So tell me where's the crime in that?"

"Veronica?" Gillette said without even attempting to raise his voice.

I knew what was coming, and I wanted to ignore him, but I needed him too badly.

"Veronica," he said again.

"Yes?" I finally replied.

"Don't say another word." Then he said to his cops, "What did Curtis and his boys have on them?"

Harry had to exhale first. "They were clean, sir," he replied, looking at me.

"Did you check his vehicle?" Gillette asked.

"Yes, sir. It was clean."

"Why am I not surprised?"

"Probably should have got the K-9 unit on it," Mac said. "I'll bet they would have sniffed something out. Certainly more than what Jarrett was carrying."

Harry, with his dirty self, wouldn't be outdone. "But since your new policy, Chief, makes it clear that we're to arrest anybody who's found with drugs in our community, no matter what amount, who they are, or who they know"—He looked at me—"That's exactly what I did."

"You did the right thing," Gillette said.

Dirty Harry smiled for the first time since I'd had the displeasure of knowing the man. His smile, however, brought a frown from me. Gillette backing him meant that he wasn't going to back me. I could rot in jail from here to eternity for all he seemed to care.

"And take me off that damn speaker!"

"Yes, sir." Harry quickly picked up the phone.

I was then treated to "Yes, sir," so many times, it made me nauseous. What in the world could Gillette be ordering him to do that required that many replies?

Then Harry looked at me and smiled. "Run a check, yes, sir," he said.

I knew I was through dealing now. I leaned my head back and sighed. Only God could help me now.

After Harry hung up the phone, he seemed quite pleased with himself.

Big Mac asked what the chief said, but Harry was too busy unlocking my cuffs from the chair and shuffling me to my feet.

"Let's go," he said, as he escorted me, not back to my cell, but to a small room off from Booking.

The holding cell, I imagined. There was a bed in there, and a table with two chairs, but nothing else.

Harry pushed me inside as if I was some hardened criminal, stepped back out himself, and then locked the door. But I didn't trip. I had no reason. Every bit of this nightmare was nobody's fault, nobody's blame, but mine.

I sat down on the small twin bed, crossed my legs, and tried my best to pray. At first I prayed my heart out, promising God all sorts of things if He got me out of this one. But then I got tired of hearing my own self and lay back on the bed, my feet still firmly on the floor.

I covered my face with my hands and couldn't stop myself from crying. I'd done it this time. Got myself into one heck of a mess this time. And the way Gillette so quickly agreed with Dirty Harry, all but sealing my fate right then and there, was just another prime example of how alone in this world I truly was.

I lay on that bed in that small room for well over an hour, crying and agonizing, before I finally let go. And let God.

Lord, help me. Please, help me. I've gotten myself in a terrible situation now, and I need Your divine intervention. Please rule in the hearts of these men, Lord, so that they may find favor in me and somehow drop the charges. I come to You as your daughter, Lord, undeserving, guilty as sin, ashamed of the decisions I've made. But I come boldly unto Your throne of grace, and ask You to drop the charges for me. Please, Lord. Please drop the charges.

I kept praying and praying, as the tears dropped like goblets of rain from my eyes. And then, as if a load had been lifted, as if rest could finally come, I fell asleep.

Nearly forty minutes later, I was awakened by the sound of an opening door. When I opened my eyes and looked up, Don Gillette was walking in.

ELEVEN

He closed the door behind him and began walking slowly around the room, his wing tip shoes pounding loud and heavy on the hardwood floor. He wore a different suit, this one brown silk, and he also wore a matching derby hat. He merely glanced at me when he first entered the room, and although his face looked hard and uncompromising, I could still see that glimmer of concern in his eyes.

I sat up and latched onto that little hope. Maybe he did care enough about me that he'd find a way to get me out of this jam. It was a slim hope, to be sure, but I also knew that God was able to change things even in the thorniest of circumstances.

Gillette took off his hat and tossed it on the table. Then he stood in front of me, his hands in his pant pockets, his face a seeming mask of anger. "So you're running with Juno now?"

"No," was all I could manage to say.

He frowned. "What do you mean, no? My officer pulled you straight from Curtis's truck and arrested you."

"I know that."

"Then don't you tell me no."

"I didn't mean no. What I meant was that it's not like—"

"Veronica, were you or were you not in an SUV with Juno Curtis?"

"Yes, I was in there, but it's not like you think. I wasn't just hanging out with him. He was helping me."

"Juno Curtis was helping you?"

"Yes."

"Juno Curtis the drug dealer was helping you?"

I couldn't go on. He had every right to be disgusted.

"What was he helping you to do? Get high?"

I looked at him angrily. "I don't get high."

"No crackhead does. That's the miracle of it. You ask any crackhead anywhere in America, and they'll declare they'd never been high a day in their lives."

"I'm not a crackhead, all right. I don't do drugs."

"No, you don't do drugs. You just like to keep them in your bra."

I stood up. "I'm not listening to this nonsense." I tried to move as far away from him as I could possibly get in such a small room.

Gillette grabbed me by the arm and pulled me back in front of him. "Don't you walk away from me, young lady. Don't you realize what that junk can do to you, Veronica? Didn't they teach you anything at Juilliard besides playing some darn piano?"

I started to fire back at him, but then I looked into his droopy, hazel eyes. I realized where that anguish was coming from. It had to be his dead wife all over again. The lies, the deception, the hurt, and the pain. He'd probably sworn to never let another woman take him through anything remotely resembling that again. Now here I was taking him through it. Why he cared so much? was the question.

"I don't do drugs, Gillette," I said in a deflated tone. "I'm not like that."

I don't know if he understood what I meant, but he immediately released my arm, placed his hand to his forehead, and began walking around in the room. He moved to the opposite side, and leaned against the wall.

"What was Curtis helping you to do?" he asked me.

On this I sat back down. "Find some people."

"Who?"

I exhaled. "The people who broke into my house."

Gillette stared at me. "Somebody broke into your home? When?"

"Tonight."

"Tonight?"

"While I was in church, yeah."

Gillette hesitated. "Somebody breaks into your house, and you enlist the help of Juno Curtis?"

"It didn't go down like that."

"You didn't call the police. Oh, no. You wouldn't dare do anything as sensible as calling law enforcement, but you turn to Juno Curtis. A thug."

"It wasn't like that, Gillette."

"You know what, Veronica, just—" He shook his head, exhaled, and then leaned back against the wall. "Did they steal anything?"

"No. Yes. I mean, I don't know yet. Look, it wasn't like I went running to Juno like that. He heard me screaming, and he came to see what was going on. That's how it happened. And then one thing led to another, and before I knew it, they were talking about chasing them down, and I just went with them. I didn't think about it first."

"You were screaming?"

He asked in a voice so low, I wondered if he was suddenly choked up or something. I even looked up at him.

"Yes," I said. "I walked in on them."

"You mean to tell me they were still there when you got home? They were still in your house?"

I nodded. "Yes."

"Good Lord, Veronica. Did they hurt you, did they try to—"

I started shaking my head. "No, thank God. They didn't touch me."

Gillette exhaled, visibly relieved.

"But that's how I hooked up with Juno. It was spontaneous, Gillette. Wasn't no plan in that."

"Did you see the guys who broke in?"

"No. Not to where I could identify them or anything like that. They just seemed young, that's all. One dude had the number twenty-three on the back of his jersey. An old Chicago Bulls jersey, I think. And they got away in an old souped-up-looking Pontiac."

"It was a Pontiac that tried to run you over in front of Hard Times."

"I know. But I couldn't tell you if it was the same car or anything. It would be mighty strange that all of these different Pontiacs were gunning for me, but it all happened so fast."

"And you don't know if they stole anything?"

"They didn't steal anything valuable, I know that. It was like they were looking for papers or something."

"Something like Taneka Dupayne's diary?"

I looked at him. "Yeah. Like that."

"I'll have some of my men get over there and dust for prints, see what they can see."

I nodded. "Thanks."

"You should have called the police, Veronica."

"I know. And I would have. But Juno was right there, and he said he would take care of it."

"So you let him."

I nodded. I knew it was the wrong move, but at the time, I was so desperate to know who had invaded my house, I wasn't half thinking. I just wanted to know.

I jumped at the sudden knocks, which caused Gillette to look at me curiously. Then the door to the small room was opened, and Dirty Harry first peeped inside and then came in with papers in his hand. He seemed downright gleeful.

"Sorry to disturb you, Chief, but I have that information you requested." He began walking toward Gillette, those papers, no doubt my rap sheet, being reached out to him. "It says here that she was arrested—"

"Okay," Gillette said.

Dirty Harry hesitated, as if he didn't understand. "Sir?"

"Thank you for getting the information. That'll be all."

Harry glanced at me before looking back at Gillette. "I thought you wanted to know if there were any priors on her, sir. And there are. It's all here," he said, referring to the papers he still held outstretched in his hand.

"I don't need to review it right now, Officer, but thank you."

Harry was through. I could tell he wanted to look at me again, to make sure I was the same female he'd pulled from Juno's truck with crack cocaine in her bra. But he didn't look my way. He didn't even look Gillette in the eye again. He simply nodded his head and said, "Yes, sir," and then hurried out of the door, closing it vigorously behind him.

I looked at Gillette, knowing instinctively that that couldn't possibly be the end of it.

He walked around the room nearly three times, in deep thought, and then he grabbed a chair, placed it directly in front of me, and sat down. He crossed his legs, placed his hands on his lap, and then looked me dead in the eye. "I want you to tell me, leaving nothing out, everything there is to know about your past. And I mean everything, Veronica."

I swallowed hard. I always knew that that past of mine would someday do me in, I could always feel it in my bones, but if I was going to go down, I might as well go down with my version of the facts. Staring at a rap sheet wouldn't harbor the details, the extenuating circumstances, and I knew it.

I pushed my glasses up on my nose. "Where do I begin?" I said with a smile Gillette didn't return, so I just got on with it. "As you know, my parents died in a car accident when I was fifteen years old. After a few months of foster care, I was released to my aunt, my father's sister, to live with her in Newark. She didn't want to take me, believe that, but I guess she knew she had no choice. There was nobody else, and I was still so shaken up by my parents' death, I didn't care either way. I mean, Neka, God bless her, tried to take custody of me. She even tried to break me out of the group home they had me staying in, but Neek was only sixteen, so naturally that didn't pan out. So I didn't care what my aunt did. She could take me, not take me, it just didn't matter to me. I missed my parents desperately, and that was all I cared about."

"So, to make a long story short, I ended up with Aunt Lucille. And it was worse than I could have imagined it would be. It was awful." I scrunched up my face, the pain still there.

When I looked again at Gillette, tears were already trying to well up in my eyes. "She was awful," I continued. "She just seemed to hate the sight of me for some reason. But I had no choice, she had no choice, and there we were, me and Lucille, or, excuse me, Lucinda, as she preferred to be called. That was her stage name. Lucinda Jarrett. She worked in this club in Newark, this strip joint called the Loopback. Richard, that's the dude you saw earlier today in that Corvette, his father owned the club, and he was the young manager."

"And my aunt was their featured stripper. Oh, she had skills, all right. Figured I had 'em too. That was why, as soon as I turned sixteen, she started badgering me about joining the fun. She wasn't taking care of no sixteen-year-old, she kept saying. It was time I started paying my own way. And her and Richard stayed on my case. They just wouldn't let up. And then all of these men kept coming around, and they were all groping at me, trying to get next to me, and it was just a bad scene. But I still wasn't stripping for nobody. So when Lucille gave me an ultimatum, that I either pony up or leave, I left. I hit the streets."

I looked at Gillette, who was staring at me.

"You didn't have any other relatives at all? Somebody who could have helped you out?"

"Nope."

He frowned. "Nobody?"

"Nobody, except good old Lucille. And she wasn't havin' it. She was all about the party, all about having fun and looking out for self."

"How did you survive?"

"The best way I knew how. Doing it to them before they did it to me. I used to cry when I first got to Jersey—You know how a kid can be—but that got old fast. Nobody cared about my tears. Lucille certainly didn't, so I got tough. That's how I survived. I stopped caring too."

"And you hooked up with the boyfriend."

"Not at first. But after about a month of that street life, after about a month of half-starving to death, sleeping on the streets, yeah, I started working for him. I had to do something."

"So you became a stripper after all."

I immediately began shaking my head. "No."

Gillette looked at me hard.

"I'm not lying, Gillette, all right. I told you I wasn't stripping for nobody. I did some cocktail waitressing for him, was his bartender sometimes too, although I had no business even being in the joint. But I caught on fast, and he could see it. I was smart, at least smarter than any female he was used to. And he knew he could trust me. So he made me his dealer."

Gillette looked astounded. "His dealer? Drugs?"

"No, Gillette. Cards. Gambling? I became the house dealer. Richard had himself an illegal gambling ring going on in the back of the club. He taught me how to cheat people out of every dime they had on them, especially his drunk, rowdy customers. And after a while, I got real good at it. He said it was like I was a natural con."

"How admirable."

"I didn't mean it like that."

"Go on."

I hesitated, but knew I had to swallow the little pride I did have and keep going. "So one night, while I was doing my thing, we got ourselves raided. I mean, those cops came in like Osama bin Laden was up in there. They knocked down doors, knocked over tables, busted up the whole place. Even shots were fired."

Gillette's look changed.

"That's right," I said. "Some of those fools started shooting at the cops. That's how crazy it got. They even claimed I had shot at one of those cops, but that wasn't even true."

"You had a gun?"

"Yeah, but it wasn't even loaded. Richard just gave it to me for show."

I could tell this story of mine was beginning to sound slightly worse than Gillette was banking on. His face seemed tense-filled.

"Was anybody hurt?"

"A few of our customers, yeah, but nobody too seriously. But we were all hauled in. Richard got me a lawyer, and he was able to get the attempted murder charge dropped against me. It wasn't true anyway, but in exchange, I had to plead guilty to some bogus drug charge."

Gillette exhaled. "You had drugs on you?"

"Yeah, but I wasn't using drugs."

"Then what were you doing with them?"

I closed my eyes. "Richard had me supplying some of his gambling customers whenever they wanted to get a hit sometimes."

"So you were dealing more than cards in that back room."

I hesitated before nodding.

"So you pled guilty to possession with intent, and then what happened?"

"I got probation since I was a minor, and at the time it was my first offense, thank God, but, man, did that scene scare me. That's when I made up my mind that I had to get my act together. Had to clean up my act. And I did. Sort of."

"What do you mean, sort of?"

"I mean, I did stop the dealing, drugs and otherwise, but I started running with Richard. Thought I was so in love with him."

"And that's what you call cleaning up your act?"

"It wasn't like that, Gillette, all right. It wasn't like today the judge puts me on probation and tomorrow I run into Richard's arms. I knew he was bad news. But I was back on the streets, trying to make a living, and the world just wasn't cooperating with that plan."

"I thought you professed Christianity. Why didn't you turn to the Lord. To the church?"

"I didn't profess anything then. I didn't know what the inside of a church, a Bible, or anything else remotely resembling Christianity looked like then. And everybody just seemed out to get me. I don't know. Dudes on the street were trying to get next to me every time I turned around; girls on the street wanted to beat me up because the dudes seemed to favor me; and the cops—" All I could do was shake my head. "There was this one cop, this sergeant, who just wouldn't stop harassing me. When I wouldn't sleep with his crusty behind, he planted some weed on me and got me busted again. He planted that junk, I ain't lying, but because I was on probation, they gave me ninety days, anyway."

Gillette just sat there, staring at me, so I kept on talking.

"It's when I got out of jail that I hooked up with Richard. He was talking all that sweet talk, all that jive, and yeah, I fell for it. I sure did. I was sixteen, still a kid basically, and he was twenty-three and great-looking, so naturally I just knew I was in love. He said everything I needed to hear, and came from a wealthy family, I thought he was the man of my dreams. The answer to my prayers."

I looked at Gillette. He tried not to show a reaction, but his face had taken on a harder edge. He was probably just imagining me shimmering down some pole at Richard's club, although I never did it like that, but why would he take my word for it? He didn't know me like that.

"Then one thing led to another, and I ended up moving into his place."

Gillette gave me a look of disapproval.

"You can give me that look all you want, but I did what I had to do. I had nothing, Gillette. Nobody. Richard at least treated me like I was something special to him, better than what the streets had to offer me, and it was all good for a while. Until the lying and cheating started. And the women. Then it all went downhill. I mean all."

"So I started getting me a new plan. I knew I couldn't rely on Richard anymore than I could have relied on my dead parents, or my aunt, or anybody else in this world for that matter." I frowned. I remembered how alone I felt back then. "I went back to school, graduated, all the while saving every dime Richard gave me."

"As his live-in whatever."

"I had to make do, Gillette, all right. It's not like it was something I enjoyed. I hated relying totally on some man. I hated it. But I was a kid living on the streets. Don't you understand what I'm telling you? I was tired of begging folks and living from hand to mouth. I was tired of fighting off men and hiding out from social workers. I wish I knew then what I know now, but I didn't know jack back then. I thought I was in love and would always be in love. I thought Richard was going to take care of me the way my parents used to do before . . . before they died. But I'm not like that now, and I'll never be like that again. Never!"

Gillette exhaled. "Why is he in town now?"

"Don't know and don't care."

"You seemed to care earlier. At least enough to get rid of me so you could talk to him."

"Yeah, because I needed to set him straight. He actually had the nerve to say he wanted to get back with me."

"Or back *at* you."

A puzzled look crossed my face. "Back at me? What do you mean?"

"You left him, right?"

"Yeah, I left him. It was either him or my self-respect."

Gillette shrugged. "Maybe he holds grudges. Maybe this visit of his is for payback."

"But what could he do to me for something that happened so long ago?"

"He could break into your house, for starters."

"Richard? No way. That ain't his style. Besides, I told you I saw the two dudes that did it, and neither one of them looked anything like him."

"He could have hired a couple of thugs from the hood."

"I would have believed that if some of my stuff was stolen, but they didn't snatch anything of value, at least not from what I could see. Hood rats don't break into somebody's home just to trash it."

"Did those drugs belong to you?"

"No."

"They were Juno's then?"

I looked away. "I'm not answering that."

Gillette frowned. "What could you possibly owe a dude like that? A drug dealer. Unless he's your new squeeze now."

I looked at him, unable to hide my hurt. He stared at me too, and then he stood and moved up to me. I could hear my heartbeat quicken as he invaded my personal space. Then he reached out and smoothed my wild hair with his hand.

I looked up at him and adjusted my glasses, as he placed his warm hand on the side of my face and continued to stare at me.

Then his look turned so somber, so concerned. Then he stepped back from me and yelled Big Mac's name loudly.

Big Mac hurried into the room, looking as if he was in some kind of trouble. "Yes, sir, Chief?"

Gillette began heading for the door. "Drop the charges and let her go," he ordered, and he didn't look back.

After being released from jail, and after watching the cops and their evidence technicians dust my house for prints, I spent the night at Pam's. I was just too shook up to turn down her repeated invitation.

When I woke up the next morning, however, my plan was to go home, dress, and try my best to get to work on time, to at least act as if my life had some normalcy left.

But when I arrived at home, I found myself cleaning up the disarray before I could even think about doing anything else. Which made me not just late for work, but excessively late. When I made it in, I found myself standing at the reception counter listening to another lecture from Anne.

Greta didn't have a customer and was sitting at the counter, smiling her little head off. She'd heard something. I knew that smirk of hers too well.

My heart began to pound at the thought that she could have heard about that mess last night, about my arrest, and when Anne finally shut up and left the salon to take care of some other business, I decided to find out.

"So what did you hear?" I asked Greta point-blank.

She was looking at the flat-screen television on the back wall at the *Judge Mathis* show. "Say what?" she said.

"What did you hear, Gret? Come on. I know what that smile means."

"Means nothing. That's what it means."

I folded my arms. "What did you hear?"

She hesitated again then swiftly turned my way. "I heard about the fight."

I frowned. "The fight? What fight?"

"Come on, girl."

"What fight?"

"The one between that brother in the 'Vette and Don Gillette."

What? I shook my head. "I don't know what you're talking about, Greta."

"I heard it was a sight to see. That young brother whipped Gillette's behind, they said, beat him down like a dog."

"That is such a lie! Who told you that nonsense?"

"Never you mind who told me. But I'm telling you, Roni, Don Gillette is not the brother to play the field on."

"Play the field? What are you talking about?"

"Just telling what I know."

"Just telling what you heard, which is a big difference. If that matters."

"Not at all," she said with a laugh. She swung out of the counter stool and then headed back to her workstation.

I shook my head as I went behind the counter. Gillette was going to just love this. Now Greta and her grapevine had him fighting for me and getting beat up in the process. Terrific. Just terrific.

After a half hour more of *Judge Mathis*, the twelve o'clock news finally came on. Our police chief, as fate would have it, was a part of one of the reports on tap for the day. Liz Steward, the local state attorney and the woman both Anne and Greta had mentioned as one of Gillette's females, was standing beside him at some sort of press conference that was apparently held earlier that morning.

To say that Miss Steward was gorgeous would be an understatement. Tall and big-breasted, she had dark skin as smooth as chocolate, and when she smiled, she lit up the room. She and Gillette looked so dazzling together.

If he could have that, why would he want some jailbird, some anything-but-glamorous female like me? That woman put criminals behind bars, not do stupid things to get behind them. But he did come to that jail to see about me. And, praises be to God, he did go against every rule in the book and order his men to set me free.

I turned up the volume to see exactly what this press conference was all about, and Greta, being Greta, laughed, as if I was only doing it just to hear Gillette's voice.

Gillette and Ms. Steward, after discussing other cases I wasn't familiar with, announced that Taneka Dupayne's murder had been solved and that Jeffrey Collins, who was himself found murdered a week ago, was her killer. When the reporters pressed for motive, Gillette told them that Jeffrey murdered Taneka as revenge for his brother's death. He then told them about Willie Barnes' love for Taneka, about Taneka's drug habit, and about Willie robbing people to pay for that habit.

What amazed me was how not one reporter questioned that theory. Why would Jeffrey killing Taneka avenge his brother's death when Taneka wasn't the one who killed his brother? And who killed Jeffrey? But not one of those reporters bothered to ask or probably even cared to know.

Taneka's death was never big news around Melville. This was evident as Gillette, Liz Steward, and the entire press corps surrounding them quickly went on to what they probably considered weightier matters. Like the small-time robbery suspect Liz Steward was prosecuting, who decided to rob what he thought was a bank, but was actually the building that housed the Police Athletic League.

Everybody laughed when Gillette talked about the robber telling the desk sergeant, "Stick 'em up, and give me all of the money in the drawer," only to find himself with twenty guns drawn on him.

"Don't let them get away with it." I could still remember Neka begging me that fateful night that now seemed so long ago, and I felt so helpless, because I knew, as the powers-that-be stood on that television screen laughing their hearts out, that was exactly what they were doing.

TWELVE

The case may have been closed in the eyes of Melville's power elite, but it didn't feel closed to me. Gillette said that many cases are closed with loose ends, but Taneka's case was just a little too loose for my satisfaction. Besides, my behind was now on the line too. I wasn't just some outside observer anymore. I needed to know why Neka had been targeted in the first place, and why did I end up on that hit list too.

And that was why, after work, I found myself, not in the comfort of my own home, but in the heart of Dodge, on a street they called "the Strip," asking around about Jeffrey Collins in particular, but also about his brother, Willie Barnes.

I parked my car in front of a hair salon and walked the Strip as if I was a regular there. I had on my dark green pantsuit and stiletto heels, but many sisters were dressed up on the Strip, and not just the hoochies either. There, boosters reigned, selling their movies, music, earrings, necklaces, pocketbooks, cell phones, tennis shoes, and just about any commodity that could be sold.

One brother, a dude in a wheelchair, was even selling a microwave that was sitting on his lap. I couldn't see how the legitimate businesses, the barbershops and pool halls, the clothing stores and liquor stores, could compete with the boosters, but their establishments appeared to be thriving too. One thing about poor people, they spend money, a contradiction in terms, but here in Melville it was evident.

But even with all of that commerce swirling around, all of

those females walking the Strip, I still stood out like a sore thumb. Even the children roaming around, many of whom lived in the housing projects just a block away, steered clear of me, and everybody I tried to talk to about Jeffrey Collins and Willie Barnes gave me the cold shoulder.

I just wanted some facts. I just wanted to know what the word on the street, the nitty-gritty street, was about Taneka's death, and if those in the know truly believed Jeffrey Collins was responsible for that death.

But talk about the sister from another planet. Because that was how I felt. The women on the Strip looked at me as if I was intruding on their game, and the men couldn't stop hitting on me. And not one of them wanted to help a sister out. I couldn't understand it. What had I done to these people? I almost said something.

One brother, a short dude with processed curly hair, came out and told me that he smelled five-O when I walked past. I stomped back to make it clear to him that no way was I a cop. How in the world could he even think such a thing?

The sister standing by him said, "If you sleep with pigs, then you're a pig."

I tell you, my jaw dropped. These people didn't know jack about me but was judging me based on what somebody else had told them about my relationship with Gillette. I could only shake my head.

I kept on walking. I was wasting my time now, if these folks thought I was Gillette's plaything, or whatever they thought.

Then I happened upon this dude with a patch over his right eye, standing near a liquor store on the corner.

"What up, beautiful lady?" he said to me.

I really didn't want to waste my breath asking him anything, but I asked him, anyway.

To my shock, he nodded. "Yeah, I knew old Crazy Jeff and that dumb-behind Willie. Two crooks—That's what I know about them. They'd steal your arms if they wasn't attached to your body."

"Crooks, yeah," I said, anxious to keep him talking, "but the cops are calling Jeffrey Collins a murderer."

"Man, you can believe them cops if you want."

"I take it you don't?"

"Me and nobody else with half a brain. Man, Crazy Jeff wasn't gonna kill no crackhead Neka just because Delvecchio iced his brother. That don't even make no sense."

"So," I said, prodding him, "you don't think Jeff killed Taneka?"

He didn't say anything.

"Patches?" I said with a smile.

He looked me up and down. "Very funny. The name's Left Eye."

A patch over the right eye, they call him Left eye. Naturally. "So you don't think Jeffrey Collins killed Taneka Dupayne?" I asked again.

He shook his head. "I know he didn't. He and Neka been kickin' it on the Strip many days since Willie took the heat. Been doing more than that too, from what I hear."

That made sense to me. Neka's diary talked as if she and Jeffrey had a relationship too. Of course, it could have been all a ruse on Jeffrey's part and he was picking his moment. But my gut was telling me, that wasn't it.

"Besides," Left Eye went on, "who killed Jeff, if he killed Crackhead Neka? Them cops don't know, and they don't care. Just trying to close another case. But betcha I know who knows what went down."

"You do?" I asked too excitably. "Who?"

He looked around, as if trying to decide if he should say more.

"Who, Lefty?" I asked. "I mean, Left Eye. Who knows what happened?"

He looked around again, and then he exhaled and began to move away. "Come with me," he said.

I looked around. It was after eight, and the sun had long since set. I hesitated. "Come with you? Where?"

"Look, you wanna know, or don't you?"

"Of course, I want to know. But couldn't you just give me the name?"

"Man, forget this!" He moved back to lean against the wall.

"Wait, Left Eye, I'm just—"

"You just what? You the one come to me. I wasn't botherin' you."

"I know that. It's just that—"

"I thought you wanted to know what them two fools was up to, and why Neka got iced, but hey, if you too scared to go someplace with me, then keep your scared butt right here. But get on out of my face with it."

I hesitated yet again, this time for a long time, because I wasn't feeling this scene for real. But it was too tempting. He claimed to know somebody with information, serious information, about what happened to Neka, and if I was especially blessed, why I was being targeted too. How could I walk away from that?

So, against my better judgment and the spirit within me screaming no, I followed the guy. Followed him along the sidewalk, across the street, and eventually through a dingy alley that ended up being the trap I should have known it would have been.

And then it all happened so fast.

Left Eye suddenly stopped walking, grabbed me by the arm, and slung me against the wall.

I fought back, screaming and swinging, and almost got away from that clown. But, sure enough, two other dudes came running in. But they came too fast—They had to be following us all along—and before I knew anything, it was three against one, with all three pulling on me and trying to get some freebie they assumed I was giving away.

Then I heard a booming, forceful voice yell, "Police!" And the thugs that had me down took off running.

I looked up and saw that the man behind that terrifying, booming voice that answered my prayers was Don Gillette. As he stood over me and I looked up at him, suddenly all of the little strength I did have left seeped right out of me. He bent down to help me up and then lifted me into his arms.

I held tightly onto him, feeling that protection I needed right then, but as quickly as I began to feel comfortable in his arms, he let me back down. And stared into my face with a look on his own that I could only describe as dread.

"You okay?" he asked me, looking me up and down.

I was able to nod that I was.

Suddenly two men who looked like undercover cops ran into the entrance of the alley, yelling out their chief's name.

"Three of them!" Gillette yelled, as they ran past us. "Probably crossed over on Herlong. Try Normandy too."

"One had a patch over his right eye!" I volunteered, but those cops didn't wait around for my description, they were already running out the back way.

Gillette then looked at me again, his face now showing more exhaustion than anything else. "Let's get out of here."

His truck was parked on the street a few feet down from the alley's entrance, with what looked like an unmarked police car behind it, and he opened his truck's passenger door and let me in. He walked around and sat on the driver's side.

I could just feel a lecture coming on. Which I really didn't need. Nobody had to tell me I was a fool on two legs. I already knew it.

He locked the doors of his truck and looked at me.

I could sense his disgust, his anger, his disappointment, his everything, but I refused to look his way. I was too shaken, too upset with my own self, to have to see it on his expressive face.

"Of all the boneheaded, nonsensical stunts you could have pulled, Veronica, this one kind of tops it, don't you think?"

I didn't respond.

"A ten-year-old would have known better than coming out here like this."

I exhaled. He was right, but that still didn't stop me from wanting to lash out too.

"I told you to leave police matters to the police. But, oh no, not Veronica Jarrett. Why should she listen to me? Why should she listen to any veteran cop? She knows better. She's got to take her pantsuit-wearing behind on this Strip and question these roughnecks for herself, like it's the joy of their lives to give her information."

I looked at him, ready to lash back and tell him that at least I was doing something, which was more than what I could say for that sorry police force of his, until I looked into his hooded hazel eyes, eyes that were sparkling with intensity. And what I saw wasn't anger, or disgust, or any of those negative emotions I expected to see, but fear. Raw, undisguised fear. My heart dropped.

"What if I hadn't been here?" he asked. "What if those fools did what they'd intended? You think you could have beat back three men, Veronica? You think they would have let you? You could have been raped or worse. Don't you get it?"

I leaned my head back and stared straight ahead. "Yes."

"Then why do you keep doing this stuff? Why do you keep putting yourself at risk like this?"

"You closed the case. You and your DA friend." My reference to Liz Steward, a woman Gillette was rumored to be seeing, was meant to sting. I looked at him, and for a moment our eyes met, and then he looked away from me. I sighed. "You closed the case without even trying to find out why somebody had targeted me. You may not have cared, but I did."

"Not care?" He asked as if he couldn't believe I'd just said that.

"That's the way it looks to me."

"I don't care. Then why am I here, Veronica? I was keeping an eye out on you. I told my men to follow you, to keep their distance, but to follow you and see you safely home. Then they were to get back to their own beat, which involves investigating the numerous murders that have been blanketing this town, investigations they've been neglecting because of you and your little escapades."

"But I should have known that would be too easy. How in the world could I have thought that you would do something as sensible as going to work and then going home? I was stunned when they phoned and told me that you didn't go home and that an accident caused them to lose track of where you had gone, only to later find your car parked on the Strip, of all places. On the Strip! Can you imagine how I felt when they told me that? How fast I got over here when they told me that? So don't you talk to me about not caring. If anybody doesn't care based on stupid moves alone, it seems to me it's you."

"I don't have a death wish, Gillette."

"Then you need to start acting like it. Because I am telling you, Veronica, I can't take much more of this. I'm too old. Been there, done that, and I'm not doing it again. And if you don't knock it off, I'll . . . "

I looked at him. "You'll what?" I asked, suddenly scared all over again.

"You know what," he said without a moment's hesitation.

And I did know what. He'd leave me, that's what. He'd put a definite end to whatever kind of relationship we were trying to build and absolve all involvement with me. There was a part of Gillette that I couldn't see doing something that cold. But with the other part, the part that had been hurt so bitterly before, the thought of leaving me would be as easy as walking out a door. That was the part that put a lump in my throat.

The two cops came back out of the alley, one so winded, he had to lean against the outside wall.

Gillette immediately got out of the truck and walked over to them, getting a report I wasn't even trying to hear. It was obvious that those thugs got away.

I looked at Gillette as he listened to his men, his broad back turned to me. He was a well-built brother, muscled from his thick thighs to his straight back, the jeans he was wearing fitting him tightly across the butt. Yet his body seemed beat-down, slumped, as if his warning that he couldn't take much more of my antics was as much physical as it was emotional.

When he dismissed his men and got back into the truck, his face demonstrated that exhaustion.

"They got away?" I asked, although I already knew the answer.

"Yeah." He said that as if it was my fault, and cranked up his truck.

"What are you doing? What about my Beamer?"

"Your what?"

"My car. I can't leave it in this neighborhood."

"Do you listen to yourself sometimes? This neighborhood is safe enough for you to roam around in, but it's not safe enough for your car? You're a gem, you know that? A fifty-carat diamond gem." He shook his head again. "I'll take you to your little car, all right, then you get in it and take your behind home." He began driving off, in the opposite end of the Strip.

"I'm not going home," I said hesitantly. I just knew that would provoke yet another argument. "I'm staying at Pam's house for a few days."

"Why?"

I hesitated.

He looked at me. "What?"

"I told you somebody tried to break into my house."

"You also told me it was no big deal, that Juno Curtis could handle it."

That wasn't what I'd told him at all, but what difference did it make? "I don't know what's going on, Gillette, and it's bugging the daylights out of me. That's why I'm staying at Pam's, until I can find out what's really happening. That's why I came here. I need to know why Neka had to die and why somebody decided to target me too. And, what with Richard here in town, I just don't know what his connection is to everything that's going on, if there is a connection. Or if he's just stalking me for his own twisted pleasure."

Gillette stopped his truck, just stopped it in the middle of the street, and looked at me. "Stalking you?"

"I didn't mean—"

"Since when has he been stalking you, Veronica?"

"I didn't mean it like that."

"Veronica!"

"Since the night Neka died, okay. He called me on the phone. It was the first time I'd heard from him in years. Then yesterday after you left, he said that we'll be together whether I want us to or not, or I could end up like Taneka."

Gillette leaned back, his eyes trained on me. "He told you that?"

"Yes."

"Did he know Dupayne?"

"No. At least not to my knowledge. He said he knows everything about me, and he knew I was her friend, or something like that."

"And you didn't think this bit of information was important enough to share with me?"

"I didn't. I wasn't thinking about it that way."

"Oh, I'll bet you wasn't."

Gillette just sat there. And then he nodded his head, as if he'd made a decision. He radioed for one of his men to come and get my car, and to pop the lock when he did. When I looked at him, astounded, he began driving again, and driving straight out of Dodge.

"You aren't going home with Pam tonight," he said casually. "You're going home with me."

THIRTEEN

Gillette's home was located on the edge of town, near Lake Bradford. The long, narrow driveway that led to his front door was surrounded by so many trees, it looked almost eerily isolated. Finally, we came to an L-shaped gate that parted for his truck, and closed behind us. The driveway then took on a circular, horseshoe shape as it veered round a courtyard with a small, flowing waterfall and a three-car garage on the side.

The home itself was one of those big, brick, Dutch colonials with a steep set of steps and a wraparound front porch.

My first thought, when we got out of the truck and headed for the big double door entrance, was that this was just too much. Leave it to some ex-nightclub-owning bad boy like Don Gillette to even consider living in a mausoleum like this. And to live here all alone, in my view, was criminal. But he didn't see the crime, apparently, as he swiped a card through a slot and his front door parted and let us in.

Whoa! I nearly stopped in my tracks when I did enter, causing Gillette to bump into me. But I couldn't help myself. I was just that surprised.

Based on the exterior, I expected the inside to be just as museum-like, filled with expensive, if not tasteless antique furnishings and all varieties of famous French paintings. But the interior was wholly contemporary, full of light and glass, an open floor plan surrounded by a massive window that overlooked the lake. The furnishings were modern and white leather, and the granite fireplace almost took up a wall onto itself.

A place like this, so open and inviting, I could easily see Gillette propped up in his recliner by that fireplace, reading his newspaper and enjoying his jazz.

Of course, I had no idea if he read anything at all or listened to music of any kind, but that was the thought that entered my mind as I entered his world. A world, I admit, I wasn't all that comfortable in. A world, based on his sudden awkwardness, he wasn't all that comfortable having me in.

He told me to sit down, which I did, on the large leather couch. He then grabbed a cordless phone from off a nearby table and sat down beside me, his weight lifting me up and sinking him down. He was leaned back, slumped and determined to find comfort.

Meanwhile, I was on the edge of my seat. I was sure his eyes were trained on me, since they usually were, anyway, but I was too wound up to worry about it.

"This is Gillette," he said over the phone. And you are? Rawlings? Jake? Good, is Vince there? Yes. No, no need for that. You can do it. I want you to pull up everything there is on a Richard ah—What's his last name, Veronica?"

I looked back at him. "Pargeter."

"A Richard Pargeter," he said into the phone. "*P-A-R*"

"*G-E-T-E-R.*"

"*G-E-T-E-R*. Pronounced *Par-gee-tar*. I want the full monty, local, state, federal, right. Right. His last known address is—" He looked at me again.

"New Jersey. Newark. He owns the Loopback club."

"Newark, New Jersey. He owns a strip joint called the Loopback. Right. He's in town now, driving a yellow Corvette. If it's spotted, I want to be contacted. That's right. No, morning is good. All right, Sergeant. Good night."

Gillette pressed a button and tossed the phone over in a chair, and then he stretched out his legs.

I stiffened. It seemed the more relaxed he became, the

more uptight I felt. I pushed my glasses on my face and decided to talk, which I often did whenever I was jittery.

"I really don't think Richard's involved in any of this," I said. "He's never been violent with me."

"Stop minimizing it," he replied, his head leaned back on his sofa, his eyes practically closed.

"I'm not minimizing anything. I'm just saying that I don't think he would harm me. He's not like that."

"Something's up. A man doesn't travel a thousand miles to hook up with a woman he knows hate his guts, unless he has something new up his sleeve to win that woman back."

"Win me back? Please."

"You said he wants you."

"He doesn't know what he wants. He never has. When he called me that first time I just knew he was talking noise, just trying to aggravate me."

"Did he threaten you then?"

"Not really, no. He was up to his old tricks, telling me he was going to expose my past to my church and my job, that kind of thing."

Gillette lifted his head and then shook it. "You're a piece of work, Veronica, you know that? Why didn't you tell me any of this sooner?"

"There was nothing to tell. Richard's always talking smack. That's how I looked at it."

"And you spent the night at your girlfriend's just for the fun of it?"

"I told you somebody broke into my house."

"Richard's threat about Taneka had nothing to do with it?"

"No. Yes. It all had something to do with it. I'm just tired of it, Gillette, I'm just . . ."

I leaned back on the sofa and found myself so close to Gillette, our arms touched. I looked at him, at his mouth first, his wavy hair, and then into his eyes. They seemed so caring right at that moment, so tender, that I could feel tears welling up in my eyes.

His reluctance was obvious, as his entire body seemed to suddenly stiffen, but he placed his big arm around me anyway and drew me to him.

I lay my head on his shoulder and allowed the tears to flow freely. I used to never allow people to see me cry. Yet that seemed to be all I wanted to do whenever I was around Gillette.

I began wiping my tears away with the back of my hand, feeling silly, but Gillette's own hand lifted my chin and looked into my teary eyes. He stared. I stared.

"What am I going to do with you?"

Since I didn't know, I didn't answer. But he kept staring. I expected him to tell me something cliched, like everything was going to be all right, but he didn't say another word.

"Do you get it, Gillette?"

A perplexed look crossed his face. "Get what?"

"Life."

He almost smiled. "No."

"Even at your age?"

He did smile this time, those lines of age suddenly appearing on his handsome face. "Even at my age."

"Which is?"

He snorted this time. "None of your business."

I smiled, and laid my head back on his shoulder. He continued to hold me as he rested his chin on the top of my hair. I felt so relaxed at that very moment that I became suddenly daring.

"Tell me about yourself," I said to him.

"Why in the world would I want to do that?"

"Because I'm curious."

"Curiosity killed the cat."

I smiled. "I'm not a cat. Just curious."

He sighed. "There's nothing to tell."

"Come on."

"I mean it."

"You owned a nightclub."

"That's right."

"What was that like? I heard it was the place to be, boy."

There was a hesitation before he spoke, as if I had touched a nerve. "It was a lot of work, Veronica. A lot of hard, demanding work."

"Is that why you sold it?" I looked up at him.

He hesitated, his broodiness back in force. "No."

"No?"

"No."

"Then why did you sell it?"

He sighed again. "Is this really a conversation we need to have?"

"I'm just trying to find out more about you, that's all. I've heard a lot of things about you, but I want to know for myself."

He looked at me. "What have you heard?"

"Lots. Believe me."

"Such as?"

"Hey, I'm the one asking the questions this time."

"What have you heard, Veronica?"

I exhaled. You just couldn't kid around with him at all. "I heard that you're tough."

"And?"

"And that you're very committed to ridding our streets of drugs."

"Keep going."

"And that you're a womanizing playboy who never let anybody get too close to you."

Gillette didn't say anything after that one. I looked at him hard. "Is it true?"

"What do you think?"

"Come on, Gillette. How should I know? That's why I'm asking. Since I'm all in your house and all, I figure I might as well get to know you better."

"You can begin by not calling me Gillette."

"Everybody calls you Gillette."

"That's my point. I want you to call me *Donald*. My name."

A lump was caught in my throat and I swallowed hard. "All right, Donald, although I like *Don* better. *Donald* is so geeky."

Gillette smiled. "Either one."

"Now answer my question. Why did you sell Big G's?"

He looked at me. I guess he thought that little privilege he'd given me would be enough to shut me up. He was mistaken.

He removed his arm from around me and leaned forward. He grabbed a cigarette from a gold case on the cocktail table before us, picked up a lighter, and lit up.

"You smoke?" I asked, unable to conceal my surprise.

"Occasionally." He tossed the lighter back on the table. Then he smiled and looked back at me. "When somebody's bugging me."

"So, why did you sell it?"

He turned back around and hesitated longer than I thought was necessary, but then he said, "My wife died. And there was no getting over that. So I sold out."

"She died?"

"Yep. Drug overdose. *Crack* overdose." He looked back at me. Then he looked away again. "And it messed me up."

"I heard you did all you could for her."

"I've never done all I could for anybody."

"But you did do all you could, Gillette. I mean, *Don*-ald. I heard how she was something else."

"Veronica?"

I didn't like the sound of that. "Yes?"

"I don't care what you've heard, you understand? Especially as it relates to my wife. She was a good woman who had a problem. A problem I couldn't help her solve. And it destroyed her, me, and everything else in its wake. All right? Does that answer your question?"

"Yes, dang. Don't take my head off."

He smiled at this, leaned back, and placed his arm back around me. He was in such a slumped position, we were now shoulder to shoulder.

I looked at him. "So is it true?"

"Is what true?"

"Is it true that you're a player. That you have all these women?"

He looked away from me, took a drag on his cigarette, and didn't even bother to answer.

"Don? Is it true?"

He leaned forward again and began snuffing out his cigarette in the ashtray as if he was suddenly upset. "I'm not getting into that, Veronica. Not with you or anybody else."

So it is true. "What about us?" I asked him.

He hesitated. "What about us?"

"Am I just another one of your females? More or less?"

He looked back at me. Rubbed his thumb across the side of my face. Then he leaned back. "You're not in a category with any other females, Veronica. You're in a class all by yourself."

I wasn't sure if that was a compliment or a put-down. "Meaning?"

"Meaning, you're a special lady."

"To you?"

"To me."

My heart soared. Then I thought about the more crucial matter. "What about God?"

He looked at me.

"I know you said you used to go to church, but do you believe in Jesus Christ?"

He hesitated. "Yes."

"So you're a Christian then?"

"Not a very good one, Veronica. I have a ways to go on that front."

"Pray. Talk to the Lord about it. He'll work it out."

He nodded. "I know," he said, but I could sense he really didn't believe it. Then he let out one of those interminable exhales of his. "We'd better call it a night," he said.

"Call it a night?"

He stood on his feet. "It's late, and I have a long day tomorrow, and you need your rest, so we'd better both get to bed."

I stood to my feet too. "Bed?" I said, suddenly uncomfortable again.

"Yes, bed. It's what people generally use when they need to get some sleep."

"But I can't. I mean, it won't . . . Gillette—Don, it won't look right for me to stay here."

First he laughed. Then he looked at me. "What?"

"It won't look right."

He stared at me. "You're serious?"

I did feel doll-like at that moment, but what could I say? I meant it. "Yes, I'm serious."

"You mean to tell me you care about that? About what people think?"

"Yes, I care. I have to."

"You're a grown woman, Veronica. You don't have to do anything."

"I have a past to live down, Gillette," I said, deciding that calling him by any first name just didn't feel right, "and a God to glorify. I don't want people confusing what I used to be with what I am now."

"And you actually believe people are that discriminating? Well, I've got news for you, young lady. They aren't. When they place you in a box, there's no getting out of it. You're in it for life, so you can forget that."

"That's still how I feel."

"Well, I don't share your feelings. I don't care how it looks, and I don't care what people think. But until I get a better read on just what this Richard Pargeter is up to, you're staying put."

"But it won't . . ." I began saying, my face filled with concern and anguish.

Gillette exhaled. "Don't worry, Veronica, I'm not going to attack you in the middle of the night."

"That's not what I meant."

"I'm a womanizer. You said so yourself. I have this great harem of females running around my house. Isn't that what that grapevine told you? So since I have more women than I can possibly handle as it is, you'll be perfectly safe with me." He began walking toward the stairs. "Now that that's settled, let's get to bed."

I didn't like his domineering ways, not one bit, but for some crazy reason I did like him. This difficult man was doing something to me that I never dreamed would happen in my lifetime. He was knocking my socks off, making me feel unlike anything I'd ever felt before.

And I liked it. Didn't like his ways, didn't like that temper of his at all, but as I followed him across this massive room and up his winding stairs, amazed that I wasn't insisting upon going my own way, I knew I liked Donald Gillette.

Like everything else in Gillette's home, the guest bedroom was large too, with a king-sized poster bed, an elongated sitting area, and an adjacent bath. *Just beautiful.* "I'd like to meet your designer," I said to him in jest, but he seemed too preoccupied to respond.

"You should have everything you need in here."

"If not, I'll just holler. Where will you be?"

"Down the hall."

Could you be more specific. "Right."

He looked at me. "Good night, Veronica."

"Good night."

He continued looking at me, as if he was looking for a sign. Then he leaned toward me, and my heart began to pound.

He hesitated, probably because of my sudden flinch, but then he kissed me on my lips, and I didn't resist. Then he pulled me to him, encircled me in his big, warm arms, and kissed me passionately, his need almost as ferocious as mine. When the kissing stopped, he held me. For a long time.

But when he removed his arms from me, he seemed almost embarrassed. He rubbed his soft, wavy hair, looking around at everything but me.

"The bath is through those double doors to your left," he said in a now raspy voice, "and there's some fresh shirts in the closet, some fresh linen. Feel free to shower, whatever. Call me if you need anything else," he said, still not looking at me. Then he left.

At first I felt a little frightened. What am I getting myself into? I wondered. I didn't know if this man was serious about his Christianity, let alone if he was even my type.

But I also felt excited. A lot in my life made no sense at all these days, yet for some odd reason my feelings for Gillette did. Made all the sense in the world.

I showered and went to bed thinking, not about what that scum on the Strip tried to do to me, but about those feelings I had for Gillette. Feelings that should have left me more than a little uneasy, more than a little restless. But I wasn't restless at all. I slept well that night.

FOURTEEN

I woke up to the sound of crickets on the lake. For a moment I thought I was dreaming, lying in a soft, warm bed without a care in this world. The more I snuggled deep into the silk comfort of that bed, the dreamier I felt. Until I felt a hand touching me, and my eyes flew open.

I was lying on my back, the bedspread to my waist, and somebody's hand was resting against my side. At first I wasn't sure who could possibly be in my home, especially since I lived alone. Then I thought about Gillette, and the fact that I was in *his* home, and that's when I saw him. He was seated on the edge of the bed, fully dressed in suit and tie, his already sleepy-looking eyes looking drowsily at me.

"Didn't mean to startle you," he said with that crooked, half-smile of his.

"What is it?"

"I wanted to make sure you didn't oversleep."

"Oh no!" I said and quickly sat up. "What time is it?"

"It's early. Not even seven. Settle down."

My heart relaxed from its sudden pounding, and I did manage to lie back down and smile at Gillette, who seemed content this morning, happy with himself, as if our closeness last night didn't do him in as he might have feared, and he was therefore grateful.

I was grateful too. There was something about him that warmed my heart, and the thought of getting to know him better was no longer a burdensome thought, but was becoming an exciting proposition. For him, too, I would guess, especially given the way he kept his hand pressed against me, which, in my wakefulness, even I could appreciate.

But then he began rubbing me. That changed everything. It felt wonderful, too wonderful, but no way was it appropriate.

I turned away from that touch by lying on my side, and he smiled weakly, as if my hint wasn't as subtle as I'd intended, but I could also see a tinge of hurt behind that smile.

"What time did you say it was?" I asked him, to move on from the awkwardness.

"Almost seven. What time do you have to be to work?"

"Ten."

"Plenty of time. Get on up and get dressed. I'll drive you home." He gave me a pat on my hip and stood up, as if that was all he needed to do to get me out of bed.

I had on my underclothes. I wasn't getting out of any bed until he left.

He actually began laughing, however, when he realized it. "Modest?"

"Christian," I said quietly, and the laughter in his eyes began to vanish.

He kept those same eyes trained on me, however, as he began rubbing his forehead and taking on that frowned, stern look he often displayed whenever he seemed to be in deep thought. What he was thinking so deeply about was a mystery to me. Eventually, he left, and only then did I get up.

We arrived at my house less than an hour later, in Gillette's Porsche, his hands changing gears and slinging corners so fast, we probably arrived there in record time. And just as Gillette had promised, my Beamer was parked proudly in the driveway. And it didn't appear any worse for wear either.

He got out of his car and opened the door for me, and then walked with me all the way up on my porch.

I turned around and extended my hand, but he didn't shake it. "Thanks for seeing after me," I said, as if I could possibly be one of those prim and proper sisters who could handle being "seen after."

Even Gillette knew better than that. He didn't buy that act for a second. He took the keys that I was holding in my other hand and began unlocking my door. Which I didn't appreciate at all.

"I got it, Gillette," I said.

"I want to check inside."

"Check inside for what?"

"Stop denying the obvious, Veronica, all right," he said irritably, and walked on into my home. I wasn't sure if he was talking about my feelings for him or the fact that my home had been recently burgled.

I was thankful that I kept a clean house, because Gillette seemed determined to check out every crack and crevice in it. He even looked under my bed, which was amazing to see. Here was this big man on hands and knees making sure no bogeyman was lying in wait for me. I knew he couldn't possibly accord every female in distress this kind of hands-on service, so I felt honored.

But it horrified me too. Gillette wasn't falling in love again. He all but told me that last night when he made it clear that if I messed up again, that was it for our so-called relationship. His interest in me or in any woman, then, could only be of the physical variety, despite my modesty, as he called it, not the deeper, emotional closeness I was beginning to yearn from him.

We made our way back into the living room, and he started wiping off his big hands with his handkerchief.

"All clear, Chief."

He glanced at me. He didn't quite get the joke, and then looked back down at his hands. "You go on to work," he said, spouting orders as if I was one of his cops on the force. "Then go over to Pam's and stay put. I'll pick you up from there later this evening."

"Pick me up? But I'll have my own car. Why would you need to pick me up?"

He looked at me then. "Why do you think, Veronica? I don't know what this boyfriend of yours is up to, and you don't either."

"He's not my boyfriend. And Richard wasn't the one who attacked me in that alley last night, nor was he the one who broke into my home Sunday night."

"You don't know if he was behind it or not."

"He's not like that, Gillette." I know, he told me to call him Donald. It was next to impossible, however, while he was getting on my nerves, which, incidentally, was practically every moment we were together. "And I'm not trying to defend him either, but I just can't see Richard doing something like this."

"Veronica?"

I exhaled. I didn't like the sound of that. "Yes?"

"Just do as you're told for once in your life. Stay at Pam's until I get there."

"If you're so insistent that I stay at your place, why can't I just drive on out there after work and keep Pam out of it?"

He sighed, as if I was just this really dense person. "The idea is that you be alone as little as possible."

"But I'll be alone as soon as you leave here."

"You'll be all right here. I've checked the place out."

"Then check it out again tonight and let me stay here, if that's all it takes."

"Veronica."

"I'm just saying, Gillette. Goodness." Then I exhaled. "I don't like this. I feel like my life is being snatched from me. And I don't like it."

He considered me. "I know how you feel, but there's lots of things we don't like. You'll just have to deal with it."

"You are such a comfort," I said snidely. "Anybody ever tell you that?"

"Look, Veronica, if there's a better way, let me in on it, because I can't find it," he said, frustration in his voice. "Once this is over, you'll have your life back, I promise you. But right now you have to be cautious."

"I don't like depending on people. That never works. People always let you down in the end. But they can only let you down if you let them pick you up. Which is what you're trying to do with all of this 'blanketing me' business."

He began walking toward the door. I halfway expected him to say forget it and keep going, but he turned around and looked at me.

"There's nothing wrong with being independent and standing on your own two feet. I hope you stay that way. But you're taking it too far. You're taking too many unnecessary risks."

"Last night, for instance."

"Yes, last night," he said sharply. "What would have possessed you to go on that Strip, a place like that, nosing around as if you didn't realize where you were? Didn't you know what kind of people hang out in that area? If I ever catch you doing something like that again, I declare I'll . . ."

He exhaled after his little outburst and placed his warm hand on the side of my unruly hair. He stared at that hair and began rubbing it in place, and then he looked at me.

"Speaking of last night," he said. "We took care of it."

I frowned. "Took care of what?" Then I understood. "You mean they caught the scum that cornered me in that alley?"

"Yes," he said, looking at my hair instead of at me.

"Including Left Eye?"

"Including Left Eye."

"But how did you know who they were? Or where they were?"

"I know all of the bad guys in my town, especially one who

wears a patch. Besides, it might have been dark last night, but I caught enough of a glimpse of everyone of those clowns to ID them myself. I tracked them down later."

I shook my head. "You're confusing me, Gillette. When did you do all of this? You were home with me last night."

"Yes, I was. Until you fell asleep." He looked at me. "Then me and my men went and took care of it."

I couldn't help but look perplexed. Talk about never understanding a man. This proved my point entirely. "But if you caught them, doesn't that mean I have to go downtown and pick them out of a lineup or something? Don't I have to identify them to make a case?"

"No," Gillette said firmly, again looking at my hair. "We were able to get him and his boys on other high crimes and misdemeanors without involving you. Your name's staying out of it."

I knew what that meant, that Gillette had probably planted something on those thugs to pad his case. Which was disturbing. Which was exactly what had happened to me once upon a time. But if such a move would keep that scum from hurting some other dumb, unsuspecting female, then I wasn't about to lose any sleep over it. But that still didn't make it right.

"If you're thinking about manufacturing some evidence to protect me, don't even try that. I'm not afraid to identify those jerks."

Gillette exhaled as if I'd just offended his mama. He removed his hand from my hair and with a jerk lifted my chin up to his face. "You think I would do that?" he asked, a frown fixed on his face.

"I said *if* you did it."

"You think I would manufacture evidence, as you call it, just to spare you from identifying a suspect?"

I felt like crap now. I felt like the sister who thought the brother had wanted her, only to find out that he wanted her credit card. "I wasn't sure."

"Don't flatter yourself, Veronica, all right." He then released my chin and began rubbing his forehead, as if I was
driving him crazy. Then he looked at me and actually smiled.
"What am I going to do with you?"

"You can start by loving me, and caring for me, and being
there for me." It was my wish list, my heartfelt, dream-like
wish list, but Gillette didn't have to know that. That was why
I kept the smile plastered on thick. But even with my smiling,
his handsome, already intense face, had taken on a far more
mortified look. "It was a joke, Gillette," I quickly added.

"I'd better get to work," he said in a subdued tone. He
was still frowning, still seemingly perplexed, as he opened the
door of my home and walked outside onto the porch.

I stepped out beside him, my arms folded, my heart still
ramming with the embarrassment of my confession. My smiling hadn't fooled him for a second. He knew I meant it. He
knew I wasn't the type of female to joke about matters of the
heart.

He still seemed bothered by my comment, it seemed to me,
as he placed his hands in his pants pocket and looked up
one end of Elkin Street and then the other. When he looked
across the street at that old familiar apartment complex, he
sighed.

"Stay out of other people's business, Veronica."

Where did that come from? "Other people's business?"

"That's right. Leave it alone. You don't know trouble until you start getting caught up in other people's. And steer
clear of that Richard Pargeter." He looked at me, as if to gauge
some reaction.

I didn't give him the satisfaction.

After a moment he began looking around, once again, at
that apartment complex across the street. "Ever thought of
moving into a better neighborhood?"

"Sure, I thought about it. Then I looked at the prices in

those better neighborhoods and thought again. This is all I can afford. Besides, it's not as bad as it looks."

"Yes, it is."

I half-smiled. "Whatever, Gillette."

Gillette continued looking around my neighborhood, his face frowned with concern.

I frowned too. "I can take care of myself."

"Think so?"

"I know so."

"I can help you out if you want to move."

"Help me out how?"

He hesitated. "Buy you a place."

Buy me a place? So that I could be beholden to him as long as I lived in that place? So he could have certain privileges with me? No way. "No thanks," I quickly said. "I'm all right where I am."

He continued to stare at me, as if he wasn't convinced at all, then he began walking down the steps. "Go to Pam's tonight," he ordered as he went.

"Yes, sir, Chief."

"Very funny."

I smiled. Then it occurred to me what day it was. "Oh, I forgot," I said, and he turned my way again. "I have choir rehearsal tonight."

"Tonight? Can't you get out of it?"

"Of course, I can't get out of it. I'm the choir director. I have to be there."

He looked so distressed by this minor news.

I quickly added, "I'll call you when I'm done, and if you're still insistent on picking me up and carting me around, you can pick me up from there."

He seemed a little upset with my flippancy, but he nodded and walked on toward his car. But when he got into his car, he just sat there staring at me.

At first I thought he was admiring the view, I even smiled at him, but then I realized he was more than likely waiting for me to take my admirable behind indoors. So I did. And he left.

Later, after I'd showered, dressed, done something to that long, thick, wavy hair of mine, and was about to get into my car and take myself to work, I saw that Juno was now outside. He was out on his stoop reading a newspaper. I threw my briefcase and purse in the car and walked across the street to where he sat.

He was trying to act all funny, reading the paper and not giving me a second glance. He was probably still fuming over what happened Sunday, when I almost refused to hold his dope for him, but I eventually took it, so I didn't know what was his problem. Besides, I should have been the one with the attitude, not only about going to jail for his behind, or being stunned senseless when I realized what I was really holding, but because I still wasn't so certain anymore that he wasn't connected to Neka's death, or to any of those close calls I'd been having lately.

But I seriously doubted his involvement. Juno was a thug in many ways, but even thugs had other sides.

"What's up, Juno?" I said as I approached him.

He barely glanced at me. "'S up?" he said with a lilt of his twist-plait head.

"Aren't you going to thank me?"

He looked at me then. "Thank you? Thank you for what?"

"For holding that bag for you. What you think?"

"Oh, that."

"Yeah, that. Crack, Juno? You selling crack?"

"No, I ain't selling no crack. You know me better than that, cuz."

"Don't even play me like that, Juno. Crack was in that bag of weed I thought I was taking off your hands, and you knew it."

"I didn't know nothing. Why would I have crack in a bag of weed, girl?"

"You put it in there when you saw that cop. You knew you were through if he caught you with crack, and you knew I wouldn't have agreed to hold no crack for you."

Juno didn't say anything to that, which was all the confirmation I needed.

"Thanks. But you and me both know that your boy Gillette wasn't about to let his little princess rot in nobody's jail cell."

"His little princess? Man, you crazy."

"Oh, I'm crazy?"

"Yeah, you're crazy if you think that man holds me in some high regard. That is so not true. Trust." I could have added that I'd uncovered evidence just this morning, when I gave my heart to him on a silver platter, and he gave it back.

"So I guess that means you're out on bond, right?"

I frowned. "No, I'm not out on bond."

"Then how you got out? Gillette don't play that about no crack. Everybody knows that. Ain't no way you was gonna be released unless somebody with top authority had you released. I know that game too well, girl. See, I know a brother like Gillette. A nice, young, church-going sister like you, yeah, he'll look out for you for now. He's always on the lookout for fresh meat."

"Maybe he released me because I told on your butt."

Juno smiled, showing his gold teeth. "Not a chance. You don't rat. That's what we like about you. Snitching? That ain't you. I knew that wasn't gonna happen."

Little did he know. If Gillette had said I had to stay in jail and face the music, I would have been singing like a canary on crack, telling on everybody. That was just how certain I knew I could never again do the jail thing.

"So tell me, Roni, what do you see in that guy? I mean, he look good and got a bad ride and living large out there wherever he lives, but he ain't exactly no good, church-going brother."

"He's just a cop investigating a homicide, Juno."

"Yeah, right. Is that why you stayed all night with the joker? I saw him bring you home earlier. What was he investigating all night? You?"

"You know what, believe whatever you wanna believe, okay."

"So I'm lying? Am I lying?"

"Whatever, Juno, all right. Just forget it."

"You the one came over here badgering me."

"I came over here to thank you, I mean, for you to thank me—Oh forget you!"

Juno laughed.

"I really want to ask you about Jeffrey Collins and Willie Barnes."

He hesitated, looking at me. "What about 'em?"

"You knew them, didn't you?"

"What's that to you? Trying to get the four-one-one for your boyfriend?"

"I'm trying to find out what happened to Taneka."

"That's what I don't get about you." He folded his newspaper. "You're a smart girl, supposed to have all this education. You don't even look half-bad, but the dudes you pick."

"What dudes you keep talking about, Juno?"

"But what difference does it make, right, Roni? I mean, Gillette is a high roller, right. Mean green all the way. Since that's apparently what you want."

I rolled my eyes. It was hopeless. But that, of course, didn't stop Juno.

"Think about it. Gillette could buy and sell this whole town twice over. You ever wonder why a brother like that would stick around here? He even left one time and came back. That's crazy. Something's up with that brother. I don't care what you say. Brothers like Gillette don't become cops, they pay off cops, they have cops on their payroll, but they don't become one. Now you ridin' around in his Porsche, staying all night at his big house, or wherever he had you."

Then he added, "And I thought you was a Christian."

"I am a Christian, whether you want to believe it or not. And nothing happened between Gillette and me. He was just helping me out."

"Right."

"He was! But forget you." I frowned. "You collected rent on Neka's place," I said to him in a matter-of-fact tone.

He looked at me. "So."

"So why didn't you tell me, Juno?"

"Tell you? Why I needed to tell you? You ain't no police."

"You told the police then?"

"Girl, you out of your mind! What I look like, telling cops my business? Get out of my face with that *wang!*"

I exhaled. He was definitely not feeling me today. What I'd done to him, except try to keep his behind out of trouble, was beyond me. "What can you tell me about Jeffrey Collins and Willie Barnes?"

"Ask their mama. What you asking me for?"

"You don't have to get nasty, Juno."

"What you mean, nasty? I'm telling you the truth. Ask their mama."

I looked at Juno. He had his Ice Cube look going now. He wasn't joking. "Their mother lives in Melville?"

"Yeah, she live here. What you think?"

Amazingly, that had not even occurred to me. Of course, she would live here. Not every family was nonexistent like mine. "Do you know where she lives?" I asked him.

"You know where Hard Times is?"

"Yes."

"Go to Hard Times and look across the street. That's where she lives."

Taneka's parents owned Hard Times rib joint, and the mother of the man who supposedly killed her lived across the street. Talk about connections. They were beginning to pile up around Taneka.

I thanked Juno and hurried to my car. Although Gillette would have what Pam calls a hissy fit if he knew, on my lunch break I would pay mama a visit. She may not know much, or even want to talk to me, but it wasn't as if I had anything to lose in trying.

After having lunch with Anne, I drove over to the home of a woman I would soon come to know as Elvira Barnes. When I made it across town to the small, brick-front house across the street from Hard Times, a small woman with pure white hair and wrinkled, blotchy skin answered the door. I told her I was trying to find out who might have killed her son Jeffrey, which was partly true, and she let me right into her house that smelled of mothballs and furniture polish.

When we took a seat in the small living room on the plastic-covered antique sofa, she asked if I was with the police. I feared the truth would be the end of her hospitality, but I told it anyway. "No," I said.

"Good," she replied and relaxed even more. "They've been asking me all kinds of questions I can't answer. All sorts of questions. I didn't see Jeff on no regular basis. Not here lately, anyway."

"But y'all used to be close?"

"Oh, yes. Me and both my boys. And neither one was worth sweeping out the door, no, they wasn't. But they didn't deserve what they got."

"Murdered."

"Right."

"What about Jeffrey and Willie? Were they close?"

"Yeah, they were. Real close. They were half-brothers, you see. Different daddies. But it hurt Jeff to his heart when Will got killed. He blamed that girlfriend of Will's."

"Taneka Dupayne."

"Right. Her mama and daddy own that sorry excuse for a restaurant across the street. That's how Will met her. Used to see her around the place, prancing around. This was before she got into them drugs. She was a pretty girl then, real smart. Will had it bad for her."

I remembered *that* Taneka well. Even I wanted to be like her then. "Why did Jeffrey blame her for Willie's death?" I asked Ms. Barnes. "A cop killed Willie."

"He knew that. But she was the one who used to play with Will's mind. Jeff was convinced she pushed Will into robbing that man."

"So he could supply her drug habit?"

"That's what them newspapers been saying, and the chief and all them. But that's not what Jeff was telling me. He didn't think drugs had nothing to do with it."

"He didn't?"

"No, ma'am, he shole didn't. Will was already spending all his money on Neka. She was getting enough drugs to satisfy her craving. Somebody else, maybe more than one, was involved in this. Jeff was certain of it."

"Did he say who? Did he suspect anybody?"

"He never told me no name. Don't even know if he knew himself. But he was sure other folks were involved. He always believed it was some kind of conspiracy, that Neka set Will up to be killed."

"But why would she do something like that?"

"How would I know? When Jeff was telling me all that stuff I was half-listening, I even told him he better leave that kind of talk alone. But he kept on talking it. He was obsessed with it."

"And he never said why?"

"They killed his brother, thanks to Neka. And he was gonna get her for it. He told me that much."

I exhaled. "So you believe the police theory that Jeffrey killed Taneka?"

"I don't know about all that, 'cause that wasn't what he was talking to me about."

"What do you mean?"

"He was talking like he was gonna make her suffer for a long time. Make her life a living hell was the way he used to put it. He never said nothing about no killing her. How she was gonna suffer if she was dead?"

"By the way she died, maybe?"

Ms. Barnes shook her head. "Jeff wouldn't have killed nobody. He got a long record. He been in and out of jail for many things, but he ain't never been accused of murdering or even attempting to murder nobody."

I heard what she was saying, but I also heard what she'd already said.

"You said yourself, Ms. Barnes, that he was obsessed with avenging his brother's death. Maybe that's what made it different. Maybe he wanted to do to Taneka what he felt she did to Willie."

She shook her head again. "My boy didn't kill nobody. Neither one of them."

"But, ma'am, it's an established fact that Willie killed Mason Lerner, the chairman of the board at Harbor House."

"'Cause the police say that's what happened don't establish nothing in my book. Will might have tried to rob that man. My boys were crooks, I'll be the first to tell anybody that, but I just don't believe he killed him."

Was it a mother's denial, or was this mother on to something? I couldn't say. Gillette seemed so convinced that Willie Barnes was the shooter. He said it had been investigated by the police and community groups alike, and I had the impression that there was no question of Willie's guilt. Now his mother was talking something completely different.

I looked at her, but I didn't know what to say to her. My inability to respond, however, apparently exposed my amateur status because Ms. Barnes suddenly became suspicious of me and was ready to give me that old heave-ho.

"Now what newspaper you said you worked for?"

I told Ms. Barnes that I didn't work for any newspaper, but was just a curious citizen, which caused her to promptly ask me to leave. Which I promptly did.

FIFTEEN

I left Ms. Barnes and headed straight for Harbor House. I wanted to see if there could possibly be any connection between that place and Neka. According to Ms. Barnes, Jeffrey believed that Neka had set up Willie in an attempt to help somebody else. Maybe that somebody else had a connection to Harbor House, a facility for ex-cons, and that was why the chairman was chosen as a mark.

Or Maybe Neka was having some sort of relationship with the chairman herself and Willie found out about it, and, in a jealous rage, killed him, never intending to rob him. Maybe that was why Jeffrey blamed her for his brother's death. It wasn't much to go on, but it was all that I had.

As I turned onto the long stretch of Monroe Avenue that led to Jasper Boulevard, the street where the newspapers stated Harbor House was located, I pulled out my cell phone and called Queen Anne's.

Greta answered.

"Hey, Gret. What's up?"

"Trying to get out of here. Where you at?"

"Listen, is Anne there?"

"She's here, but she's with an irate customer. Minnie done messed up some female's head, girl."

"For real?"

"You should see her. Looks like Wolfman Jack's sister. Talkin' about she was tryin' out this new Chicago hairstyle. It was Chicago all right, 'cause it shole looked like that sister had been through some mighty wind when Minnie finished with her."

I shook my head. Reminded myself to talk with Minnie. Again.

"Anyway, what you doing on the road? Aren't you supposed to be at work?"

"Could you tell Anne I'll be in later on? I've got to take care of some business."

"Take care of what business?"

"Just tell her what I said, all right."

"I'll let her know. But she ain't gonna like it." Then she added, "And Gillette won't either, for that matter."

How in the world did Gillette's name find its way into this conversation? "Excuse me?"

"You heard me. Gillette ain't gonna like it. He already called here twice looking for you, and he was highly pissed when I told him you wasn't here. I wonder why."

I wonder too, I thought, especially since last I looked, it was still a free country. What did the man expect? Me to just sit still like some wound-up doll until he came and picked me up? "Just tell Anne what I said." I quickly flipped my cell shut.

I pulled into the parking lot of Harbor House and was surprised to see that it looked more like a large apartment complex than some halfway house. It probably could have housed more than two hundred ex-felons. I parked my car out front and walked around in search of the office. I found it near the back of the complex.

Just as I was about to enter the open door, my cell phone began ringing. I looked at the display. Melville Police Department. I rolled my eyes.

"How did you get this number, Gillette?" I said before he could say a word.

"Where are you?" he barked.

"How did you get this number? I never gave you my cell phone number."

"I'm a cop. You didn't have to give it to me. Now where are you?"

If there was a bossier man than Donald Gillette, I'd hate to meet him. "I'm taking care of business."

"What business?"

"My business, Gillette."

"I thought I told you to stay put."

"You told me a lot of things, but that doesn't mean I have to do what you tell me."

"Veronica."

"What's with you?" I moved away from the office door, in case my voice was rising. "Why did you call my job like that? You know what kind of gossip goes on in beauty shops. People will think—"

"You think I care what people think? You think that nutcase that's gunning for you cares what people think? I can't afford to keep pulling my men off their assignments so they can run behind you."

"I didn't ask you to have anybody running behind me, to begin with. In fact, I told you not to do it, so don't try to act like it was my bright idea when I never wanted it from jump."

Gillette sighed. "Where are you?" he asked me again.

"I told you I had to take care of some business."

"What kind of business?"

"Business, Gillette. It won't take but a few minutes, and then I'll be back at Anne's."

In a way it was wonderful that he could be this concerned about me. But in another way it was a bit disconcerting. Was he so worried about my whereabouts because he knew something I didn't know, and he was frightened for me? Or was he just controlling like this, one of those men who had to know your every move? I couldn't handle anybody trying to handle me, not for a second, and if that was Gillette's bag, he may as well get a new one now.

But then again, I thought, maybe his concern had nothing to do with me. Maybe he was more worried that I would uncover some conspiracy that touched his department, or his men, or maybe even him, and he wanted me to back off. I just couldn't see Gillette as one of those crooked cops I'd come to despise. But given all of this madness around me, I wasn't taking anything for granted.

"Sorry?" I said when I realized he'd asked me another question.

"I said, 'Why don't you just tell me where you are?' What's so difficult about that?"

"It's not difficult, it's just . . . Listen, I appreciate your concern, all right, I really do, but I'll be finished in a few minutes. It's not a big deal."

"I didn't say it was a big deal. I just don't want anything else to happen to you."

"I'm all right. I'm just checking on something."

"Checking on what?"

"Just something, Gillette, all right."

"It's about the Dupayne case, isn't it?"

I didn't respond.

"Is it about the Dupayne case, Veronica?"

I exhaled. "Yes."

"Why can't you let well enough alone? That case is closed. What's the point in dredging it back up?"

"I have some questions that I need answered."

"Still?"

"Still."

"And my answers aren't good enough for you?"

I decided to just tell the truth. "If that's the way you wanna put it."

There was a pause. A long one.

"Just be careful."

"I will."

"We still haven't been able to run down that Pargeter character."

"Okay."

"Which means you still may be a target. You know that, right?"

"Yes, I know it."

"You drive me crazy. You know that too?"

I smiled. "I'm beginning to figure it out."

"How long do you think you'll be?"

"Just long enough to find out what I need to find out, and then I'll head back to Anne's."

"Call me when you make it back. As soon as you make it back. If that's not too much to ask."

"I think I can manage that. Bye, Gillette." I closed my phone before he could make any more demands.

I couldn't help but smile. He drove me crazy, too, but it was a good crazy, a kind of welcomed craziness.

I went into the office. A tall woman with long blonde hair and a quick smile was seated behind the only desk in the small room. She introduced herself as Rachel Fielding, the facility director, and then offered me a seat.

Before I could say a word, she reached behind her and grab-bed a thick folder off a long table and then opened it. "All right," she said. "Now how did you hear about our facility?"

"Newspaper," I said, unsure why she asked.

"And you've been out how long?"

I hesitated. "I don't think you understand," I said, somewhat offended. "I'm not interested in becoming a resident here. I just need some information."

"Oh, I'm sorry," she said with a ready smile. "Most people who walk through that door aren't looking for anything but a place to stay. I guess I've fallen into a routine, which is never wise. I apologize."

"It's okay."

"Now that I've botched that little encounter," she said, smiling even warmer now, "let's start over. As I said, I'm Rachel, the director, and you are?"

"Roni Jarrett. I'm here to find out some information about a friend of mine. A Taneka Dupayne."

She shook her head. "Doesn't ring a bell. Should I know her?"

"She was killed a few weeks ago."

"Sorry to hear that. Really sorry. But I still don't think I know her. She wasn't a resident here."

"I know. I was just trying to find out if she may have had some connection to somebody here."

"Why would you think she would be connected to Harbor House?"

"A few months ago her boyfriend killed Mason Lerner."

"Our chairman? Her boyfriend would be Willie Barnes then?"

"Right."

"Now that was just a terrible, awful shame, and so senseless. It happened right in front of the House. I'll never forget it."

"So you were employed here when it happened?"

"Oh, yes. I was in this very office. Mr. Lerner had just left the office, in fact, and was heading for the parking lot."

"Detective Delvecchio wasn't with him?"

"Not initially, no. He was on the grounds, in the rec room, talking to the residents about avoiding re-arrests, something he did for us on a regular basis. But then he met up with Mr. Lerner in the parking lot. That's when Barnes fired the shot."

"Was there any prior knowledge between Barnes and Mason Lerner that you know of?"

"You mean, was Barnes ever a resident here? No. He was an ex-con with a long sheet, but he never stayed here."

"What about Mason Lerner? Was he married?"

"In other words, could he have had a relationship with Barnes' girlfriend?"

"Right."

"As I said, I didn't know her, but I knew Mason very well, and I can tell you unequivocally that he wouldn't have had that kind of relationship with her or any other young woman. Old either."

How could she be so sure? Then it came to me. "He was homosexual."

"Yes."

"Great."

"Excuse me?"

"No, I mean, that doesn't help my weak little theory any."

"You think your friend's murder was a little too close in time to her boyfriend's, don't you? And that's what's making you think there might be a connection?"

"Right. And since Willie Barnes was killed here, I don't know, it seemed like a logical place to inquire."

"But he was killed by a policeman, by Detective *D*."

"Who just so happened to be here. I don't know, maybe Taneka knew Delvecchio would be here lecturing, and she somehow got Willie to attack Mason Lerner at that time, trying to set him up maybe."

"Set up Willie Barnes?"

"For Delvecchio to shoot him, yeah."

"But why would she want to set up her own boyfriend?"

"That doesn't seem very likely, does it?"

"No, it doesn't. But I know what you mean. Coincidences bother me too. Our chairman before Mason also died under suspicious circumstances."

I looked at her hard. "He did?"

"Oh, yes. Of course, the official word was that he drowned while swimming at his vacation home in Hilton Head, but I never bought that for a second."

"You believe he was murdered?"

"I do. I mean, Myron Bernstein, our chairman before Mason, was an excellent swimmer. I'm talking professional caliber. I believed it even more after Mason was murdered. Two chairmen of the same board die within six months of each other? Come on. That's too much of a coincidence for me to abide."

"Did you go to the police with your suspicions?"

"I went to Detective D. first, since he's one of our best volunteers and just a wonderful advocate for our residents."

"Delvecchio?"

"Oh, yes," she said, as if she was surprised by my shock. "He's a wonderful, caring cop. The best."

So much for my crooked cop antenna, I thought, although Rachel Fielding didn't necessarily have to be right either. I mean, for all I know, the sister could have the hots for Delvecchio and would praise him whether he deserved it or not.

"And what did Delvecchio do? Did he look into it?"

"Not his patch, as he likes to say. But he did get me an audience with his boss."

"With Don Gillette?"

She nodded. "Yep."

"How did that go?"

"It was interesting, to say the least. And a total waste of time."

"Gillette wasn't a believer?"

"I have no idea. He listened, didn't ask any questions, and said thank you."

"That was it?"

"That was it."

"But, surely, he had to see that there was a connection there."

She nodded. "You would think. But all Detective D. said was that Gillette looked into it."

"And?"

"And nothing. Hilton Head authorities are sticking by their story. It was an accidental drowning then, and it's still an accidental drowning in their eyes."

"But in your eyes, no."

"No way. I mean, come on. One chairman drowns accidentally, and then his successor is murdered? All within the span of a six-month period? But it didn't add up to suspicion in their minds. So I gave it up. What could I do anyway? I'm just a center director. But all of these new coincidences with Barnes and his girlfriend certainly make my original line of reasoning intriguing again, if nothing else."

"I'm sayin'."

Rachel nodded. "I mean, first Barnes kills Mason, then Detective D. kills Barnes, but a few months later Barnes' girlfriend turns up dead too?"

"And his brother."

Rachel looked at me. "Willie Barnes brother? He was killed too? Are you serious?"

"I am serious, girl. And I don't know if the answer lies on Willie Barnes' end, or the chairman's end."

"What are the police saying about all of these killings anyway?"

"Nothing anymore. The case is now closed, far as they're concerned, at least the part concerning Taneka. According to them, Barnes' brother killed her because he blamed her for Willie's death."

"Sounds far-fetched to me, but that's Gillette for you. Never met a more stubborn man in my life."

I stood up. "Thanks anyway, Ms. Fielding. I won't keep you any longer."

"Call me Rachel, please," she said, smiling and standing too. "I'm not that old."

"I hear that." I turned to leave. Then, as a thought occurred to me, I turned back. "By the way, has anyone been selected to replace Mason Lerner as chairman yet?"

"Sure has. Only a few days ago, matter of fact. The board went local this time and decided to select a hometown man, a very active member of our community."

"Who?"

"Dr. Alan Simms," she said with a wonderful smile.

I was certain I didn't hear her right. "Alan Simms?"

"Yes. You know him?"

Do I know him? I was stupefied, no other word for it. I think my mouth may have even flown open.

"Are you okay?"

"I'm okay. I'm fine. I just . . . Thank you again for your time."

"You're quite welcome, honey."

Alan was the new chairman of Harbor House? My Alan? It terrified me. Because if Rachel Fielding was right, and the back-to-back deaths of the chairmen weren't coincidental at all, then Alan could also become the new victim as well.

I dismissed choir rehearsal early when I saw Alan about to leave the church. Sister Finch didn't like my early dismissal. Pam would have loved it if she was here, but the others didn't seem to care either way. But sometimes you have to do what you have to do.

Alan had been on my mind ever since I left Harbor House. Just in case there was something weird going on, I had to let him know.

I grabbed my briefcase and purse and hurried out of the sanctuary. Alan was standing on the steps of the church saying good-bye to one of the deacons, his suit hanging like an oversized sack on his thin frame. *Poor man.*

"Alan," I said as I hurried down the steps, "glad I caught you."

"Hello, Sister Jarrett. I thought you and the choir were still at it."

"We just broke up. I wanted to talk to you."

"Oh yeah?" he said, a hopeful lilt to his voice.

"Yeah."

He hesitated, staring at me. "I'll walk you to your car."

As we began to walk, I didn't quite know how to come out and say it.

Alan smiled. "We could discuss it over dinner, if you like," he said, trying once again.

I shook my head. I hated that he was always putting me in a position of turning him down, but there it was. Another rejection. Sometimes I wondered if I was like that old joke, where I wouldn't want to join a club that would have me as a member.

In any event, I told him, "Thanks, but no, thanks," and kept on walking.

"I heard about you and the chief."

I stopped walking. "And what did you hear?"

"That it's getting serious."

I began walking again, with him keeping pace with me. I wasn't going to deny it, but I was still curious. "Where did you hear this?"

"Around, you know. People are talking."

"They should rename this town, I'm telling you, because that's all people seem to want to do around here."

"Just remember what kind of man you're dealing with, Roni. Donald Gillette is not the settling-down kind of man."

"And I'm not the settling-down kind of woman," I said with a weak smile, "so you have nothing to worry about."

"I'm just telling you. From what I've heard, he dates a lot of females—"

"If you heard that from the same folks who act as if they have all of this knowledge about me, then I would strongly advise you to question your source."

"It's old news, Roni."

"That still doesn't make it true."

"Fine," he said as we arrived at my car door and stopped walking. "Defend him if you want."

"I'm not defending him, Alan."

"I'm just letting you know the deal. That's all I'm doing. Gillette has been known to date a lot of women around town, whether you believe it or not, and I would hate for your name to get mixed up with theirs."

I looked at Alan's handsome, concerned face and dropped the attitude. He was only trying to warn my stubborn butt. "Sorry about that. And I feel you. I really do. I understand what you mean. But don't worry. If Gillette does have this harem of women, I won't be in it."

Alan smiled. "That's my girl."

I quickly clicked my lock/alarm and opened my car door. I suddenly felt a mighty need to get away.

Alan placed his hand on my hand. "I thought you had something to talk to me about?"

"Oh, my goodness, I forgot just that fast. You're right, I do. It's about Harbor House."

"Harbor House?"

"Yes. You've been appointed the chairman of their board, haven't you?"

"I have. Why?"

"I'm not sure, Alan, but something's up over there. I think somebody may be killing off the chairmen."

Alan at first was stunned, as if I was having a senior moment or something, and then he smiled. 'You're kidding, right?"

"No, I'm not kidding. Did you know that the chairman you're replacing was murdered?"

"He was the victim of a botched robbery attempt, Roni. It wasn't some planned, calculated murder."

"Nobody knows that for sure. It was just assumed that Willie Barnes was trying to rob that man. But what if he wasn't? What if it was intended to be just what it turned out to be. A cold, calculated murder. And what about Myron Bernstein?"

"Who?"

"The chairman Mason Lerner replaced. He was murdered too. Sort of. Well, officially he drowned at his vacation home, but there are those who don't believe that for a second." I wanted to give Rachel Fielding's name, but I couldn't. Alan, as chairman, was technically her boss, and might not take too kindly to her running her mouth off to an outsider, especially a nosy one like me.

"But the police believed it was an accident."

"Sure they believed it. But come on, Alan. First Bernstein, then Lerner, and who knows if there were others before them."

Alan shook his head. "You aren't making a whole lot of sense, Roni. Two chairmen died, okay, and maybe they both died under suspicious circumstances, maybe, but I don't understand how you leap from that to 'Danger, danger! Will Robinson!'"

"Willie Barnes, the man who killed Mason Lerner, was Taneka Dupayne's boyfriend."

"Ta-who?"

"Taneka. The girl who was found dead in that alley on Hazelhurst?"

"Oh, yes. The one you had spoken with."

"Right."

"She was Willie Barnes' girlfriend?"

"Yes. And then Willie's brother was found murdered."

"I thought the police said the brother killed Tanese—your friend."

"That's what they're saying, yes."

"But you disagree."

"I don't know. Maybe they're right, but maybe they aren't."

"Roni."

"I just want you to be careful, Alan, that's all."

Alan smiled and touched the side of my face with his long, narrow hand. When Gillette did that very same thing to me, I felt as if I was on fire. With Alan, I just felt uncomfortable.

"That's nice of you to be concerned about me, Roni, and I will be careful."

"Thank you," I said, moving away from his touch.

And as soon as I did, I heard a tire squeal and turned to the sound. But it was too late to see anything, because gun-fire erupted, the same *pop-pop* sounds I remembered from that night my house was sprayed.

But now was different. I didn't have the protection of a house, nor the protection of a big desk. I was in the open, wide open, with nothing to shield me.

Then I felt a push. A hard, violent push that took my breath away and knocked me to the ground. Then I heard screams, presumably from choir members who had already come out of the church, as the gunfire seemed rapid and endless. And there was the sound of tires squealing again. Then an eerie silence.

I was so terrified, so shaken with fear, I didn't even look up. I couldn't. I just lay there, as the sounds of screaming recommenced, as the sound of feet running seemed as if they were coming to overtake me.

I covered my head for some reason, as if I was expecting some onslaught, but then I felt hands on me, and the familiar voice of our church deacons.

"Are you all right, Sister Jarrett?" Deacon Wenn asked, grave concern in his voice.

I didn't know if I was all right or not. I began to sit up.

I heard somebody scream, "Doctor Simms!"

That's when I remembered Alan was standing next to me.

"Are you all right, Sister Jarrett?" Deacon Dopson asked. He and Wenn began helping me to my feet.

"Yes, I'm fine. I believe I'm fine. But what about Alan?" I looked behind me and discovered Alan's lifeless body lying face down on the asphalt, blood everywhere. "God, no!"

"Stay calm, Sister Jarrett," another deacon, I couldn't tell who, was saying to me.

"Somebody call nine-one-one," I said feebly.

The church members crowded Alan, crying to Jesus, and looking around as if they expected another drive-by.

I looked at Deacon Dopson. "Somebody needs to call nine-one-one," I said again

Deacon Dopson patted my hand. "We have, Sister," he said, staring at Alan's body. "We have."

"Is he going to be all right?"

"Pray for him."

"But he's been shot!"

"Pray for him, sister," he said again. "Pray for him."

He tried to contain me, but I broke free and pushed my way through to Alan's side. He had indeed been shot, the blood proved that, and when I saw him lying there so help-less, I fell to my knees.

Alan was still breathing, trying to hold on. I could feel it in my bones. Trying with all he had to fight back the darkness, the evil that was overtaking us all.

SIXTEEN

I didn't realize Gillette had been called to the scene until I saw his truck come to a screeching halt in front of the church, and he hurried out. He was in jeans, a winter-white turtleneck, and an unzipped bomber jacket. I was so glad to see him, so relieved, I almost lost all restraint and ran to him.

But I didn't move. I was still so shook up. I wasn't all that certain if I could move even if I wanted to.

Gillette just stood there scanning the scene, looking like a man tired of scenes like this. And his eyes were searching too, because they didn't stop their scan until they locked onto mine. There was a definite change in his look when he saw me, with a kind of fatigued weariness overtaking him, and his broad chest rose and then fell into what seemed like an exhausted exhale.

He started heading my way, his eyes refusing to leave mine. But one of his men intercepted him, literally walked into his path, and began giving him what I could only discern was a blow-by-blow on what went on out here tonight.

I continued sitting immobile there in the chair that had been provided for me and watched as Gillette began to take charge of the scene, barking out orders and looking toward the street, apparently in the direction of where the shooter had taken flight.

I watched him at work, desperately wanting him to remember that I needed him too, but he was too focused on his job to so much as to look my way again.

I looked over at Alan. I knew he was in seriously bad shape, but I looked anyway.

Ever since my church members had pulled me away from him, saying my hysterics were only making it worse, they had tried to staunch the blood before the paramedics could arrive, but he had already lost so much. Now he just lay there, his eyes closed, his body as stiff as the gurney they put him on.

The paramedics were working feverishly on him, doing all they could to stabilize him. When they finally managed to get him to where they were ready to lift him into the ambulance, my mobility returned.

I didn't hesitate. I stood up and hurried for my Beamer, to get ready to follow them.

The cops had already cordoned off my car with crime scene tape, so I had to stoop underneath it to get to my ride. But a hand as hard as steel grabbed me by the arm before I could make my move and pulled me back. It was, of course, Gillette.

"Whoa! Not so fast!" he said, putting his strong arm around my waist.

"I've got to get to the hospital, Gillette," I said anxiously, looking at the ambulance, looking back at him, but he would not let me out of his grasp.

He seemed to feel my pain, because a pained expression crossed his face too. "There's nothing you can do at the hospital tonight, Veronica."

"How bad is he? What did the paramedics say? They wouldn't tell me anything. Did anybody talk to them?"

"It's bad. They seem to think it's really bad. He'll probably be in surgery most of the night."

I turned and looked at Gillette. He looked as grim as I felt. "Surgery?"

"They'll do what they can for him, don't worry."

"You mean he's . . . he might . . ." I suddenly became panicky. "I've got to go to him," I said, trying to pull away. "I've got to make sure he's all right."

"He's in good hands, Veronica," Gillette said, refusing to let me go. "There's nothing you can do for him tonight."

"I can be there for him. I can wait there for him."

"You can wait at home, which is what you're going to do." He looked beyond me, his arm still around me, and yelled, "Vince!"

"What are you doing?"

"He'll take you home."

"I don't need anyone to take me home. It's Alan that's in trouble. I'm okay."

"You're a long way from okay, kiddo."

"But I still don't need anybody taking me anywhere."

Gillette looked down at me. "I heard you the first time," he said, a little annoyed.

"You hollered, Chief?" Delvecchio walked up, staring at Gillette's arm around me, and then at Gillette.

"Any luck with the witnesses?"

"Nothing we can build a case around, if that's what you mean. They all saw it generally, but mainly were getting out of the way. Although a few of them said that Miss Jarrett here was with Simms when the shooting started and would have seen more than they saw." His big head bobbed my way. "We need to get a statement from her."

"Not tonight," Gillette said, to his everloving credit.

Delvecchio sighed. "Her memory is fresh right now, Chief."

"I understand that. Did anybody see the shooter?"

"You mean other than her?"

"I didn't see anything," I said, offended. "I was just trying to stay alive too. If it wasn't for Alan pushing me to the ground, I might not have succeeded."

Gillette looked at me hard. "He pushed you down?"

"As soon as the shooting started. He saved my life."

Gillette hesitated, and then grasped me tighter after I said that, as if I was imparting some heavy news he hadn't even thought about before.

Delvecchio kept on talking. "If we can't talk to her, we got nothing. Nobody saw the shooter. The car was too dark, they said."

"Any make on the car?"

"Old-looking, maybe a Chevy, maybe a Pontiac, maybe a Ford. We got all three versions. But whatever make it was, it did have tinted windows, and it was dark in color. That's all we got."

"Terrific."

"You said it," Delvecchio echoed.

"The car that nearly ran me over in front of Hard Times was an old Pontiac. And the guys who broke into my home, they left in a Pontiac. Why don't you put an APB, or whatever it's called, out on an older-model Pontiac with dark, tinted windows?"

"We already have, Chief Jarrett," Gillette said sarcastically and then looked back at Delvecchio. "Was anybody else hit?" he asked him.

"No, sir, thank God. Just Simms. Want me to get a couple men over to the hospital?"

"Yeah, I guess we can put somebody out there, although I don't think Simms is what this was about."

"I know what you're saying. And what about all of these church members?"

"Let 'em go, but make sure we can get in touch with every one if we need to."

"Sure thing. Anything else?"

"No, that's it. Wrap it up."

"I'm on it," Delvecchio said, glancing at me again, and then heading back toward the crowd of choir members and police officers.

I folded my arms. As soon as I did, Gillette removed his bomber jacket and placed it across my shoulders. He didn't wrap me in his arms again, but in a way this gesture of giving me the coat off his back was even more telling. Although what it told, I hadn't quite figured out.

"We were talking about it," I said to him.

"Talking about what, honey?"

That word of endearment touched me mightily for some reason, but I kept going. "We were talking about Harbor House. Alan's the new board chairman. I was just telling him how I thought the chairmen were being targeted and he could be a victim too."

Gillette frowned and looked at me. "Chairmen targeted? What are you talking about?"

"Rachel Fielding told me—"

"Rachel? When did you talk with her?"

"Today. Earlier. That's when she told me about Myron Bernstein."

"Veronica, I thought I told you to stay out of our investigation."

"I'm not in it. I was just trying to understand what's going on. That's why I went over there. I didn't even know about that other chairman until she told me about him."

"There was nothing to know about him. He drowned, according to the police, the coroner, and anybody else who's looked at the case. Except, of course, you and Rachel Fielding, neither of whom has looked at anything, both of whom leap to conclusions as if they know everything."

"Why would a trained swimmer drown like that, Gillette?"

"A trained swimmer wouldn't. But a drunk trained swimmer would."

"Drunk?"

"Yes, Veronica. That's what looking into the case entails. You get the full story, the toxicology reports, the works. Not just the Rachel Fielding version."

"But still, Gillette, who's to say somebody didn't pour liquor down the man to where he passed out, and then they shoved him in the pool or whatever he drowned in?"

"Who's to say they did?"

"The coincidence of it says so. It's too much of a coincidence. First Myron Bernstein drowns, then Mason Lerner is killed, and now Alan's been shot. Three chairmen, three accidents?"

"Don't be ridiculous, Veronica. How can you even try to equate the three? One drowned, one was murdered, and one may very well just happened to have been in the wrong place at the wrong time."

"Alan?"

Gillette exhaled, a worried look on his face. "Yes."

"Why would you say that?"

"Because it's a fact. That shooter could have been gunning for you," he said with a frown. "And it probably had nothing to do with the Taneka Dupayne case."

"But why would somebody be after me?"

"Heard from your ex lately?"

"Not Richard again."

"Yes, Richard again."

"I told you he doesn't swing like this. All of this hit-and-run stuff, this ain't his thing."

"Who else could it be, Veronica? Tell me that. Pargeter hits town, tries to hit on you, and you turn him down cold. After that, somebody nearly runs you over. Then he warns you that you could meet with the same fate as Dupayne if you don't change your mind. After that somebody breaks into your house."

"You're wasting your time on that theory, Gillette. Richard is a player, not a killer. He's into that psychological warfare, not the physical stuff."

"People evolve."

"Not like that, they don't."

"You know, okay."

"I know Richard."

"Yeah, you know him. You know a lot of things. Let's go."
He took me by the arm and began moving toward his truck.

I pulled away. "I can drive."

"Your car is part of this crime scene. When my people finish, I'll have somebody bring it to you."

"But what about Alan? I've got to get to the hospital."

"You can see Alan tomorrow. Right now you're going home. With me."

"No," I said with a frown.

"Veronica."

"No. I'm tired of this, Gillette. I'm going home to my own bed, and if whoever it is doesn't like it, then he can come and see me there."

I sounded far more confident than I felt, but I meant every word. God is my protector, not Donald Gillette. He didn't like it; his displeasure was all over his face. He knew he had no choice in the matter. He didn't say another word, which was fine by me, but he did take me home.

Gillette's truck pulled into my driveway, and I thanked him quickly and got out. My plan was to say good night, send him on his way, and then catch a cab to the hospital.

He got out of his truck and walked with me to my front door.

I still tried to play the game. "Thanks," I said with a smile I didn't feel. I handed him his jacket and unlocked my door. But when I moved to walk inside, he began following me.

"Just hold on, all right," I said, poking him in the chest and backing him up. "What do you think you're doing?"

"You won't come to my house, so I'll just have to stay at yours. At least for the time being."

"But I don't want my neighbors to see where some man's truck stayed all night at my house, Gillette. I told you these people run their mouths around here."

"Then fine. I'll call one of my men to come and pick it up."

"Pick what up?"

"My truck."

"Gillette! That's not the point."

"Look, this is the fourth time somebody has tried to do you harm. Until I figure out who, what, and why, I'm sticking around."

"I wasn't the target tonight."

"You don't know that."

"Why would somebody want to harm me? It doesn't make sense."

"There have been two unusual events in your life here lately: your friend Taneka was murdered, and your ex-boyfriend Richard Pargeter has decided to pay you a visit. Since the evidence seems to rule out any Taneka connection, my money's on Pargeter. You talk about coincidences. He shows up and all hell breaks loose in your life. Yet you see no connection whatsoever. But this far-fetched story you and Rachel Fielding have concocted about the chairmen of Harbor House's board being targeted is loaded with connections, let you tell it."

"If you knew Richard, you'd rule him out too. Shooting at people and trying to run people over with a car isn't his bag, I'm telling you. It's psychological for Richard. He'll play with your mind."

"And attempting to kill you over and over doesn't play with your mind? Come on. I'm staying, Veronica."

I didn't like it, but what could I do about it? It wasn't as if I was bursting with confidence right now. I stepped aside and let him in.

Gillette did what was becoming his routine of checking throughout my house before he returned to the living room and finally settled down in a chair.

I was already settled down, too tired and confused to even care what he was doing. I was sitting on the sofa, my legs underneath me, my head tilted back against the headrest, but I could see him.

He crossed his legs, and then looked at me.

"What?" I asked, in no mood for his staring routine tonight.

"Go to bed."

"I'm fine."

"No, you aren't. Go to bed."

"Gillette?"

He hesitated. "What?"

"Stop ordering me around."

He exhaled. "Stop calling me Gillette."

"Stop calling me Veronica."

"That's your name."

"But that's not what people call me."

He considered me. "You care an awful lot about people, don't you?"

"What does that have to do with your ordering me around?"

"Nothing. You brought it up." He said this with a wave of the hand. "Go to bed, Veronica. Get you some rest."

"I'm fine."

"Would you tell me if you wasn't?"

"Alan!" I said and grabbed for the phone.

"What?"

"I forgot about Alan! What kind of friend am I?"

"A tired one."

I called 4-1-1, got the number to the local hospital, and called the main number.

"I'm calling to check on my friend," I said anxiously into the phone. "Alan Simms. He was brought in tonight with a gunshot wound." *Or wounds.* I didn't even know. All I saw was blood.

But the woman on the other line didn't care, asking me if I was a relative.

"I'm a member of his church," I said. "He's our auxiliary president."

"We can only release information to relatives of the patient, ma'am."

"But I was with him," I said. "I've got to know if he's all right. You can at least tell me if he's all right, if he's still alive."

Gillette suddenly appeared at my side and removed the phone from my ear. He sat down on the sofa beside me, his bulk and familiar sweet scent causing me to want to cozy up against him.

"This is Chief Gillette," he said forcefully into the phone. "Who am I speaking with?"

And that was all it took. Gillette asked for information, and he got it. Plenty of it, by the way the conversation went. Then he hung up the phone.

"What did she say? Is he all right?"

"He's in surgery. And will be for some time."

I exhaled. "Did she say how he was doing? How bad it looked?"

"She's a desk clerk, Veronica. What is she going to know about the severity of a gunshot wound? I told her to have Kayla phone me when she's done."

"Kayla? Who's Kayla?"

"She's the surgeon."

"Oh! But you didn't leave your number. How is she going to phone you? She might think you're at the station. Or at home."

"She knows my cell number."

"The surgeon?"

"Yes."

I frowned. "Why would the surgeon know your cell number?"

Gillette hesitated. "She's a friend of mine," he said and then looked at me.

It didn't take a rocket scientist to know what that meant. "Gotcha."

And then the silence came, where even the ticking of the clock sounded deafening. We sat side by side on my sofa, both buried in our own thoughts, for what seemed like an eternally long time.

Finally, Gillette touched my hand. "Go on to bed, Veronica. You aren't helping Alan like this, and you're definitely not helping yourself."

"I'm okay."

"No, you aren't. Go to bed."

After hesitating, I gave in. I was too exhausted to put up a fight. "You'll awake me as soon as your—as soon as the doctor phones you?"

"Yes."

"I mean it, Gillette. I won't forgive you if you wait until morning."

He smiled. "I'll awake you," he said.

And he did, nearly five hours later.

I was in a deep sleep. I could feel him shaking me but was still unable to respond to it. All I knew was that I was being shaken.

When I was just about ready to resign myself to the turbulence, I began to hear his voice, and then slowly I began to understand the words he spoke.

I opened my eyes. He was seated on the side of my bed staring at me, his hand resting on my shoulder, and he appeared to be scolding me.

"You'll sleep through a hurricane."

"What?" I yawned.

"I should have let you sleep."

"Then why didn't you?"

"Perhaps I'm a man who wants your forgiveness."

I frowned. "What?" Then I understood and became fully awake. And bolted upright.

"She called?"

"Settle down, Veronica."

"What did she say? How is he?"

"He's fine. He's a very blessed young man. The bullet did penetrate through his chest."

I gasped.

"But it missed his heart. The doctor expects a full recovery."

"Thank you, Jesus!" I threw my arms around Gillette. "Isn't it great?" I said, my face now buried into his shoulder. "This is the best news!"

I didn't realize Gillette had his arms around me too until I felt him pulling my body closer to him. He lifted my chin up to his face and stared into my eyes.

I suddenly felt so unnerved. "I'm so glad you woke me up to tell me, Gillette."

"Me too," he said, his voice now lowered, his eyes now hooded.

He began kissing me. On the side of my face, my neck, my chest.

When he began unbuttoning the long shirt I was sleeping in, I tried to pull away from him then, but he tightened his grip.

"We can't, Gillette."

"It's all right, Veronica," he said in an even huskier voice, and tried to continue kissing me.

"No, it's not all right," I said, pulling away from him.

"And why not?" he asked, an edge of frustration in his voice.

"Because I'm a Christian, Gillette. Why you think? I'm trying to be pleasing in the eyes of the Lord. I'm trying to live my life that way. And you and I both know that letting you grope all over me ain't pleasing in nobody's eyes but Satan's."

He seemed disturbed by my words I could tell. He looked at my disheveled clothing and then at my flustered face, and then he stood up from my bed.

"Gillette," I said, feeling strange, feeling as if we at least needed to talk about it.

He let out a harsh exhale. "You've had a tough night, Veronica. I apologize for taking advantage of that."

I frowned. "You weren't taking advantage of anything."

"Go back to sleep," he said softly, as if he just knew I had no idea what he was taking advantage of. "I'll see you in the morning."

SEVENTEEN

He didn't see me in the morning. He was already gone by the time I woke up. My car, however, was parked in my driveway as he'd promised, making me focus more on getting to the hospital to see about Alan than worrying about Gillette and his many moods.

But they wouldn't let me see him. He was in recovery, the nurse said, and no visitors were allowed. I did ask to speak with Kayla (I didn't know the woman's last name), explaining that she was the surgeon who operated on Alan, and was told to wait.

I waited in a small room near the nurses' station. A tall, bosomy woman who appeared to be in her late thirties, a beauty with big brown eyes and jet-black skin, came into the room. Immediately I could see her with Gillette. He seemed to go for the voluptuous types, if she and Liz Steward were any indication, maybe even the full-figure types, which I was not. Although she was still in scrubs and looked exhausted, her beauty could not be denied.

"Ms. Jarrett?" she asked as she approached me. She took the stethoscope that was in her hand and flung it around her neck.

"Yes," I said, rising, feeling dwarfed, compared to the tall doctor.

"I'm Dr. Caldwell. How can I help you?"

"I'm here about Alan. Alan Simms. I understand you're the surgeon who operated on him."

"And you are?"

"Veronica Jarrett."

"We've established that," she said with an unfriendly smile. "I mean, are you related to him in any way?"

"Oh! Well, no. I'm a member of his church. The music director. And I'm his friend."

"As I'm sure you're aware, I'm not allowed to divulge any information about a patient's well-being outside of family members."

"I understand. I just need to know if he's okay."

"He's in recovery."

"They told me that, but I'm trying to find out if he's going to be all right."

She considered me. Then she pulled up the sleeves on her scrub coat and folded her arms. "If there are no infections or any other complications I don't foresee at this present time then, yes, he should make a full recovery."

I exhaled. "Thank God."

"Yes."

"Can I see him?"

She quickly shook her head. "Not right now, you can't. Maybe later. But, again, only if there are no complications."

"Oh, thank you, doctor. Thank you so much."

She smiled weakly but did not immediately walk away, as I had fully expected her to.

She, in fact, was staring at me.

"Is there something you aren't telling me, doctor? "About Alan?"

She said suddenly, "You know Gillette, don't you?"

I started to deny all. For some reason I felt as if I was on the spot here. But I couldn't lie. "Yes," I said.

She nodded, still staring, a sadness sweeping over her pretty face. "He told me about you."

That stunned me. "Did he?"

"Don't be modest. It's unbecoming. You know you love it."

I didn't care for the way she put that at all. Why would I love the fact that Gillette mentioned me to one of his females? But as I looked into the eyes of this beautiful, successful doctor, and saw the envy there, the insecurity, the hurt, I dropped all pretenses.

"What exactly did he say about me?" I asked her, attempting to smile off her little comment.

"He said you were young."

I waited for her to tell me more. When she didn't, I frowned. "And that's all?"

"He said you're impulsive; that you're too daring for your own good; that you get on his last nerve every time he spends more than two minutes with you."

I screwed up my face. That didn't exactly sound like words of endearment to me.

"And," she added hesitantly, "he said that he wish he'd never met you."

The doctor and I exchanged awkward glances when she said that. We both knew there was nothing harsh about her words. Given Gillette's background it was obvious he did not want to be drawn to me. But apparently, just as it was for me, it wasn't something he could help.

"Now that we know what he thinks of me," I said, deciding to play it off, "what does he think about you?"

She looked at me as if I already knew the answer to that riddle and was toying with her.

"Clearly not enough," she said, not with flippancy, but with regret. She turned and was about to walk out of the sterile room.

To our shock, Gillette was walking in.

"Hey," she said, regaining her composure, smiling a smile so grand, I wondered how she could find the strength to surface it.

"Hey," Gillette said, looking past her to me. "How are you, Kay?"

"Good. You?"

"I'm good."

"I didn't expect to see you here this morning."

"Thought I'd come by and see how Simms was doing. I was told I could find you in here."

"He's still in recovery," she said, as professional as she had originally been with me. "Barring any complications, he should be okay."

Gillette nodded and again glanced my way. "That's . . . a blessing."

"Considering what could have happened, I'd say it's a miracle."

Gillette looked at her and exhaled. "Yes."

Then silence ensued. It was only then that he looked at me without glancing and then looking away. "Hello, Veronica."

"Hi."

"I see you've met Kayla."

"Yes. She was very helpful."

There was a hesitancy in Gillette. "Was she?"

"Yes. Very."

He nodded.

"Well," Kayla said, removing her stethoscope from around her neck, "I'm late for a consultation, so I'd better get going. Miss Jarrett—" She nodded toward me, and then, without looking at him as she left, added, "See you around, Gillette."

When she left, Gillette put his hands in his pant pockets and moved over by me. I folded my arms.

"Feel better?" he asked me.

"Much," I said. "In fact all. Looks like Alan's going to pull through."

"Yes. Thank God."

"Thank God."

"So," he said, "what did Kayla tell you?"

"No more than what she said to you, that if there's no complications—"

"I mean, did she discuss anything else with you?"

"She seemed to imply that she has a relationship with you," I said, fishing myself, "if that's what you mean."

"She implied that, did she?"

"She did."

He said nothing to that.

"Well? Is it true?"

"She's a friend of mine, I told you that."

"What kind of friend?"

"A friend."

"In other words, none of my business."

I told Gillette I had better get to work and I hurried away from him. I should have known better all along. I'd been warned by everybody and their mamas to steer my heart clear of this man.

By the time I made it to work, Queen Anne's was all abuzz about what happened last night at Zion Hope. Greta, who was giving a customer a thick cornrow, was talking as if she'd been right there, spouting out all kinds of false information, while Ernest, who hadn't been there either, was agreeing with every word.

Let them tell it, Alan was gunned down by some jealous husband who thought he was having an affair with his wife. I tried to set them straight, since I happened to have witnessed the whole thing, but they all but told me, as Gillette had all but told me not an hour earlier, to mind my own business. So I did and went into my office, leaving them to bask in the shame of all of their tall tales.

By the time I made it back up front to check the status of our station-to-station supplies, the talk had changed to national politics. *What a relief.*

Greta noticed I was at her station, bending down to see the

amount of supplies she still had underneath her counter. She smiled, staring at me.

"What?"

"You know what, don't even trick that," she said. "Who branded you?"

I almost rolled my eyes. What was she talking about now? "Who branded me?" I asked with a frown. I said it so loudly, Ernest looked too. "What on earth are you talking about?"

"Your neck, college girl. Don't act like you don't know. Don't act like you didn't see all that this morning."

"See all what?"

"She's talking about your bloodsucker, Roni," Ernest said, trying not to smile.

"My what?"

"Don't pay her no attention. She's just trying to push your buttons."

"But what's a blood sucker? What do you mean?"

"Passion marks," Greta said.

Ernest couldn't help but laugh.

"Passion marks?"

"Hickies. They all over your neck, girl," Ernest said.

"As if she didn't know."

I didn't know, although it should not have come as a surprise to me, given how me and Gillette had carried on this morning, but I wasn't about to get into that with them. I, in fact, was about to go and check it out for myself when the front door clanged and I saw Richard, of all people, standing in the salon.

I also saw Greta nudge Ernest, and Ernest immediately stepped from behind his stylist's chair and began hurrying toward the front to offer his assistance.

I cut him off at the pass. "I got it, Ern," I said as I moved toward the front counter.

Greta smiled. "She got it, Ern," I heard her tease. "A good-looking man, she got that."

"What are you doing here?"

He removed his shades and, as was always his way, smiled. "Is that how you greet your customers, ma'am?"

"What do you want, Richard?"

"What do you think I want? I want you. You got a problem with that?" Then he lowered his voice. "In front of all of your coworkers here."

"Where were you last night?"

"What?"

"Where were you around eight o'clock last night?"

"Why you wanna know that? What happened?"

"As if you don't know."

"What have I done this time? First, you accuse me of offing your little crackhead friend, then you accuse me of shooting up your house. Now what?"

"Not in here, Roni," I heard a voice say.

I looked around and saw Anne coming out of the break room. The salon had gone pin-drop quiet, and all eyes were on Richard and me.

Anne shook her head. "Take it outside."

I grabbed Richard by the arm and took him outside. Before I could get out of the door, I heard Ernest say, "Does Gillette know?" And laughter followed his little remark.

Greta added, "And I thought she was a Christian."

More laughter followed.

I let go of his arm as soon as we stepped outside.

He, of course, smiled. "Been a long time since I felt your touch, girl. Felt good."

I folded my arms. I wasn't in any kind of a mood for his brand of humor.

Then his smile left. "I see you been busy," he said, looking at my chest. "Dang, girl! Who's the dude? Don't tell me it's Mr. Porsche."

"Why are you in Melville, Richard? And don't tell me because you're so in love with me. I know your butt. You don't perform selfless acts. Now give and give it straight."

"I'm here for my health."

"Yeah, right."

"I miss you, Roni."

"You're hopeless, you know that?"

"Well, I do."

"You're a suspect."

That got his attention. That annoying smile of his even left his face. "A suspect in what? I didn't kill that girl."

Although I didn't say that he did kill Taneka, and I didn't mean to imply that he did, I ran with it anyway. "The cops don't know what you did or didn't do."

"I wasn't even in town when that girl got iced."

"Brother like you got connections. Who's to say you didn't hire somebody to do your dirty work? I wouldn't put it past you."

"Girl, you crazy."

"Especially since you seem to know so much about her, and how, in your words, the same fate would visit me if I didn't cooperate with your butt."

"You told the cops that? Are you out of your mind, Roni?"

"You threatened me, Richard."

"I was just playing with you, girl. You know I wasn't gonna hurt you."

"The same way you didn't hurt me when you got me fired from my job in Jersey?"

He shook his head. "I can't believe you're still on that."

"Just don't try to act like you're some reformed angel all of a sudden who treated me all angelic, because we both know better than that."

"How could you tell those cops I threatened you, Roni? Now they may try to pin some murder rap on me. I'll be dog-gone, girl. How could you do this to me?"

"Why are you in Melville, Richard?"

"What that got to do—"

"It's got everything to do with it! I've been telling the cops that you aren't capable of harming a flea, let me tell it. But I'll change my tune faster than that Corvette of yours can change lanes, if you don't cut the bullcrap and tell me what's going on."

He looked cornered, as if he finally understood that I wasn't playing his sick games anymore. He shook his head, and exhaled, but he didn't say anything.

"I'm serious, Richard."

He frowned. "All right, but not here."

"What do you mean, not here? I'm not going anywhere with you."

"Just up the way, Roni, dang. Just so we can talk privately."

"Forget it, Richard. Say what you got to say."

He looked around as people walked past continually, some even just hanging around nearby. Even I had to admit that our location wasn't the best place for a conversation like the one we were probably about to have.

He looked at me. "I can't talk about it here. Let's just walk."

I resisted even that.

"Please, Roni. You'll be out in the open. I can't hurt you out in the open."

He could certainly hurt my reputation, however, I thought. But since it was probably already damaged beyond repair, thanks to the all-knowing, know-nothing Gretas of this world, I hollered inside to Anne that I was taking a break, rolled my eyes at that giggling Greta, and began walking with Richard along the sidewalk up Bay Street.

Just as I was about to tell him to get on with it, he said, "Okay, I know you don't think my coming to town has anything to do with you. But it does, Roni."

I started to turn around right then and there, but Richard grabbed me by the arm.

"Just hear me out, all right. After that, if you still don't want to have anything to do with me, then fine. I'll leave you alone, I promise you. You'll never see me again." A pained expression crossed his face.

I snatched from his grasp, but decided to hear him out.

He looked around again, as if he wasn't at all satisfied with the busy location. Then he gestured for me to follow him to the side of the strip mall concrete block building, to a narrow passageway between the building and a supermarket, but I ignored his gesture. This was as far as I was going with him.

When he still wouldn't get on with it, I looked at my wrist, as if I had a watch on it. "You have five minutes."

"Okay." Then he took a deep breath. "I'm in trouble, Roni."

"What kind of trouble?"

"I bought a club in Miami."

"Another strip joint you mean."

"It's a legitimate club, Roni. My biggest one yet. But I got into some trouble with these guys."

"What guys?"

"Some guys, all right. Some boys from Jersey. They fronted some cash for me. We had an agreement, but you know how the boys can be. They broke the deal."

"The boys? You mean *Mafia*? Richard, I know you wasn't that crazy."

"We had a deal, but they said they wanted their money back, and they want it, with their brand of interest, right away. The club is just getting off the ground, Roni. It hasn't been open a month. And they already putting all of this pressure on me."

"What does any of this have to do with me?"

"I told you I need you. You was the best, Roni. If you could do it again . . ."

I frowned. "Do what again?"

"Deal. Run the backroom for me."

"Are you crazy?" I couldn't help but yell. "You must be out of your pea-brain mind!"

"You can make a lot of money, Roni. Way more than you been making playing a piano at some church or doing hair in some beauty shop."

I was about to read the brother real good, tell him what he could do with that kind of money, when I heard squealing tires, the same sound I had heard when Alan got shot, when I was nearly run over in front of Hard Times.

I froze in place, terrified that it was happening again.

"What the heck!" Richard said as if he couldn't believe his eyes.

I allowed myself to look too. The big wheels of a big F-150 jumped the curb and crossed the sidewalk, nearly blocking us in. It looked weird as all get-out, but when I realized it was Gillette, my pounding heart began to ease.

Gillette jumped from his truck looking as if he was ready for a fight, and his expression became even harsher when he made his way in front of Richard. He wore one of his Italian suits with the matching derby hat, although it was obvious he wasn't about to let his wardrobe deter his intent.

"Gillette," I said, terrified by his look.

He ignored me as he grabbed Richard by his collar and slung him into that same passageway Richard had tried to persuade me to enter.

"We were just talking, Gillette!" I said frantically as I hurried behind them.

Gillette slung Richard against the wall. "Talk to me!" he yelled. "You want to talk so much! Talk to me!"

"Who are you?" Richard yelled back. "Some jive-behind cop, what I figure. And you got the hots for her too, don't you?"

"Richard!"

"What are you doing in my town?" Gillette asked him, his arm pushed into Richard's throat, his hat sitting back off his head.

"I didn't know you owned a town."

"What are you doing here? I'm not asking you again."

"I came to see my girl."

Gillette slammed him so hard against the side of that building, I had to cringe.

"Okay!" Richard screamed, the pain searing his face. "I
need help. That's why I'm here. Roni's help."

"What kind of help?"

"Help, man. Help."

"When did you get in town?"

"That Sunday when she was at her house with you."

"And before then?"

"Wasn't no before then. I had to be in Miami that Monday
morning. I stopped in town to talk to Roni first."

"About what? Pargeter, don't play games with me!"

Two uniformed officers appeared in the passageway, one of
them with his weapon drawn.

"Everything okay, Chief?" he said as they hurried toward
us.

"Put that gun away," I said to the officer, as I wasn't at all
interested in becoming a victim of some accidental police
shooting. "Gillette!" I yelled. "Tell this fool to put that gun
away!"

Gillette finally looked at his officers. "Holster it," he ordered, and the jerk did as he was told.

"You okay, sir?" the other cop asked.

"Wonderful," Gillette said, looking at Richard again. "Isn't
that right, Pargeter? Now you heard me. What's your business
with Veronica?"

"It's my business."

Gillette slammed him harder against the wall.

"I wanna talk to her, okay. That's all I want."

"You phoned her the night Taneka Dupayne was murdered."

"So? I didn't know no Taneka Dupayne. I didn't even know she was dead until I started nosing around the hood asking about Roni. Some of the girls mentioned that this crackhead had been killed and that she and Roni were tight. And I didn't find that out until that same Sunday I got in town. Roni wasn't home the first time I went by her crib, so I started asking who Roni hung with, junk like that. That's all I did."

"You threatened her."

"I was just playing around, man, just talking smack. Roni knows I wouldn't hurt her like that."

"So your story is that you came to town on Sunday, and on Monday you drove to Miami?"

"I had to be in Miami that Monday morning. I drove down that Sunday night."

"When did you get back in town?"

"Today. Just now."

"Try last night. Around eight. You saw Alan Simms chatting it up with your girl, as you call her, and you tried to take him out."

"Who's Alan Simms? What are you talking about, man? I was still in Miami last night."

"I ought to haul you in on attempted murder, Pargeter."

Richard began to panic. "I was still in Miami last night, man. Check it out. I wasn't released till early this morning."

"Released?" I said before I realized it. The idea of Richard in jail, somehow, didn't sound right.

"Some dude got in my face, one of my so-called business partners, and they arrested us both." He looked at me. "That's why I need you, Roni. Those boys don't be playing. That was just a warning. I need you to come back with me."

All eyes seemed to be on me, as if I was actually considering his wish. "No way, Richard."

"Heard that, Pargeter?" Gillette said.

"Roni—"

"No. I'm sorry about your situation. I really am, but I'm

not getting back with you. Not ever. Not after how you treated me, what you did to me. I can't. I won't."

A flash of hatred crossed Richard's face. "So it's like that,
huh?"

"That's right."

"Brother can't be forgiven?"

"I *have* forgiven you."

"Sure, you have."

"I have. But I won't forget what you did."

"Girl, get a life. And keep your forgiveness. Keep it. And
who knows, when I find the right property to purchase in this
'Hoboken town' and I open up me a club here, I might even
consider making you my featured stripper."

I would have decked him myself if I was close enough, but
Gillette held me back. He looked at his two officers. "Cuff
him, frisk him, and haul his"—Gillette glanced at me—"tail
downtown."

"But I didn't do anything!" Richard yelled as the trigger-
happy cop began cuffing him.

"If his jail story checks out, escort him out of my town."

"Yes, sir, Chief," Trigger-happy said.

Trigger-happy, along with the other cop, pulled Richard
out of the passageway.

Richard looked back at me as he moved with their pull.
"I'm gonna remember this, Roni."

"Remember it!" Gillette stepped in front of me. "I want
you to remember this!"

"Let's go!" Trigger-happy slung Richard out of the passageway.

Gillette, with his back straight and his hands on his hips,
stood with his back to me for longer than I expected. Then he
finally looked my way, his handsome face more pained than
lacking in strength.

"You okay?"

"Yeah," I said, trying to lighten his impossibly heavy mood. "I'm okay."

"Can you answer a question for me?"

I folded my arms. *Here goes.* "Yes."

"Why, in the name of simple, basic common sense, would you have even thought to go anywhere with a clown like that?"

"He wanted to talk with me."

"And that's all it takes? He wants to talk, so you gladly oblige him?"

"It wasn't like that, Gillette."

"You know what, Veronica, just . . ." He paused for a long time, and then he moved his hat back in its upright position on his head. Stared at me as if he just couldn't fathom me anymore. "Did he harm you in any way, did he?"

"No," I said, wanting desperately to further explain myself. But from the look on his face, now wasn't the time. "He didn't do anything to me."

He nodded, his tired eyes looking at my neck first and then at me. This was not his day, those eyes seemed to say, and I was the number one reason. Especially after our little bedroom scene earlier this morning that got out of hand. And I still had the marks to prove it.

He sighed yet again, looked down at my neck again, and then reached out his hand to me. "Let's get you back to the salon," he said, and I gladly took his hand and followed him.

EIGHTEEN

Alan was in a private recovery room on the fourth floor of Melville Memorial. Deacon Montgomery, who had been seated at Alan's bedside, stood up when I walked into the room, and Sister Finch, who had been roaming all over the place, sat down.

I was so glad to see Alan awake and seemingly alert, I refused to let that woman bother me. I hurried to his bedside.

"You all right, Sister Jarrett?" Deacon Montgomery asked as I walked over. I guess the look on my face said it all.

"I'm fine, Deac. How's Alan?"

"Blessed and highly favored, that's how he is. The doctors say he's gonna pull through just fine."

"Stop talking about me as if I'm not here," Alan said in a voice so low and raspy, it was barely discernible.

"How you doing?" I asked him.

"Great," he said. "Can't you tell?"

"You're still above ground and able to talk about it, so I think you look wonderful."

"I feel like a truck decided to park on my chest," he said just above a whisper.

I squeezed his hand. "Thank God you can feel anything at all after how you looked last night. How long have you been awake?"

Alan looked at Deacon Montgomery. Deac shrugged and said, "He's been in and out, a few minutes at a time. He's still pretty doped up."

"Painkillers," Alan said.

"And they aren't really working," I said.

He nodded, or at least attempted to. "Correct." He cleared his throat.

"Have a seat, Sister Jarrett," Deac offered. "You don't look so good yourself."

"Thanks a lot, Deac."

He smiled. "You look tired is what I mean."

"I know." I sat down on the chair by Alan's bed.

"Long day at the salon?" Alan asked in his raspy, low drone.

"Very. That's why I couldn't get over here sooner. All kinds of requisition orders came in one behind the other. I had been bugging suppliers all last week about their late deliveries and then *bam*. Everybody shows up, on top of our normal flow of customers. It was a madhouse."

"Like that half-price hairdo day," Alan said.

I laughed. "Not quite that bad."

"At least it's something familiar to you. Nothing like this."

I looked at all of the tubes attached to his chest and arm, at the obvious pain he had to be in, and my heart squeezed in agony itself. He was helping me, and looked what happened to him.

"If it wasn't for you pushing me to the ground, it would probably have been me lying there." Another lump in my throat. "Thank you," I was finally able to say.

"Thank God," Alan said. "He's the Savior, not me." Then he looked at me. "Did I hurt you when I pushed you down?"

I smiled, and then laughed. That was my Alan. "Of course not, Alan. You didn't hurt me at all. You even shoved like a gentleman."

Alan had to smile on that one. "Good."

"I hear they caught the shooter," Deacon Montgomery said.

I looked at him. "They what? When, Deac?"

"When, Finch?" Deac turned toward Sister Finch.

She harrumphed a little, but she responded, "Sometime earlier today, all I know. They say Chief Gillette almost put the man in the hospital."

"What you say?"

"Put him in the hospital?" I asked. Gillette was a lot of things, but he wasn't like that.

"That's what they said. They said he was kickin' the man like he was a dog. Beat him down. Beat him to a pulp."

Deac shook his own bulldog head. "That's a shame before God. Don Gillette sometimes act like he's above the law around here, the way he carries on. And the mayor and city council sit right back and let him do his thing."

"What the mayor gon' do? He's scared of Gillette same as everybody else. Just because he used to own some nightclub and got a piece of money. Now I ain't saying those aren't bad men he be arresting, don't get me wrong, but still, he ain't got no call to nearly hospitalize folks just because they ain't living right. From what I hear, he ain't either."

"Amen to that, Sister," Deacon Montgomery said.

"Who did they arrest?" I asked.

"Some boy from out of town. Name of Randy or Rodney or something like that. Drives one of them fancy sports cars. You know him," Finch added. "You know him well. Least, that's what I heard."

"Are you talking about Richard?"

"That's the one. Richard somebody."

"They didn't arrest Richard for that shooting. They're just holding him long enough to check out his story. Then he'll be released."

"You sure, Roni?" Alan asked.

I nodded my head. "Yes, I'm sure. I was there when it all went down. That's why I can't understand why they don't have a cop outside your door right now. They don't know who did this to you yet."

"Maybe they know more than you think," Deac said.

"I doubt that," I said. "Did anybody let Gillette know that no one's here?"

"'Course we let him know," Finch said. "But he don't think Dr. Simms was the target." She looked at me.

"He doesn't know that for sure," I said, rightly, and for once in my life, Sister Finch agreed with me.

She added, "If you ask me, he just don't like Dr. Simms."

"Oh, Finch," Deac said.

"He don't! And we all know why too."

Both Finch and Deac glanced at me, but I ignored them. I, instead, looked at Alan. "Is there anything I can get for you?" I asked him.

He smiled. "You're too good to me, Roni."

I smiled at him and touched his arm. "I still say you look fabulous."

"Yeah, I look terrific."

"I'm just so sorry it happened. One minute I'm telling you about those chairmen at Harbor House, the next minute you're shot down, fighting for your life."

"Harbor House?" Sister Finch asked. "What Harbor House got to do with this?"

"I'm chair—" Alan began coughing.

"He's chairman of the board of Harbor House," I said for him.

"Chairman of the board of a battered women's shelter?" Finch asked. "Why would they pick a man to be the chairman of the board of a women's shelter?"

"Oh, Finch," Deac said, "that place ain't been no women's shelter for a good while now."

"Women's shelter?" I said, surprised.

"It ain't no women's shelter?" Finch asked.

"No," Deac said. "Where you been?"

"I been right here in Melville. Where you think I been?" Then she collected herself. "What did they turn it into?"

"Some kind of halfway house for ex-offenders."

"Ex-offenders?" Finch said. "You mean convicts?"

"Ex-convicts, yeah."

"Well, I do declare. I had no idea."

"Wait a minute," I said, my mind racing. "Harbor House used to be a shelter for battered women?"

"Yeah," Alan said, looking at me. "For many years before they changed it over. Why, Roni?"

"A shelter for battered women?" I said more to myself than to anyone in particular, my mind in overdrive now.

I couldn't stop considering the possibilities. I'd always suspected Taneka was connected to that place, to Harbor House. What if she had been a battered woman once upon a time who sought refuge there? What if her abuser found out about it and wanted revenge? But if that was the case, why would he start killing the chairmen after it was no longer a shelter, and why kill Neka at all? And so long after she'd been out of that place? What kind of revenge was that? I didn't know, but I knew I had to find out just what was going on.

I stood up quickly, told Alan that I'd be back to see him later, and took off. He tried to call me back, and the others wanted to know what was wrong with me too, but I didn't wait around to tell them. All of this craziness might very well be all about revenge, just as Gillette had said. Not a brother's revenge, but a man's revenge, a brutal, domineering, petty man, who could have simply abhorred the idea of anybody else giving his woman shelter.

I hurried down the hospital halls toward the elevator.

I was within blocks of Harbor House when I first heard the sirens. I assumed automatically that it was an emergency vehicle seeking to rush past my Beamer in search of some car wreck or other disaster.

I realized how wrong I was when I looked in my rearview and saw Gillette's big truck coming up behind me, a siren sitting on his dashboard and blaring at me. I couldn't believe it. I started to ignore it, wondering who could he possibly have watching my every move like this anyway that he could find me at will? That was disturbing to me. That was a little too much for me.

He started blowing his truck horn when I wouldn't pull over, gesturing for me to get over now.

I got over, and he pulled behind me and got out of his truck. He walked around to the passenger door of my car, got in, and sat down. That irked me too.

"I don't appreciate being followed all the time, Gillette."

"Where are you going?" he asked me, staring forward rather than at me.

"How do you find out my every move like this?"

"Where are you going, Veronica?"

"None of your business."

He looked at me this time with a look that was withering.

I exhaled. *That man!* "Harbor House," I said.

"Why?"

"Because I want to check on something."

"On what?"

"Gillette . . ."

"On what?"

"On Taneka's connection, all right."

He frowned the way he always did when information didn't jive with his reality. "What connection?"

"That's what I'm going to check out. Harbor House used to be a battered women's shelter. Did you know that?"

"So?"

"So? I think Taneka might have been a resident there before." He stared at me longer then looked forward.

He was dressed casual for him, in a blazer, jeans, and a

baseball cap, but his serious look hadn't mellowed. "You need to leave this alone, Veronica," he warned.

"I can't leave it alone."

"Why not?" he asked, looking at me again.

"Because it affects me. Because I promised Neka. She told me to not let them get away with it and I can't."

"You don't even know who *they* are."

"But I've got to find out."

"Stay out of this, Veronica."

Why was he so insistent on me staying out of it? Was it just concern, or did he know something? "I can't," I finally said. "And I'm not going to."

Our eyes met when I said that. Then he looked away.

"Drive," he ordered.

"Excuse me?"

"Let's go."

"Let's go? Where do you think you're going? I don't need you there with me."

"Yeah, right. Just drive the car."

"But what about your truck?"

"Let me worry about my truck. Just drive the car."

I exhaled, even shook my head. Who did he think he was? But I got back into traffic and drove the car.

At Harbor House, Rachel Fielding wasn't nearly as cooperative as she had been when I last visited her. It was Gillette. She stiffened up, became formal, spoke about HIPPA rules and confidentiality, and went on and on as if he'd arrest her if she even thought about cooperating with me.

Gillette stood near the door, his hands in his pockets, his face staring, not at me for a change, but at Rachel. Which didn't help.

"I know what you're saying, Miss Fielding," I said. "And

I'm not here just to pry. But I believe the answer to what happened to your chairman and to Alan Simms is here at Harbor House. You yourself told me you didn't believe in all of these coincidences. Well, Alan makes chairman number three that's met with some sort of tragic event, one behind the other. What more proof could you want now?"

Rachel glanced at Gillette then looked at me. "I could lose my job."

"For helping us find out who tried to kill the chairman of the board? Come on, Miss Fielding, what's up with that?"

"I would prefer a warrant."

Gillette pushed away from the wall he'd been leaning against and walked toward Fielding's desk. "It's okay, Rach," he said. "Go on and tell her what she wants to know."

"This isn't your call, Chief. We have our own rules and regulations here."

Gillette let out a sigh that told her in no uncertain terms what he thought about her rules and regulations. "Tell her what she wants to know," he repeated.

Rachel sat straight back. She didn't care for Gillette, and it was obvious, but she understood his authority. She glanced at me, glanced back at him. Then she went to a back room in the office.

Gillette sat in the chair next to mine.

"Was that necessary?" I asked him.

"It's getting results, isn't it?"

"She wants to help. You didn't have to push her around."

"Who's pushing? I don't have all day for this wild-goose chase of yours."

"Then why don't you go on about your busy day? I didn't ask you to follow me."

"I didn't say you did."

"Then why are you here?"

"Because you're here."

I rolled my eyes. "You are so . . ."

He looked at me. "I'm so what?"

I searched for the word. When I found it, I felt triumphant. "Difficult."

"And you're not? Ha!"

"I don't know what good this is going to do," Rachel said as she returned from the back room carrying a thick file. She sat back down and went through it. "Dwayne, you said?" she asked me.

"Dupayne," I said. "Taneka Dupayne."

She searched and searched some more. Then, to my relief, she nodded, looking surprised. "Yes, she was here, actually, when this place was still a woman's shelter. Off and on, she seems to have been a regular here."

"That means she was definitely the victim of abuse then?"

"Definitely. She was here before the changeover." She continued flipping through the file. Then she looked up at me. "I remembered it."

"It?"

"Yes. An awful scandal. I didn't remember Taneka's name, though."

"What scandal?" Gillette asked, surprised.

"It was all in-house. It never made the papers or anything, no police were involved, but I remember it. She was the one who got caught up in the drug exchange."

I looked at Gillette. He was staring at Rachel.

"What drug exchange?"

Rachel exhaled. "During the time when Myron Bernstein was chairman, when Harbor House was still a battered women's shelter, we had a director here that was badly mismanaging the facility. The checks and balances of today were not in place then, and since Myron and all of the board really were very hands-off, the director, his name was Jody Loman, was a loose cannon, doing whatever suited him."

"You knew about it?" Gillette asked her.

"Oh, no. I was in the crisis center then, not in the residential facility, so I had no idea, at least not until after the scandal broke."

"Rachel, what scandal are you talking about?" Gillette asked.

"Jody, Mr. Loman, would supply residents with drugs in exchange for sexual favors."

"Gave them drugs?" I said. "Battered women?"

"Yes."

"But why would he?"

"He played on their vulnerability," Gillette said. "Was this Loman the only person getting these favors from the residents?"

"And certain members of his staff, yes. He was fired, of course, but the board became increasingly concerned about the liability. That's what led to the changeover."

"It changed over from battered women's shelter to a facility for ex-cons?" I asked.

"Right."

"How would that help their liability?"

"Ex-cons can take care of themselves. That vulnerability factor," she said, looking at Gillette, acknowledging his earlier point, "is usually not there. Not the way it is with abused women, anyway."

"And this scandal was just swept under a rug?"

"You can say that, yeah. Nobody was aware of it, anyway. At least nobody outside of the circle here. And it certainly wasn't something we intended to broadcast."

"It was illegal," Gillette pointed out. "It should have been broadcast."

"I just worked here. I didn't make the decisions."

"Was Taneka a problem resident while she was here, Miss Fielding?" I asked her.

She looked through the file. "No," she said, still reviewing the file. "Not at all, according to the notes. She was one of our better residents."

"So her drug addiction wasn't a problem here?"

While Rachel reviewed the notes again, Gillette and I exchanged glances.

Then Rachel began shaking her head. "According to this, Taneka Dupayne didn't have a drug addiction problem initially. She apparently called herself falling for one of the staff here, one of Jody's people, and he began supplying her. That, according to what I'm reading here, is how she became hooked."

Me and Gillette looked at each other. Gillette leaned back and let out a harsh exhale. Then I looked at Rachel, to make certain I had heard her correctly. "Are you saying, are you telling us that Taneka was not on drugs when she first came to Harbor House?"

Rachel nodded. "That's what I'm saying. She apparently was a good kid who just happened to have gotten hooked up with the wrong man, and unfortunately at that time, the wrong facility."

I was heartbroken by this news. To think that Taneka came here for help and ended up being abused even worse was devastating to hear. But I would bet the farm that that's the motive. Somebody, Taneka's father or uncle or even her abusive boyfriend, became angry about what Harbor House had done to her and sought revenge, going after the head man in some sort of twisted play on the belief that if they cut off the head of an organism, the rest of the body will die.

Willie might have been that crazed, abusive boyfriend who decided to kill the first two chairmen, and Jeffrey, learning of Neka's involvement before Willie died, might have killed her too, to avenge his brother's death.

But who tried to kill Alan last night, since both Willie and Jeffrey were dead? That was the question to me.

Before I could ask it, Gillette asked Rachel, "Who did Taneka name as her abusive boyfriend? Was it Barnes?"

Rachel looked through the file pages, her eyes determined now. "No, matter of fact it wasn't. The name we have here is Luther Montgomery," she said, looking up.

My eyes shot up at her. "What did you say?"

She seemed surprised by my response. "Miss Dupayne listed her abusive boyfriend as Luther Montgomery."

Luther Montgomery? Deacon Montgomery? Then, as if a light bulb had just clicked on, I thought about what Neka had said to me in my living room the night she died. *"You're a church going lady, Roni. You're the only one I know can promise me. Promise me, Roni. Promise me you won't let them get away with it."*

I always wondered why she would have mentioned that I was a churchgoing lady. Was it because going to church meant that I would be more trustworthy? Or did she call me a churchgoing lady because the man she feared, her tormentor, was a churchgoing man?

And he went to *my* church.

I jumped to my feet, suddenly putting in place that last piece that had puzzled the daylights out of me.

"What is it?" Gillette asked, standing too.

"It's him," I said, almost too stunned to breathe.

"Who's him?"

"It's him. He goes to my church."

"Luther Montgomery attends your church?"

"He's our head deacon."

"What?"

"And he's at the hospital with Alan, Gillette." As if that oral pronouncement woke me up, I began running for the door. "He's at the hospital right now!"

I couldn't move fast enough. The only reason I knew Gillette was running behind me at all was because I heard him talking on his cell phone, yelling for some squad cars to get to

Memorial. He probably told them why, and what to do when they got there, but I was too terrified to hear him.

We arrived too late. The entire fourth floor of Memorial, where Alan's room was located, had already been cordoned off and was now swarming with cops. Gillette wouldn't even allow me to go beyond the nurses' station at the front of the hall, right near the elevators.

"Maybe I can talk to him," I said.

Gillette looked at me as if I'd just insulted him. "You will stay right here, Veronica," he said firmly. He moved away from me and then hurried toward Delvecchio, who was hurrying toward him. Other detectives began to surround the two men, while the uniforms stayed near Alan's room, awaiting further instruction, I assumed.

"He's about as loony as a caged hyena, Chief," Delvecchio said.

Gillette folded his big, muscular arms and pushed his baseball cap off of his forehead. "What went down?"

"Couple uniforms got here first, but as soon as they tried to open the door of Simms' hospital room, that idiot inside starts shooting."

"Shooting?" I yelled and hurried toward Gillette and Delvecchio.

A plainclothes man, however, put an arm out to stop my sudden progress and to keep me just out of the reach of Gillette. "Not so fast, lady," he said to me as Gillette was asking Delvecchio if anybody was hit.

"Not out here. Inside, we don't know. The shooter says he'll fire another round if we come any closer."

I looked at Gillette anxiously. He had to get in there, to get Alan. Gillette, however, seemed deep in thought, almost too calm. "Is there anybody else in the room besides the patient?"

"Unfortunately, yeah, there's a woman. A Bernadette Finch. And get this, boss, the shooter is a member of Simms' church and Finch is the choir director."

Was *the choir director*, I wanted to say.

"It's personal," Gillette said.

Delvecchio shook his head. "It's personal. And that ain't the topper. You ain't gonna believe this one."

"Try me."

"Mister Nut Brain, or whatever his name, says he'll talk to no one, he'll negotiate with no one, except Veronica Jarrett."

NINETEEN

"Veronica?" Gillette asked, his voice unable to hide his shock.

"That's what the man is demanding," Delvecchio said, as me and Gillette stared at him in disbelief. "And he wants her in there with him, and he wants her in there now."

Gillette exhaled bitterly then looked at me as if I somehow orchestrated this whole thing.

"He's not being reasonable at all, Chief. He says he's shooting everybody in sight if we don't get Jarrett in there. He wants it his way or no way."

"Tough," Gillette suddenly said, as if looking at me made up his mind. He began moving away, toward Alan's room, the men that had been surrounding him now following him as if he were a movie star and they were the paparazzi. "Nobody gives a darn what he wants!"

"Gillette, wait a minute," I said, to try and get him to remember that Alan was in that room too, but he kept walking away. I tried to follow him then, but a uniform this time, who had been guarding the elevator, suddenly grabbed me and held me back.

"Don!" I yelled.

He turned around and glared at me, as if I was a burden he didn't need at this particular moment, but then he told Delvecchio to hold on and walked back toward me. The uniformed officer backed off then.

"What is it?" he asked with a frown on his face, as if he already knew what I was about to suggest.

"Let me talk to him."

"Forget it," he said and began moving away again.

I touched his arm just enough to get him to stop and turn around again. "You heard Delvecchio. He said he'll shoot those people if I didn't talk to him."

"I'm not about," he said way too loudly, then, realizing that his men were watching, grabbed me by the arm and pulled me further aside. "I'm not about to let you go anywhere near that room!" he said, this time lower.

"But you have to, Gillette. Those innocent people can die if we don't do what he says."

"We don't know if they haven't already died, for one thing. We don't know what's going on. And I'm not sending another hostage in there for that nutcase to harm, you understand me?"

"But Gillette—"

"I said, do you understand me?"

"But—"

"Veronica!" he said through clenched teeth this time, daring me by the modulation of his voice alone to make another sound. But my heart was pounding and I couldn't remain silent the way he wanted. Alan Simms was too good a man, a man of God, for me to sit back and remain silent.

"He'll kill Alan if we don't do something," I said.

He swiftly took me by the arm again and was about to head to the elevators, as if he was throwing me out of the hospital completely.

Delvecchio, God bless him, intervened. "He will, you know," he said as he approached us, and Gillette looked at him. "He's sick, Chief."

"Have we confirmed that Simms is still alive?"

"No, but—"

"What if he's not? What if that choir director isn't, either? But we send her in anyway?"

"We get confirmation first, Chief," Delvecchio said.

I began nodding my head. He was, by far, the more reasonable of the senior cops here today, as Gillette didn't seem to be thinking this thing through at all. He just didn't want me in there period, regardless of whether or not it was the best way to proceed.

"Maybe she can calm him down, at least long enough for us to come up with a workable plan, Chief. That fool in that room, he ain't playing."

Gillette exhaled angrily again, his hand gripping my arm in a painful squeeze. "She's not going in there."

"Look, boss, this is me, all right. This Vince. I know you care about her, but—"

Gillette frowned. "Don't you dare come at me that way," he said to his detective. "You think I'll sacrifice two innocent people who just might still be alive, because of feelings you've decided I have for somebody? You know me better than that."

"But if she can just talk to him—"

"I said no. Now how many times do I have to say it? He wants to kill her. That's what this is about, make no mistake about it. And there's no way that's going to happen." He began moving me toward the elevators.

I looked back at Delvecchio, who threw up his hands in frustration, and began hurrying back toward Alan's room.

"Gillette, please," I pleaded as he pulled me along. "I can help."

"No."

"I can buy you some time."

"No."

"But why?"

"Why do you think?"

"Because you're being possessive and stubborn. That's what I think."

As soon as I said it, a gunshot fired. I turned around hastily just as those cops began frantically scrambling to get away from Alan's room door, one knocking over a hospital cart in his haste.

Gillette and Delvecchio, however, stooped down as they drew their weapons and began running toward Alan's room. I began moving in that direction too.

"I'll blow her brains out, Gillette. I mean it!" I heard Deacon Montgomery's voice even from where I was, and it was frightening. "I want Sister Jarrett in here, and I want her now!"

"You can talk to me, Montgomery!" Gillette yelled as he motioned angrily with his gun for his cowardly fleeing men to start coming back toward the room. "Is everybody all right in there?"

"I want Roni, and I want her now!" he yelled again and then fired yet another shot, causing Gillette's men to run for cover again.

"Okay!" Gillette yelled to Deac.

Delvecchio, sensing, as I was, that Deac's patience was all but out, started running down the hall toward me, motioning wildly for me to hurry to him. I broke from my sudden paralysis and hurried to him, an officer right on my tail.

Gillette, however, was still trying to calm Deac down. "We're trying to find Jarrett now," he yelled. "You've got to give us time!"

"I've given you all the time I'm giving you. If I don't see Roni's face in two minutes, I'm dropping bodies, Gillette. I ain't playing with y'all!"

It was now Devecchio's turn to grab me by the arm and hoist me forward, toward Gillette.

"What you need her for, Montgomery?" Gillette asked. "You have hostages already."

"She understood," Deac said as Delvecchio pushed me past Gillette, positioning me, no doubt, to make a quick appearance in the doorway of Alan's hospital room.

Gillette pulled me back and protectively placed his arm around my waist. He looked at Delvecchio with contempt. "She understood what?" he asked Deac.

"She understood the light in Neka, and she cared for her. She was the only one who cared."

"But you killed Taneka, Montgomery," Gillette said. "Why didn't *you* care?"

"I didn't kill her," Deac said in a hoarse way, his voice breaking. "How can you say . . . I could never . . . " Then, just when it seemed Gillette had hit a chord, Deac's voice changed again. "If I don't see Veronica Jarrett in one minute," he screamed, "you'll have to bring body bags up in here!"

Gillette looked at me and if anguish could be described, it was all over his face. I felt suddenly sorry for him. He seemed to absolutely hate the position I was being placed in, but he knew, like I knew, that Luther Montgomery wasn't playing.

"I've got to do it, Gillette."

"She's got to." Delvecchio seemed a little too eager to get me in that room, but he was right. There was no other way.

Gillette reluctantly began to loosen his grip on my waist. When he removed his arm, however, and I was hurrying away, he took my hand and gently pulled me back. Then he yelled into Alan's room, "Miss Jarrett's coming in, but you've got to assure us that the hostages are still alive."

"They're still here! For now."

"You've got to show us, Montgomery. Send the lady out."

"I ain't sending nobody out!"

"One for one, Montgomery. We're giving you Miss Jarrett. Give us the lady."

"No! Send Roni in here, or I'll give them all to you right now—in fifty pieces!"

"Now is the time, Chief!" Delvecchio rightly demanded.

Gillette still wouldn't let go of my hand. He looked at me, his beautiful hazel eyes now stunned. "Stay near the door," he ordered, "and if you so much as suspect he has other ideas in mind than thanking you for being sweet to his girlfriend, which I'm certain he—" He exhaled. "You get the heck out of there if you suspect anything, Veronica. You hear me?"

I nodded. "I understand."

"Don't you dare play hero on me."

"Heroine," I said in an attempt at levity.

Gillette wasn't amused.

"I won't try to be the hero, Gillette, okay. I just want to make sure Alan's all right."

His look changed when I said Alan's name so lovingly, and that was exactly why I had done it. His death grip on my hand finally relinquished and I prayed silently as I hurried toward the room.

Before I marched on in, I felt a sudden urge to announce my arrival, remembering vividly how easily Deac enjoyed discharging his weapon. "It's me, Deacon Montgomery," I yelled.

"Roni?"

"Yes, sir. I'm getting ready to come in."

"I'll shoot Bernadette if you try something funny!"

On an ordinary day anybody threatening to shoot Sister Finch would have been a comforting thought, but this was no ordinary day. If Luther Montgomery was behind any of the violence that had occurred here lately, this man was dangerous beyond anything I could even imagine. I wasn't about to take him lightly. I said a silent prayer again, for all of us, exhaled to regain control of the butterflies in my stomach, and opened the door of the room.

Alan was still in bed, looking helpless and terrified, and Deacon Montgomery was standing beside him, behind Sister Finch, his revolver to her head. She was literally shaking with fear, looking worse than Alan, while Deac was sweating, looking evil and crazy and unlike anyone resembling the kindhearted man I thought I knew. *What drove him to this?* I wondered. *Taneka? Love? It hardly seemed possible.*

"Close the door all the way!" he yelled, pressing the gun harder against Finch's temple.

"I will, Deac," I said, "but you gotta let Sister Finch go."

"I ain't lettin' nobody go!"

"You'll have me and Alan. She'll only be in the way."

"I can take care of that right now. I ain't got to let her go to get her out of the way."

This man was crazy, I could see it in his eyes. "Deac, please," I said, "no more bloodshed. Let's talk this out. But please let her go, Deac, please."

Sister Finch seemed oddly touched by my plea, and even Deacon Montgomery acted as if he was moved.

As soon as Montgomery released his arm from around Sister Finch, he hurried to Alan and placed his arm around his neck, his gun now pressed firmly against Alan's face.

Sister Finch looked back as she was hurrying out, and to her credit, she looked worried, but she kept on going. When the door slammed shut behind her, I could hear her scream, "Don't shoot!" to the overeager cops in the hall and was then, by the sound of it, rustled away.

I exhaled and looked at Deac. "Why don't you let Alan go too, Deac. Look at him. What good is he to you?"

"He's one of them. He ain't going nowhere. They ruined my baby's life, and he's one of them. Now he's got to pay."

"But, Luther—Can I call you Luther, Deac?"

"Call me whatever you wanna call me. Nothing never stopped you before. You and Dr. Simms the only folks that calls me Deac. I let y'all. I let y'all do a lot of things. I let you get away with a lot of disrespect."

"Okay, Deacon Montgomery, let's just try and figure this out. I don't understand what's going on here. You said Alan was one of them. Who are 'them,' and what did they do to you?"

"They ruined my baby. How many times I got to tell you

that? My Neka. They destroyed her. She was fine till she went
to them."

"Went to who?" Alan said, barely above a whisper. His
voice was growing weaker, and so was the look on his face.

"Harbor House, that's who! You know who. You one of
them now. You knew it all along. She was fine till she went to
y'all. Now look what's happened. Look what's happened!" He
pressed the gun firmer against Alan's head.

I nearly panicked, as I started toward them, but Deac's look
terrified me. I stayed where I was.

"They ruined her, didn't they, Deac?" I said to him, attempting to get his mind off that gun, at least momentarily.

He began nodding his head. "Neka wasn't on drugs or anything else when she went to Harbor House. But what I don't
understand is, why was she there, Deac? That was a place for
abused women then. Who was abusing her?"

"Nobody was abusing her! We got into a little argument,
that's all. A little shoving match. She didn't need to go to no
place like that. But she didn't think she needed me no more.
Called me an old man, said she was just using me anyhow.
I knew she was just talking. She loved me, but she was listening to the wrong people, you see. I didn't know it at the
time, but I figured it out. Willie was my friend, somebody I
threw jobs to every now and again. I even hired him to follow
Neka around, make sure she didn't get into any trouble while
I was working and running my business. I own a couple convenience stores around town. You didn't even know that, did
you, Roni? You never asked. You never cared about nobody
but yourself, did you, Roni? Just like Willie."

"Willie Barnes?"

"Yeah, Willie Barnes. Who you think? That's how come I
knew Neka had went to that place. Willie told me. I tried to
get her out. With all I had, I tried. But they wouldn't even
admit that she was there. Said they'd call the police on me if I

showed my face around their establishment again. But I knew she was there. I already knew that. So I waited.

"I knew she'd come back to me. I knew Neka, see. They didn't know her. She didn't belong to them, she belonged to me! She would come back to me. And, sure enough, she did. She got out of that place and came running back to me, but it was already too late. She was already hooked on them there drugs. Because of that place."

"That's why you hired Willie to kill Mason Lerner, isn't it, Deac? Because of what they'd done to Neka?"

"It wasn't like that. It was Myron Bernstein first. He was in charge when they ruined my Neka. So I had to get rid of him first."

"But the police said Myron Bernstein drowned. They made that clear."

"He drowned, all right. With help."

"You paid Willie Barnes to do it?"

"Are you crazy? What man like Myron Bernstein gonna let some joker like Willie Barnes come anywhere near him? No, I took care of that man myself. It was my pleasure too. He was in charge when they ruined Neka. He knew me from my civic work, see. We even served on the mayor's civil rights commission together once upon a time. He knew me. Gladly invited me in, offered me a drink. I drank with him too. I drank with him all right. Then did what I had to do."

"But why didn't it end there, Deac? They got rid of Harbor House as a women's shelter after that scandal that destroyed Neka. They turned it into a place for ex-offenders."

"That wasn't because of Neka! That was because they knew no woman in her right mind was going to go to a place like that no more, unless, of course, she wanted to get hooked on drugs. They had to change it to keep that government money coming in. There's big money in running places like that. That's what you don't know, Roni. That's what you don't understand. Who better than ex-cons to move up in there? They'll stay anywhere. That's why they did it. They thought they'd change the membership, and everything would be forgotten. But, no. Never. I was gonna keep reminding them about what they did to Neka. Every time I looked into her face, a face that used to look so beautiful, a face that started looking like a ghost of herself, I knew I had to keep reminding them."

"And that's why you hired Willie to take care of the next chairman?"

"That's right. And it worked out perfectly. It was pure luck that that cop was there. Willie was a hustler, a crook. Everybody knew that. Naturally they'd blame his death on an attempted robbery. He was a brother with a gun. What else was he doing? Assassinating somebody? They don't see brothers doing that. Just like they wouldn't even dream of thinking of me as drowning somebody. That's just the way it is."

"Was that the end of it?" I asked him.

He frowned. "The end of what? Ain't no end to this! What you think this is? A game? Willie's brother, that fool, Jeffrey Collins, killed my baby. Left her dead in that alley like she was a dog in the street! Ain't no end to this. I had to take him out. What you think?"

"So you killed Jeffrey Collins?"

"When he admitted to me that he was the one that killed my Neka, you better believe I killed him. But that wasn't it. That wasn't near 'bout it. It was you. You was supposed to be first, Roni."

"Me?"

"She came to you. That's what everybody was saying. They said she came to you for help, and you wouldn't help her."

"That's not true, Deac."

"Shut up!" he yelled.

This thing was beginning to spiral even more out of control. I could feel it.

"She came to you, and you didn't do right by her. So I got to get you too, Roni."

"It was you who shot up my house, and who tried to run me down in front of Hard Times?"

"Of course, it was me! I wanted you to suffer too. Had them boys break into your house and everything. To make sure you understood that I could do anything I wanted to do to you. Then that Gillette started acting like he was your shadow, hanging all out with you and following you around. But I kept on trying. I had to. I took care of Jeffrey and had to take care of you too."

"Then I find out that Simms' was named the new chairman of that hellhole called Harbor House. I couldn't believe it. It was like y'all was toying with me. I always told Neka that I wouldn't let them get away with what they'd done to her. I always told her that. And she'd cry and fall into my arms. She wanted me to kill 'em all. She hated what they'd done to her. And Simms joined up with a pack of wolves like that? That's when I put him on the list. Had to get him just like I had to get you."

"Y'all didn't do right by Neka, Roni. Y'all didn't do right." He paused, as if he had to catch up with his own racing emotions. "I almost had you last night, after church. I almost had both of y'all. But he pushed you down. I got him, but I still didn't get you. And I got to finish him."

"Deac, listen to me," I said, moving ever so slowly toward the foot of Alan's bed. "Alan didn't know anything about Taneka, Deac. He didn't even know her."

"I don't care. Neka's dead. Dead, you hear me? Now he's got to pay."

Then the gun suddenly pivoted away from Alan's head. For a slight second I felt relieved, as if maybe I was getting through to him somehow. But then the gun kept pivoting, slowly but surely, until the barrel was pointed at me.

"First you," Deac said, "then him. You didn't help my baby. She came to you for help, and you didn't help her. You got to pay too, Roni."

I knew I was in deep trouble, and I started praying even harder. *Dear God, what to do?*

Deac fired his weapon directly at me. I screamed the name of Jesus with a deafening shrill, and ducked by reflex, my hands covering my head, but the bullet never came. Never discharged. It somehow had jammed.

I looked up, ready to shout hallelujah, to praise the Lord from the top of my lungs. It was a miracle, after all.

Deac wasn't through. He looked at the gun, shocked that it didn't fire, and immediately pointed it at me to try again.

I cried out, "Help me, Lord!" in a blood-curdling scream. And then, as if I'd been told to do so, I found my hand reaching for the tray of uneaten food sitting on a cart at the foot of Alan's bed.

Alan reached for Deac's gun at the same time, and then, as in a chain reaction, a number of things happened in rapid succession.

I grabbed the tray from the cart and threw it violently at Deac. His finger immediately squeezed the trigger of his gun.

Alan flung his entire broken body off of the bed and threw himself, like that tray, at Deac, knocking Deac's hand and the now firing gun upward as he did.

I ducked, and as Alan and Deac fell hard to the floor, the cops kicked down the door with a force that shook the walls.

Gillette, Delvecchio, and seemingly the entire Melville Police Department, came charging in. Gillette grabbed me, Delvecchio grabbed Deacon Montgomery, and the other cops rushed to aid poor Alan.

Gillette pulled me up and into his big, warm, burly arms. I was still so dazed, so shocked, that I appreciated the warmth. But as soon as I tried to relax, to enjoy his protection, he pulled me away from him and held me at arm's length.

"Are you okay?" he asked, looking me up and down.

"It jammed," I said, my entire body shaking. "The first time he fired, he should have killed me, but I yelled the name of Jesus and the gun jammed. The gun wouldn't fire, Gillette. It wouldn't fire."

"It's all right," he said, pulling me into his arms again.

I closed my eyes, as if I could blink away the shock, the horror, of what had just transpired, but I couldn't.

Deacon Montgomery was still there. I looked at him. He was being manhandled by the cops, cuffed and frisked, that faraway, crazed look still in his eyes. That was a man I truly thought I knew. But he would have killed me today, if my prayers weren't answered. He would have killed me, accusing me of something that wasn't even true. But truth didn't matter. He was hell-bent on getting his revenge. And nearly got it. All in the name of what he thought was love.

I looked at Alan, a man who truly knew what love meant. They were laying him back in bed, his narrow face wrenched in pain.

"Get the doctor in here," some cop was demanding, and movement was being made.

It would be that surgeon Kayla, no doubt, Gillette's lady friend. One of probably far too many to mention. Another twisted version of man's love.

And that was why, as if by yet another reflex, I broke away from Gillette and went to Alan. I owed him everything, this man I never seemed able to do right by, even my own life now.

Before I could thank him, before I could show him an ounce of my gratitude, he told me in a weak voice to thank God, not him. "And pray," he said, his voice barely audible. "Pray."

And so I did.

TWENTY

It was Greta's thirty-sixth birthday, and Anne thought it would be a blast if we all took her to lunch at the Dale. It would not have been my first choice of gift for her—A muzzle would have been more like it—but as Greta's supervisor, Anne pointed out, I couldn't exactly not participate.

So I participated, sitting at the double-long table we pulled together and watched Greta fawn all over herself with adulation, talking about, she was so thrilled, she couldn't believe it. This was her best birthday ever.

I wanted to puke, I'm sorry. Especially when she finished spewing out adjectives and started throwing down on the gossip, a local mortician and his wife the subjects of her sharp tongue this time. I knew something was coming when she leaned forward at her perch in the middle of the group and whispered, "Chile, did you hear?" to Ernest.

Naturally, Anne, Minnie, and all of the rest of the stylists leaned forward and bent their ears too, to hear what thus saith Greta Crenshaw, as if she spoke the gospel truth.

I felt negative the whole time. Anne said that I was letting off such bad vibes lately that she wondered if I didn't need counseling or something. I wanted to cock an attitude, pull out a stunned, how-dare-she look of my own, but I couldn't even front like that. Because she was right. I needed something.

Ever since that day in the hospital, which had now been nearly two weeks ago, I'd been feeling incomplete, as if that horror show was unending within my soul. I tried to snap out of it, especially on those days when I visited Alan, which was most days after work, but even he could see that I wasn't myself. He went so far one day as to recommend a minister in town that I should go and talk to, noting that I was still relatively new in the faith and probably needed a strong hand of guidance.

I took the name and number, and thanked Alan for his concern, but never even thought about following up. Somehow I didn't feel that my mood had anything to do with my faith. I couldn't say what the problem was, at least not to where I was willing to admit it, but that wasn't it. And maybe the problem was just me being me, or me feeling the aftershocks of that horrid day, but somehow I doubted it.

"Roni would know," I heard Anne say.

I looked across the table at her. "Know what?" I asked, revealing my true lack of interest in their various conversations.

"I told y'all she wasn't paying attention," Ernest said. "She's just here."

"I didn't hear the question, Ernest. Goodness."

"It wasn't a question," Anne said. "Gret was speculating on what was going to happen to Luther Montgomery, but I told her that you would know."

"Me? Why would I know?"

"You know," Anne said with a smile.

I frowned. "What?"

"Come on, Roni. I thought maybe Gillette told you something."

"Why would Chief Gillette be telling me anything about his police investigation?"

"You know why," Greta said, smiling too.

I stared at her. "No, I don't know why."

Ernest laughed.

"Somebody's in a bad mood today," he said.

"As a matter of fact, I haven't even spoken to Chief Gillette since I gave my statement to police on the day they arrested Deacon Montgomery, so I don't know what y'all talking about."

"That ain't what I heard," Greta said in that lip-smacking, all-knowing way of hers.

I just shook my head. Luther Montgomery nearly killed me over some false rumor about how I had refused to help Neka in her final hours on earth, and instead of the rumor mill stopping its churn, given the damage it nearly caused, it had picked up the pace.

Now me and Gillette were supposedly super-tight, some romantic item, when, in truth, given his total absence in my life over these past two weeks, the man probably didn't know or even care if I was alive or dead. But was that pesky little detail of any interest to Miss E.F. Hutton and her crew? Of course, not.

"What did you hear, Gret?" Ernest asked.

"I heard that a certain party at this table, who shall remain nameless, and one chief of the Melville Police Department have been hanging out together, not every now and then, but every single, solitary night, *night*, mind you, since Luther Montgomery was arrested."

"That is such a lie!" I said loudly, causing others in the restaurant to look my way.

"Let's lower our voices, ladies," Anne said in her singsong voice.

"Why do you repeat such lies, Greta? You never go to the parties involved to see if any of those tales you, quote, unquote, hear all the time are accurate. You just tell it anyway. Deacon Montgomery nearly killed me based on a lie like that, but that doesn't even faze you, does it?"

"All I know is—"

"No, you answer my question. Does the fact that somebody, namely me, nearly died behind the kind of gossip you love to tell matters to you?"

"Lower it, Roni," Anne said.

"I heard what I heard," Greta said, equally as loud, but receiving no rebuke from Anne. "Now if it's not true, oh well. I didn't start the rumor."

"No, you never start it, do you? You just spread it around like a cancer. It's just fine laying dormant, you know, doing no harm whatsoever. Until you get a hold of it and start spreading it around. Until you start telling it like you think it is."

"Now you can just step off right there, college girl," Greta said, her head bobbing, her fingers moving around as if she was practicing sign language. "You ain't about to sit up in here and try to lay your problems at my feet. I wasn't the one who refused to help Neka."

"Refused to help, Neka?" I said, an exaggerated lilt in my voice. Neka had never even asked for my help, at least not in the way that they meant. But who was going to believe my report? Certainly not Gossiping Greta and her army of listeners. So I didn't bother. Just ignored the sister the way I should have all along.

And, sure enough, she eventually changed the subject, this time to what one of her customers had told her about some activist in town, and I tuned her out completely. Until she said that old familiar name.

"Gillette?" she said.

I immediately looked at her and then toward where she was looking. And, sure enough, Donald Gillette, in one of his best tailored suits, was just being escorted to a table."

"What's he doing here?" Greta said.

"He has to eat like everybody else." Anne then waved in Gillette's direction. "Hello, Chief!"

Gillette looked our way with the coolness of someone accustomed to being recognized and called out. But when those lazy, hazel eyes of his moved over to mine, my heart raced faster. I could see the change in him.

He looked as if he had forgotten I existed, and had to suddenly stand corrected. He began walking over without hesitation.

Anne began shaking her head. "Gots to give you your props, Roni. That's a good-looking brother there."

"Hello, Anne," he said casually.

Anne smiled. "Hello yourself. I haven't seen you in a month of Sundays."

"Been taking care of yourself?"

"Not as good as you been taking care of yourself. You better-looking every time I see you, Gillette. Tell me your secret."

Gillette smiled that crooked smile of his. "I can always count on you for an uplifting word."

"Got that right."

Greta began clearing her throat, which made me want to strangle her.

Anne got her point. "You know my staff here, don't you, Chief?"

Gillette's eyes, which seemed purposely fixed on Anne, began moving away from her and toward the rest of us. To my relief, he barely glanced at me.

"Yes, I think I do."

"And Roni, of course," Greta said.

Gillette had no choice but to look my way. "Yes. How are you, Veronica?"

"I'm fine." I could barely manage a smile.

"She's in her own world these days," Anne said. "But you know young people. They don't ever focus on anything for too long."

Where in the world had that come from? Was she trying to insinuate that the reason I hadn't heard from Gillette in over two weeks was because I was no longer interested in him? That it was all on me?

I looked at Gillette, who seemed almost embarrassed.

"I'd better let you folks finish your lunch," he said. "Good afternoon." He began moving away.

My heart sank. It was all I needed. More rejection.

Greta, however, started smiling. Any sensible woman would have left well enough alone and ignored the witch. But I was a long way from sensible, especially at that particular moment. "What's so funny?" I asked her, frowning.

"You, that's what. That man ain't stuttin' you."

"What?"

"You heard me. He looked at you like you was just another face in the crowd."

"So?"

"You know it hurt. Don't even try that."

"Child, please."

"Probably gonna go home and cry."

"Whatever, Greta."

"So let me make sure I understand you," Anne said to me. "Are you telling us that you and Don Gillette are not an item anymore?"

I wanted to roll my eyes. What was with these people? Had they never heard of boundaries? Privacy? Ain't none of your business?

I began standing. I felt so exhausted, I could barely stand up. "I'm going back to the salon," I said to her, which should have told her what I thought about her question. "Bob Allen from Mercer Beauty Supply is supposed to come by this afternoon."

"In other words, you tired of us," Anne said.

"Not in other words," I wanted to say. "See you when you get back." I began walking out of the restaurant, and Greta's little smart remarks started before I barely left the table.

Once outside, however, I could at least breathe again. I stood there momentarily, feeling weak, feeling as if I could burst into tears at any moment. Maybe it was indeed that ordeal with Luther Montgomery that had me behaving so crazy lately, or maybe, as everybody else seemed to believe, I was just crazy anyway. But I knew something had to be done. Something was wrong with me. I couldn't continue in the state I was in. Maybe Alan was right, and my problem was directly related to my faith. I hadn't been a Christian for very long at all. I still had a lot to learn.

I began walking away from the Dale. We all rode in Anne's SUV and therefore I had no wheels of my own in which to escape, but that wasn't about to stop me. I couldn't bear the sight of them right now. I'd walk all the way back to the salon, if it meant not asking them for any favors. Or maybe I'd just call a cab.

But before I could decide either way, Gillette came out of the Dale and called my name.

I stood there with my back turned to him, my head jerked back as I braced myself for more emotion. Since the day we'd met, I seemed unable to do anything right in his eyes anyway, as if I was nothing more to him than a nuisance, a problem, and today, thanks to my abrupt departure, he probably still felt that way.

"Veronica," he said when he walked up to me, willing me to turn around to him.

I turned around, and my breath caught. His face didn't look accusatory, as I'd fully expected, but showed concern.

I swallowed. "Yes?"

His breath apparently caught, too, as he seemed momentarily paralyzed also when I faced him, his intelligent hazel eyes searching mine, drilling into mine.

For a brief period I returned his stare, and wanted to cry because of the warmth and sincerity that I saw there, but I'd had too much disappointment for one lifetime. I looked away from him.

"You forgot your jacket," he said.

And for the first time I saw that he was indeed holding up my thin, shirt-jacket that went with the purple pantsuit that I wore. I removed it from his grasp. "Thanks," I said, hugging it to me.

"Put it on," he said in that direct way of his. "It's chilly out here."

I was downright freezing, and it wasn't because of the weather either. I put on the jacket.

"I don't know if you've heard yet, but Montgomery did confess. Told us everything he had told you."

"That's a good thing, right."

"Oh, yeah. The best we could have hoped for."

"So what does it mean? They'll put him on death row?"

"No. Just the opposite. In exchange for his confession and a guilty plea, the prosecutor's recommending life without the possibility of parole."

"In jail forever."

"Certainly for his natural life, yes."

"And for what?" I said, shaking my head.

"Agreed. But let this be a lesson to you. Never underestimate the power of evil, Veronica. It's out there, and it's real."

"I already knew that."

"And that's why playing detective is a dangerous game. Not recommended for amateurs."

"You don't have to tell me. Believe that. The next time somebody asks me to promise to do something for them, I'm heading for the hills. I declare I am. Who? You won't see me mixed up in anybody's business ever again."

"Good." Gillette smiled a weak and feeble smile at best, and was quickly overcome by that concerned look in his eyes. "How have you been?" he asked me after a moment.

"Okay."

"That's not what I've been hearing."

I almost rolled my eyes. What was with these people and their great need for all of this gossip?

"I can't help what you've been hearing, Gillette."

"Alan's worried about you."

I looked at him. "You saw Alan?"

"I did."

"When?"

"Three, four days ago at the hospital. He says you're not yourself lately. Said I should check on you."

"And you were so concerned that you rushed right over three, four days later to tell me?"

I sort of blurted that one out before I could pull it back, and even Gillette seemed caught off guard by it. I closed my eyes. Could this day, this life, get any worse?

"Forget I said that," I said, opening my eyes. "I was just talking. Forget it. So how did you say Alan was doing? How did he seem to you? Your doctor friend, Kayla Caldwell, says he's improving a lot by her standards, but I don't know. Two weeks in the hospital and tubes still all in him isn't showing remarkable improvement to me."

He took his hand and placed it on the side of my face, the warmth of that hand causing me to almost lean into it. It was obvious that he hadn't forgotten my outburst at all.

When his hand lingered on my face, contrary to what I thought it would do, I looked up and into his eyes. And being the emotional wreck I'd been lately, I wanted to cry. Very few times in my entire adulthood had I cried in front of a man, and every one of those times was in front of Gillette, as if he and he alone understood what a struggle this life has been for me. But there won't be another time, however, I decided.

His gaze on me was so penetrating, I almost failed to hold back the tears. I tried to look away from him, to control myself, but his hand kept turning my face back to him.

"How are you, Veronica?" he asked me again, this time much more deliberately, and he looked like a physician with curious eyes, trying to diagnose a serious ailment.

"I told you I was fine."

He continued staring at me, diagnosing me, and then he brushed his finger across my lip and let me go. "Since your meal was interrupted," he said, his hands now in his pant pockets, his muscular chest suddenly straining the fabric of his tailored suit as if it was now puffed out, "how about going somewhere with me for lunch?"

I shook my head. "No thanks."

He seemed surprisingly hurt.

"I mean, I'm not hungry."

"Why did you leave?"

"What?"

"Why did you leave the Dale? Is it because I showed up?"

I couldn't believe his vanity. "Sometimes it's not about you, Gillette."

"Then why?"

"Because I wanted to leave. Is that a crime now?"

"Have lunch with me, Veronica."

I almost fell for it, but I thought about his last two weeks of silence and got serious. "I couldn't eat right now even if they force-fed me."

"Dinner then," he said in a pained expression.

I shook my head. "Can't. I promised to sit with Alan tonight until visiting hours are over to tell him all about my day, which is never much to tell, but he likes to hear it."

Gillette exhaled. "In other words, you've made your choice."

I frowned. "Excuse me?"

"You've made your choice, and it ain't me." He said this with a weak smile.

"Gillette, what are you talking about? What choice?"

He hesitated, as if he couldn't understand why I wouldn't understand him. "At the hospital, when you went in to talk with Montgomery—"

"What about it?"

"I thought, after I came in and held you, but you left my arms and went to Simms, I thought that you'd made your choice."

He seemed embarrassed, as if he absolutely wasn't accustomed to rejection. Welcome to the club, I wanted to shout.

"No," I said, not entirely sure if I wanted to disabuse him of his mistaken notion just yet. But I was never good at subterfuge. "I wasn't making any choice. I was trying to comfort Alan. He needed comfort right then."

"So what you're telling me," he said with a hopeful look in his eye that, after the briefest of moments, turned more sober, "what you're saying is that Simms is not your boyfriend?"

"My boyfriend?"

"I just want to make sure I understand what you're saying."

"Gillette you"—I shook my head—"You never cease to amaze me. I mean, why are you here? What is this about? Fifty girl-friends aren't enough for you, so you've got to have fifty-one? Is that it?"

"You know that's not it."

"You've got to conquer them all?"

"Is that what you think of me? What people have told you about me, not what you've come to know yourself?"

He said this as if I'd just betrayed him, which would have been impossible, it seemed to me. He was the one who'd started it, after all, and like the idiot I truly was, I finished it with a flourish. I decided to quit before I got any farther behind. "I'm sorry," I said, looking into his eyes. "I didn't mean to say that. This just isn't a great time for me."

He nodded, staring at me. "What about tomorrow?"

"What about it?"

"Will you have dinner with me tomorrow?"

I stood there, staring at him for a change, and I considered everything that was this enigma called Donald Gillette. I thought about his everpresent anger, his impatience, his bossiness. Then I considered all of those times he came to my defense, all of those times he could have left me to my own craziness, but he came anyway. I also considered the unflinching support he'd given me, not constantly by my side, that wasn't his style, but when I needed him most. And I considered that odd, almost heartwrenching sadness that always appeared quietly in the furthest recesses of his beautiful hazel eyes. And I sighed. I couldn't help myself. The eyes won out.

"Depends on how I feel tomorrow," I said, thinking the entire time, tomorrow couldn't get here soon enough.

READING GUIDE QUESTIONS

1. What moral responsibility did Roni feel that led her to go to the police on the day after Taneka's death?

2. Describe the past relationship between Roni and Taneka. Do you believe that their past friendship warranted Roni's decision to find out what happened to Taneka?

3. What was it about Roni's behavior, past and present, that gave Don Gillette the most concern?

4. Who was Juno Curtis, and what secret did he keep from Roni?

5. Was Roni's arrest her fault, or was Juno more to blame?

6. Why was Roni torn emotionally between her feelings for Gillette and her friendship with Alan Simms?

7. What role did gossip play in Roni's Christian walk? Discuss specifically Roni's beliefs on the appearances of evil.

8. What role did gossip play in Taneka's murder investigation? How did it nearly cost Roni her life?

9. Discuss Roni's relationship with Don Gillette, and her relationship with Alan Simms. Which man would be a better life partner for her as she seeks to grow closer to the Lord?

10. Discuss Greta's birthday luncheon and what events led to Roni's anger. What role did Gillette play in her anger? What role did gossip play in her anger? Was her anger justified?

BIOGRAPHY

Teresa McClain-Watson is the author of seven published novels, including *Before Redemption* and *When He Hollers, Let Him Go*. She currently resides in Florida with her husband John. She can be contacted at www.teresamcclainwatson.com.